ALL OUT OF LOVE

Boys of Riverside

Gracie Graham

For everyone who has ever been friend-zoned and gotten their heart broken but still believes in love. This one is for you.

CHAPTER 1

GRAHAM

I ALWAYS HOPED THAT if I died young, it would be at the high point of my life. Long after I made Mackenzie Hart, my best friend for the last six years, my bride or signed my first NFL contract. Maybe after I've had my first child. Certainly not like this. I never thought my demise would be a result of my massive mistakes and the rejection from the only girl I've ever loved, while I struggle to come to terms with the fact that my happy family is actually one giant facade.

I'm sitting in the back of the black SUV Crenshaw arrived in, a blindfold tied tightly around my eyes. It wasn't long ago he and Frankie showed up on my doorstep and strongarmed me into their car. Gravel rumbles under the tires, matching the pulse jackhammering behind my ribs while my thoughts drift to everyone I left behind at home. I'm supposed to be at our belated Thanksgiving dinner for my cousin, Atlas, since he got out of the hospital. Now he and Mackenzie most likely think I bailed on them. My father will probably chalk it up to another of the many ways I've fucked up and disappointed him.

I wonder what they'll think when they find my body blown to bits in the woods. Will they ever discover it's because I owed a gambling debt I couldn't pay?

Unlikely.

At least, I assume Crenshaw and Frankie abducted me to take me wherever the hell we are now to teach me a lesson. Less messy that way. No witnesses. Nothing to clean up. No one to hear me scream.

The vehicle comes to a stop, and there's nothing but silence before the driver and passenger doors open and slam closed again. I'm already expecting it when the back door flings open and two hands roughly yank me out.

The cold air bites my skin as they drag me by both of my arms over the lumpy ground.

I don't even fight them. I don't yell or shout or plead or try to escape the vicelike grip they have on me. There's nowhere for me to go even if I did. And I'd be foolish to think there's any chance of me escaping unscathed.

Abruptly, we stop. There's a moment of silence—of noth-ingness—before a hard blow to my stomach knocks the wind out of my lungs. I fold in half, the breath wheezing inside my chest. I cough, stumbling slightly as I try to keep my balance when the cold hard sting of metal strikes me in the back of my calves. My cry pierces the quiet, my legs buckling beneath me as my knees hit solid ground.

Suddenly the cloth is ripped away from my eyes, leaving me to blink into the waning light of day.

Trees surround me, their bare limbs reaching into the sky like arthritic fingers. In the distance, the hoot of a barred owl echoes in the still evening air. Its presence is both ominous and eerie, and despite how dire my situation is, it somehow still creeps me the fuck out.

Frankie blocks the gravel road from view with his burly form. In his hands, he holds a crowbar. Beside him, Crenshaw buffs his nails on his coat, seemingly bored with the situation. "The way I see it, we can do this the easy way or the hard way. You can use my phone, call and beg Daddy for the money, and we all win. Or, you can lose the ability to use your hands." He casually shrugs. "The choice is yours."

I think of my father, his reaction to the news that I gambled away ten thousand dollars in a debt I can't pay, and I shake my head. I'd rather die than admit to him how badly I fucked up.

My life is a mess, anyway. What the hell have I got to lose at this point?

"I can't do that." I take a deep breath, sucking at the air greedily because I know the moment the words leave my mouth, I'm fucked. "But if you give me more time, I can get you the money."

Crenshaw barks out a laugh. "You've had a month already."

"Surely, people owe you a lot more than I do. My debt is probably a drop in the bucket to you. What's another couple of weeks?" I ask, stalling for time.

Crenshaw grins, a cruel twist of his lips. "Even if what you're saying is true, I'm not in the business of IOUs. If I let everyone who owed me pay me when they felt like it, I'd be waiting a lifetime." He steps forward, kicking dust up with his booted feet. "I was a poor man once," he whispers, his voice low and menacing, "and I have no desire to be that man again."

His gaze flicks to Frankie as he stands, his expression cold as frostbite. "Carry on."

Frankie lifts his leg and plants the sole of his shoe on my back, pushing me down. My hands catch on a fallen log, stopping the momentum of my fall.

My thoughts race as I think up another argument, another way to get myself out of this mess. "I have stuff I can sell," I say, grappling for a solution.

"Not fast enough."

Frankie towers over me, the crowbar clenched in his meaty fists. I panic as the gravel crunches beneath Crenshaw's feet. He squats down in front of me until he's eye level, staring at me like I'm a bug under a microscope. "You know, it's a shame, really. I thought you and I had a good thing going. A partnership, if you will. You were more than happy to take my money when offered, more than happy to collect your winnings when things were going well, but the moment they went south, you took no ownership of your actions. You're fumbling for a life raft even though you already popped a hole in it. Now . . ." He leans closer, his voice soft as he says, "Frankie, here, is going to smash this crowbar over your knuckles. He'll take it to each of your fingers, shattering all the delicate bones until they resemble two slabs of meat and you can no longer throw a football. Then he'll finish with your knees. Because nothing is free, not even for golden boy Graham Scott, and you owe me."

He straightens and turns his back on me while my chest swells up like a balloon. Above me, Frankie raises the crowbar.

Oh, shit!

I squeeze my eyes closed, so tight, I see spots, and when I blink them open, the glint of iron careens toward my hands.

"I'll work for you!" I blurt. "Whatever you want."

Wincing, I wait for the blow. But it doesn't come.

I open my eyes while my stomach flips. One of Crenshaw's hands is raised in a silent command for Frankie to stop.

I think I might be sick as my hands tremble against the rough bark of the log and I realize what I said gave Crenshaw pause. "I'll work. Do just about anything to pay off my debt as long as it doesn't involve telling my father."

The air rattles in my lungs as Crenshaw slowly turns, head cocked. "You'll work for me?" he asks.

My thoughts race as I recall my pleas. "Y-yes," I stutter. I'll pay you in whatever way I can."

Crenshaw scratches his chin, a wrinkle of concentration marring his otherwise smooth brow. "Interesting."

He nods to Frankie and motions for him to lower his hand. I watch as the crowbar falls to Frankie's side, and he takes a step back.

Holding my breath, I wait as Crenshaw's dark eyes narrow. "Ten thousand dollars, plus interest."

I nod, exhaling. "Okay."

"You'll work every last dime off doing whatever I want. Any job I need."

Swallowing, I stare up at him, knowing I have no choice unless I want to end up seriously mutilated—or worse. "Fine. I'll take any work you give me until my debt is paid off," I say, pushing to my feet. I wince as my legs burn from the blow of the crowbar to my legs earlier.

Crenshaw closes the space between us until he's in my face, and I have half a mind to use whatever strength I have left to strangle him.

My gaze flickers to Frankie behind him. I'd do it if I thought Frankie wouldn't kill me first.

"It's a deal," Crenshaw says, his tone deadly. "But remember one thing." He pokes a finger into my chest. "You mean shit to me. You're just a dumb, privileged, rich kid from a small town who owes me, and I'll think nothing of putting a bullet in your head myself if you so much as think about going to the authorities or refusing work. You'll be ten feet under before you even have a chance to say your goodbyes."

I somehow manage to nod through the tightening in my chest.

"I'll be in touch," he says. Then he takes one step back—two, three—until he turns and gets in the passenger side of the SUV, and it's not until he closes the car door that Frankie so much as moves an inch.

Once he joins him, they back down the gravel driveway while my lungs try to play catch-up. I gasp for air as my pulse continues its frantic pace, and I glance at the nothingness around me, wondering where the hell I am, how I'm going to get home, and why it feels like I just made a deal with the devil.

CHAPTER 2

SKYLAR

I TAKE A SIP of my beer and groan when I see Brad sauntering toward me and my best friend, Mallory. "Incoming!" I hiss, trying to avoid eye contact.

Mal groans. "Oh my gosh, can't he get a hint? I mean, seriously, dude. Desperate much?"

I snort and take a sip of my beer.

"Ladies," Brad says as he comes to a stop in front of us. He runs a hand over his curly dark hair, which is gelled into place within an inch of its life. "Can I get you guys another drink?"

I glance down at my bottle, which only has a few sips left, and though I'd like another, I'd rather not have Brad thinking I owe him anything. "No, I'm good, thanks," I say.

Mal's lips curve at the corners, but she says nothing. She hates Brad, mostly because he's been trying to hook up with me for more than a year now, and no matter how many times I tell him in no uncertain terms that I'm not interested, he doesn't seem to want to listen. He even went as far as to get a job at the hotel where I work, although he denies that's why.

"Okay, sure." He glances around him before nodding toward David, another one of our classmates at Oak Ridge, who's racking the balls at a nearby pool table. "We're about to get a new game started. You ladies wanna join?"

I purse my lips as if I'm considering it. "Nah. I think we'll just watch."

"Yeah, there's nothing I want more than to watch you bend over a pool table, Brad," Mal says with a roll of her eyes, but Brad must think she's serious because he takes a step closer.

I can smell the bourbon on his breath, and I try not to cringe as his gaze drifts to my mouth. "You gonna be my cheerleader, Skylar?"

"I might puke," Mal mutters.

Either he doesn't hear Mal or he chooses to ignore her.

I press my lips closed, trying not to laugh. "Yeah, sure," I say.

A smug smile stretches over his lips as he steps away and picks up a cue stick, gawking at me as he chalks the tip, and it takes everything in me not to burst out laughing. When he finally turns and breaks the pool balls, I sigh and turn back to Mal. "Now, where were we?"

"About to upchuck the contents of this beer bottle? Seriously, Skylar, if I were you, I'd remove your implants just so you don't have to listen to his sorry ass anymore. You'd have the perfect excuse to ignore him." She taps her ear and winces.

"'What?'" she says loudly, doing an impression of what she imagines I'd say. "'I can't hear anything. Don't have my ears in, so sorry!'"

I tip my head back in laughter.

I was born completely deaf, but after a surgical procedure when I was five years old, I have cochlear implants installed, which allow me to hear as close as humanly possible to a hearing person. Still, if I don't actually wear the implants, I'm completely deaf and rely on reading lips if I want to know what someone is saying.

"I mean, he's not that bad," I say, trying to be nice.

She shoots me a look that says *you've got to be kidding me.* "He's repulsive."

I roll my eyes, because even though there's not a single bone in my body that's attracted to Brad, he's not quite as bad as she makes him out to be. In fact, a lot of girls at Oak Ridge would love to be with Brad.

I, however, am not among them.

"Whatever." Mal waves me off. "I just can't wait until the Oak Ridge Scholarship for the Arts is awarded and you're named, so you can finally blow him off and not worry about it backfiring."

I sigh. "Agreed."

Brad's mother is the principal at Oak Ridge, and coincidentally, a crucial part in deciding the scholarship recipient. Ever since I applied, Brad has made it known in no uncertain terms that my chances of winning will be much better if I give him a chance.

I hold my beer bottle out and Mal taps hers to mine. "To winning and following my dreams," I say.

"And finally telling dipshit he can kiss your ass."

I chuckle. "That, too."

"Speaking of the scholarship and college, have you given any thought to how you're going to break the news to JD?"

I blow out a long breath and the dark hair around my face flutters. JD is my overprotective brother, who raised me after both of our parents died, which gives an interesting dynamic to our relationship. He's my brother and friend and both of my parents all wrapped into one, while I'm his entire life. He has very little outside of work, and it'll kill him when I tell him I want to go away to school. Which is exactly why I have yet to broach the subject.

"Not yet," I say, glancing down at my nails, taking in the chipped blue polish.

Brad glances up from the pool table and bites his lower lip, his gaze flickering down my body while I fight a grimace.

"Well, you better figure it out because that scholarship is yours. Twenty bucks says Brad will wait until you win, then take credit for it."

I arch a brow. "Of course he will. Last week, he all but told me he could put a good word in for me if we came to O'Malley's to hang out tonight. So, here we are." I spread my arms out.

Mal narrows her eyes on me. "I was wondering why we came here tonight, since you normally avoid it."

I shrug. She's right. Even though O'Malley's serves us, it's not my favorite place due to the live bands. I like a good concert as much as anyone else, but not if I just want to hang out with my friends and talk. The live music makes it really hard to follow the conversations around me. If I go to see a live band, it's for the experience. The lyrics aren't easily decipherable, so I mostly enjoy the beat of the music, the vibrations, and dancing. But to carry on a conversation? Forget it.

Mal's gaze returns to Brad, a scowl darkening her features. "What a pig. You should've told him to go to hell."

"If only it were that easy," I murmur, hearing the desperation in my voice.

Sometimes I feel like a caterpillar, just waiting to emerge from its cocoon and turn. But in order to become a butterfly, I have to get out of here, away from the shelter of my brother's presence, to somewhere I can be free to spread my wings and fly.

And so I have to win the scholarship money. It's the only way to prove to JD I can take care of myself and do this on my own. The only way I can think of to set myself free.

GRAHAM

By the time I reach the end of the gravel road, darkness has fallen.

I burst through the grove of trees out into the open and peer around me to get a feel for my surroundings. A car passes on the street in front of me as I suck in huge gasps of wintry air, enjoying the cold bite of it in my lungs.

I'm still in disbelief that I managed to escape Crenshaw's clutches and he agree to me working off my debt. Regardless, I'm cautiously grateful.

I take another step forward and amble down the side of the road with a slight limp, thanks to the crowbar to the back of the legs. Had the blow been to the front of my kneecaps or my shins, I have no doubt I wouldn't be walking at all. But here I am.

A quick perusal of my surroundings tells me I'm no longer in Riverside, my hometown. Nothing is familiar, which doesn't surprise me. So much adrenaline and fear had been pumping through my blood on the way here, I failed to calculate the passing of time. For all I know, I'm more than an hour from home.

Neon lights beckon from up ahead and as I approach, I realize it's a dive bar of sorts called O'Malley's. Beside me, a sign for the I-75 catches my eye. With any luck, I can borrow a phone from someone inside and get a ride.

I push through the heavy steel doors, surprised to find it rather busy for a bar seemingly in the middle of nowhere. The soft hum of music plays in the background, along with the snap of cue balls at a nearby pool table. Up ahead, a massive oak bar with an array of booze bottles on display beckons me, so I decide to push my luck and see if I can get a drink. If the crowd is any indication, they have no problem serving minors here.

The bartender eyes me a moment before sidling up in front of me. Slinging a dishcloth over his shoulder, he places his hands on his hips. "What can I get ya?"

I don't hesitate. I take the opening as my gaze settles on the whiskey behind him. I could drink half the bottle, and it still wouldn't be enough to help ease the anxiety gnawing on my insides like a dog with a bone.

"I'll take two fingers of Jameson, thanks."

"Sure thing." The bartender drifts to the selection of booze, pulls down the green bottle of Irish whiskey, pours some into a highball glass, then slides it my way.

I lift the cup to my lips, hearing Atlas's voice from months ago inside my head. *It doesn't take much for me to recognize bad patterns when I see them. I lived with an addict my whole life . . .*

I squeeze the edge of the bar top with my free hand as the memory floats away, and though I know I should adhere to the subtle warning in Atlas's words, I don't. The pain in my legs and my ribs throb like a fucking toothache. Besides that, I'm too in my head, too wrapped up in the abyss of my failure, so I ignore it and take a sip, grateful for the burn of alcohol working its way down my throat and into my chest. With any luck, after a couple more, it'll hit my ribs and legs next.

Once I drain the glass, I order another, recognizing the familiar pang of a headache blooming at the base of my skull.

By the time he slides me the next glass, I've already decided to get wasted. "Do you have a phone I can borrow by chance?" I ask him, knowing I'll need a ride.

The bartender hesitates as if he might tell me no before he digs in his back pocket and places an iPhone in front of me. "Thanks."

I pick it up and stare at the keypad on the screen, debating on who to call. The guys will have too many questions, ones I don't want to answer. Atlas and Mackenzie will be pissed, and there's no way they'd be satisfied with whatever lame ass excuse I give them for why I have no idea where the hell I am. Telling them the truth isn't an option. The less people I involve, the better. Mackenzie would freak the fuck out and try to convince me to get help from either her father or my own, and I can't afford to do that. I'm already on Crenshaw's radar. He'd skin me alive if I even thought about going to the authorities, and the great Cal Scott, the former professional football player, would never let anything sully his reputation, not even his son.

Which leaves me one option. *Peters.*

He's the only one that knows about Crenshaw and my gambling, so I'm not risking anything by calling him. Besides, in a roundabout way, he got me into this mess.

Without overthinking it, I quickly dial his number, relieved when he answers. "Peters, it's Graham. Hey, I need a ride, man."

"Dude, I have plans. Do you think I just sit around waiting on you to call?"

"I'm at O'Malley's, a bar off I-75," I say, ignoring him. "Just get your ass here, will you?" Lifting my gaze, I catch the bartender heading my way and lower my voice. "It's half your fucking fault I'm in a bind. You owe me for getting me involved with Crenshaw."

"Shit, man. What did you do?" he asks as I hear the slamming of a car door in the background.

"Just get here, will you?"

"I told you not to mess with him."

I sigh, not in the mood for warnings from a pothead who got booted from Riverside's football team this year. I may have messed things up, but he has zero room to give anyone a lecture. "Just move your ass, okay? I'm already two drinks in and plan on being blitzed by the time you get here." I stab the end button and hand the bartender back his phone as he eyes me warily.

"Listen, we run a low-key place here. We don't want any trouble, and we have the local PD on speed dial," he says, as if I'm some low-key delinquent.

I roll my eyes as I lift my glass, drinking another swig of booze. "No trouble from me," I say, my smile tight.

He hesitates, then leaves to take someone else's order while I nurse my drink and wait for Peters, trying hard not to think about the shitshow my life has become. Atlas's recent accident and time spent in the hospital may have diverted me from my problems for a moment, but the events of the last few months can no longer be shelved. It just so happens the consequences of my actions took this long to rear their ugly heads.

Discovering my father had an affair with my cousin Atlas's mother and has a love child no one ever knew about. Looking my mother in the eyes every single fucking day and feeling like I'm lying to her because I know the truth about her marriage and what an utter sham it is. Dealing with the narcissist that is my father and facing the excruciating choice of being the one to tell my mom about his infidelity, or praying she figures it out on her own. Losing both my best friend and the only girl I've only ever had real feelings for—deep feelings—in one fell swoop. Gambling money I didn't have and being faced with working for a criminal or have my fucking limbs broken.

Yeah, my life is fucking sunshine and rainbows.

Most of all are the head games I play with myself. The what-ifs and the weight of my regrets that bear down on me like a steamroller, pressing me flat against the pavement.

I know I need to come to terms with the fact that I'm in a completely different place in my life than I thought I would be, but that's easier said than done when nothing looks like I imagined. My life is a fucking dumpster fire, and all I seem capable of is holding the kerosine and lighting the match.

Maybe Crenshaw was the final blow. Maybe this is where it ends, because it sure as hell feels like reckoning day.

I glance around at my surroundings as I rattle the ice in my glass. The bar gives way to a scarred wooden dance floor, which is currently empty, though the band setting up equipment in the corner of the room tells me that might soon change. Booths line the back wall, only a few of which are occupied with pool tables wedged between them. A couple of guys, who I estimate to be about my age, play on one of them while two girls watch from a high-top table nearby.

One of them, a brunette, grins as she turns and whispers something to her friend, and despite how scarred my heart is, attraction tugs on my guts. Proof I'm not dead yet. There's no denying how striking she is even from a distance in the soft light. Long, dark locks reach her waistline, perfectly framing an angular face and full lips that spread into a beautiful smile.

A throat clears behind me, and I realize I'm staring. Turning, I catch the bartender eyeing me with a smirk before he nods toward my glass and I tip it back, swallowing down the final dregs of whiskey and sliding it to him for another.

By the time Peters shows up, my head buzzes from the alcohol, making it easier to pretend my ribs and legs don't hurt like a motherfucker. "It's about damn time." I turn to him.

"It took me forty minutes to get here," he says, his tone pissy. His gaze flickers to the almost empty glass in my hand before he snatches it from me and sniffs at the liquid. "Whoa." He sets it back down, eyes wide, and whistles. "Whatever that is, it smells like goat's piss." He eyes me, then, "How many have you had?"

"Enough."

His lips thin. "So, Crenshaw, huh?"

I nod, my expression grim.

"What kind of trouble are we talking?" Peters leans against the bar while I wonder why the hell I ever thought hanging out with him was a good idea.

"I gambled more than I should have. Got in over my head. I owe him ten thousand dollars."

Peters whistles for the second time. "And I assume you don't have it?"

"You assume correctly." I take another sip of my drink, knowing it might numb my aching bones, but despite how many I have, I can't outrun my problems no matter how much I wish I could. "He wanted me to go to my father for the money, but I'd rather die first. So, here I am," I say, spreading my arms wide.

Peters shakes his head as he looks at me. "You want my advice?" He leans closer, his cool gaze focusing on mine. "Do it. These guys don't mess around. Swallow your pride and crawl to Daddy. It's better than the alternative, no matter how much of an ass he is."

"And owe Cal, instead?" *Show him how much I screwed up?* "Fuck that. I'd rather Frankie cut my fingers off one by one with a butter knife."

I can still picture the glint of the crowbar as he raised it above my hands, and I have no doubt he'd do whatever Crenshaw asked.

Peters scoffs and shakes his head. "You might just get your wish."

He has no idea.

"Luckily, it shouldn't come to that. We have an agreement. I'm going to work for them to pay off my debt."

"What's that now?" Peters cocks his head, cupping a hand around his ear. "Because it sounded a whole hell of a lot like you just said you're going to work for him."

I toy with my glass, running a finger through the condensation as I mull over the situation. It sounds crazy when I say it out loud, but from where I'm sitting, I have no choice. "I struck a deal with him. It's done."

Peters's eyes widen, and it's not lost on me that it's the most emotion I've seen from him since he got his ass kicked off the football team. "Dude, no."

"It's fine," I say, my tone matter-of-fact, trying to sound like it doesn't even faze me, even though my insides quake at the thought. In truth, the idea of working for Crenshaw makes me break out in hives.

Someone behind me bumps my stool, his obnoxious laughter ricocheting like a machine gun. I glance behind me and realize it's the guy from the pool table. He has curly hair and, with an obnoxious smile, he leans into his friend and says, "Do you see her rack in that sweater? I mean, shit, man. It's like she's just begging me to stare at her tits."

My gaze narrows, flickering over his stocky form and pretty boy face. From the leather cuff around his wrist, his baggy jeans, and leather jacket, he looks like the wannabe bad boy of some cheesy boy band. Nothing about him is particularly special, though I can tell he thinks it is based on the air of arrogance surrounding him.

I follow the direction of his gaze, wondering who he's talking about when I realize it's the brunette from earlier. My gaze drinks her in once more, drifting to her low-cut sweater, and a swell of anger I have no right to rises inside my chest.

Boy Band catches me looking and winks like we're fucking besties.

I scowl, then force myself to turn back around, shoving down my savior complex. If he wants to ogle her and talk about her like she's a piece of meat, let him. I don't know her. It's not my business.

"Listen, man." Peters stands and steps closer, glancing around him, checking if someone might hear. "I know Crenshaw runs the Play House, but that's not where things end with him. Word is he has this whole underground casino. Like, big time. We're talking millions of dollars of illegal activity going in and out. You don't want any part of that. You saw what he did to you over five figures. Can you imagine what he'd do to someone for ten times that? Think about it; Crenshaw doesn't get his hands dirty. He has someone do that shit for him. Are you really ready to get caught up in all that?"

My stomach squeezes. I'd rather not think about it.

Instead, I clutch the glass in my hands, my chest tight, because what other choice do I have? Run to my father?

Hell no.

"I said, let's dance." The lecherous tone of Boy Band's voice assaults my ears once more like nails on a chalkboard.

I take the last sip of my drink, pressing my fingertips to my forehead as I try to block him out so I can fucking think.

"No. I already told you I don't want to," a female voice says, and I freeze because I'm pretty certain if I turn around again, it'll be *her*.

Bitter laughter follows. "Come on, I promise you'll have fun."

My teeth grind together as I glance at Peters, like, *can you believe this prick?*

He raises a brow at me and shrugs as I turn in my chair at the same time Boy Band grabs the girl's waist and pulls her close. He leans down and says something in her ear I can't hear while her cheeks heat and she pushes away from him.

"Get off, Brad!" she says at the same time her blonde friend makes a beeline for her, but the idiot just laughs.

Fuck, I'm not in the mood for this shit.

I slide off my chair while Peters shakes his head, mouthing the word no, but I ignore him.

Placing my empty glass back on the counter, I direct my stony gaze at Boy Band while he grips the girl's wrist in his baby hands, ignoring her weak protests.

I might not be able to solve my problems in a night, but I can solve hers and put this asshole in his place. "I'm pretty sure she told you to back the fuck off," I say, my voice hard.

The jerk pulls away from the girl, giving me an up-close view. The clear amber shade of her eyes and the sprinkle of freckles across her nose make me forget my next move.

Boy Band sneers at me and scoffs. "Okay, buddy. Don't act like I didn't see you leering at her, too. You're probably just pissed I'm the one she's talking to. Mind your own business, bro."

I cross my arms over my chest while my temperature rises. "I'm not your bro."

The girl uses his momentary distraction to yank her arm free and start for her friend who looks ready to tear the kid's throat out.

That makes two of us.

"Whatever," Boy Band mumbles, then turns back around and cups his hands around his mouth, following her as he shouts really fucking loudly, "Did you not hear me?"

"I wouldn't do that if I were you."

With a laugh, the guy turns back around. "Or what?"

The girl with the eyes takes notice of our escalating confrontation and pipes in. "I'm fine. He's fine. I can handle myself."

I ignore her as my lip curls. Suddenly, the culmination of everything I'm feeling mounts inside my chest, and my fists tighten. "Today is not the day to fuck with me."

"Oh, yeah?" Boy Band steps closer, assessing me with his eyes. "You don't look like too much of a threat to me," he says, turning to his friend with a chuckle.

I roll my head on my neck, knowing the last thing I should do is react, especially when I'm drunk. But my emotions are high, and I'm feeling triggered. I don't know this girl, and maybe she *can* take care of herself, but I'm finding it hard to give a shit even though I should grab Peters and go. I have no skin in this game.

"That's what I thought." The douche smirks, snapping the final thread on my self-control, and before I can stop myself, I lunge at him with my fist, popping him in the nose.

I feel it crunch as a scream curdles his lips and he cups his face, bending over at the waist. "What the fuck?"

"I warned you," I say, standing over him, my voice cool, despite the pulse ticking in my jaw. "I told you to leave her alone."

"What the heck are you doing?" The girl whose honor I defended rushes over, mouth gaping as she places a hand on Boy Band's back—only she doesn't call him Boy Band when she leans over, asking him if he's okay. She calls him Brad. Like she knows him.

What the hell?

"I'm doing you a favor," I say. I'm hoping that should be obvious, but the second the words leave my mouth, the punk straightens and growls as he barrels past her and toward me like a linebacker. A shoulder hits my chest, knocking the wind from my lungs.

I cough as my back hits the bar top, and I wince as my already bruised ribs scream. Whatever relief I found in the alcohol instantly vanishes.

But I accept the pain, welcome it.

Because the pain makes me forget more than the booze.

Hissing, I push him off me and raise my fists at the same time he throws a right hook and misses. I retaliate with an uppercut, hitting him square in the jaw. His head snaps back and he loses his balance, falling backward into his friend as the girl shouts for us to stop and the bartender jumps the bar, a baseball bat in hand. Boy Band comes at me, fists clenched with so much momentum, he doesn't register it when the bartender braces the bat against my throat, pinning me down, and his fist connects with the bartender's chin.

The bartender roars in anger while I raise my hands, palms up, so he knows I'm done fighting, but it's not enough to cool the venom in his tone as he barks, "You're out of here! All of you."

The girl steps forward, ready to protest as he spits on the ground beside his feet. "Don't even think about it, sweetheart," he says. "I know you're underage, so just go."

The girl huffs and stares daggers at me before she spins on her heel and heads for the door, motioning for her friend to follow.

From behind the cover of the bartender, Boy Band points. "I'm pressing charges."

I lick my swollen lip, then wink at him like he did to me earlier as he disappears out the door. Once he's gone, the bartender releases me, and I head for the exit while Peters follows, his stride short and clipped, his face a mask of anger. "I can't believe I drove all the way here for this shit. You're losing it, man. You're in enough trouble as it is, and now you're playing knight in shining armor to some chick you don't know and getting in bar brawls—"

"Shut up," I snap as we burst outside and the cold air hits my skin.

"Fine. I'm out, dude," Peter's says as he strolls away, and I watch my ride leave me.

Fucking great.

The nameless girl stands on the sidewalk as if waiting for me, but instead of giving me the thanks I deserve, she's following Boy Band around like a lost puppy. "Brad, hey, we're still cool, right?"

"Back off," he snarls at her, shaking off her hand as he retreats to his car in the lot.

I watch as she stares after him, muttering to herself, leaving me to wonder if I misread the situation and she came with him before she whirls on me. Immediately, her gaze finds mine, and I'm transfixed as she steps closer. Her eyes are even more breathtaking when she's angry, like the color of gold sapphires with little flecks of copper and brown. I can't help but stand in the same spot, frozen as I stare.

"You!" She jabs a finger in my chest, her brow pinched. "What the hell was that?"

I blink and glance around me as if she's talking to someone else, because surely, she's not angry with me. "Excuse me?" I say after a moment, wondering how in the hell I feel sober after so much whiskey. "You're mad at *me*?" I ask like the notion is impossible.

"Of course I'm mad at you!" She throws her hands in the air, her cheeks flushed with color, and I catch a hint of an accent in her voice, or maybe it's just naturally husky, but there's definitely something different about it I like. Something infinitely sexy I can't quite put my finger on. "You have no idea what you just did," she continues, "and for the record, I can take care of myself, thank you very much."

I scoff. "Right. Sure seems like it."

Her nostrils flare. "What the heck is that supposed to mean?"

"It means, I sat by and listened for the last ten minutes about how nice a rack you have, as well as every other body part assessment from that asshole, then sat by while he pawed you and ignored your wishes to back off. Sorry, but I was raised with more respect for women than that."

Miraculous, considering who my father is.

I step closer, until we're only inches apart, and I catch a hint of her perfume. It's floral and spicy at the same time, and I fight the urge to close my eyes and inhale. "You're welcome," I say like the smartass I am.

She narrows her eyes, and her lips part. If I weren't so pissed, I'd think it's hot. Okay, I still think it's pretty fucking hot, even with my rising temper. Still, I prefer anger to attraction, because one hurts more in the long run, so I ignore it.

"For your information, I go to school with that creep. And, yeah, Brad might be arrogant, and a little douchey, but he's harmless otherwise. And, not that it's any of your damn business, but I can't afford for him to hold anything against me right now."

I laugh, a bitter sound. "Okay, well, I don't even know what that means, but you're right about one thing. The guy was being a total douchebag."

She practically vibrates as she says, "Why is it that everyone assumes I can't handle myself? Why does everyone think I need someone to come to my rescue, like some white knight on his steed?"

Her words echo Peters's from moments ago, which only pisses me off further. "So your panties are in a twist because a man dares to come to your rescue?"

"Don't talk about my panties," she snaps.

I scoff, fighting a laugh as I make a show of checking her out. Hard not to with a body like that—curves in all the right places and a face to die for, even if she is a little hot-headed.

"You must be one of these guys with a hero complex. Some wannabe Kent Clark. Ever occur to you that by laying hands on a guy for being obnoxious makes you every bit as toxic?" She steps forward and pokes a finger in my chest. "This might be hard for someone like you to believe, but not all girls need rescuing and you caused me more harm than good in there just now."

"And how is that?"

A siren bleats from down the road as flashing red and blue lights swirl over our surroundings. Seconds later, a cruiser slows down and pulls beside us into the parking lot of the bar.

You've gotta be freaking kidding me.

My blood runs cold as I realize the bartender wasn't joking when he said he keeps the PD on speed dial. Either that or Boy Band made good on his promise.

My stomach pitches as the police officer steps out of his cruiser.

Cursing, I pinch the bridge of my nose, unable to believe this is actually happening.

Then again, this is my life now; maybe I shouldn't expect anything less.

The officer steps closer, his gait even as his gaze flickers between us. "Someone call in a fight?"

CHAPTER 3

SKYLAR

I STARE AT THE cruiser with a frown as the boy responsible for getting me kicked out of O'Malley's disappears into the back seat.

"Whoa, did he really get arrested?" Mallory stumbles outside, after heading back in to grab our bags. "How long have I been gone? I've only been inside for a few minutes."

Long enough to miss our entire exchange.

I reach for my bag and take it, following the trajectory of her gaze as the cruiser pulls away from the curb and stops at a nearby traffic light. "I'm so screwed," I say.

Brad looked certifiably pissed when he stepped out of his car and approached the officer. I have no idea whether he's pressing charges or not, but if the acidic look he gave me is any indication, he'll probably screw my chances of winning the Oak Ridge scholarship.

I rake my hair back with my hands, then let them drop to my sides as I exhale. I'd been so close. The scholarship was at the tips of my fingers. I put up with Brad's shit for months, only for it to be ruined by a hot stranger with a savior complex.

Mal glances around us. "What sewer hole did Brad disappear into, anyway?"

"After recounting his side of the story to the police, he took off," I say. "I doubt anything will come of the arrest. When the guy protested and tried to explain he was defending me, the cop told him they'd sort it out at the station. I don't even know if they would've taken him in if it weren't obvious he'd been drinking."

"Poor guy. He deserves a medal." I shoot her a glare, and she throws her hands up. "What?"

"That poor guy probably just screwed me over."

"Oh," Mal says, registering what I'm trying to tell her. "Right."

"Brad's furious, like this is somehow my fault." I shake my head. "I can't imagine being humiliated like that in front of Dave and the entire bar, for that matter, went over well. It was clear who was gonna come out on top in that fight." I sigh as Mal grabs one of my arms and loops it with hers as she begins to walk toward her car.

"If you ask me, Brad deserved an ass whooping, and I quite enjoyed watching it."

"Putting up with Brad was a small price to pay if it meant more than half of my college tuition would be paid for," I point out. "Besides, that guy didn't even know me, yet he swooped in and played the hero. I mean, who does that? Now, thanks to him, my entire future is in jeopardy."

"I'm sorry," Mallory says as we reach her car and she unlocks it.

I sink inside while she settles in next to me and starts her car. Once the engine rumbles to life, she cranks the heat and bites her lips, stifling a smile.

"What?" I ask, eyeing her warily.

"Nothing. I mean, it's just . . ." She shrugs, then breaks out into a grin. "Did you *see* him?"

"Who?" I ask, pretending I have no idea what she's talking about.

"Um, your knight in shining armor? The guy that came to your defense? He was beyond hot."

"So, you like your men in cuffs?" I ask archly.

Mal's dark eyes fall to mine as she wiggles her brows. "Maybe."

I scoff.

"He doesn't strike me as the submissive type. Coming to your rescue was definitely an alpha move."

"Whatever." I roll my eyes. "Jailbirds aren't my thing and neither are violent hot heads who think the rules don't apply to them."

"I think it's sexy. He defended you. What's not to like?"

I shake my head, in a foul mood after getting kicked out. "I'm not having this conversation."

Mal pulls out and we somehow wind up beside the cruiser at the next light. The brooding boy in the back seat glances over at us and Mallory purrs.

I smack her, motioning for her to go as the light turns green. "You're seriously unhinged."

Mal laughs, unfazed by my insults. "Is there really not even a tiny part of you that thinks it's hot having a guy fight for your honor?"

I hold a finger up. "Correction. He wasn't fighting for me. He doesn't even know me. He probably had a bad day and took it out on Brad because he's an easy target, that's all."

Mal purses her lips as if considering. "Maybe. But when I was grabbing our bags, I thought I saw you talking to him. Did you get his number?"

"Get his—" I snap my mouth closed, then shake my head when I see Mal vibrating with laughter. She's teasing me. "Of course not," I say, just to be clear.

"Shame. Did you see his eyes?"

I cross my arms over my chest, feeling oddly defensive because I did notice his eyes. When he looked at me, I felt them sear clear to my soul.

Still doesn't mean I have to admit that to her. "He has eyeballs. So, what?"

She stares at me, slowly shaking her head like I'm stupid. "They're the brightest, prettiest green I've ever seen. They're not even the color of real eyes. They're like bright moss. Or shelled pistachios. Or—"

"Shelled pistachios?" I snort. Clearly, she's gone insane if she's lusting after eyes the color of a shriveled-up nut.

"And did you see his body?" she continues, bringing her fingers to her mouth in a chef's kiss.

I smash my lips together in an effort to stifle a laugh. "I saw that he was wearing a T-shirt with no coat in December when it's freezing outside, which only confirms he's crazy."

"Hey, if crazy looks like that, I'll take it." She grins, then sobers when she takes in my scowl. "I wonder if we call the jail, they'll give us his digits?"

My gaze narrows.

"Kidding!" she says, though I really don't think she is. "So, what now?"

I sigh. "I don't know. Wait and see how big of a hit to Brad's ego this is? Start searching for other ways to pay for college just in case?"

Mal taps her hands on the steering wheel as if thinking, then glances over at me. "I think you should ask your brother for help. Tell JD the truth. He loves you, and he wants what's best for you. He'll come around to the idea of you going away to school eventually and help you in any way he can. It's what he does."

"I'm not so sure, but even if he wanted to help, if I make it into the School of the Art Institute of Chicago, it's crazy expensive, and he's already sacrificed so much for me so many times. I don't want to do that to him anymore. It's time he used his money on himself."

After our mother died of cancer when I was only two, my father was never the same again, and a year later, he, too, died. JD says it was a broken heart. Ever since, JD's taken on the role of caretaker, protector, and provider. It's a role he takes seriously. One I can never repay him for. He's given me a good life; one I may not have had if it weren't for him. My parents weren't wealthy people. They were working class and barely scraping by, from what he's told me. When I was born profoundly deaf, they planned on enrolling me in sign language and going that route, but after they passed, we lived with our uncle for a short time during which JD did a ton of research on my condition and treatments. By the time he turned eighteen later that year, he already had a job and was saving to take me in on his own. We moved out of my uncle's house into a small apartment, where he raised me. He borrowed money, scraped, and saved to pay the hefty price tag for cochlear implants. Paid for speech therapy all through grade school so I could hear and speak like other kids, all while pulling us out of poverty. To this day, I have no idea how he did it, but I'll be forever grateful.

Which is exactly why I can't bring myself to tell him I want to leave, nor can I ask him for any more help to do it. How do you tell the one person in your life who has sacrificed everything for you that you appreciate it, but it's no longer enough?

Mallory's car backs down my driveway as I make my way to the garage where I let myself inside using the keycode for the man door. I head past JD's Porsche, which tells me he's home, to the door that leads to the house, and enter into the mud room.

Hanging my coat and purse on one of the hooks, I kick off my shoes and pass the washer and dryer, then stroll into the massive kitchen to find JD manning the stove. Even though it's Saturday, he was still at work when I left to hang out with Mallory. Judging by the dress pants and shirt rolled at the sleeves, I assume he just got home.

He turns when he hears me, and I can't help but smile at the sight of him in our mother's old apron with the rosebuds on it. The juxtaposition between his sharp, masculine features, and the ruffled floral fabric is almost comical, yet he somehow pulls it off.

"Hey," I say, taking a seat in one of the stools at the kitchen island.

"Hey, I wasn't expecting you home yet. How's Mal?"

"Good. We decided to call it an early night. A band was warming up at O'Malley's, and I wasn't in the mood," I say, knowing it's as good of an excuse as any with the added bonus of being partly true.

His gaze flickers over my face, searching for the truth in my excuse. Whatever he sees must confirm my statement and put him at ease because he simply nods and turns back to the stove. "I just got home a bit ago. You hungry? I'm making stir fry."

"Sure, I can eat," I say at the same time my stomach rumbles.

I watch as JD adds soy sauce, fresh ginger, and honey to the pan of vegetables. Cooking is one of the many things he taught himself and excelled at after my parents died. For years, he watched cooking shows until he learned his way around a kitchen. Now he cooks and it feels as if he's been doing it his whole life.

While he finishes up, I set a place for both of us at the table, and a few minutes later, he sits beside me, our plates heaped with stir fry and jasmine rice.

I take my first bite, contemplating tonight's turn of events. Though I typically try to avoid Brad outside of school and work, when he proposed putting in a good word for me if I hang out at O'Malley's, I couldn't pass up the opportunity. But now look where it got me . . .

Serves me right for playing him like that. I know damn well he wants to go out with me, just like I know I have zero interest in him.

I glance over at my brother out of the corner of my eye, watching him eat. The muscle in his jaw works as he chews and swallows his food, then picks up his water glass to take a sip.

Guilt settles in the pit of my stomach. I hate that I don't have his support where my future is concerned. Then again, I haven't exactly given him a chance, have I?

"Wanna watch a movie after we eat?" he asks, glancing up at me. "I was thinking of a comedy. Something silly stupid like *Mall Cop* or *Grown Ups*."

Comedies are his tell, so I ask, "Rough day at work?"

He grimaces and grunts out a response I can't decipher, and I wonder if he garbled his words on purpose.

I take a bite of my food, eyeing him as I eat when Mal's words come back to me. *He loves you and he wants what's best for you. He'll come around to the idea of you going away to school eventually.*

I imagine telling him the truth. That despite everything he's ever done for me, I want to venture out into the world on my own. That I'm stifled here. Overprotected. And though he means well, sometimes I feel smothered, like I have no voice when he went to such great lengths when I was a kid to ensure I had one, literally.

I want to go to art school in Chicago; it's always been my dream. I want to be a part of something bigger and better than this suburban life can offer. I want to surround myself with different cultures and people and the hustle and bustle of the windy city. I want to study art and find inspiration in the uninspired. Sketch until the charcoal coats my skin and my fingers ache. Live my life with the constant stain of paint under my nails. I want to move away. Go off on my own. Find myself.

I inhale through my nose, gathering my courage as I open my mouth and will myself to say the words, to spit them out before I can stop myself. "JD?"

"Yeah?" he asks between bites.

I imagine what he'll say. I picture the pain in his eyes, the implication that despite everything he's done for me, it's not enough—*he's* not enough. Yet, I'm all he has. We have no family to speak of, other than our uncle who moved away, and after devoting his life to raising me and ensuring I had a childhood he could only dream of—of having every advantage in life—he has very few people surrounding him he can call a friend. Because the kind of success he's achieved doesn't come without sacrifice, and I can't do it. I can't say the truth because I know how much it will hurt.

It seems so unfair that he chose to put me first, only for me to turn around and choose something different, reject the life he's given me.

At my silence, he looks up and catches me staring. My lower lip trembles, and immediately, his smile begins to fade.

I bite back the words, swallow them whole, nearly gagging on their bitter aftertaste.

"Um, you forgot the cashews," I choke out, even though I could give a crap less. Still, they're my favorite, and he always uses them instead of almonds or peanuts.

He blinks as if this wasn't what he was expecting, and I can't blame him because cashews aren't what I was thinking about. Not at all. But then he glances down at his plate and his cheeks pinken. "Oh, shoot. I must've got distracted. Hang on." He scoots back from his chair and heads to the massive pantry where he pulls out a can of cashews and returns.

With a pop of the lid, he sprinkles a generous amount over my food before doing the same to his own plate and smiling over at me. "I knew something was off. Better?"

I nod even as my stomach sinks. "Better," I mumble, and I tuck into my food. Mostly so he won't notice my frown or the ghost of discontent hovering inside my words.

CHAPTER 4

GRAHAM

I SIT IN THE sterile atmosphere of the clinker, with my head between my hands. Cinder block walls surround me, along with a painted concrete floor. Two other dudes take up residence on the wooden bench beside me. One has teardrop tattoos under his eyes and a gold tooth. The other reeks of alcohol and is currently slumped over, his white T-shirt stained with lord knows what while the sound of his snores fill the background.

If I weren't at an all-time low, I might find humor in the situation. Graham Scott, Riverside's golden boy, waiting to be bailed out of jail. Only I could somehow get arrested for playing knight in shining armor to a girl who'd rather be talked down to and ogled by a creep, than have someone defend her.

I hear the sound of footsteps grow closer. The metal doors clang, the sound of metal on metal making me wince. "Scott?"

I raise my head and stiffen when I see the guard motioning for me.

I stand and step forward, wary of who might be behind my release. I called Jace, my good friend and teammate, but that doesn't mean he kept it to himself. If my father's here, my ass is toast.

"You're out of here," the guard says, and when he steps to the side to allow me passage, Jace comes into view, and the tension in my body vanishes.

His mouth spreads into a shit-eating grin when he sees me, but he says nothing as the door clinks shut behind me. Leaning against the wall, arms crossed, his gaze flickers over me. "Oof. Bad night?"

I roll my eyes. "Shut up."

Jace chuckles and follows behind me. "Grumpy. You know, I expected this kind of behavior from Atlas. I mean, if he had called me up late on a Saturday night to tell me he's in the slammer and needs a ride, I wouldn't even bat an eye. But you . . ." He shakes his head, his voice dripping with humor. "It's like the Scott cousins have done a complete role reversal."

I pause in front of the heavy glass doors that lead outside. "Can we just lay off the sarcasm and get the hell out of here?" I push through the doors without waiting for an answer, grateful for the feel of the brisk December air.

"Your wish is my command," he says as he follows me outside. "You know, I'm flattered, really. I mean, I was your one call?"

He places a hand over his heart. "That's pretty special. Means a lot, bro."

I groan and make a beeline for the parking lot where I see his truck idling in the front row. Serves me right for calling him. Jace never can take anything seriously, but out of our crew, I thought he might be my best option for taking things at face value and not looking too closely.

"I'm not gonna lie," he continues as we approach his truck, "when you told me you got in a fight and were arrested, I assumed you'd be worse off. But you look good. Maybe the slammer agrees with you. You know, not everyone can pull off a life of crime and come out of it looking like James Dean."

I pause to glare over at him, and he stretches his arms out toward me. "Do you need a hug? It looks like you could use a hug. Come on," he says, waving me forward when I just stand there, "bring it in."

I flip him the bird because right now I have no words, and he laughs, unfazed, before he promptly turns and unlocks the doors.

I get inside, waiting as he rounds his truck and takes the driver's seat. Once he's behind the wheel, he turns to me. "So, in all seriousness, what the hell happened?"

I sigh, and part of me wishes we could just stick with the jokes. I prefer it to the truth, which makes me look like a moron.

"There was this punk talking about some girl and being disrespectful. He wouldn't leave her alone."

Jace groans and leans his head back. "Please, tell me this isn't about a girl. What is it with you and girls, Scott? Don't you see the pattern here? They're always getting you in trouble."

I shoot him a scowl. "It's not like that. I wasn't interested." Though I'd be lying if I said she wasn't hot. "But this guy was being a total prick and harassing her, so we exchanged words, and the next thing you know . . ."

"You were getting arrested."

"I only got a couple hits in," I say, on the defense. "It's not like I kicked his ass." I scrape a hand over the rough stubble of my jaw. "The worst part is the girl was pissed. Totally turned on me for coming to her rescue."

"It was probably her boyfriend just being a douche," Jace says, and I can hear the barely restrained laughter in his voice.

"It wasn't her boyfriend. I'm not a complete moron," I grump. "She was angry, said she knew the guy and could handle herself, that she didn't need a man to do it for her. Then she went on about how I screwed something up for her. Who the hell knows."

Jace splutters out a laugh. "Oh, man. That's classic. So, you try to play Prince Charming, get arrested for it, and she's pissed?"

My lips thin, which only makes him laugh harder.

Speaking in between gasps of air, he says, "Shit, man. You really know how to pick 'em."

"Would you shut the hell up and drive?" I snap. "I already said it wasn't like that."

He arches a brow. "So you're saying this chick wasn't hot?"

I say nothing, silently staring at the window.

"That's what I thought."

"I would've defended any woman in the same situation. To imply otherwise is just dickish."

"You're right. I'm sorry." His expression sobers, though he doesn't sound sorry, and the pinched set of his mouth as he holds back his laughter only confirms this. "Seriously though," he says as he takes the ramp for the interstate, heading toward Riverside, "who would've thought that out of all of us, you'd be the troublemaker? Mackenzie really fucked you up."

My gaze darkens as I glare at him. "Don't say it like that. This shit isn't her fault."

She may have been a catalyst in my life turning to crap, but I own my mess.

"So, what are they charging you with?"

I lift my shoulders. "I don't know. For now, the kid hasn't pressed charges even though he threatened to. If I'm lucky, they'll drop everything. If not, I'll probably get charged with disorderly conduct and underage drinking."

"And what are you gonna tell your father?"

"I'm not gonna tell him shit."

"Come on, dude. You know he'll find out about this. Even though you weren't in Riverside, the man has his pulse on everything."

"I'm eighteen. They have no reason to call my parents," I say, hoping it's true. If my father finds out about this, he'll kill me, and the last thing I need is him breathing down my neck about one more thing when I have enough to deal with already.

"But he could probably pull some strings, get you out of it, right?"

He could. I know he could. But just like my debt to Crenshaw, I'd rather eat a dog turd, then crawl to him for help. So, I grunt and mutter, "I'll figure it out," even though I have no idea exactly how I'm going to do that.

Exhausted from the conversation and the day's events, I lean against the passenger window, pressing my forehead to the cold glass as I close my eyes. First Crenshaw, now this. My problems are stacking up, but the solutions are running thin. And sooner or later, they're all going to catch up with me.

CHAPTER 5

GRAHAM

I QUIETLY CLOSE THE door behind me and snap the lock into place. All the lights in the house are off, and though I know it's too much to hope my parents are asleep, I can't help but pray I might catch a break just this once.

Taking care to keep quiet, I move through our massive foyer and past the sitting room to approach the staircase when a figure emerges from the shadows. I know instantly by the broad shoulders and the way he moves it's my father.

"Where the hell were you?" He steps into a sliver of light from the window, and it gives enough illumination that I can make out the angry lines of his face.

It feels like days ago that I was standing in the foyer with Mackenzie and Atlas when Crenshaw arrived, rather than mere hours. But I simply shrug in response, saying nothing because what can I say? Certainly not the truth.

"You leave during a family dinner, just take off, and I'm supposed to accept it? Do you know how embarrassing that is?"

"Hmm, I don't know. As embarrassing as discovering your father had an illegitimate child with your cousin's mother?"

Before I can react, my father slams me against the wall beside the staircase in one rough movement. He braces his forearm against my neck, pinning me on the wall as he presses against my windpipe until I cough. "I will not have you speak to me that way in my own house. Do you hear me?"

I say nothing. Instead, I grip his arm with my hands, sucking in a breath as I stare at him with so much pent-up rage, I nearly combust from it.

"I don't know what the hell has gotten into you these past few months, but I've had about enough of your attitude and your disrespect. You fight with me every step of the way even though I'm trying to help you," he seethes while my fingers dig into the flesh of his arm. "Now, I'm going to ask you again. Where. Were. You?"

He leans up slightly so I can speak. "Out," I snarl, before I push him off me.

"You know, it wasn't just me you disappointed today. It was Atlas and Mackenzie."

"I'll deal with it."

"And your mother, too," he shoots back. "What about her?"

I laugh and shake my head. Of course he would use her to make me feel bad when he has no fucking right to talk. The gravity of his secrets has been weighing on me for weeks. It's fucking killing me keeping his infidelity from her. Every time I look her in the eye, every time she gives my father a hug or kiss or speaks kindly of him, his secrets eat away at me a little more, gnawing on me from the inside out like some kind of parasite, and now he's gonna talk to me about disappointing her?

The fucking audacity.

"I don't see anything funny about this," he snaps.

"No, you're right, Dad." My smile fades, my humor vanishing with it. "None of this is funny, but for you to sit here and talk to me about disappointing Mom after everything you've done?" Anger glints in my eyes as I shake my head. "Well, that's a whole new level of fucked up, even for you."

"The things I did are in the past."

I take a step closer to him, my lip curling in disgust. "If only they'd stay there, right, Dad?" I stare at him cooly, watching as a vein pulses in his forehead.

"You pull a stunt like this again, and I'll—"

"What?" I cut him off, my hands balling into fists.

I have at least a couple inches on him, more muscle mass and stamina, and as I stare down at him, a fist clenching in my gut, I want to see if I can take him. I will him to lay his hands on me again, so I can find out.

"You'll what, Dad?" I repeat. "You've already destroyed this family. You've hurt us in all the ways that count." My gaze flickers over him, revulsion twisting my features. "There's not much more you can do to me that'll hurt any worse than the things you've already done."

His mouth parts, and for the first time since I've known him, he appears to be speechless. Nothing comes out, but I'm surprised putting him in place does nothing to ease the ache inside.

I turn away from him and start up the stairs, done listening to him.

"You'll come back here right this instant, so we can talk about this!" he shouts to my back.

I pause, glancing back at him, sadness descending over me like a pair of heavy drapes. "I'm done talking. But don't worry, I'll keep all of your dirty little secrets. Just don't expect me to act like we're a family."

I enter school with dread sinking in the pit of my stomach. I've fielded more than a dozen calls and texts from Atlas and Mackenzie since Saturday. Facing them today is inevitable, and though I've thought a lot about what I'd tell them, I still have no answers.

Several girls greet me before I even make it to my locker. I never realized before how wrapped up in Mackenzie I was, how I must've been completely oblivious to every other member of the female sex while I was pining over her. Ever since she and Atlas became an item, it's like the floodgates have opened and every chick within a five-mile radius is throwing their hat in the ring for a chance to get my attention. I wonder how long it's been this way and I just didn't notice?

I try to smile and be polite, but my heart's not in it. I'm too nervous about the impending confrontation I know I'm about to have.

With my head down, I make a beeline for my locker just as Jessica Turley sidles up beside me. I enter the combination and pop it open as she pushes her blonde locks off her shoulders and snaps her gum. "Hey, Graham."

"What's up?" I say, barely glancing her way as I gather my books.

"Um, so I was wondering if you wanna hang out after school?" Her cheeks pinken as I slam the door closed and glance over at her.

Jessica's a nice girl. Pretty, too. But I'm just not interested. Part of me wonders if I ever will be, or if Mackenzie broke something inside of me too deep to heal.

"Actually, I can't, I'm sorry. I promised the boys I'd hang with them," I lie. Just because I have zero desire to start something with Jessica, or anyone else for that matter, it doesn't mean I want to hurt her feelings.

"Oh." Her face falls. "Okay . . . I just thought . . ." She steps forward and leans into me, close enough her lips brush my ear as she whispers, "If you change your mind, and you're lonely, give me a call. Anytime. I think I can help." When she steps back, she bites her lower lip and her gaze flickers down my body.

I clear my throat, unsure of what the hell to say to what I'm pretty sure is an offer of a booty call when a shadow falls over us, and I glance behind her to find Atlas, arms crossed over his chest. Jessica takes one look at him, correctly reads his body language, and scurries away. Whether it was the muscle ticking angrily in his jaw or the murderous gleam in his eye, I'm not sure. Maybe the combination of both. Whatever tipped her off, I have half a mind to follow.

Beside him, Mackenzie's forehead creases with worry as she looks me over, her cool, blue eyes taking me in. "Graham, what happened—"

"Where the hell have you been?" Atlas snaps.

We've come a long way since he first moved to town at the beginning of fall. There was no love lost between us, and even though we're far more civilized around each other, and we've come a long way since the beginning of the school year, it's not like he and I are besties now; there are times where our "friendship" is still touch and go. Like now.

"Good morning to you, too." I force a smile, but it goes unreciprocated. Sighing, I glance around me, relieved to see we don't have an audience. "Listen, I'm sorry, okay?"

"You're sorry?" Atlas's brows rise to his hairline. "We come to your place as a favor to *you*, and you disappear before the appetizers are even served, leaving us to fend for ourselves. If anyone knows how much I hate your father, it's you. I never would've gone there on my own. We went for you, because you asked us to."

"I know." I rub the back of my neck. I can't even imagine the situation if it were reversed. If I were in Atlas's shoes, I'd be more than pissed.

"We saw you." Mackenzie waits, and my gaze flickers to hers, but I give nothing away. "We saw you leave and get in the car with two guys."

Shit. I hadn't even considered the fact that they might've seen me leave with Crenshaw and Frankie. "Yeah, uh . . ." I sniff and scrub a hand over my face. "Some friends unexpectedly showed up right after you guys got there, and I had some stuff to take care of that couldn't wait."

I have nearly forty-eight hours to create a story they might buy, and this is what I come up with?

"They were older than you, and from the looks of it, not your friends," Atlas quips, and I can tell he's not buying one second of my bullshit story.

"Graham . . ." When Mackenzie steps forward, I glance away from her, but it doesn't stop her from placing a hand on my arm and dipping her head to catch my eyes. "What's going on? You're disappearing with no explanation, leaving us high and dry without so much as a text. Strange men are showing up at your house and forcing you into their car, and then you show up at school acting like it's normal and nothing happened."

I don't know what to say, so I opt for nothing, shoving my hands in my pockets instead.

I'm a coward. If I had any balls at all, I'd just come clean to everyone. But I don't. And it's not just because I don't want shit from my father. I don't want everyone else to know just how bad I fucked up. If Mackenzie knew the mess I'd gotten myself into, it would only confirm that she chose the right boy, and everyone would see me for who I really am. A loser. A screw up. Just another golden boy who caved under the pressure of trying to be perfect.

"I'm worried. Like, really worried," she continues. "I know something's up. Are you in trouble?"

I say nothing, and my jaw tightens.

"Is someone angry with you, or . . . I don't know." She pulls her hand away, frustrated with my lack of response and rakes her hands through her hair. "You can tell us . . ." She bites her lip and glances up at Atlas who hasn't so much as flinched. "I know a lot has happened with the three of us this year, but I thought we were getting better. I thought we were okay."

"We are," I say, balling my hands into fists, frustrated.

"Then what's going on? Tell me. You can trust us, you know that, right?"

I swallow and open my mouth to speak. For a moment, I contemplate telling her. I imagine blurting out everything that's happened in the last month. From gambling and winning and feeling on top of the world, then losing and owing massive debts, to this weekend, when Crenshaw showed up at my place to collect.

Movement catches my eye behind them, and I zero in on Peters who shakes his head in warning, and it's the reminder I need to keep my mouth shut.

My image isn't the only reason for staying quiet. I can't imagine Crenshaw would take kindly to my spilling the beans to Mackenzie, a police chief's daughter.

Sanity snaps back into place as I press my lips together. The last thing I want to do is risk putting Atlas and Mackenzie in harm's way because I can't handle the pressure. This was my mistake—my debt to pay—and I won't bring them into this. I refuse to jeopardize anyone else just so I can feel a moment of relief from the weight of my secrets.

Atlas follows the trajectory of my gaze, and his expression turns to stone. "Does this have to do with that fucker?"

"Listen, I don't expect you to understand—"

"He's trouble."

"This isn't his fault." I sigh and shake my head. "I totally get why you're angry about Saturday. If I were in your shoes, I'd be pissed as hell. And I get you're worried, but I can't tell you what's going on."

Alarm flickers in the blue of Mackenzie's eyes before she steps forward, and I can see the fight brewing within her as she opens her mouth to protest. I reach out and place a hand on her shoulder. "You have to trust me." I stare into her eyes as my words sink in. "Everything is going to be all right. I'm fine, and I'm handling it."

"You can't be serious. You expect us to just accept this?"

"You have to," I say, my tone firm. I glance between them before I hold her gaze once more. We've been friends a long time. That has to count for something. "Do you trust me?" I ask her.

Her eyes search mine for a moment before she nods, though I can see her reluctance to concede.

"Then trust that I'm fine. Maybe I can't tell you exactly what's going on right now, but I have everything under control."

My hand falls to hers. I give it a little squeeze before I nod at Atlas, then take this reprieve as my chance for escape. My feet carry me down the hallway toward my first morning class.

Facing them did little to ease the fist tightening in my chest, and when my phone vibrates in my pocket, I half expect it to be them, demanding more of an explanation. But when I slide it out of my jeans, a number I don't recognize flashes on the screen.

With a frown, I answer and bring it to my ear. "Hello?"

"Tonight." a deep baritone booms over the line. "Five p.m., sharp."

Crenshaw.

"We'll text you an address. Go to the front desk and ask for Franklin."

Fear needles my spine. The air turns thick as soup and I find it hard to breathe. "What will I be doing?" I ask, but as I wait for an answer, the line goes dead.

I grind my molars when he ends the call. Dozens of questions run through my head as I reluctantly shove the phone back in my pocket, knowing I won't get an explanation, only realizing I might live to regret ever going to the Play House even more than I already do.

CHAPTER 6

GRAHAM

THE REST OF SCHOOL passes quickly. I take a calculus exam I'm pretty sure I fail. The only thing I can focus on is meeting with Frankie at five. Miraculously, I somehow manage to choke down my food at lunch and make it through the day without further prodding from Mackenzie and Atlas. But these are meager wins in what is sure to be a losing day.

By the time I arrive back home, my stomach is a tangle of knots. All I can do is think about what Peters said, about how Crenshaw never gets his hands dirty.

When it's time to leave my house, I head to the address Frankie texted me while my stomach roils. Focusing on the road ahead is all I can do to keep my nerves from completely wrecking me and my lunch from making a reappearance. When I finally arrive at the address, I'm sure I must have the wrong place.

I find parking alongside the road across from the towering buildings, and blink at the black building number etched on the glass beside the door. It's the right place, of that I'm sure, but I'm so dumbstruck at what I see that I can't seem to make my arms and legs move to exit my vehicle.

In front of me sits the Bardot, an upscale boutique hotel and restaurant. The massive building towers between the other businesses and shops. Potted pines flank the huge glass doors, white twinkling lights brightening their branches in the softly falling snow. A giant pine wreath with a large red bow hangs on the center of the building, overtop a massive glass window.

It's swanky, yet inviting, and the total opposite of what I expected. I pictured a darkened alleyway. Or a vacant building. Something similar to the Play House perhaps, but definitely more private and far more sinister than this modern hotel.

I double-check my phone to ensure I have the address correct before I exit my car and cross the street, pausing in front of the large glass revolving doors to calm my nerves. For some reason, the ambiguity of the place scares me more than if I had shown up at some kind of underground crime ring.

But maybe I'm overthinking it.

Snowflakes dance around me, their delicate beauty mesmerizing, yet fleeting. As I take a deep breath, a gust of wind whispers through the street, carrying the faint scent of luxury with it. Apprehension and anticipation wash through me in an uncomfortable combination, and though the door beckons me forward, promising answers to the questions that have plagued my thoughts since the moment I agreed to work for Crenshaw, it's hard to make my limbs move.

With a surge of determination, I push open one of the heavy glass doors, and step inside. The interior is both elegant and sophisticated with clean lines and bright colors. Crystal chandeliers cast a warm glow over soft leather furnishings. The sound of hushed conversations and clinking glasses fills the air, intermingling with soft jazz playing in the background. It's as if I've stumbled upon a hidden sanctuary, concealed within the heart of the city.

More confused than ever, I navigate through the buzzing crowd, my eyes searching for a familiar face, any hint of Frankie or Crenshaw's presence. I have no idea what I'm doing here, but Crenshaw strikes me as the type of guy that dips his toes in many pools. Maybe he's going to have me work my debt off legitimately? Or maybe that's wishful thinking . . .

I continue toward the front desk when the guests clear, and the face of the receptionist comes into focus. The sight of her is like a punch to the gut. But it's not her flowing chestnut locks, high cheekbones, or rosebud mouth that grabs my attention. It's those eyes—those amber eyes with flecks of gold and copper that seer me to the bone. Those same eyes from Saturday night.

"*You*." She sneers.

Several seconds pass before I can speak. I'm too shocked at the odds of coming face-to-face with the nameless girl whose honor I defended.

"Shouldn't I be the indignant one?" I ask. "After all, you did get me arrested."

"I did nothing of the—" She stops abruptly, her jaw set as her cheeks flush with emotion.

"What are you doing here, anyway?" I ask.

"I work here, you dunce cap." She rolls her eyes and crosses her arms over her chest, drawing my gaze to the swell of cleavage rising above the neckline of her dress while she pierces me with a look. "Please tell me you're not a guest. I would've taken you for more of a Motel 8 kind of guy."

I choke on a laugh. I've never met someone so combative before in my life, but I kinda like it. Her attitude has a way of bursting the bubble of anxiety ballooning inside my chest, and for a moment, it's easy to forget why I'm here. In fact, I quite enjoy getting a rise out of her. I could see it quickly becoming my favorite sport. Maybe it's because Mackenzie and I always got along so swimmingly; everything between us was always easy, smooth sailing. These choppy waters are a refreshing change of pace.

Wait . . . why the hell am I even comparing her to Mackenzie?

"Hoping I might ask you back to my room?" I wink.

Her pretty jaw drops, and she scoffs so hard I think she swallowed a bug. "Back to your dungeon is more like it. I prefer my men with a little more class. Sorry, not sorry."

At the same time the words leave her lips, another employee hurries behind the desk, and I'm shocked for the second time today, because it's the asshole that ate my fist on Saturday night.

I scrub a hand over my mouth moments before Boy Band lifts his head and says, "Hey, Skylar, did you . . ." His voice trails off as he meets my eyes and recognition widens the darks of his, bringing out the bruises on his face.

A black eye gives way to a bruised jaw and fat lip. Shock moves through his normally smug features, and when he glances at *her* for an explanation as to why I'm here, at their place of work, I want to pop him in the eye a second time.

"What the hell is he doing here?" Boy Band asks, straightening.

Skylar sighs, and I can't deny I'm glad to see I'm not the only one who irritates her.

"I was just trying to figure that out. Did you need something?" she asks.

He blinks over at her, as if he expected a different response. "Uh, yeah. Did they happen to fax over the final numbers for the guest list of the Hawthorne wedding by chance?"

"Yeah. Hang on." She turns away from him and opens the desk drawer in front of her while Boy Band glares at me over the counter and I work on smothering a smile.

"Here it is," she says, turning and handing him an envelope.

He takes it from her and leans in, brushing a kiss over her cheek as he says, "Thanks. You're a lifesaver."

My jaw tightens while Skylar blinks, her mouth parted in shock. "What the hell was that?" I hear her mumble as he winks and leaves the reception desk.

Once he's out of ear shot, I take a deep breath, trying to smother my annoyance. "So, Brad's your type? Really?"

"You remember his name?"

Unfortunately.

Her amber eyes turn venomous as she glares a hole straight through me. "What the hell are you doing here? Wait. Don't tell me. It's to get a room with a view before you pick the highest window to jump off," she says, her voice saccharine. "Am I right?"

My lips twitch. "Sorry to disappoint, but I'm here to meet with Franklin," I say, remembering what Crenshaw told me. I assume Franklin is Frankie, but I can't be sure, and I'd be lying if I said I wouldn't be relieved if it turned out to be someone else entirely.

The color drains from her face. "Please tell me you're not Graham Scott?"

When I don't answer right away, she squeezes her eyes closed, muttering under her breath before she opens them once more and says, "Please tell me you are *not* the new guy I'm training?"

I grin and spread my arms. "Guilty," I say, even though truthfully, I have no idea what the hell I'm doing here. All I know is the little I was told in the clipped phone call.

"This *cannot* be happening," she mutters.

"Afraid so, sweetheart."

Her little hands ball into fists on top of the desk while she utters, "I'm a professional. I'm a professional," over and over.

"You finished?" I ask once she pauses for a breath. "Now that we have that established, am I supposed to go somewhere . . .?" I ask, swallowing my nerves at the thought.

"Unfortunately for me, you're in the right place." Her smile tightens. "Franklin had something come up, so he asked me to show you around and fill you in on your job duties before you meet with him."

Relief sweeps through me. Anything to put off the inevitable. "This should be fun." I grin.

"If fun is sticking an electric prod in your eye, then yes." She lowers her head, taps something into the computer screen, and the printer beside her comes to life. Turning back to me, she says, "If I'm going to be training you, then you should know I'm deaf. I wear a cochlear implant, so I can hear, but it's helpful it you face me, speak clearly, and don't garble your words."

"I don't garble." I huff, trying not to show the surprise on my face. I never would've guessed she was deaf. Not that one would know by looking, but . . . "So, that's why you have the sexy voice," I say as it clicks into place.

Shit. I wince, realizing I just said that out loud.

"What?" She blinks as if she didn't hear me right, and it dawns on me maybe she didn't.

"The sexy voice. You have this sultry, Miley Cyrus sort of vibe going on. It's fucking hot. I mean, until the actual word vomit ruins it," I say with a smirk.

She narrows her eyes, but her cheeks heat, and I can't tell if it's a blush from calling her voice sexy, or anger from the latter insult.

She murmurs something in the back of her throat, then turns to the printer and grabs a small stack of papers. "Well, at least I have a new goal in life."

"And what's that?" I ask.

She slaps the stack into my chest. "Either getting you to quit, or getting you fired."

SKYLAR

The moment Graham leaves to meet with Franklin in the employee break room, I hurry away from the receptionist desk. His words play over and over in my head as my feet carry me down the short hallway to the conference room.

So, that's why you have the sexy voice.

I try to remain unaffected. I push his words to the farthest recesses of my brain, letting them roll off me like raindrops. But they're still all I can think about.

Because someone, namely a hot boy, thinks my voice is sexy.

I don't know if he's the first person to think it, but he's certainly the first one to say it.

After all the grueling years spent in speech therapy; all the times when I was young and I got made fun of because my voice sounded funny those first handful of years, or I mispronounced something, it feels cathartic. Surreal.

My voice is naturally raspy, and when I don't have my implants in, it drops even lower. Never in a million years would I have thought someone might actually *like* my voice, let alone call it sexy.

Figures the first one to think so is Graham.

I grimace and find Brad in the conference room, his head bent over a stack of paperwork.

I have no idea what his little display in front of Graham meant, but I'm dismissing the little voice in the back of my head telling me he only kissed my cheek to piss Graham off, and hoping it's a good sign instead. Never mind the fact that he completely ignored me at school today; it's a minor detail, one I'm inclined to ignore.

Clearing my throat, I wait until he glances up, then step into the room. "Hey . . ."

He sits the pen in his hand down on the desk and leans back in his chair. "So, are you two dating?" He nods toward the hallway. "Is that what Saturday night was about?"

"What?" I flinch. "No. What on earth would make you say that?"

"Uh, because he gave me a black eye for coming on to you, and suddenly, he works here. It's not a giant leap to think—"

"*No.*" I wave my arms a little too emphatically. "I don't even know him. He was a stranger to me until the other night."

Brad arches a brow, then shakes his head and mutters something I can't quite hear.

My eyes widen. "You don't believe me?"

Brad's lips thin, and for a moment, I don't think he's going to answer, but then he says, "I find it a little hard to believe that some random decided to get into a bar brawl over a girl he doesn't even know. And why? Because I had the nerve to check you out? Because I wanted you to dance with me? And I'm supposed to believe it's some cosmic coincidence he shows up here today?" He scoffs and stares back down at the papers on his desk.

I step forward, anger curling my hands into fists. "Yes, that's exactly what I expect you to believe because it's the truth. And to be fair, I can see how it might have looked as though you were bothering me."

"I should've pressed charges," he says with a shake of the head.

I wave a hand out in front of me. "Be my guest."

Brad's mouth hardens and he narrows his eyes. "You really wouldn't care?"

I shoot him a look that says, *what do you think?*

"Okay, then," he says, tapping his pen on the desk while he eyes me. "If you and Rocky Balboa out there aren't an item like I say you are, then prove it."

I sigh, suddenly, unsure of whether kissing Brad's ass is worth it. I should tell him to go to hell and be done with it. "How?" I ask, eyeing him warily.

"Go out with me."

I bark out a laugh. "Are you serious?"

He lifts a shoulder and smiles. "Go out with me and I'll believe the two of you aren't together, and I won't interfere with your chances at winning the Oak Ridge scholarship."

All the air rushes from my lungs.

I shouldn't be surprised by his request. He's been working up to this for weeks; he just finally found an excuse to coerce me.

But I can't be bought, and I don't like boys that assume I can. No matter how badly I want to win that scholarship, I won't sacrifice my integrity to do it, so I say, "Go to hell," and slam the door on my way out.

CHAPTER 7

GRAHAM

I INHALE AS I head in the direction Skylar pointed, toward the employee break room. I guess it was too much to ask to merely work at the reception desk in a hotel lobby. Of course Crenshaw would have something else in store for me, and I wonder exactly what that is as I hover outside the door labeled *Employees Only*.

My stomach does a backflip as I push the door open and step inside.

Frankie stands by a small kitchenette fixing a cup of coffee. He turns when he hears the door open and takes a sip, eyeing me over the rim of his cup with his beady eyes before he says, "Boss is waiting for you. Come on."

He turns without another word and brushes past me back out into the hallway, taking the first turn, and standing in front of the elevators. A stab of the finger on the button and the doors slide open. Waving for me to get in first, he follows me inside.

Once the doors close, he pulls an employee badge out of his pocket and holds it in front of the card reader. It beeps once and flashes green before the car lurches and begins to move. "Everything you're about to see and hear is confidential. You are not to talk about it with anyone, not even another employee. Understood?"

I nod, swallowing.

"If you slip up even once, it'll be the first and last time. Do you catch me drift?"

"Understood," I say, a hint of nerves in my voice.

"The elevators take either an employee badge or a guest key-card. You have to use it if you're going to the bottom floor, but only when you're alone for the reasons I just gave you. Only certain people have access to the basement. You're one of them."

Wiping my clammy palms on my pants, I focus on slowing my racing heart when the elevator dings and the doors slide open. I hold my breath, my mouth turning to sawdust, and Frankie steps out, allowing me the space to breathe. When he motions for me to follow, I hurry behind him on rubbery legs, wondering what in the hell we're doing in the basement, knowing nothing good could possibly come of this.

With cautious steps, I venture forward, drawn deeper into the unknown when we reach a large steel door. Frankie swipes his card once more and we push through, stepping beneath an ornate archway.

My eyes widen as I scan the yawning mouth of the hidden room before me. It's unlike anything I've ever seen before. If I thought the Play House was impressive, this is remarkable.

An underground casino stretches out before me like a mirage, something only my imagination could conjure. But I'm not imagining things, nor am I dreaming. The space in front of me is real.

The air crackles with energy as I absorb what certainly must be Crenshaw's biggest secret and largest accomplishment. From the looks of it, the Play House is child's play compared to this, and as my gaze sweeps across the dimly lit expanse, I remember something Peters said to me the night at O'Malley's. *I know he has the Play House, but that's not where things end with him. Word is he has this whole underground casino. Like, big time. We're talking millions of dollars of illegal activity going in and out.*

Looks like he was right.

The T-shaped room is cavernous, illuminated by the seductive glow of slot machines, their colorful reels spinning in a mesmerizing dance. A poker table stands at the epicenter of the room, where players sit, straight-faced, engaging in a high-stakes battle of wits. The clatter of dice on the craps table echoes through the space, intertwining with the symphony of laughter and clinking glasses that emanate from the expansive bar at the end of the room.

With bated breath, I follow Frankie deeper into the space where Crenshaw waits, clad in a navy-blue suit that fits him like a glove. He holds a cigar in his left hand. Tendrils of smoke curl into the air around him as he turns his eyes on mine. "Graham," he greets me. "Welcome to the Gentleman's Club."

I scan the room with wide eyes as my mind races. "What is this place?" I ask. Even though it should be obvious, I can't seem to wrap my head around the fact this place exits in secret.

"It's an exclusive casino. Not everyone knows about it, and just like the Play House, not just anyone gets an invite to play here. Running a place like this on top of a legitimate enterprise like the Bardot is no small feat. And there are certain . . . duties"—he waves the cigar in his hand in the air, creating a ring of smoke—"that ultimately go hand in hand with my line of work. Eventually, we will summon you to help with them. In the meantime, you'll work the front desk of the lobby. We have a small staff downstairs, but everyone who works at the Gentleman's Club also works at the Bardot. It's easier to cover our tracks that way."

My chest tightens, and the lightness I felt in Skylar's presence earlier vanishes. "So, the hotel is . . .?"

"Let's just put it this way, the Bardot is a legitimate business. However, it's also a convenient way to conceal the money the casino pulls in."

Money laundering. Shit.

I scrub a hand over the scruff on my jaw, knowing I'm getting more than I bargained for as my eyes dart around the room, imagining what this place must look like packed with bodies rather than the few that are here now and wondering what he'll have me do.

"Where do I come in?" I ask, afraid of the answer. "I can't imagine how I can help you with this."

His eyes meet mine and the corners of his mouth curl as he steps closer, until he's so close the sweet scent of the smoke from his cigar burns my nose. "You'll do whatever I need, when I need it," he says, his tone flat. Then he slaps a hand on my shoulder and winks. "Why don't we just leave it at that for now, huh?"

A bead of sweat rolls down my back as he takes another puff on his cigar, a halo of smoke swirling around him. "Before you go back upstairs, I have a few ground rules. Frankie already told you about the confidentiality of what's in the basement?"

"Yeah." My gaze flickers to Frankie, who stands behind Crenshaw, stone-faced, sipping his coffee. "Only go on the elevator alone. Don't ever mention anything about this place or the basement to anyone, including employees."

"Also, the name Crenshaw, is never to be uttered beyond these walls. Ever. It's every bit as secret as the Gentleman's Club. You're not to acknowledge you know any of the clients who frequent the casino, nor any of the other employees here. If you don't work with them upstairs, you don't know them. Every single thing about this place, the people, and what goes on here is to be protected. Frankie is Franklin above ground, and if you have even the slightest lapse in judgment and slip up, it'll be the last thing you do."

He stubs his cigar out on the bar top, blowing a final stream of smoke in my face. "Think you can handle that?"

Do I have a choice?

I exhale, my gaze flickering around me as I nod.

"Good. Both jobs will work toward paying off your debt to me, but anything you do for me down here, pays more. For now, you can go. Be sure to report for your training in the lobby tomorrow, same time."

I turn, my mind spinning as I cross the room toward the archway I entered with Frankie.

"Oh, and Graham?" he calls after me.

I pause, glancing over my shoulder as his lips pull into a smug smile. "You didn't think I'd let you off that easy, did you?"

CHAPTER 8

SKYLAR

*H*OW? THAT'S ALL *I wanna know.*

How in the world did he get hired here?

The million-dollar question has been running through my head ever since he stepped through those doors yesterday and I discovered he was the new hire.

His eyes flicker up and down my body as I direct him to stand against a blank wall and tell him to smile before I snap a photo with my phone, then return to my computer.

"You know, I feel like we got off to a bad start," he says, rocking on his heels in a casual way that irritates the crap out of me.

"Uh huh." I upload the photo to the computer, only half listening as his badge prints.

"Why don't we start fresh?"

I glance up at him to see if he's actually serious, one hand on my hip while I drum my fingers on the counter with my other, staring at his stupidly handsome face trying to find a flaw.

There's gotta be something . . .

A wart.

A hairy mole.

Boogers in his nose.

Ear hair.

A pimple the size of Texas.

Something!

Damnit, I find nothing.

I scowl when the laminating machine beeps, and I turn back around, even more irritated than I was only moments ago. Until I get a glimpse of his badge and feel the telltale tug of a smile pull at the corners of my mouth. "Here," I say, slapping it into his chest.

He takes it from me, and our fingers brush while I try to ignore the zap that courses through me; it's like I've touched a bare wire.

"What the hell is this?" He frowns, his eyes trained on the photo.

"Oh. Your employee badge. Everyone has them. It gives you access to different rooms and floors of the hotel, depending on your role here."

He huffs and rolls his eyes. "I know what it is, I just . . ." He holds it out in front of my face as if I hadn't been the Picasso behind this masterpiece.

"What?" I shrug, stifling a smile.

"It's terrible. It doesn't even look like me. Look at the face I'm making. It looks like my skin is melting. What the hell went wrong with the printer?"

I peer down at the badge, my eyes narrowed into slits, then blink back up at him. "Looks pretty accurate to me," I say as I turn and greet a customer at the desk.

"You have to retake it," he says from behind me.

"No can do."

The heat of his glare burns into my back while I check a patron out of their room and print them a receipt. When they leave, I wish them a great day with the biggest smile I can muster, all while ignoring the boy beside me.

"So, Skylar, huh?"

I glance over at him to see him eyeing my badge. "That's my name, yes."

"Cute." He flicks the plastic card attached to the lanyard around my neck, muttering under his breath, "For a viper."

I shoot him a look that lets him know exactly what I think of him when he asks, "So, the implants you mentioned earlier . . ."

"What about them?"

"Can I see one?"

I blink up at him, unsure of whether he's being a dick or genuine, but his expression remains smooth, serious. With a sigh, I lift my hair so he can see the device curled around the top of my right ear and the circular implant on my head close behind it.

"Wow. That's pretty cool. I never would've known."

"My hair usually hides it," I say, surprised at his open curiosity. I'm used to people either being rudely nosy about it or completely ignoring the fact I'm deaf. So, Graham being openly inquisitive is refreshing in an odd way.

Not that I'd tell him that.

"So, without them . . .?"

"Can't hear a thing. Which is good news for me."

"Why's that?"

"Because when the sound of your voice grates on my nerves and I want to be rid of you, all I have to do is turn them off," I say sweetly. Graham frowns, which makes me want to smile. "Now," I clap my hands together, "ready for training?"

Over the course of the next hour, I give him a tour of the first level of the Bardot, inform him of some of our more important policies, show him how to use the computer, and explain reservations, rates, and bookings. All the essentials. And in that time, I still haven't figured out how to get him to quit or get him fired. All I know is I can't stand to be around someone who will not only undermine me but purposefully get under my skin at every turn. Work is my happy place. I enjoy it here and find the monotony of my job relaxing. There's a special kind of peace in being good at your job, but Graham's presence threatens to ruin anything and everything good about this place.

"You know, for such a pretty little thing, you really shouldn't frown," he says as I go over the room service charges. "It makes you look all pruney."

I grit my teeth. "Oh, I'm sorry. Is this better?" I tip my mouth up in a smile so wide, I feel like the Joker.

"Never mind." He cringes.

I drop my smile, and the urge to punch him in his stupid mouth with his stupid full lips hits a crescendo. "Despite what you think, I don't need your approval, and women aren't just pretty little things meant for the enjoyment of the male gaze. Expressions exist for a reason, to convey one's feelings. And I have a feeling I'll be scowling a lot more often after today," I mutter, "so get used to it."

He chuckles, covering the sound with his hand. Why does he find everything I say so dang funny, when I'm being perfectly serious?

"Hilarious, but I'm not buying it." He rounds the front desk where he cages me in with one hand planted on the counter and the other on the back of my chair.

Swallowing, I ask, "What's not to buy?"

"You're so attracted to me, you don't know what to do with yourself. I can see it in your eyes."

I scoff while his green eyes bore into mine, and I think, *you're not wrong,* before my stomach backflips into denial. "Please. I'd rather pour hot sauce on my retinas than look your way with any sort of desire."

"Whatever you say." He smirks.

Franklin walks by the reception desk and the smirk falls. Immediately Graham straightens, his posture as rigid as his expression.

Interesting. He's all cocky swagger with me, but intimidated by authority.

While Franklin grabs something from the storage closet, I take the opportunity to study Graham in the silence. My gaze dips to his mouth. He's standing so close, I can see how soft his and full lips look.

A moment later, Franklin disappears down the hallway once more and Graham's relief is palpable as he focuses back on me as I struggle to remember where we left off. "You clearly want me to be attracted to you, which tells me *you're* the one attracted to *me*. I bet you just can't stand it that I'm not throwing myself at you. Let me guess?" I tap my chin as if deep in thought. "Your privilege screams money. I'm guessing you're one of the most popular boys at school, too."

My gaze homes in on the biceps straining against the fabric of his dress shirt. "Probably quarterback of the football team." I roll my eyes because I'm sure I'm right and it's so cliche. "Most likely to be Prom King. I bet girls just throw themselves at your feet. Am I close?"

The flicker of muscle in his jaw confirms the truth, and I'm about to tell him so when we're interrupted by the sound of footsteps.

"Well, who do we have here?" Rosa asks as I turn to her.

Dressed in her usual polo shirt and dress slacks, with her hair pulled back in a bun, her presence makes me smile. Rosa's been in housekeeping at the hotel since its inception and is one of the Bardot's most valued employees. She's also the closest thing I have to a mother, the voice of reason in my life when I feel as though I'm falling off the deep end.

"This the new guy?" she asks, glancing from me to Graham with a toothy grin.

"Unfortunately," I grump.

Rosa's smile fades, and I can understand why. I'm normally not this rude, especially not at work. But Graham somehow brings it out in me.

"She has all the manners of a feral barn cat, doesn't she?" Graham says, and I fight the urge to prove him right and claw his eyes out.

Instead, I hiss while Rosa chuckles, eyes wide as she glances between us. Extending a hand, Graham takes it in his while I try not to stare at how large and strong they look. "Graham Scott," he says.

Rosa smiles. "I'm Rosa Diaz. I run the cleaning crew here at Bardot, and my kids are all grown, so I'm here most days. If this one gives you any trouble," she says, motioning to me, "just holler."

"Traitor," I mumble while Rosa grins.

"Nice to meet you, Rosa," Graham says with a smile. "It's refreshing to see at least someone with manners around here." He winks at me, then returns his perfect smile back to her. "Something tells me I'll be taking you up on that offer."

When Rosa laughs, her whole body shakes. "It'll be nice to have a strapping young man around here. We could use you."

He puffs his chest for show, and I want to barf.

"Ugh. Don't encourage him," I say. "His head is already five times the size of the Empire State building."

Rosa places her hands on her hips, her eyes bright. "At least he's easy on the eyes. We could do a lot worse."

"If Shrek is easy on the eyes, then sure." I shrug.

A smirk plays on Rosa's lips. "Girl, why are you playing?" She swats at me. "He's exactly your type. He's exactly *everybody's* type."

My cheeks heat. If I had a mirror, I'm sure they'd be red as a tomato.

Is she trying to kill me?

An incoherent sound bubbles from the back of my throat. "You can't be serious?"

"All that sandy hair. Muscles for days. Those gemstone green eyes and that charming smile. Oof, he's like a more muscular, masculine version of Harry Styles without the accent."

"The accent is half the turn-on," I say, pulling at straws, but I can hardly think with Graham's laser beam eyes glaring holes in me. "Everyone knows a great accent instantly elevates your looks."

"Oh, honey, back in my day . . ." Rosa hums suggestively in the back of her throat, and I want to murder her. Or die. I'm not sure which. Maybe whatever comes first.

I open my mouth to defend myself, to tell her how grotesque I find him and that he's nothing like Harry Styles—*nothing!*—but the ogre beats me to it. Placing a hand on his chest, he offers Rosa what I'm sure is his most charming smile. "Rosa, don't tease me like that. My heart can't take it."

She tips her head back and laughs. "Boy, you be lookin' like you stepped off the cover of GQ."

"Pfftt." I roll my eyes. "Let's not get carried away," I say, but they ignore me. It's like I'm not even here.

"Too bad she's trying to sabotage me," Graham says, shaking his head sadly. "It's only my first day and she's already gunning for me. Just look at my badge," he says, holding it out. "Do you think it's because she's jealous of my beauty?"

"Oh, dear." Rosa gasps and covers her mouth as she takes in the photo in all its glory. It's probably my best masterpiece to date.

"You know what they say?" I singsong, feeling smug about my handiwork. "The camera never lies."

Rosa glances between us, humor dancing in her eyes. "Surely, Skylar can retake it, huh?"

"Nope. Sorry." I cross my arms over my chest. "Out of ink. What an inconvenience, isn't it?"

Rosa stares at me for a moment before she bursts out laughing. "I like this." She motions between us. "Anyway, I'm off the clock, so I better get going." She turns for the door, calling over her shoulder. "Don't let her scare you off, you hear?"

"Not a chance," he mutters, his eyes on the side of my face while my cheeks burn even hotter.

Is it too late to find a new job?

GRAHAM

It's only been two days since I started working with Skylar. Two days where the unease of making a deal with Crenshaw has been diminished by her presence. He's yet to call on me to join him in the Gentleman's Club, but I know my days of skating by at the front desk are numbered. Eventually, he'll call on me for more, and when he does I won't like whatever he asks of me. But in the meantime, bantering with Skyler takes the edge off.

I try to imagine what it would be like working with anyone else in this situation, and I can't. The knot in my stomach every time I catch a glimpse of Frankie or think about what Crenshaw has in store for me indicates I'd be a walking time bomb of nerves. Skylar's biting remarks loosen the knot. Her sweet face and raspy voice somehow make me forget I'm in way over my head. Her presence calms me, her sarcasm soothes me, and I find myself looking forward to each and every exchange, rather than dreading my time here like I should.

Someone clears their throat, and I glance toward the sound to find a female guest waiting for help. She smiles slightly, and it showcases her already obvious beauty.

"Can I help you?" I say with a flirty smile I know will irritate Skylar. I can feel her gaze, as we speak, boring into the back of my skull.

"Yes," she all but purrs, batting her ridiculously long eyelashes. "I was hoping I could get a few extra towels? I like to take long, luxurious bubble baths."

Bat, bat, bat.

I roll my eyes inwardly, because she's trying way too hard, which is a total turn-off. Not that I'd let Skylar know her interest in me is unwelcome. I quite like the glare she's currently aiming my way.

"Oh." Skylar moves closer to the woman and squints. "Do you have something in your eye?" She points to her fluttering lids and the woman abruptly stops.

"What?" She touches one of them, and I wonder if she's checking to see if her false lashes are still there. "Uh, no."

Skylar rolls her lips inward, fighting a smile that forces me to stifle one of my own.

"Excuse my colleague's rude behavior," I say, mostly to annoy her. Leaning further over the counter, I grin. "I can appreciate a good bubble bath. What's your room number?"

"212."

"Got it." I wink, and I'm pretty sure I hear a gagging sound come from Skylar's direction. "We'll have some sent up for you."

She grins. "Do you hand deliver them yourself?"

Skylar gapes before she snaps her mouth shut, her nose crinkling in in disgust.

"Unfortunately, I don't," I say, trying my best to sound contrite. "Sorry to disappoint."

"Damn," the woman mutters, then turns and heads for the elevators.

Once she's out of earshot, Skylar arches a brow. "Gross. She's nearly twice your age."

I laugh and lift a shoulder. "So? Age is just a number." She scoffs. "No harm in looking. Or flirting," I say, my tone teasing.

She's the third woman this week to practically throw herself at me. I think Skylar referred to the others as "thirsty," which got a good chuckle out of me.

"Whatever." She grimaces and walks around the desk. "I suppose I'm the one hand delivering those towels?"

"I mean, I figured it might be unprofessional to get mauled on the job. But if you want me to, I can take one for the team."

"You're despicable."

"If I'm so despicable, why is it that I can be charming to so many of our guests while you seem to scare them away?"

"Right. You're such a charmer," she says like it's farfetched when we both know it's not. "That's why I got more tips than you last week."

I tap a finger on my chin, pretending to ponder. "Ah, yes, the elusive 'generous tips' phenomenon. I'm yet to experience it myself."

"Maybe if you spent more time working on your customer service skills and less time perfecting your hair and flirting with cougars, the universe might reward you, too, and the men, who are the ones who actually tip, would take notice."

I point, pushing the real reason I'm here—Crenshaw—to the back of my mind with the easy banter. "First, how do you know the men aren't giving you tips because they're checking out your rack?" My gaze flickers pointedly to her chest.

"Um, barf," she says.

"Also, it's sexist to assume men tip better." I place a hand over my heart. "And cold. You wound my masculine sensibilities, Skylar."

She rolls her eyes and pushes on my arm. "Like anything could wound you or your massive ego."

"Only you, Skylar." The sincerity in my voice startles even me as her eyes meet mine, searching to see if I'm serious. A hint of a smile plays on my lips, but I try and keep my expression neutral. Our flirting is harmless. It means absolutely nothing—a distraction for why I'm really here, the one thing keeping me sane at the possibility at any moment Crenshaw could call on me.

The air crackles between us before she turns away.

"You may think I wear a scowl all the time, but I'll have you know, there are plenty of men who hit on me while I'm working."

I raise a brow. "Oh, yeah?"

She nods, taking a step closer until she's in my face. "Plenty." She meets my eyes, so I know just how serious she is, even though I can tell she's bluffing. Though I have no idea why men haven't come onto her. She's witty, whip smart, and gorgeous—the perfect combination.

"What's the best pickup line they've used?" I ask, unable to help myself.

She blinks. "What?"

"The best line." I cross my arms over my chest. "Give it to me."

"Uh . . ." She shifts on her feet, panic flickering in her eyes. "Um . . ."

"You don't have one, do you?"

"Of course I do."

I wave a hand out in front of me, waiting for her response.

"One time, a guy leaned over the counter and trailed a finger up my arm and said, 'Besides being sexy, what do you do for a living?'"

I'm pretty sure I've seen that same line from a cheesy Facebook meme, but I don't say so. Instead, I scrunch my nose. "But you work here. He obviously knows what you do for a living. That's so stupid. It doesn't even make sense to use that line."

She rolls her lips, nodding. "I know. Precisely the point," she says, waving her arms around. "Now you see my plight. The options out there are pretty dismal."

When I narrow my eyes, she keeps rambling.

"See what I'm up against? That's why I'm holding out for someone truly special. Maybe a mature college boy who knows what he wants, unlike all of the juvenile boys I know."

As soon as the words leave her lips, her cheeks flush a bright shade of pink.

"Right." I roll my eyes. "Because there couldn't possibly be immature college boys, or conversely mature high school boys that know what they want, for that matter."

"Conversely?" She blinks up at me as if shocked by my well-rounded vocabulary.

"It's when you state something that's the reversal of—"

"I know what it means," she snaps.

I raise my hands in the air, my lips quirking.

"As I was saying, I'm holding out," she says, buckling down. "The boys our age are . . . well, let's just say they're not exactly Prince Charming material."

"Are you implying that I can't be Prince Charming material?" I point to my chest.

She scoffs. "You?"

"I'll have you know"—I step forward, so close, I can smell the sweet scent of her perfume, and my stomach flutters—"that I can be romantic. In fact, I guarantee you I could sweep you off your feet if I wanted to."

She swallows, a pensive look in her eyes. "So why are you single?"

"How do you know I'm single?" I arch a brow.

"Call it an educated guess." She stares up at me, and my breathing picks up.

The last thing I want is to talk about past relationships.

I shrug, then step back. "Maybe I don't believe in love."

"Oh, of course, you're jaded. I should've guessed," she says, irritation spiking her words. Though I'm unclear on why my opinion on love should irritate her so much. Then again, everything about me seems to annoy her.

I shrug. "Not jaded."

"Riiiight." She brushes past me and gives me a little pat on my chest. It's clearly meant to be condescending, but her expression darkens as she lingers over the wall of muscle beneath my shirt. "You know, Graham," she clears her throat, her breathing shallow, "you should work on being a little less predictable."

I laugh just as Frankie—or Franklin—rounds the corner and the sound dies in my throat. He shoots me a caustic look, his gaze calculating as it lingers to the place where Skylar's hand touches my chest.

Noticing my stare, Skylar drops her hand and turns toward Frankie and smiles while a bead of sweat prickles my spine.

"Graham, can I get help with something a moment?" he asks.

"Sure." I step away from Skylar but not before I note the smug look of satisfaction on her lips.

I follow Frankie down the hallway where we pause at the elevators and he wordlessly scans his badge before we descend.

I barely look at him as we ride the elevator down to the basement, and I wonder what Crenshaw has in store for me.

When the elevator dings and the doors open, I wipe my clammy palms on my pants and step out, following behind Frankies as he pushes through the double doors and makes his way through the grand entryway, past the poker tables and slot machines. When we round the corner, I spot Crenshaw at the bar, same as the first time I came here.

He swirls the liquid in his glass, his brow pinched as his dark gaze penetrates straight through me. It's a full minute, during which I fidget with the cuffs of my sleeves, my pulse pounding in my ears, before he speaks.

He takes a sip of his drink before he steeples his hands. "It's time I give you more than just desk work. I have a small job."

A bead of sweat rolls down my back. It feels like someone has me in a choke hold. I'm two seconds away from a full-blown panic attack, wondering what in the hell he'll have me do. I remind myself to breathe through the vice grip on my lungs. And because I can tell he's waiting on something from me, I ask, "What do you need?"

Turning, Crenshaw snaps his fingers, and Frankie steps forward, handing him a thick manilla envelope. "For your first assignment, I need you to drop this off. You'll wait until the end of your shift, then head to the address on the back and slide it inside the mailbox, flip the flag up, then disappear. Got it?"

I stare down at it like it's a ticking time bomb, wondering what's inside. Drugs? Cash? I have no idea, but I don't like being the messenger. Worse yet, I have no choice.

My hands shake as I reach out and take it, surprised at its weight. "What is it?" I ask, not sure I even want to know.

Crenshaw cocks his head and smirks before he lifts a finger and waggles it in my face. "No questions." Then he nods toward the way I came. "Go."

Two hours later, I grip the steering wheel of my car while the glow of the lamplight above illuminates the street before me. My hands ache, the skin pulled tight over bone. A headache blooms in the front of my head while I stare straight ahead. It's been twenty minutes since I stashed the envelope in the mailbox at the address Crenshaw gave me, yet no one has claimed it.

I shouldn't be here. I shouldn't be waiting to see who retrieves it in the vain hope of getting a glimpse of what's inside. But part of me needs to know what I had a hand in, because I suspect coming from Crenshaw, the contents of the envelope can't be anything good.

Still, there's not a single soul in sight, and I'm well aware I could be waiting here all night and still leave empty-handed. I wait a while longer, my thoughts drifting to Skylar, wishing she were here to distract me, and wondering if her presence at work will be enough in the coming days and weeks to divert my thoughts from Crenshaw and all the things he'll have me do for him in the future.

I glance up and down the empty road once more, taking one last look at the mailbox before I pull away from the curb. I pass it with a sinking in the pit of my stomach. I may never know what the hell was in that envelope. Maybe it's better I don't. In fact, I'm almost certain it is, but it doesn't make it any easier to leave it and walk away.

CHAPTER 9

SKYLAR

I'M CONVINCED SOMEONE IS trying to punish me. I'm not sure I could be any more annoyed than I am at this very moment. Or maybe it's the fact that I'm waiting on Mallory's phone call that's making me extra prickly. It's only been a few days since the night at O'Malley's and though Brad hasn't mentioned the Oak Ridge scholarship, I have no idea where I stand. The list of finalists is supposed to post any minute, and I'm waiting on the phone call that will either make or break me. If I'm on the list, I have every confidence the scholarship money will be mine. But if I'm not . . .

Well, I can't even think about that possibility, because at the moment, I have no other options. It's the only way I have to show my brother that I'm more than capable of providing for and taking care of myself.

"Hey, someone said the water thing is out." Graham's shadow hovers above me as I scroll through a list of possible art scholarships I found online.

"So, fill it," I say, my tone flat.

"What about the stuff in it?"

I sigh as my gaze drifts to the crystal beverage dispensers. "You mean the fruit?" I ask like he's a total moron.

"Yeah. Do I need to do anything with that?"

"No," I say, going back to my reading. "Every morning, the kitchen has fresh fruit set aside for this and whoever's on front desk at the time cleans the containers and swaps it out."

"Okay." He stands there, still hovering when Franklin passes by the reception desk.

I say hello as he grabs something from the supply cabinets, watching as Graham's easy demeanor shifts. He stiffens as his gaze follows Franklin's every move, and I wonder if he's worried about getting in trouble for fraternizing on the job.

Graham tenses further, his posture rigid as Franklin passes by us once more, then heads through the lobby, back down the hallway. Once he's out of sight, Graham deflates and his questioning gaze returns to mine.

Taking pity on him, I wave him off. "Just use tap water. In the kitchen. Go."

When he returns a few minutes later, he checks a family—husband, wife and their teenage daughter—into their room.

My gaze drifts up to him, watching as a lock of sandy hair falls in his eyes while he speaks. The teenage girl stares up at him with pink cheeks and doe eyes, hanging onto his every word.

I try to push aside my annoyance. He really does have the most spectacular eyes, warm and vibrant, unlike the odd amber, hazel color of my own.

Just one more reason to hate him, I think, begrudgingly.

I tear my gaze away from him, immersing myself back in my search when the phone rings. I pick it up and answer as Graham hands the family their keycards.

"Hey, lady." Mallory's voice fills the line, and I suck in a breath as I try and decipher the nuance of her voice.

"Is the list posted?" I ask, wishing I were there to see it myself.

"It is."

Her clipped response does nothing to ease the anxiety in my chest. "And . . .?"

She sighs, and I can practically hear her shoulders slump as she says, "I'm sorry, honey."

"I'm not on it," I confirm, a sinking feeling in the pit of my stomach.

There's a long pause, then, "No."

All of the air rushes from my lungs. Any hope I had that Brad might not be a douche and ruin this for me go up in smoke.

"There are other scholarships, Skylar. Other ways to get money for school," Mallory says.

"It's December, Mal. I'm running out of options and you know it." I shake my head, feeling the press of tears sting the back of my eyes. "Maybe I'm not meant to go. Maybe I should just forget it. Stay here. Work at the hotel for the rest of my life."

The thought depresses me.

"You can always tell JD. Be honest with him, and I'm sure he'll understand. He'd probably give you—"

"I don't want him to pay my way through school. Gosh, Mal, he's sacrificed enough. He's given his life up for me. How can I tell him I want to leave him, then ask for him to pay the way?"

"It's not like that."

My throat aches and I hastily swipe at my eyes at the same time Graham looks my way. His expression softens, and I hate the concern I see there, so I shift away from him. Give me his sarcasm any day, but his sympathy? That's a hard no.

I lift my chin in case he's still watching and will the tears to stop. Feeling sorry for myself will get me nowhere. "Accepting his help would be exactly like that," I say.

"Don't give up, Skylar."

My chin wobbles. It's taking everything for me not to cry. "I gotta go. Thanks for staying after school to check the list." I hang up without waiting for her goodbye, ignoring the heat of Graham's gaze on the side of my face as the flames of anger reignite in my chest.

If it weren't for him, my name would be on that list. I'm sure of it.

Chapter 10

GRAHAM

I STARE AT MYSELF in my bathroom mirror. My T-shirt is damp with sweat and my athletic shorts hang low on my hips. Football season might be over, but I still go to the gym almost every day. Athleticism and muscle are forged year-round, not just in season, and though I have no idea if I'll be playing ball next year at college, it's more a force of habit than anything. That, and it's about the only thing helping relieve my stress these days other than a bottle of Jack, and since I'm trying to cut back on stupid decisions, Jack Daniels will have to party without me.

Not that I have much time for partying these days.

Between school and my job at the Bardot, I have no time for anything else. When I told Crenshaw I'd work for him, and he agreed, I knew he wouldn't let me off easy, but I also hadn't expected to be at the hotel almost every fucking day. The guys keep calling and asking me to spend time with them. Even Mackenzie and Atlas are wondering where the hell I am when the crew hangs out at Roasted, the local coffee shop, after school. I know I should just tell them the truth, or at least a partial truth, about where I'm spending my time, but it'll only open me up to more questions, and I don't have the energy for that.

Then there's Skylar.

It's been more than a week since my first day, and the girl is still every bit a pain in the ass as she was the moment I met her. Inside her chest is a block of ice, but for reasons I can't explain, she brings out a side of me I don't recognize. Around her, I find I'm more playful, carefree, and bold, whereas I'm normally reserved, cool, and calm. Biting remarks and playful banter aren't normally a part of my vocabulary, but the more I'm around her, the more I find I like the dynamic between us. At the very least, it's entertaining enough to help me forget what's going on at home and the ever-present threat of Crenshaw hovering over me like a blanket of angry thunderclouds.

My phone buzzes on the bathroom sink, and I pick it up to see Jace's name flash across the screen.

Shit.

I run a hand through my sweat-damp hair, contemplating whether I should answer. I know he wants to hang out, but I've been blowing him off, and if I don't pick up, Teagan will call next, then Knox. Maybe even Atlas. Who knows how long I'll be working for Crenshaw, which means sooner or later, I'll have to give them some sort of explanation. These guys are like a dog with a bone with zero chill.

I swipe the screen, then pick it up and bring it to my ear. "What's up?"

"We're hanging at the cabin tonight. You in?" Jace's breath puffs into the phone. In the background, I hear a steady hum, along with the pounding of feet, which is how I know he's running on the treadmill.

"Nope. Not tonight."

"Why the fuck not?" I hear Teagan say in the background. *Great. They're together.*

"Because I have shit to do. Besides, aren't you guys the ones who suggested I stop drinking so much? If we go to the cabin, that's all we'll do."

"Well, yeah. But we never said to be a total buzzkill. It's Crow's Creek, man. The cabin means we can crash, so none of us have to drive. We haven't hung out in ages. Dude, think about it. The last time we all got together was when we won State, and Atlas found out his dad overdosed, then practically launched himself off a fucking roof. We need this."

I pinch the bridge of my nose, sensing they're not going to take no for an answer, at least not without a fight.

"Maybe that should tell us something. When we all hang out, it's dangerous. Bad karma. It's—"

"Cut the bullshit," Jace says as the humming of the treadmill in the background comes to an abrupt stop. "Even Atlas and Mackenzie are coming, and they're usually so busy sucking face and reciting sonnets, or whatever the hell it is they do in their spare time, to grace us with their presence for more than an hour."

I turn and lean my back into the sink. "Ooh, sounds right up my alley. Watch the former love of my life hang all over my cousin."

"Shit." Jace scoffs. "Aren't you used to that by now? Besides, I thought you were over that and everything was cool?"

I sigh. "I am."

Mostly.

But sometimes it still fucking hurts when we're all together. A single look between them, the sound of her laughter, or even the hint of apple blossoms in the air can send me spiraling without warning. The only difference between now and months ago is I handle it a whole hell of a lot better. I recover quicker. These days, I'm able to lick my wounds and move on; an acquired trait I'm rather fucking proud of.

"Then give me one good reason."

An image of Skylar pops in my head.

Hell. Here we go . . .

"I have to work," I say.

Jace chuckles. "Yeah, okay, buddy."

"Seriously."

"What the fuck do you mean you have to work? Like, for your dad? At your house?"

"No, like a real job. You know, punch a time card, get a paycheck. That kind of shit."

"You got a fucking job? When?" he asks, his tone ripe with disbelief.

I roll my eyes and exit the bathroom, because apparently, this is gonna take a while. I sink down on the edge of my bed and sigh. "About two weeks ago."

"Why?"

I contemplate my options. I can lie through my teeth or . . . or what? I can't exactly tell him the truth. *Oh, I owe ten thousand fucking dollars to some thugs who threatened to smash my hands to bits, and who knows what else if I don't pay, so I'm working off my debt.* Yeah, that'll go over really well. Hell, he probably wouldn't even believe me, so I go with the first thing that pops in my mind.

"A girl."

"A girl?" Jace repeats like he didn't hear me the first time. "I'm sorry, I think the line is breaking up. It sounds like you just said *a girl*. Do you hear this shit, T?" Jace says, his voice muffled. "Graham said he got a job because of a girl."

"No way," Teagan says in the background.

"Why is that so hard to believe?"

Shit. I know why it's so hard to believe. I'm still not 100 percent over Mackenzie yet. Hell, I just used her as an excuse not to join them at Crow's Creek, and now here I am telling them I'm so interested in some random chick they've never heard of that I got a job. Real believable.

Smooth, Scott.

"So, you got a job because of a girl. To, what, impress her? Spend time with her?" he asks, his tone incredulous.

"Yeah, I met her at a bar. She was pretty chill," I lie, because Skylar was anything but chill. "There was a spark of interest, something there for the first time since everything with Mackenzie. So, when I found out the place she works at was hiring, I applied for a job. I figured it was the best way to get to know her without the pressure of actually dating, since she doesn't go to Riverside."

It must be believable because for a moment, Jace is speechless. There's nothing but silence on the other line, and I give myself a mental pat on the back.

"Sounds like a rebound chick," he finally says. "Is this a rebound thing?"

I throw my free arm out as I shout, "No! I don't know . . . maybe?"

"Did you even think to consult us before getting a job?" he asks, and I can hear the hurt in his voice. "I mean, shit, man. When are we supposed to see each other?"

I press my fingers into the front of my skull. "Am I supposed to ask you before I wipe my ass, too? We see each other all the time at school, Jace."

"It's not enough," he says, his tone sullen.

I bark out a laugh. "You sound like a chick."

"That cuts deep, bro. Men have feelings, too."

I pinch the bridge of my nose, unsure of whether to laugh again or cry. "Listen, it's temporary. Besides, sooner or later, we'll all be going separate ways, anyway."

"Exactly. This is our final year together. Our last hurrah, and now I find out you've abandoned us for a piece of tail? That shit doesn't sit right with me, bro."

I scrub a hand over my face. "I'm sorry. Listen, I'll try to stop by after my shift, okay?"

"You're just saying that to placate me."

I press my lips together, half amused, half annoyed. "I promise. But, listen, I have to go."

"Fine." He sighs. "This chick better be a fucking ten. And be prepared to tell us all about her because we have questions. Serious questions."

I shove a hand through my hair, wondering what the hell I've gotten myself into. "Yeah, okay, fine. Later, I promise."

I hang up and chuck my phone to the side, then stand, heading toward the bathroom so I can shower and change before I need to be at the Bardot when there's a knock on my door.

My muscles instantly stiffen, a knee-jerk reaction at knowing my father might be on the other side. "Yeah?" I call out, hoping for my mother instead.

The door pushes open, and I see it's him. His gaze flickers over my gym shorts and sweat-stained T-shirt with a hint of approval. "Get some training in?"

I fight the urge to roll my eyes. Why can't he just call it a fucking workout? Why does everything have to be about training for football?

"Yeah, sure," I say, my tone bored.

"Good. Because I have a surprise for you." He nods and a small smile splits his lips. "Get showered up and changed. Something nice—a dress shirt and trousers, then meet me downstairs."

"Why?" I ask, my expression wary.

He smiles and raps his knuckles on my door frame. "We're headed to Penn State."

I frown. "What do you mean we're headed to Penn State?"

Dad beams. "What can I say? Your hard work paid off. They're interested in signing you and invited us to come tour the campus. I spoke with them a couple weeks ago but forgot to tell you."

My brows rise to my hairline.

Forgot to tell me? It's my future we're talking about here, and he didn't think it pertinent to fill me in?

It's just like him, riding my ass for years to play harder, do better and be the best, only for him to call the shots when I get to the finish line. The news shouldn't shock me, but after we won States, life went into a tailspin. He lost his brother to an overdose, Atlas had his accident, and everything else got put on the backburner. Including football. But I should've known that wouldn't last long.

My mind churns as I contemplate how the hell I'm going to travel to Penn State today when I'm supposed to work for Crenshaw. It's not like I can shirk this responsibility. Crenshaw doesn't strike me as the type that'll let me blow him or my debts off without repercussions.

I shove a hand through my hair and shake my head. There's no way around it; I have to tell him.

"I can't," I say.

"You *can't?*" My father huffs out a laugh. "Listen, you and I may have had our differences recently, but it's no reason to screw with your future."

I pierce him with a look. "This has nothing to do with your affair," I spit. "As much as I'd love to punish you by refusing a tour and screwing with recruitment, not everything involves you. I just . . . I have somewhere I need to be today, and I can't cancel."

The amusement in his expression fades as he takes me in. "You're serious?"

When I say nothing, he steps closer, pointing a finger at me. "You can, and you will."

Laughter bubbles in the back of my throat. "Wow," I mutter with a shake of the head. "You're unreal, you know that?"

He has balls to bark orders after everything he's done. I could expose him. I could tell my mother about Storm and Marie. Sell his story to a news outlet. Do any number of things to screw him over. But if he thinks for one second that I'm going to drop everything and do his bidding after all he's done to our family, he's insane.

"Nothing is more important than this. We're talking about your future here. And so far, the only other school that's interested isn't even a double-A. It's shit. Penn State is in the Big Ten. *This* is how you get noticed. *This* is how you come one step closer to a career in football. It's what we've worked so hard for. Playing for a good school isn't just important, it's fucking essential."

It's what *we've* worked so hard for? You've gotta be fucking kidding me.

"Then maybe I'm not meant to play football!" I bark out. "Don't you get it? I'm not you. I'm not good enough. Isn't that what you've been telling me for years? That I'm not there yet? I've heard it every single day. All the things I do wrong. All the areas in which I need to improve. You, more than anyone, should know I don't have what it takes, but now all of a sudden you want me to believe I do?"

"Everything I've said to you, I said to push you." He throws his hands out. "I made you better. Coached you. If I've been hard on you, it's only because I want to see you succeed, to see you reach your full potential and accomplish your dreams. Hell, you have it in you to be one the greats, to be even better than I ever was. Don't you see that? But you need to give a shit, Graham. Feel the fire in here." He points to his gut. "You need to have the drive. You always used to. So, tell me when that changed."

My stomach sinks, and the anger drains from my face.

Maybe he's right. Maybe I did lose my drive.

Or maybe I simply realized along the way that this was his dream, not mine.

But I don't say that. I can't. Because as pathetic as it is, I don't want to disappoint him more than I already have. After everything he's done, after he showed me how selfish he is, there's still the little boy inside me that seeks his approval—needs it to survive.

"So help me, if this is about Mackenzie . . ." he starts.

"It's not about Kenzie," I snap.

He stares at me a beat before he smooths a hand down his dress shirt with a nod. "Good. Then do whatever it is you need to get ready because we have to leave within the hour if we're going to make it."

"I told you, I can't." *Fuck it.* "I have to work," I add. "And I can't just call out after two weeks."

"You have to . . .?" He stares at me for a moment as if trying to work out whether I'm serious or not. "Is that where you've been lately? I just assumed you were at the gym or training."

When I shake my head, he tips his head back and laughs. "You don't need a job. I can give you whatever you want. *Football* is your job. Now, stop playing around and get ready."

I glance away from him, unsure of why I expected a different response when he's never made an effort to understand me a day in his life.

"I'm serious. I have to go to work today. You'll have to reschedule with Penn State."

"Reschedule?" His laughter fades, and the tendons strain in his neck as his eyes harden on mine. "You have thirty minutes to get your ass in the car."

"Or what?" I clench my jaw as we face off.

"I'll take your car. Won't be easy getting to and from work without a ride now, will it?"

Panic ripples beneath the surface of my skin. "You can't do that," I say, even though I know he can.

"Oh, I can, and I will. And that's not all. I'll make sure you have no access to your bank account or emergency funds. I'll take away your phone. Your computer. I'll ensure you have zero ways to communicate with the outside world when you're within these walls."

Fuck.

My palms begin to sweat as I curl them into fists.

"I'm eighteen. I can move out," I say, but the argument falls flat. Without my trust fund and having blown what was in my checking account, I don't have the funds.

He snorts. "I'd like to see it. You'll quickly realize you prefer your privileged life to the one you can provide for yourself."

Resentment curdles in my stomach like sour milk.

How am I supposed to get to the Bardot without a car when it's all the way in the city? Even if I found a ride today, what about every other day? I'm already broke, so taking an Uber isn't an option. Losing my phone would mean I'd have no way to call

Crenshaw to apprise him of what's going on, and if I miss work so soon after starting, he'll be pissed. In fact, I don't even want to contemplate his response.

He might renege on our deal and ask for his money, and then I'm back to square one. Only, this time, I'm positive he'll break my fingers one by one. Or worse.

Either way, I'm screwed.

CHAPTER 11

GRAHAM

THE DRIVE TO PENN State goes as expected. Dad and I hardly speak, and Mom carries the weight of the conversation. Despite the beef with my father, I should be celebrating this trip, excited at the prospect of playing football at such an amazing university, but I feel nothing. Instead, it's like someone has placed a weighted blanket on my emotions, smothering them.

When we step foot on campus, I try to tell myself it's because I'm worried about what will happen when I don't show up for work today. I tell myself I'm just pissed at my father. I sell myself a million lies for why I'm not completely and utterly stoked to be here, but none of them feel right.

The campus is beautiful in wintertime, so I can only imagine how gorgeous it is in the spring and the fall when the trees have their leaves and the flowers bloom. Despite the chilly weather, the sun shines overhead, casting its golden glow over the tree-lined walkways and the impressive buildings as we tear through the heart of campus.

Since it's the weekend and their winter break has begun, we pass very few students. The campus is quiet and serene. It's also huge with everything spread out over thousands of acres.

I try to picture myself here, but for some reason I can't sharpen the image in my head, and when we draw closer to the football stadium, I hold my breath. It towers in the distance, and as we approach, it's even more impressive in person than I ever could have imagined. Riverside has spent a lot of money over the years updating our stadium and ensuring we have the best equipment money can buy, but it pales in comparison to the sight of the Beaver Stadium, home of the Nittany Lions.

James Franklin, Penn State's coach, smiles at us from outside the main gates. His handshake is firm as he introduces himself and guides us through the entrance into the stadium. The moment I step out onto the field, I suck in a breath, expecting the elation and awe that such a stadium should inspire. But all I feel is . . . overwhelm.

I turn in a circle, staring up at the stadium lights, the yards of grassy field spread out before me, and the tens of thousands of seats. I imagine them filled with a hundred thousand screaming fans, and my stomach squeezes.

I can feel everyone's eyes on me as I take it in. They're waiting for my reaction, a response to the thought of being granted the privilege of playing here, but I'm having a hard time coming up with something to say when my emotions are all tangled up inside.

"Wow," I breathe.

"Impressive, isn't it? The television broadcasts just don't do it justice. It gets me right here, every time." Coach fists a hand over his chest. "Running out onto this field never gets old."

I swallow, tearing my eyes away from the stadium to the coach. I remember a time when running out onto a field with a hoard of screaming fans blew my mind; it filled me with adrenaline. Playing here would most certainly put me in the spotlight. As the quarterback, I'd take center stage, something that I once dreamed about. Just a couple years ago, I would've given anything to play for a team in the Big Ten. But as I stand here, trying to provoke some semblance of enthusiasm at the prospect of becoming a Nittany Lion, I realize at some point, it stopped being my dream and became my burden.

We talk for a few more minutes with my father monopolizing most of Coach's time and attention before he leads us off the field and briefly shows us the locker rooms and the workout facility. The equipment is state-of-the-art, everything gleaming under the bright lights as Coach talks about training, the staff, and their physical therapy program.

"We sure do hope you'll be joining us in the fall, Graham. You're a fine quarterback, and we'd be glad to have you." Coach claps me on the shoulder.

"Thank you, sir. I'm honored," I say, wishing it was how I really felt.

"We'll give you time to consider everything and will be in touch with your folks about the details, of course." He glances at my parents, who nod in approval. "In the meantime, feel free to stick around and see a little more of the campus. And don't forget to hit up the creamery." He leans toward me, cupping a hand around his mouth. "Peachy Paterno is the best."

I force a smile, relieved when my father pulls him aside and they chat for a few minutes, mostly because the spotlight is no longer on me.

"You okay?" My mother bumps my arm.

"Huh?" I turn to her, startled. I was so lost in thought I almost forgot she was still standing beside me. "Yeah. Yeah, I'm fine." I stare after my father. Something he says makes Coach laugh, and I wonder what they could possibly be talking about. I can only imagine what he'd say if I turned down their offer.

"It's a beautiful campus," she says.

I murmur my agreement, my gaze still trained on Dad.

"But there are tons of beautiful colleges."

Her words draw me up short, and I turn to her. "Not ones I can play football at."

Mom picks a piece of lint off her winter coat. "Football isn't everything." She says it so casually, I wonder if I heard her right.

"According to Dad it is."

She meets my eyes, the bluish-green of them swirling with emotion. "But your father can't play for you. This is *your* decision, Graham, your life. And nobody can tell you what to do with it." My heart pounds in my chest as she gives my arm a little squeeze while I blink down at her with surprise. "Not even your father."

I think about my mother's words all through dinner, even when my father won't stop talking about the football program and my future in the sport. I mull them over on the drive home, too. My father acts as though I don't have a choice but to sign with them, like it's a no-brainer, and maybe it is, but there's something freeing in knowing my mother thinks otherwise.

By the time I get home from Penn State and rush over to the Bardot, it's pushing ten o'clock, which means my shift is almost over and the night shift guy, Jack, is set to take my place. I have no idea what I'm hoping to accomplish by showing up this late. I suppose I'm wanting to mitigate the damage of my earlier no-show.

I step into the lobby, and stop in my tracks when I set my sights on Skylar. She must've covered for me when I didn't turn up earlier, and I wonder how she feels about that even though I already know she's probably pissed.

Her chestnut locks spill over her shoulders like a waterfall as she leans over the counter, chatting with a blonde girl I vaguely recognize as her friend from the night at O'Malley's. Sometimes, when she doesn't know it, I steal glances at her and imagine what it would be like if Mackenzie never hurt me. If I was just a normal guy who hadn't completely fucked up his life.

I wonder what it might be like if the smiles she gave me were warm and flirty, rather than the byproduct of the disdain she clearly feels for me.

I start toward her, and it doesn't take long for her to notice. Her expression turns chilly when she glances up at me with a scowl. "Well, look at who decided to show up at the last minute. Literally."

I smother any pang of desire I might have for her at the reminder we're clearly enemies. "Miss me?" I wink. Even though this isn't the time for a joke, I just can't seem to help myself where she's concerned.

"Funny." She taps her chin. "I was just telling Mal how that weird skunk smell I've been catching a hint of all week has miraculously gone." She leans forward as I approach and sniffs. "But it's back."

I roll my eyes. "Whatever. You love the way I smell, and you know it."

She scoffs. "You wish."

"Don't deny it. My pheromones make girls weak in the knees," I say, leaning toward her.

"Um, that scent is the omniscient stench of your narcissism." She leans even closer, and her floral scent drifts toward me. "And I hate to break it to you"—her lips thin—"but the only thing it's weakening is my gag reflex."

I press my lips together holding in a laugh. *Omniscient stench of your narcissism?* Where does she get this stuff? If she didn't irritate me so much, I'd be so damned enamored by her it's not even funny.

I move behind the desk and step closer while she narrows her eyes at me, as if wary of my intentions. The rapid rise and fall of her chest spur me forward as I pin her with my eyes and dip my head closer. "I don't see you gagging now."

I forget all about how I missed work and Crenshaw is probably pissed when her breath hitches, cascading over my neck and sending chills down my arms. Energy snaps between us. The air thickens, and for a fleeting moment, her focus shifts to my mouth. I urge her on, enjoying the feel of her gaze on me, before she clears her throat and abruptly spins around, her ass brushing against my thighs as she does.

"Whatever," she mutters. "When you're done getting under my skin, Franklin wants you to call him."

I swallow. Her reminder is like being hit with a bucket of ice, and though I want to crack a joke, I can't muster one through the dread pooling in the pit of my stomach.

"What? No jokes or smart retorts now?" Skylar smirks over her shoulder.

I straighten, and I catch her friend's gaze as she smiles and shakes her head. "Interesting."

I arch a brow, a silent question.

"Funny how my best friend, here, didn't mention the new guy is the same guy with the right hook from O'Malley's."

I blink over at her, only half listening through the nerves roiling in my stomach at the prospect of facing Frankie, and likely Crenshaw.

Blondie tips her head back and laughs. "Your hostility toward the new guy makes so much more sense now."

"Not sure why you're laughing. Working with him is torture," Skylar mutters.

The blonde continues, either oblivious or unsympathetic to Skylar's obvious plight of having me for a coworker. "Talk about fate . . ."

"It's not fate." Skylar and I say at the same time, then glare at each other.

"Fate implies a positive outcome of working with him," Skylar says, her voice tight. "Like there's some greater purpose, when the only purpose is to send me to an early grave."

I roll my eyes, but Blondie just shakes her head and laughs. "Did she tell you why she was so pissed that night?"

I shake my head.

"She'd been kissing Brad's ass for months, and then you ruined it with your right hook." Blondie stops long enough to offer me her hand. "I'm Mallory, Skylar's best friend, by the way."

"*Ex* best friend, if you keep it up," Skylar mutters under her breath.

Mallory chuckles as I shake her hand, and then, because I know it'll annoy the shit out of Skylar, I bring it to my lips and brush a soft kiss over her knuckles. "Nice to meet you, Mallory."

Skylar scoffs and pushes between us. "Enough of the Prince Charming bullshit, okay? You're not fooling anyone."

"I mean, I'm kind of buying it," Mallory says, which earns her a glare from Skylar. "What? I mean, look at him." She waves a hand toward me.

"Oh, I've looked," Skylar says. "In fact, the second I leave here, I'm running to the bathroom so I can upchuck my dinner."

Mallory snorts, unperturbed as she turns toward me. "Don't worry about her. She's just having some issues with her overprotective brother and her future precariously hanging in the balance. No biggie."

That makes two of us.

Skylar shoots her a look that could kill. "*Not* his business," she says between clenched teeth.

"Overprotective brother, huh?" I give Skylar the once-over. "I'm surprised. I took the prima donna over here for an only child."

"Oh, nooooo." Mallory shakes her head, ignoring the daggers Skylar sends her way. "Her parents died when she was young, so he pretty much raised her. Add in the deaf thing, and he's been in hyper-protective mode for as long as I can remember."

I risk a glance at Skylar, gauging her reaction to Mallory referencing her deafness so casually, but she has none.

"JD was always going into school roaring like a bear about every little thing," Mallory continues. "I mean, he's basically the reason she's never had a boyfriend—"

Skylar slaps a hand over Mallory's mouth, her cheeks pink. "Stop!" she hisses.

"What?" Mallory mumbles underneath her hand. "It's not like I told him you've never even had a first kiss."

"You're dead to me," Skylar says, voice tight.

I cross my arms over my chest, enjoying this nugget of information more than I should. "Well, well, well. Never been kissed by a boy, huh? With your bedside manner, I can't begin to imagine why."

"Shouldn't you go find Franklin?" Skylar asks, a cruel smile twisting her lips.

My smile falters as my stomach turns in on itself at the reminder. Once again, our banter made my problems vanish, even if temporarily.

"I'd hate to see you miss the verbal lashing you're likely to get for ditching work on your second week."

I swallow, wondering what Crenshaw has in store for me when her friend, Mallory waves a hand in my direction. "Skylar's not usually this prickly with other boys. Something about you just brings it out in her. But I'm totally here for it."

"It's his caustic charm." Skylar rolls her eyes.

"Whatever it is, the chemistry between you two is . . ." Mallory fans herself.

"Chemistry?" Skylar's eyes widen into two amber orbs. "Are you insane? What you're sensing is pure unadulterated hatred."

I scrunch my nose. "As much as I hate to admit it, I have to agree with Skylar here."

"That's a first," Skylar mutters under her breath.

"I mean, the chick did have me arrested," I add.

"Um, *no*." Skylar's eyes flicker to me. "You got yourself arrested because of your lack of control."

"I think you secretly like it when I lose control." I wink, which only makes her scowl.

"I like it. This thing." Mallory motions between us.

"We're leaving!" Skylar announces as she spots Jack enter. Grabbing her keys, she rounds the counter and shoves her best friend away from the reception desk. "Enough talking before I murder you," she warns.

Mallory's chuckle trails behind her as Skylar strongarms her toward the door. Once they're out of sight, my smile fades and the lightness in my chest disappears bringing with it the heaviness from earlier. Sparring with Skylar might be the perfect distraction, but it can't last forever, and now that she's gone, I'm faced with reality.

I give Jack a small wave as I step away from the counter and slide my cell out of my pocket. Inhaling a lungful of air, I find Frankie's name, call him, and wait as it rings.

The second he answers, my heart hammers against my ribs. "You better have a damned good reason for missing your shift," he snaps.

I swallow, knowing my excuse is futile. "I'm sorry," I say, already imagining the crunch of my bones. "I can explain."

"Meet us downstairs," he barks, and then the line goes dead.

CHAPTER 12

GRAHAM

I INHALE A DEEP breath as I walk down the hallway toward the elevators, feeling like I'm walking to the guillotine. Whatever awaits me can't be good, and I curse my father for being such a controlling asshole. If it weren't for him, I would've completed my shift and I'd be on my way home now instead of Skylar.

Skylar.

The thought of her shouldn't distract me. Not right now when my fate is in the hands of a criminal who wanted to break my bones only a short while ago. Yet from the moment I met her, she's done nothing but divert my attention. For reasons I can't explain, she captivates me, steals my thoughts, and punches through my walls to earn a reaction when I'm otherwise numb. Even from the first time I laid eyes on her at O'Malley's, when I was waist-deep in problems, her presence never let me go. All I should've been thinking about was how lucky I was at coming out of that interaction with Crenshaw unscathed, and focusing on the deal I made with him. But instead, the sight of her gripped me by the throat and never let me go.

I glance around me to ensure no one's around, then step onto the elevator and scan my badge like Frankie showed me and hit the little red button, waiting as the car starts to move. The breath stalls in my lungs, and my mouth turns to sawdust as I count the passing seconds, thinking about what Crenshaw has in store for me.

When the elevator dings and the doors open, I move on rubbery legs. Another scan of my badge, and I push through the double doors and enter the casino. I'm shocked to find it so busy. It's the first time I've been here at the height of operating hours, and with the buzz of activity all around me, it's hard to wrap my head around the fact that this place exists while remaining a secret to so many.

I hurry through the entryway, past the slot machines, and head toward the bar where Crenshaw sits, holding a cigar in his hand as he studies the room with eagle eyes. Unsurprisingly, he homes in on me almost immediately, his gaze dark and haunting as I come to a stop in front of him.

"Follow me," he stands and smooths a hand down his suit jacket. No greeting. No pretense or pleasantries. Crenshaw is all business as he rounds the bar toward the bathrooms, and pauses to punch a code into an unmarked door.

It beeps once and I hear it unlatch before he pushes his way inside, closing the door securely behind us and taking us down a short corridor to another room on the end. The space is sparsely lit and decorated. An abstract painting graces one wall, along with a giant charcoal sketch–the side of a girl's face–while the remaining walls are blank.

A large black desk is flanked by a set of chairs, one of which is occupied by Frankie.

Crenshaw motions to the empty chair next to Frankie while he holds a hand up for me to wait, then props his hip against the edge of the desk in front of us and addresses Frankie. "Any word from the electrician?"

Frankie shakes his head. "He seems to have gone off-grid."

Crenshaw curses under his breath. "We can't just have anyone fix the electrical down here. It needs to be the right person. Put your ear to the ground, will you? Let me know if you find someone."

When Frankie nods, Crenshaw turns his attention to me. "Graham, so glad you could *finally* join us."

I open my mouth and start to explain, but he cuts me off. "I'm not interested in excuses." His smile tightens as he adds, "You can make it up to us. Tonight, we're seating you at the poker table with a group of regulars. This man"—he snaps his fingers and Frankie takes out a phone, a photograph lighting up the screen. It's of a middle-aged man, with reddish hair and freckled skin—" is Daniel Miller. He's a patron, but not our friend. He owes me a lot of money, and he's been cheating. We have proof, but he's still denying it and had the gall to show up here tonight, so we're going to teach him a lesson."

"How?" I croak, my pulse in my throat.

"The house will stack your cards. All you have to do is wager and play them properly."

I open my mouth to ask another question, but a sharp look by Crenshaw draws me up short. "Don't worry about how we'll stack the deck. Let him win the first round to hook him in, then after that, you'll have the advantage. No one else at the table matters. They're not my concern. Your one and only goal is to keep this man"—he taps the phone—"in the game and crush him. He doesn't like to lose almost as much as he doesn't like to quit, so he'll keep playing long after he's lost. We're going for broke here, playing until he has nothing left and owes us a large debt. Got it?"

Bile rises to the back of my throat as I contemplate what he's asking of me. "You want me to cheat in order to punish a cheater?"

Crenshaw's gaze narrows, and his jaw tenses. "I *want* you to win back what's rightfully mine, what he stole from me."

I glance between him and Frankie, and my palms begin to sweat.

Let him win the first round, then after that, you'll have the advantage.

I think back on the elation of winning my first few hands at the Play House, and I wonder if they did this with me. In fact, Crenshaw gave me the cash to play that first night. At the time, I thought he was super chill for doing so. But the next two times I went back to the Play House, I won just enough to keep me interested, to keep me hoping I could win it all back, until I couldn't.

My nostrils flare as I squeeze the arms of the chair, wondering if they cheat with all their clients or just the easy targets.

He says Miller stole from him, but I have no idea if that's even true.

I run a trembling hand roughly over my mouth, mulling over what he's asking of me.

I want to refuse, to protest this isn't what I signed up for.

Only, it was, wasn't it?

I know what kind of character Crenshaw is. He runs an illegal business and he's successfully built his empire off lies and brute force when necessary. Yet I agreed to work for him to save my own skin, even if it meant compromising my integrity in the process.

I was a fool to get comfortable, to allow my guard to drop just because Skylar has a way of distracting me.

She can't help now, and I can hardly cry foul because my moment of reckoning has come.

Three hours later, I hang my head as I sit in Crenshaw's office at the back of the casino, my emotions raw. My gaze flickers once more to the sketch on the wall, somehow finding some semblance of solace in the emotion it evokes. Still, all I can think about is the look on Miller's face when he lost everything he had. In only a couple of hours, he managed to gamble away thirty thousand dollars.

His crumpled expression will haunt me for weeks to come. The panic when he realized if he didn't win his last hand he'd lose it all, and the resulting desperation when he didn't.

The door clicks shut behind me, and my gaze swings to the side until it finds the target—Crenshaw.

He claps his hands as he rounds my chair and props himself up against the edge of his desk. "You did good," he beams.

The elation in his voice makes me sick. My nostrils flare as I breathe through the nausea brewing in the pit of my stomach. "I won't do this shit again," I say with a shake of my head. "It's not right."

Crenshaw darts toward me so fast, I don't see it coming. One hand fists my shirt as he lifts me from my seat so we're eye to eye.

The breath rattles in my lungs as he grits his teeth. "You *will* do this again, Scott, and anything else I ask of you for that matter. Because you owe me. Or have you forgotten?"

I swallow, anger and fear swirling inside of me in a potent combination.

"I haven't forgotten," I grind out.

Just because Skylar has been running interreference doesn't mean I've forgotten. When I see her—hell, even when I think of her—she helps me to breathe a little easier. But Crenshaw's ominous presence in my life is with me every fucking second, every time I even think about work or walk inside the walls of this hotel. The brunette bombshell is merely a distraction.

"Good," Crenshaw says, his tone dark. "Because I'm not in the business of right and wrong, only making money and collecting debts. Remember that."

CHAPTER 13

SKYLAR

"**I** SHOULD DISOWN YOU as my best friend," I say over a virgin margarita at my favorite Mexican restaurant. It's only a few minutes from the Bardot, and they serve endless baskets of tortilla chips fresh from the fryer and the best queso dip in the entire county. Coming here is a no-brainer when I'm distressed.

"Okay. I'm sorry. Maybe I said too much." Mallory shrugs, and flips her blonde locks behind her back. "So, sue me."

"Maybe?" My eyes round. "You freaking told the boy who is currently the bane of my existence that I've never been kissed and never had a boyfriend. Do you know how much ammunition you just gave him?"

"Sorry." She winces. "In my defense though, I was blinded by his charming smile and the sage green of his eyes. I can't be held accountable for what I might say in front of a boy as hot as he is. It sort of just gushed out like word vomit."

"Uh huh."

"I blame you."

"Me?" I point to my chest. This should be good.

"Yeah. I wasn't thinking because I've never seen you like that with a guy before, I mean, the chemistry between you two"—she fans her face with her hand—"was off the charts."

I peg her with a glare. "No. There is no chemistry between us. Zero."

"Maybe just a little." Mal holds her fingers an inch apart.

"None. Zero. Zip. Nada," I say, unsure of why the accusation bothers me so much. "What other words are there to convey there's not a single bit of chemistry—or anything remotely similar—lurking between us?"

Mal narrows her eyes, her gaze probing. "You're awfully insistent."

"I know what you're implying with that look you're giving me." I swirl a finger at her. "You're trying to imply that I'm denying it so hard because I'm secretly really attracted to him."

"I didn't say that, but it's interesting that *you* did."

I huff, and she chuckles.

"Aren't you attracted to him, though, even just a little? Because from where I was standing . . ." She trails off at the laser beams I'm shooting her way, mostly on account of fighting the urge to lunge across the table and throttle her.

What is it about Graham that gets me so riled up? I'm usually unflappable, cool under pressure and in tense situations.

"He's a chauvinist," I say.

"Is he really, though? Because I thought him defending your honor was kinda sweet."

"Pah!" I dip a tortilla chip in queso and pop it in my mouth. "Don't forget his macho display likely cost me."

"It cost him, too," she points out. "I mean, he *did* get arrested."

"Why are you defending him?" I ask, narrowing my gaze at her like she has some kind of ulterior motive.

Mal raises her hands in surrender. "I'm playing devil's advocate here, that's all. I've just never seen you, so . . ." She trails off, searching for the right word while I sit on the edge of my seat, waiting.

"What?" I ask, impatient.

"So worked up over a boy before. It's interesting."

My brows rise. "That's one way to describe it, but thanks to you, I look like a giant L now," I say, ignoring her assessment, mostly because I know she's right, and I'm not sure what that means.

"You are far from being a loser," she admonishes.

"Right. Because you know what it's like to be eighteen and a kissing virgin, I forgot." I roll my eyes. "It's super cool."

"I think it's admirable you're not just going around kissing everything that moves."

I scoff. It's not like I've had much of a choice. As soon as guys find out I'm deaf, they instantly turn weird on me. You'd think it's contagious.

"Listen, you're just getting off to a late start, that's all," she adds in my silence.

"I bet if I weren't deaf, I'd have had my first kiss already."

Mal chucks a chip at my face, causing me to flinch. "That has nothing to do with this, so you stop that right now." She stabs the table with her finger. "You hear me? You are perfect. All the boys we know are morons. And what about Brad, huh? He wants you so much he tried to blackmail you."

A sound of disgust rumbles from the back of my throat. "I'm pretty sure he just views me as some kind of conquest. I'm not sure how genuine he really is."

Mal frowns. She hates when I'm hard on myself, but in truth, I'm more than a little jealous of her. With long blonde hair, bright blue eyes, and a rocking body, guys tend to gravitate toward her. Best of all, she doesn't come with a disclaimer. Her ears are always on. She doesn't need a device helping her to hear. She almost never needs people to repeat themselves, and she can spend all day in a loud room, crowded with people without having it drain all her energy from the sheer amount of concentration it takes to follow a simple conversation.

"Hey," she says, ducking her head to catch my gaze. "I have good news, remember? It's the whole reason I came to see you at work today, but all you've done is focus on Graham. You haven't even asked me what it is."

"Oh, right." I shake my head and dust the chip crumbs from my hands, relishing a change of topic. I don't want to think about Graham or my disability. Focusing on something good is a welcome change of pace. "I almost forgot. So, what's the news?"

Mallory grins as she reaches beside her and rummages in her purse, then pulls out a pamphlet and slaps it on the table in front of me. Tapping it with her finger she says, "Assuming it was Brad that screwed you over—"

"Which he did, because I'm not a finalist," I remind her.

"This is your ticket to college." She taps a finger over the shiny brochure. "Your chance to get out of here on your own terms."

I reach across the table and pick it up. My eyes flicker over the words as I read, "Siddhartha Art Gallery's Amateur Art Competition?" When I glance up at her, she flips it open, pointing to the inside of the pamphlet.

"There are guidelines and rules," she says, her voice rising with her excitement. "All the details are right here, but each year, there's a different art category. Two years ago, it was sculptures. Last year, oil paintings. This year, it's sketches. Can you believe it? It's like you're meant to enter."

My eyes widen and my heart flutters in my chest. "Seriously?"

She nods, her eyes bright with excitement. "It just has to be an original piece. And get this . . ." She drums her fingers on the table. "The winner receives sixty thousand dollars to the school of their choice!"

My mouth parts in shock. That's a lot of money. More than the Oak Ridge scholarship.

"But . . ." I shake my head as I push the pamphlet closed. "Anyone can enter this thing. It's not just for high school seniors."

"There's an age range. It's meant for emerging artists."

Hope swells in my chest, but I quickly tamp it down. "Do you know how hard it will be to win this? My sketches probably won't stand a chance against what other people can do."

Mal scowls. "Since when are you so negative?"

I drop my face in my hands and groan. "I know. You're right." I glance up at her again. "Sorry, I guess this thing with Brad just really threw me. I was a shoo-in for the Oak Ridge one."

"I know, but this one is even better, and your sketches are freaking amazing, Sky. Like, next-level amazing. You can win this, I know it. And when you enter and crush the competition, you'll finally see just how amazing you are."

I exhale as I stare over at her, wishing I had as much faith in myself as she does. Normally, I'm a confident person. I've had to grow a thick skin over the years. Not everyone understands my disability, and children, especially, are afraid of anything—or anyone—different.

But finding a way to pay for college myself is so important to me, it's messing with my head, making me doubt myself.

But Mal's right. I *am* super talented. Even more so, I'm a fighter.

I'm Skylar fucking Davenport, and giving up isn't an option. Once I set my sights on something, I don't stop until I have it.

With a nod, I pocket the brochure with renewed determination. Not only will I enter my work, but the competition is mine to lose.

CHAPTER 14

GRAHAM

I SIT IN MY car outside of the Bardot in the dark, wondering how I got here—to this place where I'm sacrificing my integrity to save my own ass when my phone rings.

I glance over at it and see Atlas's name illuminated on the screen. I already have half a dozen missed calls from him during the time I spent in the Gentleman's Club. Apparently, he hasn't caught the memo I don't feel like talking.

No sooner than I send it to voicemail does my phone ping with a text.

I sigh and swipe the screen open, annoyed he's interrupting my introspection when I was well on my way to a self-loathing pity party I feel like I've earned the right to.

Atlas: *On my way to your place. Need to talk ASAP.*

My gaze lifts, and I glance at the Bardot once more, the light from inside illuminating the lobby, marveling at the fact there's a whole underground world within its walls no one knows about. One I wish like hell I weren't privy to.

My phone dings again, drawing my attention.

Atlas: *Dude, where the hell are you? We need to talk. Is Cal home?*

I frown, and my stomach turns. What does he want with Cal?

My fingers fly over the keyboard as I shoot of a text of my own.

Graham: *No clue.*
Atlas: *So, you are alive.*

Okay, I deserve that. I won't deny I've been MIA lately.

Graham: *I'm not at home, so I don't know about my father. Why?*
Atlas: *I swear to God if he's there, I might strangle him with my bare hands.*

That makes two of us.

My father's done plenty to piss Atlas off in the past. I'd be the first to call him out on it, too, but in light of my shitty evening,

I'm not in the mood for his crap tonight. As always, his timing is impeccable.

Graham: *Get in line.*
Graham: *Be there in thirty.*

After I hit send, I glance back to the Bardot once more with pit in the bottom of my stomach and pull away from the curb to head for home.

The miles pass quickly, my mind spinning from today's events. The trip to Penn State, and all the conflicting emotions that went with it. Skylar. Rigging the poker game. The look on Miller's face when he lost. And now this . . .

By the time I pull in the driveway, it's no surprise Atlas is waiting for me, but what does surprise me is that Kenzie is with him. They sit in her car, the engine running, and though the fact that they're a couple should no longer faze me, I feel a momentary stab of pain when they slide out and Atlas grabs her hand.

I tear my eyes away from them and park before I get out, mentally preparing myself for seeing them together. Sometimes it's like that. I need a pep talk to get me through. Other times, it's easier. I'm not sure what the difference is. I'm not even sure it's because I'm still in love with her. I let go of her the night of Atlas's accident. Sometimes I think it's the idea of what we could've been—this fictional relationship I built with her in my head—that haunts me.

I'm not more than a foot from my car when Atlas runs his gaze over me, homing in on the badge still draped on the lanyard around my neck. "So, it's true. You did get a job. Jace wasn't bullshitting us."

"Were you already up at Crow's Creek?" I ask, remembering I was supposed to meet them.

"Yeah. Until I got a call from my mother, telling me Cal got her evicted."

I blink, unsure of whether I heard him right. "What?"

"Why don't we go inside and talk?" Kenzie suggests, her voice soft.

My gaze falls to her. It's freezing outside and she's dressed in jeans and an oversized Rebels football hoodie which I assume belongs to Atlas. Once upon a time, she used to wear mine, even though she wasn't my girlfriend. For some reason, seeing her in it hits different tonight, and it reminds me of the time I asked her to wear my football jersey, knowing what it would mean if she did.

I cringe at the memory—it didn't end well—then push it aside with the other things I hate thinking about.

I brush past them, moving onto the sidewalk while I try to get my thoughts straight. "Come on," I say, motioning for them to follow.

I pause at the front door and try the knob to find it locked, so I dig my keys out of my pocket and unlock it before pushing inside. "Dad?" I call out, but I'm answered only with the echo of my voice bouncing off the walls.

I quickly make my way down the hall and to the garage door where I find his car missing—the Lincoln, to be exact. It's the one he always drives with Mom.

"They're not home," I confirm, turning around to find Atlas and Mackenzie on my heels. "So, what the hell happened?"

Atlas begins to pace and push a hand through his hair. "My mother, Storm, and I were supposed to have brunch tomorrow."

I vaguely recall Atlas inviting me to brunch with them, but I forget the details. He's forever trying to convince me to be the bigger man and extend an olive branch where Storm is concerned, and I'm forever making excuses for why I can't. I have enough on my plate already without adding to it by getting mixed up in my father's messes.

"I remember," I say, and he shoots me a pointed look I choose to ignore.

"She called me up an hour ago to cancel because, apparently, she got kicked out of her place."

"That sucks." I shrug. "But I don't see what my father has to do—"

"Something didn't sit right with me considering she's been a good tenant, so I called the landlord. According to him, a man with deep pockets offered him double the rent to vacate the property. Conveniently, he couldn't remember the name on the check."

I reach up and scratch my head. Of all the shitty things to do

. . .

"Yep, that sounds just like Cal."

"Ya think?" Anger darkens his eyes to onyx as he pauses. "Who in their right mind would pay double the rent to leave a house empty other than someone who wants the tenant out? And your father—"

"Has a lot of reasons to want your mother and Storm gone," I finish for him. "I know." I exhale and scrub my hands over my face. I can't help but feel like if I'd just find the courage to tell my mother the truth, maybe this nightmare would be over. Maybe she'd finally leave him, he'd have no more secrets to hide, and I'd be free of this burden.

My stomach pitches with the thought, and I think I might be sick.

"So where are they now?" I ask.

"I don't know. I only spoke with her briefly. As you can imagine, with Christmas right around the corner, she was pretty upset. I think they're working on finding somewhere to stay, at least for the night. I tried calling her on the way here, but it went straight to voicemail."

Atlas pauses to place his hands on his hips. "My mother and I still have a long way to go before I can say we've mended bridges, but Storm doesn't deserve this shit." The muscle in his jaw twitches. "That kid has done nothing wrong from the beginning. He's a victim of our parents' shit just like we are. They shouldn't be having to find a new place to stay just because Cal doesn't want to take ownership of his past."

I stifle a groan as I run a hand over the back of my neck. As much as I've resisted the idea of Storm, Atlas is right. He's just a kid; he doesn't deserve to be toyed with. "You're right," I say, though I'm not sure what we can do about it.

"I mean, shit. Storm's young. He's in grade school. I know what it's like to be displaced. There was a time when I wasn't sure where I'd lay my head for the night. I don't want that for him. It doesn't need to be that way, especially with the holidays coming up. Not when Cal is so well off and perfectly capable of owning up."

"I get that my father is an ass. If anyone knows that, it's me, but what exactly do you want me to do about all of this?" I ask, feeling my headache from earlier return with a vengeance.

Atlas arches a brow like I should know. "Acknowledging Storm would help, for one."

"Knock that shit off. I have a lot going on, okay? I'm dealing with this the best I can."

"You have a lot going on?" He scoffs. "You know who you sound like?"

"Don't say it," I grind out. "I'm not my father."

Atlas steps closer, getting in my face as he pokes finger in my chest. "Then prove it. Deal with this shit."

"Guys . . ." Mackenzie pleads, likely worried we're going to start fighting.

It wouldn't be the first time.

"That kid needs us," Atlas continues, ignoring her. "How do you expect your father to own up and acknowledge him if you can't even do it?"

I match the intensity of his gaze, urging him to lay his hands on me so I have an excuse to take my aggression out on someone. Today has been a shitshow and I'd love nothing more than to release a little bit of the tension.

"We're all in this together. Remember?" Mackenzie pipes up.

I nod, because she's right, and honestly, it feels good to have someone in my corner, reminding me not to lose my shit over a mess my father created.

I take a cleansing breath and use another tact. "I'm trying to come to terms with the Storm thing, and I know it's not fair to him, but every time I look at him or hear his name, or even think about him, all I feel is guilt. Guilt over this secret. This fucking thing I'm keeping from my mother."

Atlas softens his stance. "Listen, I'm not telling you what to do, man, but I think it's time to tell her."

I stiffen, and everything inside me turns to ice. I imagine my mother's face when I tell her the man she's been married to all these years cheated on her. How he has a son she never knew about. How he paid them to stay away for years, hiding them like a dirty secret.

I envision her crumpling smile. The tears. The questions I don't have answers to.

I've contemplated telling her a million times in a million different ways since I discovered the truth, but I just can't bring myself to do it. I can't bring myself to obliterate her entire world in a matter of seconds, no matter how much I hate my father.

But I also know Atlas is right. For once in my life, my father needs to be held accountable.

I shouldn't have to bear this burden alone, but here I am, shouldering my father's sins with little choice in the matter.

He steps forward and places a hand over my shoulder as I resist the urge to knock it off. "I won't tell her for you, because it's your family. This is your decision to make. But as long as you're keeping Cal's secrets, they'll eat you alive."

CHAPTER 15

SKYLAR

THE LAST OF THE morning rush dies down. We had a million checkouts, bills to settle, and last-minute reservations for the evening to fulfill, and now that it's over, I finally have a minute to breathe. Which means it's time for me to turn my attention to my sketchbook.

I reach underneath the desk, slide my notebook out of my bag along with a charcoal pencil, then take a seat as far away from Graham as possible. We've been so busy the last couple of hours, we've barely spoken two words to each other, and I'd like to keep it that way. The last thing I want is him peering over my shoulder or asking questions while I work.

My gaze briefly flickers up at him before refocusing on the paper in my hands as I think about the last conversation we had, and my cheeks heat. I still can't believe Mal opened her big mouth in front of him.

Taking a deep breath, I bite my lip and relax my mind, allowing it to wander and find my muse. After enrolling in the Siddhartha competition late last night when I got home, I received an email this morning confirming my entry and assigning me the theme of "Fate." I realize the theme is subjective, left to interpretation by the artist, but I can't help but feel it's a difficult subject matter to portray. Happiness? Simple. Sadness? Piece of cake. Even jealousy or envy would be less complicated.

How the hell does one sketch fate when it's such an abstract concept?

I have no clue.

Virtually none.

I rack my brain for ideas. When I think of fate, it brings to mind the notion that everything happens for a reason, a theory I'm not entirely sold on. Because if everything happens for a reason, it means my parents were meant to die. My brother was supposed to give up his youth to raise me. And I was meant to be deaf. It would mean everyone who got sick or hurt or wronged did so only because it was predestined. There would be no luck or chance. Only this unseen force guiding everyone and everything in the universe. No matter how much I try, I can't seem to wrap my head around it.

If fate is a thing, then it's a cruel bitch, and we are not friends.

Still, fate is all I can think about as I begin to draw—just a little something to warm up my creative muse. I start with a sketch of my mother, but my memories are fuzzy. I was too young when they both died, so I go based off the countless photos JD has scattered around the house, rather than the picture of her I have in my head.

I'm shading in the soft angles of her face when I sense a presence beside me. "Whatcha got there?"

With a sigh, I press the sketch pad to my chest so a particularly gorgeous set of green eyes can't see it, and glance up at his stupidly handsome face. "Just listing all the ways in which I can secretly poison you when you're not looking."

"Really?" He grins and leans back against the counter. Setting his phone down, he picks up his coffee. "And how's that going for you?"

I eye the coffee pointedly. "Pretty well." I grin sweetly.

His lips twitch as he brings the coffee to his lips. "Soooo," he drawls, after he takes a sip and lowers the cup, "never been kissed, huh?"

I groan. "I should've known you wouldn't forget about that."

"Not a chance."

"Listen, Mallory is a blabbermouth, okay? She has no idea what she's talking about."

"Really?" He arches a brow. "So, she's wrong? You have been kissed?"

My mouth presses into a flat line as I stare up at him, wishing I had the ability to unalive him with my eyes. "She's not wrong, per se, but if you're trying to humiliate me or make me feel small, it won't work. I'm not ashamed of my lack of experience," I say, even though it's not entirely true. "For your information, I have standards. I don't go around just sucking face with anything that breathes."

"And I do?" He points to his chest, an irritating reminder of how solid it felt beneath my palm the other day when I pushed him back.

I purse my lips, letting my silence speak louder than words, because there's no way Graham isn't the player I imagine him to be. Not with everything I know about him. His confidence. Quarterback of his high school football team. That face and body. Those eyes.

He might as well be sex on a stick.

"For your information," he says, pointing to his chest again, "I've only kissed one girl in more than two years."

I scoff. "Yeah, okay."

"You don't believe me?" he asks, his tone incredulous.

I roll my eyes. "Puh-lease. You have 'player' written all over you."

"If that's what you think, you're terrible at reading people."

I eye him for a moment. I like to think I excel at reading people, but he appears to be completely serious. "So, what, did you have a serious girlfriend or something?"

"It was serious, I guess, but not a girlfriend."

"Well, whatever," I say, my tone indifferent. "It's none of my business." I swivel in my chair, turning away from him, ready to be done with this conversation when his hands come down over the arms of my chair, and he spins me back around.

We're so close, I can smell him—the faintest hint of leather and spice from his cologne. "So, you're telling me you haven't found one guy worthy of a first kiss yet?"

His green eyes meet mine, and my heart leaps to my throat. I swallow. "The whole deaf thing isn't exactly the best selling point, nor is it the best icebreaker with cute boys."

"That's dumb." He lifts a shoulder like it's nothing.

I eye him for a minute, slightly surprised by his nonchalant attitude. "Well, maybe it doesn't matter to you, but others feel differently. Trust me. The whole 'hey, I think you're hot. Wanna make out? By the way, I'm deaf,' isn't exactly the best sales pitch."

"Everyone has their flaws." He lets go of my chair, but he's still too close for comfort.

"Says the boy who thinks he's the exception," I murmur.

"Trust me, I know how imperfect I am," he says, and something about his tone makes me take him seriously.

"You certainly seem to be the total package," I say, then instantly regret it.

What the heck am I saying?

"You think I'm the total package, Skylar?" Graham asks, his lips quirking.

I suck in a breath, then lower my gaze, unsure of what it is about him that disarms me. "Anyway," I say, focusing back on my sketch pad, "I'm okay with waiting for the right guy."

My thoughts shift to the theme of fate for the art contest. Maybe the reason I don't believe in fate is because life is full of choices that shape our lives—the good and the bad. Regardless, I believe in choosing to mold your life instead of sitting idly by and letting life just happen. One is active and one is passive. And I've never been passive a day in my life.

"It's just a kiss, Skylar."

I glance up at him, mulling it over. "Maybe. But I don't believe in doing something for the sake of it. Anything worth doing, is worth doing right the first time around. So, whoever he is, I want him to be worth it."

Emotion settles in the depths of his green eyes, and something tells me there's a lot more going on in that head of his than he lets on.

Suddenly, I'm hit with the urge to ask, "Was she worth it?"

"Who?" he asks, though I can tell by the way he's looking at me he knows what I mean.

"The girl you mentioned, the only one you kissed in the last two years. Was she worth it?"

His throat bobs. "Yeah, she was."

I nod, once again surprised by his answer. It makes me wonder who Graham Scott really is, that maybe he's not the boy I thought he was.

"Have you ever been in love?" I ask, watching as he takes a step back, like he can put distance between himself and the question. It's invasive; entirely too personal. Especially for a conversation between two people who seem to hate each other most of the time. But I can't seem to help myself. The ghost of emotion in his eyes paints a bigger picture, it tells a story I want to know.

He clears his throat and averts his eyes. "I think so."

"You think? Don't most people know when they're in love?"

"It sure as hell felt like the real thing, but it's hard to know for sure, considering it didn't end the way I wanted." He pinches the bridge of his nose and closes his eyes, and when he lifts his gaze again, he says, "It's not a feeling I want to replicate any time soon."

Why do I feel like that's a lie? And why do I feel like everything about Graham is not what meets the eye?

"Excuse me." A woman appears at the reception desk. A young boy stands beside her, a book bag slung over one shoulder. "We checked in really late last night and were told to come down sometime this morning for a tour of the facilities?"

"Oh, yeah, sure. Are you the ones staying with us long-term?" Jack, our night shift guy, told me about them this morning so I wouldn't be completely in the dark.

"That's us," she says with an exasperated sigh.

I stand, catching sight of Graham out of the corner of my eye—the wide eyes and pale skin with a sheen of sweat.

I frown as he presses himself further into the wall, obscuring himself from view.

"My son and I were renting a place, but it needs repairs, so here we are," the woman explains, sounding less than thrilled about her situation.

I force my gaze back to her. "Well, I'm sorry to hear about that." I glance over at the boy. He's young, maybe ten or eleven with strikingly dark hair and even darker eyes, and I can tell he's going to grow up to be a heartbreaker. "And your son's name?" I ask his mother.

"This is Storm."

"Well, Storm, I think you'll be particularly fond of the pool. It's huge, and heated, too."

"What about a gym?" the kid asks. "I have to train for football."

"We have that, too." I wink. "Maybe, Graham, here, can give you a tour. He plays football, too," I say, turning toward him only to find him gone. "Oh, actually, he must've . . ." I trail off because I have zero explanation for where the hell he's disappeared to. All I know is he's acting super strange.

"Graham, you said?" the mother—Marie is her name—peers around me, eyes bright.

"Um, yeah," I say, hesitant. Suddenly, I'm not so sure I should've mentioned him.

"And he plays football," she confirms.

I offer her a sheepish smile. I have no idea what's going on, but I'm getting the feeling they must know each other.

"Um, I think so?" I say. It comes out like it's a question, mostly because I'm unsure of whether it's a good thing they seem to know each other. Based on the way Graham had been looking at her, I'd guess it's not. "Why don't I give you that tour now?"

CHAPTER 16

GRAHAM

I BURST INTO THE employee bathroom and brace my hands on either side of the sink while my stomach churns, my mind racing as I try and reason what just happened.

Marie and Storm are staying here—thirty minutes away from Riverside. No way can she afford a place like this herself. Last I heard, Atlas told me she was working at a local warehouse, stocking inventory. I'd bet money on the fact that her room is booked with my father's credit card, and I can only think of one explanation for why that might be.

He wanted to hide them, so he got her booted from her rental, and then stuck her at the Bardot, hoping the opulence of the place would stifle her complaints.

It won't take long for someone in Riverside to put two and two together and figure out who Storm is to my family and why he's there. Discovering the great Cal Scott has an illegitimate child is a lot less likely if they're in a different town.

I reach out and turn the faucet on until the water runs cold and I splash some of it on my face, then take a deep breath, but it does little to ease the pressure ballooning in my chest. Marie and Storm's presence at the hotel means every day I work is a day I might run into them. It's not as if I don't know about them. I know they exist. I realize whether I see them or not, they've still been hanging around in Riverside like the homewreckers that they are.

Okay, I'm being unfair.

I certainly know my father's role in this. I just don't understand what the catch is. Why has Marie not told my mother yet? Why is she waiting on my father when I know he'll die before admitting the truth? She says she wants Storm to have a relationship with him, but is that really all she wants?

Atlas might be able to forgive her and move on, but it doesn't mean I have to.

All I know is that ever since she stormed into our lives, nothing has been the same. My chest aches every time I sit down to a meal with my mother. When someone talks about infidelity, my stomach churns. The sight of Cal makes me sick. And now, more than ever, I crave booze to keep me steady.

My head is messed up enough without the constant reminder of my father's affair every time I step into the hotel. Just the thought has me raking my hands in my hair and tugging at the silky strands.

But Marie and Storm aren't going away anytime soon, and there's only one way to avoid them: Call my father and ask him for the money to pay off Crenshaw, so I don't have to return to the Bardot.

Either I deal with my father's disapproval and disappointment, and listen to the lectures on how he wishes I were different and that I need to get my shit together and stop fucking up. Or I continue on, working here where his transgressions will be shoved in my fucking face every day. I feel the guilt boiling in the pit of my stomach, turning sour at the thought I'm my father's accomplice because I can't bring myself to tell my mother the truth.

I hate my choices.

My mother's a righteous woman. She's everything good in our home. She'll do the right thing and force Dad to ante up, to be a father to Storm in the only way he knows how—with his wallet—and insist he forge a relationship with him. She'll stay; I know she will. And I'm not sure I can bear to watch her set her pride aside for the sake of her marriage, for a man who doesn't deserve it.

Either I hurt myself or I hurt my mother.

I release the hold on my hair and whirl around, kicking the trash can in the corner of the bathroom and sending it crashing into the wall.

Fuck.

I can't do it. I can't fucking do any of it.

But this secret, my father's mistakes, are eating me alive.

I close my eyes and wish for a drink, needing one to numb this gnawing ache inside that's eating away at me like a festering wound.

I lose track of how long I've been standing here, in this bathroom, losing my mind as I think about my limited options. I slam my palm against the wall beside me, then work on catching my breath before I push through the bathroom door and force one foot in front of the other as I stride down the hall.

Skylar's now familiar face comes into view as I approach the front desk. Storm and Marie are no longer with her—thank fuck for that—but I still have to call my father, so I walk right past her without a word.

If all goes well, I'll no longer have to work here anymore. She'll be a blip on the radar, a memory from my past. I won't have to see her anymore and endure her biting remarks. No more flinging insults, dealing with her moods, or trying to convince her I'm not the asshole she thinks I am.

She lifts her head as I pass, and I can feel those whiskey eyes on me without looking. "Hey!" she calls out. "Where do you think you're going?"

I say nothing. Instead, I raise a hand in a silent wave and head straight for the door.

"Graham?" The sound of heels clicking the marble floor behind me alert me to her presence. "What exactly do you think you're doing leaving me here to—"

"I'm quitting," I bite out. "I'm done. I'll be out of your hair starting now." I try for a smile as I glance over my shoulder, but it falls flat. "You got rid of me, after all. Congratulations."

She winces, and I see the flash of confusion cross her pretty face. "Is this about that woman and her son?"

She's observant, I'll give her that much.

"It's not about anyone else. It's about me." I turn and push through the doors without waiting for a response.

"Shit," I hear her mutter behind me as the glass swings closed.

I step outside and I'm blasted with the cold. Snow falls in large tufts, covering the sidewalk like a fluffy blanket. A vehicle passes, and I can barely make out the sound of Christmas music. Both are a reminder the holidays are less than a week away, but it doesn't feel like the most wonderful time of year. It feels like the walls are fucking crumbling around me.

I cross the street, walk the block to where my car is parked, and sink inside. Then I start the wipers and wait a moment as the windshield clears before I pull out into traffic. Once I'm on the road, I think about what I'll say to him. What words should I use to tell my father I'm a disappointment?

The thirty-minute drive passes quickly before I arrive back home, only to discover his car isn't in the garage.

Fine by me. Calling is easier anyway. This way I won't have to see the disappointment in his eyes; I'll only have to hear it in his voice.

I somehow manage to get out of my car without my knees buckling, and slide my cell phone from my pocket. Finding his number in my contacts, I hover over the call button while the breath stalls in my lungs.

I can't fucking breathe.

I press call while my heart knocks against my ribs.

"Graham?"

The sound of my name draws me up short and I spin around, eyes widening in shock when I lay eyes on the girl behind me.

Skylar? What the hell?

She stands in front of a little red car, snow clinging to the strands of her dark hair. Her cheeks are pink from the cold as she takes a tentative step toward me. I'm still trying to make sense of her presence here, in Riverside, standing in front of my home when my father's voicemail picks up, and I end the call.

"Skylar, what are you doing here?"

"I followed you," she says like it's the simplest thing in the world.

"Aren't you supposed to be at work?"

"Aren't you?" Her red lips quirk, drawing my gaze. "What's going on, Graham?"

I glance away from her, confused by the sudden ache in my chest, the one that tells me I want to tell her everything.

Fuck, why does this girl get under my skin? And why now?

"Why do you care?" I ask, my voice rough with emotion. "Since when are we nice to each other?"

Her gaze drops to the phone clenched in my grip, my knuckles white, and she crosses her arms over her chest. "Who says I care? I just don't want you to quit because then I have to cover your shifts."

I bark out a laugh.

It's a half-truth. We both know it. I have no doubt Skylar would love nothing more than to have me quit, so she can run the front desk without me. She's said as much a thousand times since I started.

The phone in my hand rings, and I glance down at it.

It's him, my father.

A wave of nausea rises in the back of my throat at the thought of telling him.

I can't do it.

I can't fucking do it.

I close my eyes for a moment, before I open them again and find Skylar has moved closer. She's so close I can reach out and touch her. And I want to. The sudden urge to stretch my arm out and run my fingers through her long dark locks to see if they feel as soft as they look, hits me like an anvil to the chest, sinking inside my gut like a boulder I can't move.

My fingers twitch with need, but I deny myself, squeezing my phone harder.

"This is your house?" she asks, her gaze shifting behind me.

I nod, my jaw tight.

"Have any coffee in that big 'ol house of yours?" she asks, tilting her head.

I motion for her to follow with a crease in my brow. Skylar and I barely know each other, so I have no idea how much she needs her job, but the last thing I want to do is be responsible for getting her in trouble, even if she has been a pain in my ass ever since the day I met her.

"Who's covering for you at the hotel?" I ask as she steps in line beside me.

"Rosa. Don't worry, she's covered for me before, so it's all good."

I reach the door and fumble for my keys as I think about the day's turn of events.

"Could you move any slower?" Skylar rubs her hands over her arms to ward off the cold. "It's freezing."

"You know you're the one who showed up uninvited, right?"

"Yeah, well, you're too slow," she complains, and oddly enough, the heavy weight in my chest shifts a little with her annoyance. "I mean, have you seen these things?" She lifts a foot and points down at her shoes. They're jet black, pointy-toed with five-inch heels. Her toes appear to be squished inside. I can't imagine they're comfortable, nor how she doesn't fall flat on her face in the snow, but fuck, they look good.

My gaze shifts from her feet to the slight muscle in her shapely calves, to the bottom of her dress low on her thighs, suddenly wishing for summer and shorter hems.

She clears her throat, motioning to her face. "Eyes up here, champ."

When I laugh, I feel a little lighter, and I can't help but think about how I've laughed more in the last couple weeks than the three months before it.

I push open the door and we step inside. Motioning down the hallway, she follows me past the massive Christmas tree in the foyer, the great room, and down the hall to the kitchen where I find the coffee pot. I add water to the reservoir and fill the basket with grinds, trying not to focus on how Sky's presence in my home unnerves me.

"Did you even measure those?" she asks, one brow raised as she eyes the mountain of coffee.

"You measure that shit with your heart."

She snorts. "So, we'll be drinking motor oil, then."

My mouth tips up as I lean against the marble countertops, watching her big Johnny Walker eyes take in her surroundings while a nutty aroma and the sound of percolating coffee fills the silence. A few minutes later, the pot begins to sputter and I grab two mugs from the cupboard and place them on the island in front of her, realizing I have no idea how she takes her coffee.

"Do you take anything in yours?" I ask.

"Do I look like a masochist?' She scoffs. "Of course."

I chuckle as I cross the kitchen to the fridge and grab the cream, along with the sugar dish off the counter, and set them down in front of her, then grab the pot and pour us each a mugful.

I lift mine to my lips and take a sip, drinking it black and enjoying the slightly bitter tang of the brew while I watch her add an obscene amount of cream and sugar to hers.

Arching a brow, I ask, "Do you want any coffee with that, or …?"

"Very funny."

"Seriously. That's not even coffee at this point. It's basically candy. Coffee-flavored liquid candy."

With an exaggerated motion, she lifts her mug and takes several noisy sips. Her throat bobs as she swallows, and I watch, entranced by the movement.

"Mmmm," she murmurs, smacking her lips as I try not to stare.

I lower my head, cheeks flushed like I've been caught looking at her naked.

"So . . ." she says after a moment. "What's the deal?"

"What do you mean?" I ask, playing stupid, even though I know damn well it won't fly with her. Skylar may be a lot of things but stupid isn't one of them.

"Cut the crap, Scott. I saw the way you blanched at the sight of those two at the desk, then you just disappear and return saying you're quitting? Super weird, even for you, which is saying something."

"Even if there was something wrong, do you really think I'm going to tell you? Aren't we enemies?" I ask, stalling for time.

"Mortal. But that's not the point. I'm not letting you leave me to handle the desk alone, so you have no choice but to tell me what the hell is going on." She cocks her head to the side as if it dawns on her. "And I'm nosy, so there's that."

I chuckle, but inside I'm screaming. While part of me wants to tell her to mind her own damn business, another part of me wants to spill my guts.

"It's complicated," I start, unsure of whether to say more.

"Look at me." She points at herself. "I'm deaf and was raised by my older brother after both of my parents died. Plus, some other stuff I'm not getting into. I'm the definition of complicated."

"No. That's just what makes you fucking amazing," I say, pleased to see a blush rise to her cheeks.

Though Skylar and I aren't in the habit of handing out compliments to each other, it's the first time she's talked about her parents and what happened to them. Sure, Mal mentioned her overprotective brother and that her parents had died, but at that point, I wasn't entirely sure everything Mal was saying was completely true. To say I'm shocked is an understatement. I never would have guessed any form of tragedy lurked in Skylar's past. She's independent, smart, and driven. Hell, the girl has balls. She's fearless. Unapologetically Skylar.

"Nice try." She lifts her mug, and I wonder if it's to hide her blush. "But don't think you're getting off the hook by giving out compliments."

I bring a hand over the back of my neck and tug on it. "Really? Because I'm pretty good at them," I tease.

"I don't care if you're freaking Romeo and I'm Juliet. We're not leaving here until you confess, and Rosa can't cover for me all day. I do have to go back at some point, so . . ." She swirls a finger in the air. "Time is of the essence."

I sigh and shift on my feet before I take a stool behind the island. There's no sugarcoating the truth, so if I'm really contemplating confiding in Skylar, I might as well tell her straight up. "The woman you showed around the hotel is my father's mistress, or ex-mistress, I guess—hell, I'm not even sure. And the boy is my half brother."

Skylar's mouth gapes, and I can tell by her silent reaction it's the last thing she expected. "Shit." She comes around the island, joining me as she drops down into a stool beside me, eyes wide with shock.

Her mouth opens again, but nothing more than hiss of air comes out.

"Yeah. That's pretty much how I feel about it, too. I only learned the truth a little over a month ago, so I'm still adjusting, still figuring out how to navigate this."

"Dang. And here I thought maybe you had an affair with the old chick and she dumped you for some silver fox with 401k and health insurance."

I arch a brow. "Seriously? That's what you thought?" I shake my head, unable to help the grin touching my lips. "You're deranged."

"What?" She shrugs. "One minute you're sharing this depressing view on love, and the next, this lady shows up and you freak the hell out. What was I supposed to believe?"

"Not *that*."

"It was a pretty good theory."

I narrow my eyes at her, then exhale. "There *was* a girl, but she only vaguely has to do with all of this," I say, unsure of whether

I want to share this part. After all, when we go back to work—if I go back to work—she can use all of this against me.

"Ooh, color me intrigued. Go on," she says, waving her hand for me to continue. When I say nothing, she groans and rolls her eyes. "Whatever you say here, stays here, okay? Consider this free therapy."

"And I'm supposed to believe that?"

"Okay, how about I make you a deal?"

"Ooh, a deal with the devil, here we go." I rub my hands together.

She rolls her eyes. "If you never bring up the fact that I'm a kissing virgin again, then I won't repeat whatever you're about to tell me."

I consider this for a moment. I like having the kissing virgin thing in my arsenal; it's just too good. But the prospect of getting everything off my chest feels a little like taking the lid off a pot of boiling water; maybe it'll stop me from spilling over and making a mess of things.

Since Kenz chose Atlas over me and losing her as my number one, I no longer have an ear to confide in. We're still friends, sure, but not like we were. And the guys can't offer me advice or listen to my problems without bias. All they want is for me and Atlas to bury the hatchet. Which we have. But sometimes it's damn hard, and I need a way to express that without judgment.

I cross my arms over my chest. "Fine. You have a deal."

"Pinky swear?" She extends her hand toward me, pinky out.

CHAPTER 17

GRAHAM

I ARCH A BROW as I stare down at Skylar's tiny finger. "Pinky swear? What are we, five?"

"Hey, the pinky swear is sacred and binding." She shoves her hand closer to mine, until it's practically in my face.

My lips twitch as I curl my pinky around hers, surprised at the jolt of energy from her touch. "You have the hands of a child," I say in an effort to chase away the butterflies wreaking havoc in my chest.

"I'm small boned, so sue me." She huffs and drops her hand, leaving me to reluctantly return mine to my coffee cup where it feels useless.

Staring down at it, I toy with the handle of my mug as I say, "I was in love with my best friend for years."

Skylar blinks. "For real?"

My forehead creases. "You sound surprised. Is it that unusual?"

She shakes her head no. "I guess it just comes as a surprise because, well, the other day you said . . . it's just, I never would've guessed you were gay."

I glare at her, my mouth a flat line. "I'm not *gay*." Leave it to Skylar to make that assumption, like I'm incapable of being best friends with a girl. "My best friend was a chick. Or *is* a chick. Hell, I don't know . . ."

"You don't know if she's a girl? Is she—"

"No!" I shout, exasperated. "She *is* a girl, I just don't know exactly what we are anymore. I mean, we're friends. I think we'll always be friends, but it's not what it was."

I pinch the bridge of my nose.

Maybe sharing was a bad idea.

"I loved her for years," I continue, because if there's one thing about me, it's that once I commit to something, I follow through. "But Mackenzie—that's her name—went through a lot of heavy shit in the last year, so I waited to tell her, and right when I was ready to make a move, my cousin moved to town. Long story short, she fell for him instead."

"Ouch." Skylar winces.

"Pretty much. And if that isn't the cherry on top of the fucking cake, my father's ex-mistress also happens to be my cousin's mother."

A puff of air escapes Skylar's lips. "Your life is like a soap opera."

I laugh dryly and scrub a hand over my face. "You're telling me."

"So, I guess I can see why you wouldn't want to be anywhere they are."

"Every time I look at them or think about them, all I can see is my mother's face. All I can picture is how much it'll crush her to discover the truth. And I know it's only a matter of time before she does, but it eats me up inside that I have this secret. I feel like I should tell her, but I just can't bring myself to do it. She gave her life to my father. She followed him around and let him take the spotlight, build his career while she put her own on hold. So, to know he fucking did this to her . . ." I shake my head, clenching my jaw until my molars ache.

Skylar leans back in her stool and blows out a long breath. "So, what are you gonna do? Are you really gonna quit just because they're staying there?"

They wouldn't be the only reason, I think. Sooner or later, Crenshaw is going to call on me to do something bigger than drop a sealed envelope at a mystery location, and I'm not sure I wanna be around when that time comes.

But, of course, I can't tell her that. I was told to never mention his name, that only a few of the employees at the Bardot even know the Gentleman's Club exists. Not that I'd tell Skylar about my debt, anyway. If she already thinks poorly of me, I can't imagine what she'd think if she knew all the mistakes I've made.

But as much as I want help, I can't bring myself to ask my father. I have no doubt it would come with a dozen strings attached, and the last thing I want is to be in his debt. So, maybe I'm stuck.

"That depends. Is this a truce we have going here?" I joke.

She glances away from me to her coffee-flavored candy drink and smiles. "Nah. The truce ends the second we get back to the hotel."

Our eyes meet and I smirk. "I should've guessed as much." Pushing back from the island, I get to my feet. "Well, in that case, I guess we need to head back to work?" I go to collect our mugs and knock one over, watching in slow motion as the brown liquid splashes on the bottom of my white dress shirt. "Shit," I say as I jump back.

"Smooth." She laughs. "Might wanna change before we leave."

I sigh and motion her to follow. "Come on."

"You want me to watch you change?" She quirks a brow, which I answer with an exaggerated eye roll.

"I was trying to be nice by not leaving you," I say, my tone sober. "But if you'd prefer to wait here in a strange house alone, where my lecherous father can walk in at any moment, that's fine by me."

"Nope." Skylar hops off her stool. "Lead the way," she says with a wave of a hand. "Besides, I'd be crazy to pass up an opportunity to see where the narcissist sleeps."

I smirk and shake my head as she follows me down the hall-way. We enter my room and I glance around, trying to see it from her eyes. The huge four poster bed with the navy-blue bedspread, the creamy walls, and shelves lined with years of trophies and awards.

I head to my closet, trying not to think about the fact that the only girl I've ever brought here is Mackenzie.

Stepping inside the walk-in closet, I choose a pale green dress shirt, and step back out to find Skylar staring at my trophy wall. When she hears me behind her, she glances over her shoulder as she reaches out and touches one of the medals, reading the inscription. "'MVP Rebel Freshman.'" She moves to the next one, reading several more of the awards out loud, and with each one, my muscles tense. "'Quarterback of the Year. Peewee Excellence in Football. Ohio High School Athletic Association Award . . .'" She goes on, but I stop listening.

Finally, she turns to me and whistles. "That's some wall of fame right there."

"Yeah. That wall about sums up my life," I say, hearing the bitterness laced in my tone.

"You don't sound happy about that."

I shrug, trying to sound nonchalant as I say, "I used to love it. I'm just not sure I do anymore."

She frowns as I start to unbutton my dress shirt.

"Um, what are you doing?" she asks, waving a hand toward me.

A smirk curls the corner of my mouth, and I shrug. "It's just a shirt. Relax."

"Just a shirt," she mutters under her breath with a little shake of the head.

Amusement plays on my lips as I drop the soiled shirt to the floor, then angle myself slightly away from her before reaching for the hem of my white T-shirt in an effort to hide my tattoo.

To this day, no one else knows what I have branded in my skin but the tattoo artist. Things went haywire the night we got them. First, with Atlas finding out his father overdosed, and then his accident. The ink on my side was forgotten. It wasn't until later, when things calmed down, the guys remembered to ask what I got. I shrugged and said I went with a Rebel tattoo like Jace, Teagan, and Knox. It was easier that way, less explaining.

I start to yank the T-shirt over my head, catching a quick glimpse of Skylar's pink cheeks before she spins around, giving me her back.

"What? Never seen a guy without his shirt before?"

"Of course. I've seen plenty of boys—I mean, men—without their shirts on. I'm just worried the sight of your bare skin might make me gag, and I hate to be rude."

I stifle a laugh, reveling in the blush spreading over the back of her neck. Part of me wants to reach out and touch it, to feel the heat surge through my skin, even though I know I shouldn't. But damn it feels good to be appreciated.

"Must be nice to be so good at something. I assume you'll be playing at college somewhere?" she asks.

"I don't know." I sigh. "If my father has his way, I will."

She spins around. "Wait. You *don't* want to play in college? Or did you just not get an offer, because I find it hard to believe—"

"I have some offers, but I don't know if I want it anymore."

"Hold up. When you say you have offers . . .?"

"The day I missed work, it was because the coaches at Penn State are interested. They wanted me to tour the facilities. It would mean a full ride, but I'm not sure I'm gonna take it. There are some small double-A colleges, too."

"You have a full ride and clearly, a ton of talent"—she motions to my trophy wall—"but you're just going to give that all up?"

"You make it sound like I'm ungrateful or something."

"Maybe you are," she blurts.

I stare at her hard. "It doesn't feel right anymore."

She bites her lower lip, her posture rigid. "I knew you were dumb, but not this dumb."

I blink down at her, shocked at her anger. "Excuse me?"

"Do you know how lucky you are to have a ticket out of here? I would give anything to have an opportunity like that."

"It's not that cut and dry.

"Seems pretty cut and dry to me. You have raw talent you're ignoring, all because—you know what?" She throws her hands up. "Never mind." She pushes past me and out of my room.

Muttering under my breath, I follow her out into the hallway even though I know I shouldn't. "What the hell put a bug up your ass? I don't see how what I choose to do with my life matters to you," I say to her back.

She turns, and her eyes pierce through me like a knife. "You're right. It makes no difference to me what you do, but I guess . . ." She bites the inside of her cheek, and I can see her mind working, the thoughts swirling in her eyes as she says, "For a moment, I thought you were different. The kind of boy that sees the value of what's right in front of him. The kind of boy that would never waste an amazing opportunity like that."

And then she turns and walks out, leaving me wondering what the hell just happened, and why it feels like I have whiplash.

By the time I return to the Bardot, I have no idea what to expect. Surely, Skylar will give me the cold shoulder. Our temporary cease-fire was so short-lived, part of me wonders if I imagined it.

But when I enter, I find Rosa at the front desk. "Skylar never came back?" I ask.

"Oh, she's around here somewhere. I think she's helping out with a big event in the ballroom that's taking place next week."

Great. That likely means she's with Brad.

The thought pisses me off.

"I'm sure she'll be by soon, dear." Rosa pats me on the shoulder. "Said you'd be here shortly. Glad you made it back."

After she turns and heads down the hall, I wonder how much Skylar told her. I get the feeling they're close, and Rosa's statement only confirms that.

I lean my elbows on the counter and rest my head in my hands while I think about everything that happened earlier. For once, Skylar and I had actually gotten along. I wouldn't believe it myself if I hadn't been an active party. Clearly, she took issue with the idea of me passing on a sports scholarship, which brings to mind the reason she was pissed I got her kicked out of the bar that night.

Is that what triggered her? She's desperately seeking a scholarship, and I want to turn mine down. I wonder if she's having trouble finding a way to pay for school; it's the obvious conclusion. If so, I guess I can see why she might be triggered at the thought of me passing on an opportunity. But still . . . I shake my head, pushing the thoughts aside because it doesn't matter.

She doesn't matter.

Skylar and I aren't even what I would consider friends, so why the hell do I care what she thinks?

It shouldn't bother me.

And it doesn't.

So, why does it feel like I'm trying to convince myself?

CHAPTER 18

SKYLAR

WHEN I ARRIVE HOME from work I check the mail, knowing JD likely won't be here for at least another hour. I got a text from him on my way home telling me not to eat anything because he's grabbing sushi. Normally, he cooks for us, but on the weekends, he often spoils me with my favorite takeout, and sushi tonight sounds amazing.

After the day I had, I'm looking forward to hanging with him while we eat, then taking my implants out for a hearing break, and losing myself in a good book.

Sometimes I need the silence to recalibrate after a long day, and today is no exception.

I take the handful of mail out of the box and make my way up the sidewalk to our house, where I unlock the front door and let myself inside. My thoughts are on Graham as I drop the mail on the kitchen island and help myself to a soda from the fridge.

His confession took me by surprise. I never would've pegged him for being so complicated, or for being the kind of guy who wears his heart on his sleeve, but from what I saw, he's both. The sarcastic, irritating man I've been spending time with is just a facade for a boy who's hurting.

I laugh to myself and shake my head.

God, he would hate that assessment.

But it doesn't make it any less true.

I pop my soda open and take a sip. He and I formed somewhat of a truce today; we crossed a line and entered new territory. At least before I ruined it and got pissed at him.

I sigh as press the cold can to the side of my face, feeling the condensation against my skin. I don't know what got into me.

Okay, I do know. I got jealous. Truly and unnecessarily jealous.

And the worst part about throwing a fit was that up until that moment, I was actually enjoying myself. I kinda like the person I saw today. But I probably put us right back into enemy territory with my little tantrum.

Shaking off my thoughts about Graham, I pick up the stack of mail and flip through it half-heartedly, most of it bills or junk addressed to JD. I rarely get anything. But when I spot a thick envelope with my name on it from the School of the Art Institute of Chicago, I freeze. I applied for early acceptance, but never in a million years did I think I would hear back already.

My fingers tremble as I turn the envelope over and tear through the flap to reveal the contents inside. Early acceptance is rare, and my hands shake as I dump the contents on the table. I paw through a couple of brochures, but when I find their letterhead, I unfold it, and begin to read.

Dear Skylar Davenport,

Congratulations! It is with great pleasure that I inform you of your acceptance to the School of Art Institute of Chicago.

I throw my hands up, and a blood curdling scream escapes my lips, piercing the quiet.

The paper flutters from my fingers, floating to the floor by my feet, but I don't care. I'm too busy doing a happy dance because my number one school of choice, one of the best freaking art schools in the country, has accepted me into their art program. Me! Skylar Davenport.

It's almost too good to be true.

I crouch to the ground and pick the letter back up and give it a kiss. This is my ticket out of Oak Ridge and to go on to bigger and better things. It's my chance to prove I can make it on my own.

I can take care of myself. I can build my own life. I don't need JD to provide for me. I can set him free, and he can finally have his life back while I build mine.

The thought fills me with so much happiness, I feel it in my arms and legs, all the way to my toes.

All I need now is a way to pay for school, which is why I'm going to win the Siddhartha Art Competition. And after I do, I'll tell JD. I'll break the news to him.

He'll take it hard at first, of course, because worrying about me is second nature for him, but after he gets used to the idea, he'll see this is the best thing for both of us. He'll see what an amazing opportunity this is, and won't fathom allowing me to let it pass by.

The click of a key in the lock comes from the foyer, and my head whips toward the sound—*JD!*

I scramble to cram the contents back in the envelope, then hurry to my room at the end of the hall where I shove it in my top dresser drawer.

Taking a deep breath, I try to calm my racing heart before I head back into the kitchen just as JD appears in the entryway.

He loosens his tie with one hand while gripping the takeout bag in his other. "Hey," he says.

"You're home early." I smile, pushing back the dregs of guilt that are swimming in my stomach.

He shrugs and brushes past me to the island, where he calls over his shoulder, "It's been a while since we've had a night together just to hang out, so I took off early."

"Awesome." I take the bag from him and arrange the takeout containers on the island as he grabs plates and napkins, both of us working in tandem; it's a routine we're used to. "Eat at the table?" I ask.

"How about the couch and coffee table? I thought we could watch a movie while we eat, and then after, I'll kick your butt in Scrabble."

"Ha! Fat chance." I grin over at him before I turn and fill two glasses with ice and tea from the fridge, then take them to the coffee table. Though I wanted a hearing break and some time to myself, the guilt from the acceptance letter burning a hole in my top dresser drawer has me reconsidering.

"Ready?" he asks, grabbing the flatware.

"Ready." We both fill our plates in silence, then take our seats on the couch where I settle in, fighting the urge to moan at my first bite of California roll.

Beside me, JD props his socked feet up on the coffee table in front of us while he finds the newest comedy we've been waiting to see and puts it on. Soon, we're both engrossed in the film, eating and laughing in all the same places. But eventually, a romance subplot blooms in the storyline, and after a kissing scene, we both grow quiet.

All these years, JD has made me his number one priority. He's never brought a girl home. Or if he has, I certainly haven't known about it.

I wonder if he's lonely.

I glance at him out of the corner of my eye, watching as he takes a bite of his sushi, and an overwhelming wave of sadness washes over me. I'm only eighteen and I want to be in love. I practically dream about it. I can't imagine how he must feel at thirty-two. Have I ever been a burden? Does he ever crave a woman's touch? Her kiss? A relationship other than the kind I can offer?

Maybe he resents me . . .

He's such a good man. He deserves so much happiness, and I want that for him. Sometimes more than I want it for myself, which is why I haven't told him about my plans to go away to school.

As if he senses my gaze, he turns to me and smiles. "What's up, bug? You're not enjoying the movie?"

I offer him a half smile, then shake my head. "No, it's not that. I just . . . Do you ever want that?" I nod toward the television where the couple dances on-screen, holding each other in their arms.

"What?" He somehow manages to smile with his lips but frowns with his eyes.

"Love. A girlfriend? Don't you get, you know, lonely?"

"Of course not." He nudges me in the arm. "I have you. We're the two amigos, remember?" He winks.

My stomach sinks and the little voice in the back of my head pipes up like it always does.

It'll kill him if you leave . . .

"Right," I say, but I push the issue. "But a girlfriend is different."

He picks at the food on his plate with a frown as if contemplating what I said. "I don't know. I guess I never really thought about it."

"Really?" I ask, because I find that hard to believe. Lately, finding love is all I can think about, and men are supposed to be walking balls of testosterone. "If not a girlfriend, you haven't even wanted a fling? I mean, don't you have . . . needs?"

He chokes on a bite of sushi, his face turning red as he coughs it up. "Skylar!" he scolds once he can breathe again.

"What?" I shrug. "I'm serious."

"I'm not talking about this with you," he says, his tone firm.

He shakes his head, and if I weren't so worried about him, I'd find his embarrassment at the subject amusing. "I just thought—"

"Well, stop thinking!" he barks. He takes a drink of his tea before he sets it back down with a clang and turns to me, wide-eyed. "Wait. You're not . . . you aren't . . . thinking about your"—he winces—"needs, are you?"

"What? No!" I all but shout. Now I'm the one who's blushing. My cheeks could fuel the California wildfires for years without burning out.

"I was just—how about let's forget I said anything."

"Sounds good to me," he says, cramming a huge bite of food in his mouth.

"But first, I just want to say that if you, you know, want a girlfriend or even a friend with benefits thing, or a fling or whatever—"

"Skylar."

"—you have my permission. You can bring whoever you want here, and I won't think anything less of you. No questions asked."

"Skylar!"

"I just want you to be happy," I nearly scream.

He sighs and reaches over, grabs my hand, and gives it a squeeze. "I know," he says. "But I *am* happy, okay? You . . .This"—he waves his hand around us—"is all I need."

I open my mouth to protest, when he rolls his eyes and says, "But if that ever changes, I promise, I'll tell you. I won't hold back, okay?"

I relax back into the couch, exhaling. "Okay," I say, because it's all I can ask for, even though, deep down, I kind of wish he needed more.

CHAPTER 19

GRAHAM

WHEN I PULL INTO the gravel driveway of Atlas's place, I'm unsurprised to see Mackenzie's car in the driveway. It's a Sunday night, so I should have guessed they'd be together. The two are rarely apart anymore.

I turn the ignition off and sit there for a moment before getting out. The porch light illuminates the snow-covered yard in front of the trailer. Dim light glows from within, and when I make my way up the short walkway to the front door and hear the soft sound of Mackenzie's laughter, I feel a pang of envy deep in my bones.

Inhaling, I raise my fist, pausing to compose myself as I knock. A moment later the door swings open, and Atlas fills the doorway while Mackenzie calls out behind him, "Who is it?"

"See for yourself," Atlas tells her as he jerks his head toward the living room, an invitation to come in.

It's the first time I've been in his place. Despite hanging out with him and the guys after school, the three of us are yet to spend a lot of time together. Though I meant the things I said in the hospital, when I gave him my blessing to be with Mackenzie, it's still not always easy for me. I let go of her that night and accepted that she and I would never be together. Put the idea of us to rest. But there are times where it still hurts, where all my old feelings creep up on me and rise to the surface. It's those times where for the briefest of moments, I forget we have no future together. Other times, I see the way they look at each other and I'm hit with a burst of white-hot jealousy. It eats me up inside, tears my guts into pieces, and I can't help but want what they have.

Hell, I thought I had it with Kenz. Discovering you're wrong about the one thing in the world you were most sure of—the one thing you would've bet your life on—has a way of fucking with your head.

I lift my head as I enter, and I'm hit by the sight of Mackenzie like a tidal wave. She stands in front of a Christmas tree, an ornament in her outstretched hand. White twinkling lights illuminate her face like an angel, forming a ring of light around her otherwise dark hair.

She steals the breath right out of my lungs.

I have no idea why the sight of her strikes me so hard tonight. Maybe it's my mixed-up emotions. They've been running high for days—weeks. Adding fuel to the fire, my earlier interaction with Skylar reminded me of how Kenz and I used to be and what we once shared. She was always the one I ran to with my problems. Just like she always knew the right thing to say to make them better.

Of all people, Skylar gave me that today.

Until she chewed me out and left.

"Uh, hey." I raise a hand in a little wave before I tuck both of them into my pockets.

"Graham." Mackenzie steps back from the tree and smiles. For a moment, she moves toward me as if to give me a hug, then pauses as if remembering herself, and wraps her arms around her chest instead.

A simple greeting, something that should come as natural as breathing between us, now feels awkward.

Atlas goes to her side and drapes an arm around her shoulders, and I wonder if things will always feel so fucking weird between us.

"Putting up the tree?" I ask, focusing on it with a smile I don't entirely feel.

"Yeah. Atlas hasn't had a real Christmas tree in years, so I convinced him it was a good idea."

Atlas rolls his eyes, but I can hear the affection in his voice when he says, "Convinced is putting it mildly. Twisted my arm is more accurate."

Mackenzie's mouth drops open and she swats him lightly on the chest while he grins down at her. "Lies. You love it. You were just telling me how much."

Sighing, he pulls her into his arms. "Fine. You know I do. Thank you, doll," he murmurs, his tone so intimate, I look away.

My stomach tightens. I clear my throat, trying to lighten the pressure on my chest. "It's, uh, it's nice."

I think of the professionally decorated ones towering in the living room and foyer of my own home. I'm not sure Dad ever really showed an interest in decorating for the holidays. I don't even know when we stopped decorating them ourselves with sentimental ornaments, rather than the sterile, professionally decorated ones we have now, but I wonder if my mom misses it. I wonder if there was ever a time when they did this together.

Atlas may not have had a Christmas tree because his father was too blitzed out of his mind to think of putting one up, but neither did I. At least not in the way it counted. Just because it appears like you have it all, it doesn't mean you really do.

"Hey, by the way," Atlas says as he releases Mackenzie and she goes back to decorating the tree, "I heard from my mom, finally. I guess they're at a hotel, so all is good for now, but I'm still hoping she can get a place back in town. Makes it so much easier for me to help out with Storm between work and school."

I know it's not meant to be a jab at me, but I feel the sting of guilt anyway. I know how he feels about Storm, just like I know he thinks I need to step up to the plate and be his brother.

"Yeah," I say, running a hand over my mouth. "That's actually why I came. I saw them today. They're staying at the hotel where I work. But that's not all. I logged into their reservation.

They're booked for a long-term stay courtesy of Calvin Scott's credit card."

Rage darkens Atlas's features. "I knew it. This has Cal's fingerprints all over it," Atlas spits, hands clenched at his sides. "Probably put them up in a fancy-ass hotel to try and look like the good guy, when really his only motive was to get them out of town."

"My thoughts exactly, and I'm going to confront him about it."

"You want me to come with you?" Atlas steps forward, but I place a hand on his chest as my gaze drifts to the girl behind him.

I know Mackenzie well enough to know she won't mind him leaving to take care of this, but he shouldn't have to. He's my father, and it's about time I call him out on his shit.

"Stay here," I say, my tone firm. "Finish putting your tree up with Kenz. He and I need to hash this out."

"You sure, dude?"

I note the relief in Mackenzie's eyes. "Positive," I say before I turn and head for the door.

"Okay, but let me know if you need backup."

"Will do." I swing the door open and step outside, curling my shoulders inward against the cold as I quickly close the distance to my car.

Surprised to hear footsteps behind me, I turn to find Mackenzie following on my heels. She hugs her arms around herself, but it's futile against the frigid air, and she shivers anyway.

"Kenz, it's freezing. Get back inside," I say, motioning toward the house.

"I wanted to make sure you're okay." Her breath puffs in the cold.

I swallow, thinking of the last time I felt "okay." The closest I've come to it has probably been when I'm sparring with Skylar.

The revelation surprises me.

"Yeah, of course," I lie. "I'm good. Why wouldn't I be?" I try for a smile, but it falls flat.

She reaches out, pressing a hand to my arm. "You'd tell me if you weren't, right? You'd tell me if you needed anything?"

Emotion swells inside of me like a water balloon. "Yeah, of course," I say, knowing it's the last thing I'll do.

"I know things are different now, but I'm still here if you need me. I still care as much as I always did."

"I know." I exhale, and the ache in my chest returns with a vengeance. "But it's like you said, things are different now."

I take a step back, and she drops her hand. "But it's okay, really," I say, meaning it.

You've found your happiness, and I'm just trying to make peace with the hand I've been dealt.

I smile through the pain in my chest, something I've gotten good at these last few months, and for reasons I can't explain, my thoughts drift to Skylar. I think about the image of her standing in my kitchen, a wide smile spreading her lips.

"I'll be okay," I repeat.

Mackenzie nods, offering me a soft smile that I return. "Okay," she says, though I'm not sure she buys it.

I turn away from her, opening the car door and sliding inside, then promptly start it and back down the driveway.

I travel the roads home, my wipers fighting the snow as it peppers my windshield. The driveway is empty, not unusual this time of year. When I click the remote for the garage door on my visor, the door lifts, and I see my father's car inside.

After I park, I head into the house, searching the kitchen and foyer. It's not until I head down the hallway that I find my father in the den, his head bent over a stack of papers.

"Where's Mom?" I ask, unable to help myself. As much as I want her to discover the truth, I still can't bring myself to cause her that kind of pain.

Dad's head jerks up, his eyes finding mine as he peers at me over his glasses. "She's at her monthly book club tonight. How was work?" he all but sneers.

"Enlightening, actually. Did I mention where I'm working? It's a hotel in the city, just thirty minutes from Riverside."

Dad tenses. To someone else, they might not notice the small change in the set of his shoulders, or the muscle in his jaw, but I do. "Is that so?" he says, returning his attention to the papers in front of him.

"Did you really think sending Marie and Storm thirty minutes away would keep Mom from finding out about them?"

"Why do you assume I had anything to do with them moving there?" he asks, removing his glasses.

"Do you ever plan on telling Mom?"

"Your mother and I have had our share of problems, but—"

"I'll take that as a no."

My father's mouth hardens as he stares a hole through me. "If you must know, her place had mold issues and a faulty furnace. It was freezing in there half the time and the landlord is a lazy shit. I did them a favor by buying out their lease."

"You expect me to believe you have their best interest at heart?" I chuckle, the sound bitter in my ears. "That's comical, especially coming from you."

"The Bardot is a fine establishment, but only temporary."

"Until you can send them away again? Preferably out of state?" I arch a brow. "Do you really expect me to believe anything you're saying right now when everything that's come out of your mouth is complete bullshit? Your entire marriage. Your relationship with Atlas. All of it has been built on a bed of lies."

Pushing back from his desk, he gets to his feet, his face contorted with rage. "Despite what you think, I'm trying to make this right for everyone."

"If this is what doing the right thing looks like, then I'd hate to see you do the wrong thing."

"You want to talk about overdue conversations?" he asks, spittle flying from his lips. "Let's talk, then. What the hell is going on with you and football? You haven't made a decision. Haven't given a verbal commitment yet. Penn State wants you, yet when we toured the stadium, you had the enthusiasm of a corpse."

"I was distracted, okay? I told you I was busy and had to work, but you still made me go."

"Signing day is only a little more than a month away and you're too busy to make a decision that will determine the rest of your life? What the hell is wrong with you?" he snaps. "There was a time where you treated football and training like it was your job, and rightly so, because it'll get you a hell of a lot further than working as a bellhop at some damn hotel. Where are your priorities?"

"Where are yours?" I shout, my breath shallow. "Where were they when you were screwing another woman?"

Dad's hands fist, and for a moment, I think he might hit me. Hell, I'd probably deserve it if he did.

"Tell Mom. She has a right to know," I grind out.

"I'm trying to figure this out. I haven't always done things the right way, I realize that."

I bark out a laugh. "That's an understatement."

"But I love your mother."

I want to believe him. I do. But he's so full of shit, I don't know where the dog pile starts and where it ends.

"Then tell her," I say, my voice thick with emotion. "Before I do."

CHAPTER 20

SKYLAR

I'M BACK AT WORK, and I can no longer prolong the inevitable. Graham is set to arrive in the next few minutes, and I might've been able to shove him to the corner of my mind after work yesterday, but I can no longer avoid him or the fact I might have overreacted due to my own frustrations because of my circumstances. In fact, I fully expect him to think I'm a complete psycho now, considering I had zero right to dump on what he wants for his future. If he did the same, I'd be pissed.

I sit behind the front desk, glancing up at the door from my sketch pad every now and then. The drawing I'm working on is of my father and a harsh look at his grief after my mother died.

My hand moves over the paper, sketching in the basic shape of his face then his body, before I begin to shade and fill in details. I imagine being so immersed in sorrow that your body shuts down. Your will to live ceases.

I darken the hollows of his cheeks, the painful crease of his brow, and the circles beneath his eyes when the hotel doors open. I glance up, expecting Graham, only to find JD barreling toward me, his face red with anger.

My forehead wrinkles in concern as I set my charcoal down and rise to my feet. I'm about to ask him what's wrong when he slaps the brochure for SAIC down, and my stomach sinks to the floor.

I open my mouth to speak, but the words stick in my throat before he slides the pamphlet toward me. "Care to explain?" he asks, keeping his voice down, despite the angry tenor.

"I-it's just . . ." I twist my hands in front of myself, unsure of whether I want to tell him the truth. Sure, he's going to find out eventually, especially if I win this art contest or I can get a scholarship another way. But I'm not ready yet. I'm still hell-bent on making it on my own and I don't want anything to jeopardize that.

Rosa appears from down the hall rolling a cart with supplies to stock the coffee bar in the lobby. Hovering nearby, she fills a tray with little creamers and sugar packets while JD tugs my arm, guiding me to the hallway for some semblance of privacy where he waves the brochure in my face.

Oh, goody. Glad he didn't forget it on the counter.

"Explain," he bites out.

"I applied to the School of Art Institute in Chicago."

"I can see that," he says.

"Right." I swallow. "Well, I got in."

He glares at me, letting me know he doesn't appreciate my evasiveness. "I got that part, but what I want to know is why you applied to this school when it's all the way in Chicago."

I swallow, completely unprepared for this conversation. Even if I were ready, the last place I'd want to have it is in the lobby of the Bardot.

"It's one of the best art schools in the country," I say because it's true.

"And?" His eyes search mine.

"*And* I got into one of the best art schools in the country," I say like it's obvious. "Do you realize how amazing that is?"

"But you don't actually plan on going there, do you?" he asks, ignoring my question.

Here it is, the moment of truth. I could tell him what I want, how a part of me feels like I'm being smothered. Admit to him that I'd rather die than stay here in Ohio, working at the hotel. That there's a big world out there, and all I want is a little piece of it. That I want to carve my place in the world.

But when I look into his big brown eyes, I see the ghost of pain in them, and that's not what comes out of my mouth. What comes out instead, is, "No, of course, not."

He frowns, but I can't help but note the way his face softens with relief.

"I mean, I considered it for a second, but then I realized how far away it was and decided that if I want to go to school, maybe I can go local."

I chew on the inside of my cheek as I think of what a bullshit lie it is.

He straightens and shifts on his feet, and I can tell he doesn't know what to do with this information. It's not what he expected, yet it's news to him, even if it's better than the idea of me moving.

"What about your job here? I thought you talked about staying on, maybe taking on a bigger role? You never mentioned pursuing art." He offers me a small shrug. "I thought it was just a hobby and you were happy with the way things are."

"I am." I place a hand on his arm, hating myself for being a coward. "Of course I'm happy, and I'm not leaving the Bardot anytime soon. At first, art *was* just a hobby. But I love it. I love to draw. And maybe it won't amount to anything, but, I don't know, sometimes I think it might be kinda cool to see if it could."

I glance down at my hands and stare at my nails, wanting nothing more than to drop the conversation. "Never mind. It's probably stupid."

I reach out and take the brochure from his hands, fighting the sting of tears pressing against the back of my eyes while he stares at me with an intensity I don't recognize.

After a moment, he exhales and his whole body relaxes as he reaches out and pulls me into his arms. I melt into him, half expecting him to tell me it's okay if I want to move away, that we'll make it work. I expect him to say he understands if I want something different from the life he's given me because he only wants my happiness, and he understands that pursuing my dreams will make me happy.

But I don't get what I expect, nor what I want.

Instead, he presses a brotherly kiss to the top of my head and gives my arm a little squeeze.

"Sorry if I overreacted, bug," he tells me, "but I can't say I'm not relieved. For a second there, I thought you were actually considering an out-of-state school. Glad it's not what I thought."

He inhales, and the tension drains from his face. "I don't know what I'd do if you left me."

A few minutes later, JD leaves, and I return to the front desk where I attend to a guest requesting room service and fresh towels, then pick my sketch back up, albeit less enthusiastic than before. I try to add detail to my father's eyes, but my focus is shot. I can't concentrate because all I can think about is how I should've told JD the truth. Rip the Band-Aid off. It would be so much easier than hovering between the truth and a lie.

But when his sad eyes met mine, all I saw was every single sacrifice he ever made to give me a good life.

Skipping college and working his butt off so that he could pay for my cochlear implants.

All the speech therapy lessons he took me to.

Playing Barbies with me on his twenty-first birthday when he should've been out getting drunk with his friends.

The endless hours he watched cooking shows so he could learn how to prepare a proper meal.

All the tea parties, lemonade stands, and days spent at the pool in the summer.

How many times did he work late into the night building his business, so he wouldn't miss dinner or taking me to some school event or a friend's house?

He did it all for me.

Every. Single. Thing.

And now I want to repay him by pushing it all away, say "thanks, but no thanks," and leave for greener pastures.

I don't know what I'd do if you left me. His words dance in my brain, taunting me until I hang my head and put the sketch back down, shoving it to the corner of the desk.

How am I supposed to go to school in Chicago when he says things like that?

I owe everything to JD.

Deep down, I know I have every right to forge my own path. Craving independence is normal—healthy, even—but it really sucks when it feels as though it's coming at the expense of someone you love.

"You okay, darling?" Rosa's soothing voice penetrates my thoughts as she places a hand over my shoulder.

I glance up at her, taking in her soft smile. She's the closest thing I have to a mother, and I nearly burst into tears at the sympathy I see in her eyes. "So, you heard that?"

"Hard not to," she says, her voice clipped, which tells me she also didn't like what she heard.

With a sigh, I flop back against my chair. "Why can't he make this easier on me? Shouldn't he want me to spread my wings?"

Rosa leans forward and cups my face in her hands. "Letting go of your children is one of the hardest things you ever have to do. Parenting is completely selfless. You give all of yourself, everything you have to someone, only for them to turn around and leave you. With JD, it's probably worse because he has no one else. He's petrified at the thought of losing you, darling."

She gives my cheek a little pat and then releases me. "But he'll be okay if you go. Maybe he'll even be happier in the long run. He might not realize it, but it'll allow him to finally spread his wings, too. Right now, he's just too close to the situation to see that."

"I hope you're right," I say, sounding as dubious as I feel.

I love the thought of JD finally *living*. The idea of him rebuilding lost friendships, dating again, and being selfish for a change fills me with joy. But I'm also starting to doubt whether that will ever happen.

"You'll see." Rosa nods as if she can read the doubt in my expression.

The front doors swing open and Graham strolls inside. A burst of cold air follows in his wake, and even from here, the vibrant green of his eyes cuts the distance between us.

"Now, if that doesn't cheer you up, honey, I don't know what will." She winks. "At least you get to work with a view."

"Rosa!" I hiss, and my cheeks instantly heat.

"What?" She shrugs, all innocence. "I may be old enough to be that child's mother, but I still have eyes, and that boy right there is *fine*."

"Oh my gosh. Gross," I say to the sound of her chuckle.

Graham greets her first, and when my traitorous gaze darts up at him, as much as I hate to admit it, Rosa's right. Not that I'd ever confess to him how completely gorgeous he is; his ego is big enough without me inflating it.

His gaze catches mine, and I realize I'm staring. "Hi," I mumble.

He joins me behind the desk and arches a brow. "So, we're speaking now?" I blink over at him as he clarifies, "Because I wasn't sure after you took off in a huff yesterday, then proceeded to ignore me for the rest of the day."

Shit. With the conversation between JD and me, I almost forgot about yesterday. Though I know I should be sorry, that smug look on his face makes me double down on my pride.

I clear my throat. "Don't flatter yourself," I say, noting Rosa's smirk out of the corner of my eye. "I wasn't ignoring you yesterday. I had some things to take care of for an event."

"If you say so."

My gaze narrows, but I refuse to give him the satisfaction of pressing the point, so I log into the computer in front of me and get back to work. But I can't do anything when I can feel his eyes boring into the back of my skull. "Can I help you?"

"Nope. Just watching to see if your head starts spinning."

I roll my eyes and turn back to the screen I'm fake-reading when he reaches for my sketch pad. My hand shoots out, but grasps only air as he lifts the notebook up before I can stop him and looks at the half-completed drawing of my father. "Hey," I say, reaching for it. "That's mine!"

He holds it higher, his forehead creased as he turns the page to a sketch of my mother. "Give it back," I yell, but my pleas are futile as he ignores me.

He turns another page, and I know what he finds. A self-portrait titled *The Sound of Silence*—a portrayal of what it's like when I take my implants out for a hearing break.

He holds the book above my head as he looks through it and I uselessly try to grab it. "You have the arms of a chimp. It's not fair," I moan.

Graham places the flat of his hand on my head forcing me back down into the chair. "Maybe your arms are just freakishly small."

"My arms are *not* freakishly small," I say in a huff, then cross them over my chest, waiting for him to finish the invasion of my privacy because there's no use at this point in trying to stop him.

After a moment, Graham glances back down at me, an angry glint in his eyes. "Too bad you don't have any sort of talent. You know, as your ticket out of here, huh?"

"It's . . . complicated," I murmur.

"Right." Graham's mouth flattens, giving the impression he thinks I'm full of shit.

I huff and tap my foot, waiting, but he still doesn't give back my sketch pad. Instead, he turns another page and a surge of panic sends my heart spiraling because I know what sketch is next. I drew it in a weak moment at work a few days ago. It's one of Graham, his head bowed, a crease in his brow while he focused on something in the computer.

I can't let him see it.

"Give. It. Back," I say between gritted teeth.

Graham chuckles, his fingers hovering over the edge of the page ready to turn it.

"Graham, I'm serious. Come on," I plead as my heart leaps into my throat.

"Kiss me."

"What?" I blink in shock, unsure I heard him right.

He stares down at my lips, and if his wide-eyed expression is any indication, he's half shocked he said it himself.

His throat bobs while I try to process his request. Did he really just . . .?

"Kiss me, and I'll give it back." The corner of his mouth twists into a smirk, but something tells me he's not taunting or teasing or joking. He's serious.

My breathing hitches as my gaze flickers to his lips while he watches me with an intensity that sends goose bumps blooming all over my skin.

With as much courage as I can muster, I step forward and slowly slide my hands up his chest, feeling the ridges of muscle beneath his dress shirt. Maybe I *should* kiss him. Maybe I should seize the opportunity, because I suddenly have no doubt in my mind that Graham excels at anything involving his mouth.

His pupils dilate. The steady rise and fall of his breath falters.

I can only imagine the critique he'd give me, it being my first time. I'd probably never live it down.

So, before I can do anything I'll regret, I snatch the pad out of his now-loose grip and take a step back. "Ha!" I taunt as I wave it in front of him.

He frowns down at me for a moment, and I'm surprised by how genuine the disappointment in his expression is. I'm not sure what's crazier. The fact that he asked me to kiss him and seems disappointed that I didn't, or the fact that I wanted to—desperately.

"You play dirty." He points, recovering the humorous gleam in his eyes.

"Well, if you recall, you lost a scholarship for me, remember?"

"This again?" He rolls his eyes. "I remember all right, and it's the last time I'll be a gentleman and come to a lady's rescue."

"Good. Because maybe women don't want men to rescue us. We can rescue ourselves," I say, mostly because I know I'm wrong and feeling salty about it.

I know Graham well enough now to know he had nothing but genuine intentions that night at the bar. Just like I also know I was wrong yesterday to go off on him. His life choices are absolutely none of my business, but I can't seem to bring myself to admit it when he's staring down at me with so much disdain.

The transition from his lust-filled gaze to one of disgust gives me whiplash.

"Are you always this strongheaded?" he asks, arms crossed over his chest.

"Are you always this self-assuming?" I ask, my voice rising with my emotions. After my interaction with JD, I'm at the end of my rope. Much more, and I'll snap.

He snorts. "Good one."

"You don't just go nosing in people's stuff," I splutter, waving my book around.

"If it's so personal, maybe you shouldn't just leave it lying around for anyone to find."

"I was working on it," I seethe. Then I shake my head. "You know what? Never mind. It's really none of your business what I do."

"I beg to differ. Using company time for personal work?" He makes a *tsking* sound before pursing his lips, and I wish they didn't look so damned kissable. It makes me loathe him even more. "Not cool."

I rise to my feet, and my hands fist at my sides while I stare him down. I'm so angry my mind goes blank, but instead of insulting him like I want to, I shake with the effort of holding back my tears.

"What, no witty comeback or snarky retort?" he asks.

"You know what? Screw you," I say, and then I spin on my heel and rush from the lobby with the sketchbook clasped in my hand

CHAPTER 21

GRAHAM

I FROWN AS I watch Skylar race from the room as if her feet are on fire, and can't help the sinking feeling in the pit of my stomach.

What the fuck is wrong with me?

First, I ask her to kiss me, then I push her so far, she runs from the room. It's like I have zero self-control whenever she's around.

I scrub a hand over my face, thinking about the last couple of minutes. The desire to kiss her hit me so hard and fast, I couldn't stop the words from coming out of my mouth.

But damn if I didn't want her to press her lips to mine in that moment.

I wanted to taste her innocence. Kiss away the biting retorts and quick comebacks. To see if her lips are as soft as I suspect they are.

But maybe I pushed too hard, went too far.

"Was it something I said?" I mutter out loud like the jackass that I am, because of course it was something I said. It's my whole fucking existence that puts her on edge.

Out of nowhere, a hand comes over my shoulder. I glance down to see Rosa looking up at me, her lips twisted in a half-smirk, half-frown. "Not your best move, sweetheart."

"It seems the only thing I'm good at is pissing her off."

"Maybe, but the fire between you two?" Her lips spread into a smile. "Now, that's passion."

I roll my lips as I stare at her and question her sanity because there is nothing passionate between me and Skylar. There's only hate.

"Give her some grace, will you?" She stares back in the direction Skylar disappeared. "She's trying to navigate some tough terrain right now, and just before you got here, she discovered she has to scale an emotional mountain if she wants to get to her destination."

I have no idea what Rosa's referring to, but I know how it feels to face an uphill battle. And though I shouldn't feel anything but irritation toward Skylar after the way she snapped at me yesterday, my chest tightens with the desire to know what's plaguing her.

My lips twitch with the urge to ask a million questions.

I want to know why she feels she has no talent, or at least not enough to go after what she wants. I want to know how she overcame the obstacles in her life, allowing them to make her stronger instead of bitter and weak. What made her start drawing? Why is she so damned insistent on doing everything herself?

Most of all, I want to know what it is about her that draws me to her, despite every morsel of my body telling me to stay away.

I want to know a hell of a lot more than I should—a lot more than I have rights to. Like what her lips would feel like pressed against mine.

Swallowing, I fight to rein my thoughts in, but shaking off thoughts of Skylar is like digging a splinter out of your hand you can't see.

"Is she okay?" I ask.

"No. That girl is anything if not resilient, but she's also not made of stone." She shoots me a pointed look, and I want to ask her more. But I'm the last person Skylar would ever want to confide in, so prying for information seems wrong.

I gaze down the hallway where she disappeared, feeling an invisible tug to follow and learn what's upset her. Certainly, it's not my request for a kiss.

Rosa hums under her breath and takes a seat in the chair at the front desk before she sighs and says, "I think I'm just gonna rest my feet for a moment. Hope you don't mind."

I glance down at her knowing expression and wonder if she's a clairvoyant. "Well, go on," she says. "No sense in us both sitting here. Feel free to stretch your legs."

It's the opening I need to go after her.

I find Skylar sitting in a chair in the break room a few minutes later, her arms wrapped around her legs, with her knees tucked into her chest. The sight of her so upset turns my stomach in knots.

I take a tentative step inside the room, wondering if she'll tell me to get lost. I'm not sure I'd blame her if she did. "Do I need to wave a white flag in surrender?"

Her head jerks up at the sound of my voice, and she quickly swipes her hands over her damp cheeks, obviously wanting to hide her tears.

Clearing her throat, she drops her legs and straightens in her chair. "What do you want?" she asks, and I'm pretty sure she means it to sound harsher than it does, but her voice is too thick with emotion to sound even remotely threatening.

"I'm sorry I looked at your sketches. I should've given them back as soon as you asked and respected your privacy."

She sniffs, those wet amber eyes staring up at me.

"But for what it's worth," I continue, "those sketches are fucking amazing, and anything that beautiful deserves to be seen."

Her mouth parts, as if she's too stunned by the compliment to speak. I wonder how I became the kind of guy who's expected to shoot barbed comments out of my mouth rather than words of affirmation. I remember a time where all I did was lift Mackenzie up. Respect for women is something I've never lacked. I've always given it so freely. Yet with Skylar, I've become sullen and prickly. It's like the second she's around, my walls come up and the daggers come out.

I shift on my feet in the silence and clear my throat when it becomes obvious she's not going to be the first to break it. "Anyway, I just wanted to tell you that. If you need anything, I'll be back—"

"I'm sorry," she blurts, and I freeze.

Of all the things to come out of her mouth, an apology was the last thing I expected.

Cocking my head, I turn toward her as if I might've heard her wrong, but she licks her lips, and adds, "For yesterday in your room, I'm sorry."

"You don't have to apologize, Skylar."

Even though she was wrong, I know without being told her lashing out had nothing to do with me, and everything to do with whatever is going on in her own life. Skylar might be short and brazen with me, but I've seen how she is with everyone else. She's not the kind of girl who begrudges someone else's choices.

"No, I do." She shakes her head and runs a hand through the length of her hair. "I took my own frustration out on you, and that wasn't fair. It's just that I desperately want to go to Chicago for school, and I want my brother's support more than I want to breathe. So, to hear that you not only have your father's support, but that he's pushing you to go to college and play football, kills me. Having JD's blessing would mean the world to me."

I take a step closer, closing the distance between us. "You and your brother, you're really close?"

She swallows, and my gaze homes in on her throat, transfixed by the movement. "You could say that. He's my brother, father, mother, and one of my best friends, all rolled into one. So, knowing he doesn't want me to leave to pursue my dreams . . ." She worries her lower lip with her teeth before she releases a breath. "It's slowly killing me," she confides. "But that's no excuse. It's none of my business what you do with your life, and even if it were, I can't expect you to want the same things I do."

I sink down in the chair beside her as the sudden urge to pull her into my arms shoots latches onto my heart. "Your brother doesn't support your art?"

Her gaze drifts up to the ceiling. "It's not so much that. It's just he can't bear the thought of me moving away. Any time I talk about it, he clams up and changes the subject, or he guilts me into staying. Just this morning, he told me he didn't know how he'd live without me if I left. Said it would kill him."

"Ouch." I wince. "That seems unfair."

"If he were anyone else, I wouldn't give a damn. I'd do what I want without a second thought, but I just can't bring myself to do that to him. Not after everything he's done for me. I know he has my best interests at heart, but he doesn't realize how desperately I want a life of my own, one of my choosing. I want something that's mine and mine alone, you know? My whole life he's provided for me, watched over me. My life has been laid out before me, and even though I'm grateful for every bit of it, I still can't help but want more."

Her gaze drops to mine, and her eyes fill with tears. "Everything I have is because of him, and now I'm eighteen and about to graduate, he seems to think that because he's given me a good life, I should be content with the status quo. But I'm just not. I'm not sure I ever will be, and I feel so selfish for wanting more."

"It's not selfish to want to pave your own path, Skylar," I say, and it dawns on me I might as well be talking to myself.

Though in my case, rather than selfishness, it's the deep-seated notion that if I don't pursue football, I'm throwing my life away. It's the little boy still seeking his father's approval.

"Then why do I feel so ungrateful?" she asks, a tear sliding down her cheek.

I reach out, brushing the moisture away with the pad of my thumb. "You can be grateful, but still have your own dreams."

"And that's what they are," she says hastily. "My dreams. I want my art and my own place. One *I* pick out, decorate, and slave away to save for. I want to be independent and live on my own terms. I want to bring a guy back to my place without my brother giving him the third degree or interrogating him. I want so many things, but he takes that desire and ambition and twists it, until all I feel is guilt for wanting these things when what I really want the most is his support."

I slowly nod, absorbing everything she's told me, and I think about the real reason she'd gotten so upset to know my father was pushing me to go to school for football. Why she'd gotten so pissed at me at O'Malley's for interfering with Brad and screwing things up. Why she takes her art so seriously. It's her fierce independence. Suddenly, everything about Skylar makes a lot more sense.

She and I are more alike than she thinks. Little does she know my father's desire for me to play college ball is his way of controlling me, in the same way her brother seems to be doing through her guilt. For years, I've busted my ass to be good enough, to live up to his expectations, and just like her, I'm so tired of doing everything for everyone else and not myself. My wings have been clipped every bit as much as hers have.

When a grin spreads across my lips, she frowns. "I spill my guts to you, and you're smiling?"

"I'm smiling," I say, tenderly brushing the hair back from her face, "because you and I are alike in more ways than you know. Your brother wants you to stay here and continue life as you know it, while my father wants me to leave and pursue *his* dreams, not my own. He's pushing me to accept a football scholarship and go to college, but only because that's what *he* wants for my future."

"You like playing football?" she asks, her eyes searching mine for the truth like it actually matters to her.

I exhale a steady breath. It's been a long time since I've felt like someone really cared about what matters to me. "I'm not so sure anymore," I answer, honestly. "I used to, but lately, well, I've spent the better part of my life trying to live up to Cal Scott's impossible expectations. I strive for any morsel of affection he might throw my way, and no matter what I do, each and every single time I fall short to the point where I'm not even sure I want to play anymore."

I rake a hand through my hair, suddenly jittery, as if I've downed a shot of caffeine. Skylar's the first person I've admitted that to, and I'm not at all sure how I feel about it.

"All I know is that I'm fucking tired of living under his thumb." I lift my gaze to hers, and our eyes lock. "If you truly care about someone, love and affection should come freely. But where my father's concerned, it's only ever been earned."

"Graham . . ." Her voice softens. "I'm sorry . . ."

I shrug and glance down at my hands, willing away the sudden thickness in the back of my throat.

"I'm lucky in that JD has loved me so fiercely, but sometimes I wonder if it's too much. Somewhere along the way, he expected me to be everything good in his life."

"That's a lot of pressure."

She lets out a half-laugh. "Yeah. I'm all he has, so the thought of losing me or things changing scares him."

My chest pinches at the image she paints. She wants her brother to love her a little less, while all I've ever secretly wanted was for my father to love me a little more.

I clench my jaw as I wonder what it would feel like to love someone so wholly, you're petrified at the thought of losing them almost to the point of dysfunction, and I realize I already know. Because I've lived it with Mackenzie. I felt that way about her, too, once.

I think about the similarities between myself and Skylar's brother with the way he feels about her versus how I felt about Mackenzie, and it strikes me for the first time that maybe the extremity of those feelings came from a place of trauma. Skylar and her brother lost their parents at a young age. I have no doubt he clung to her after that, and his fear of losing her is heightened because of it. I've been grappling for my father's attention for years, and after Kenzie's accident, I spiraled because she was the one person who was always there for me, and I almost lost her.

There's no doubt in my mind that I loved Mackenzie, but I wonder if maybe my feelings for her were enhanced by everything that happened. The way she leaned on me after the accident. How I became responsible for lifting her out of the darkness she'd fallen into. Being her hero gave me a purpose greater than football.

After she physically recovered, I'd still been so afraid of losing her to depression that I became desperate to save her. Suddenly, my life's goal became making her happy, and I lost sight of everything else.

I rake a hand through my hair, unsure of how I feel about this new perspective. "So that's why the scholarship meant so much to you," I say, shifting my focus back on Skylar.

If she has a way to pay for school herself, she won't have to rely on her brother for help, which makes it a little easier to leave for both of them.

"I can't even bring myself to tell him I'm leaving, let alone ask him for help, so if I can do it myself—completely—then maybe

I won't have to feel so guilty about going. Maybe he'll even see it for what it is: an amazing opportunity I can't pass up." She twists her hands in her lap. "I just wish it didn't feel so shitty about it."

I bark out a laugh. "I'm hiding my father's affair from my mother because I'm too damned afraid to tell her myself. Trust me, I'm an expert on feeling shitty. He's the biggest dirtbag, yet here I am. In order to protect her, I'm protecting him. Yet, as much as I hate to admit it, I still care about him. After everything he's done, I can't shut that part of myself off."

I can say I hate my father until I'm blue in the face, and maybe a part of me does, but he's still my father. All his wrongs can't negate the rights, as little as they are.

Her damp eyes search mine. "I guess loving them means we don't want to let them down or upset them, even when we're right and they're wrong."

I nod and bump her knee with mine, ignoring the way my skin breaks out in goose bumps at the contact. "Your brother sounds like a really good guy. Even if it's hard for him to accept you going away, I'm sure he'll come around."

She leans back in her chair, tipping her head back as she gazes at the ceiling. "Rosa said the same thing, but sometimes I'm not so sure . . ."

"This scholarship," I say, feeling the sting of guilt, "is it really a lost cause?"

She nods. "Yeah, Brad made sure of that, but there's another one, a competition I entered, so . . . If I can win and pay for school, then I'll tell him. I just can't bring myself to do it yet."

"And if you win, and he still doesn't see this as an opportunity you can't refuse?" I ask.

She exhales, her breath shaky. "He has to."

CHAPTER 22

GRAHAM

Graham: *Did you have to blow up my phone while I was at work?*

Jace: *I still can't believe you have a job.*

Knox: *Wait. Graham has a job?*

Teagan: *Bro. You're way behind.*

Atlas: *If it's any consolation, my phone's been blowing up all day with this stupid group text, too.*

Jace: *Soooorry to interrupt you. Did I piss the wifey off?*

Atlas: *Fuck off.*

Jace: *I'll take that as a yes.*

Graham: *As enlightening as this is . . .*

Jace: *Don't be a dick. You haven't even answered the question yet.*

Graham: *What question?*

Teagan: *Is he for real?*

Knox: *He's definitely deflecting.*

Jace: *ARE YOU GOING TO THE FOOTBALL BAN-QUET?*

Graham: *Do I have a choice?*

Atlas: *Are you trying to make Jace cry?*

Teagan: *Bro, you'll break his heart if you don't show.*

Jace: *I'll bring you flowers. *wiggles brows seductively**

Jace: *Maybe even buy you dinner . . . And I promise to wear something pretty.*

Teagan: *Something with cleavage.*

Knox: *Damn. Are you going to put out, too?*

Teagan: *Shit, maybe I wanna go with you now.*

Atlas: *I think I might be sick.*

Jace: *Easy for you to say, Atlas. You're practically married. You can get some whenever you want. The rest of us can't be so choosy.*

Atlas: *True.*

Teagan: *I can hear the smugness through the text.*

Knox: *Bastard.*

Graham: *OMG. I'll go if we can just end this text chain. It's not like I really have a choice.*

Knox: *It was the tits that got you, wasn't it?*

Teagan: *I mean, Jace does have nice pecs.*

Jace: *I think I'm getting excited.*

Atlas: *You guys are so messed up.*

Graham: *I'M LEAVING NOW. STOP TEXTING.*

I power off my phone and slide it in my pocket when I feel eyes on the side of my face. I glance up to see Skylar watching me. "Your phone's been blowing up all night."

I roll my eyes. "My friends are going through withdrawal since the season's over," I say by way of explanation.

"Ah," she says with a nod at the same time the front doors swing open and Storm wanders in, a book bag slung over his shoulder.

I turn my back to him before he can make eye contact, busying myself with something at the desk and ignoring the pang of guilt that takes hold of me. He's just a kid. I know this, and yet, I still can't help the rush of anger every time I see him. The only person who has welcomed him here is Atlas.

Not that I'd know much about it.

Atlas has been trying to convince me to reach out to him for weeks, yet I refuse.

A seed of nausea swells in my gut. The last thing I want is to be on the same wavelength as my father.

I glance over my shoulder, my expression sheepish as I search for him, only to realize he's gone. "What?" I ask, noticing Skylar's eyes on me.

"Nothing." She glances back down at the sketch pad she's been working in.

"No. You were thinking something. Might as well just say it."

She gives a little shrug. "I just feel bad is all."

My chest squeezes. I know exactly what—or who—she feels bad for, but I can't seem to help myself from asking. "About what?"

"He just seems . . . lonely."

"I'm sure he's not," I mumble, although I wouldn't know.

She glances at me like she couldn't hear me, but I don't repeat myself because it was a stupid thing to say in the first place.

"The other day, we started talking and he told me winter break starts tomorrow," she says.

"So?" I shrug, busying myself with organizing the papers lying on the desk.

"So, he just seemed sad. Like he'd rather be in school than here all day for the next couple of weeks."

I frown because I hadn't really thought about it from Storm's perspective no matter how much Atlas has badgered me about it. I can't imagine coming to a new school, joining a new football team and trying to make friends, all while knowing the reason you're here is because your mother wants you to have a relationship with your father. But as it turns out, he wants nothing more to do with you other than the day you were born, and your brother wants nothing to do with you, either. Maybe he feels like he's tearing apart my family? Maybe he feels responsible somehow for whatever pain their presence here in town causes my mother? He might be young, but he's not stupid.

For the first time, I wonder if he has any friends. I wonder if rumors have started to spread about why he's here. Just because I haven't gotten wind of any, doesn't mean they don't exist.

I don't relish the idea of the kid being lonely, and it's the first time I wonder what he does when Marie is at work. Hell, I don't even know what Marie does for a living. I've done everything I can to avoid her since she moved to town, and especially in the week they've been staying here. For all I know, she's gone all night, leaving Storm to his own devices. He might have Atlas, but how many times has Atlas told me he needs both of us in his corner? And how many times have I ignored it?

I purse my lips and place my hands on my hips, warring with my desire to shove this under the rug and the voice in the back of my head telling me it's time to grow up.

"You think I should talk to him," I say. It's a statement, not a question.

Skylar bites her lips as if mulling it over. "Look, I can't imagine how I would feel if I were in your shoes. Maybe I would want nothing to do with him, but . . . maybe getting to know him wouldn't be the worst thing in the world. Maybe getting to know him and discovering that he's pretty awesome might be the one good thing that comes out of it all."

Atlas said pretty much the same thing not that long ago, but I ignored it.

"Anyway," she says, turning to greet a guest, "that's just my two cents, but I'm sure you'll do the right thing for both of you."

I exhale as I stare down the hall where Storm disappeared a few minutes ago, wishing I had as much faith in myself, and wondering why it feels like it's been too damn long since I did the right thing.

I can see his shadowy figure moving outside. He's been out there for the past thirty minutes, and I don't need to see his face to know who it is. *Storm.*

The view of the courtyard from the front desk is mostly obscured, so I only catch glimpses of him. He tosses a football in the air, catches it and tucks it under his arm, then sprints like his life depends on it.

I only have thirty minutes for my lunch break, and Skylar's words have been stuck in my head all morning. For reasons I can't explain, she makes me want to be better—do better.

I round the desk and cram a protein bar down my throat, then hurry to the break room where I grab my coat. Once I'm back out in the hallway, I take the exit that leads to the outside courtyard and place a palm on the heavy glass door and push it open.

The cold air hits me immediately. My breath forms a puff of white, and I wonder if he won't catch his death out here, sweating in the cold.

His back is to me, so he doesn't see me as I step outside, which gives me the advantage of watching a moment longer.

He throws a perfect spiral into a net a few yards off, and my chest pinches. I have no idea how he smuggled the net in here, but it's my best guess he was given a little grace considering the sheer amount of money he and Marie are spending to stay here over the next month. That, and I was told the courtyard is filled with flowers in the spring and summer, but since it's winter, everything is dead and dried out. Snow dusts the ground, leaving the space useless this time of year.

He spins around and startles, clearly surprised to find me standing there, staring. The darks of his eyes widen before he drops his gaze, hanging his head as he turns away from me.

He thinks I won't acknowledge him; he's come to expect it.

I feel like shit at the thought.

I've had so many opportunities to extend an olive branch but chose not to. After everything my father's done, I'm blaming a fucking ten-year-old? He has no ownership of my anger, and yes, he's a reminder of everything that's happened these past couple months, but that's not on him. It's on Cal Scott and no one else.

I promised Atlas I'd give him a chance, but I never had any intentions of doing so. Maybe I've fucked up, but it's time I stop playing the victim and start trying to be the hero.

I exhale in a huff as Skylar's words come back to me, affirming what I need to do. *I'm sure you'll do the right thing for both of you.*

"Isn't it a little hard to play football by yourself?"

Storm whips around at the sound of my voice, and he looks so much like Atlas, it's uncanny: dark hair and brooding dark eyes that see straight to your soul.

Tossing the ball nervously between his hands, he assesses me for a moment, likely trying to gauge whether I'm here as an employee, a friend, or an enemy. I'm not sure it's any of those things.

"I was bored, and I don't have anyone to play with," he says matter-of-factly.

"You have me," I say. I hold my hands out for him to toss me the ball, which he does.

"Aren't you working?" he asks, scrunching his nose.

"I have a few minutes." I feel the laces and find the sweet spot with my fingers. "Your spiral is pretty good, but you need a little more snap in the wrist," I say, showing him what I mean in slow motion. "Just like that." I toss it lightly so it hits the net.

He nods and retrieves it, but when he goes to hand it back, I shake my head. "Now you try it."

A subtle grin plays on the corners of his lips, and I come to stand beside him, showing him again what I mean as he raises the ball in his hand and brings his arm back. When I step away from him, giving him room, he launches the ball and it soars into the net.

"Good. Again. But this time, to me." I jog past him and snag the ball from the ground on my way, tossing it into his chest as I continue to the end of the courtyard. I clap my hands and beckon for him to throw me the ball.

He takes a step forward, arm back, then launches the ball to me with perfect precision. I catch it easily, grinning as I do.

"Damn, kid." I tuck the pigskin under my arm as I approach. "Where'd you learn to throw like that?"

"Not my father," Storm blurts out, then as if remembering we share the same dad, his cheeks redden.

I nod as my stomach does a slow roll. "No, I don't suspect you did," I say, eyeing him warily as I come to a stop in front of him.

His gaze hardens as he glances away from me, his throat bobbing with emotion, and I can't help but feel like I'm staring at a mirror image of Atlas. He's every bit as angry and jaded as he was when he first came to town.

"What made you talk to me, anyway?" He kicks at a clump of dead grass at his feet. "Was it my mom? She's always saying I need to make friends."

A vice grips my chest as he peeks up at me, hope shining in his dark eyes.

I clear my throat. "No. It wasn't your old lady. But she's probably right," I say, thinking about the guys. As much as they piss me off, I'm not sure I could've gotten through these last couple of years without them. "Friends are pretty important."

"I had friends at my old school. Sometimes I still talk to them, but I have Atlas now, too." He stares at me intently, and I wonder if he's gauging my reaction to the mention of my cousin.

"Yeah, that's great. Atlas is a good dude." I offer him a smile of reassurance and watch as the tension in his small shoulders melts away.

"Yeah, he's pretty cool."

"It won't hurt to make friends your age, too, though."

He nods and glances at the ground. "I guess I was just waiting, you know, to see if we were even staying. But the other day Mom said we're going to see this through, and that my father's coming around."

I'm not so sure about that.

I swallow, and the air turns thick with tension until it's hard to even take a breath. Because as long as they stay in town, I'm walking around with the weight of my father's secrets bearing down on me.

Until this moment, I hadn't realized just how much I hoped they'd leave, which I suppose makes me just as bad as my father.

"Yeah, well," I shuffle my feet and my gaze drifts to the door. "I don't have the best relationship with my father these days, either. I wish I could tell you I think she's right."

His throat bobs, and I wish I could tell him something different, but I'm not gonna lie to the kid.

"Wanna go again?" he asks, pointing to the ball.

A grin splits my lips. "Absolutely."

For the next thirty minutes, we throw the ball back and forth. Sometimes we run it down the yard. Other times, we simply toss it back. We don't talk about my father or Marie, or even Atlas. All we do is play, relishing the feel of the leather in our palm and the laces between our fingers. I give him several tips and talk about conditioning, things he can do over the winter to get stronger, even at his age, and it's not lost on me this is probably the most fun I've had with a football in a long time.

Once my break is over, he gathers up his things and tucks the ball under his arm as he walks with me to the door. "Are you gonna go back to ignoring me?"

The dull thud of my pulse echoes through my hollow chest as I glance down at him. With Christmas break starting tomorrow, I'm sure I'll see him around more often than normal, and as much as I'd like to pretend he doesn't exist, I can't do that to him anymore. I'm tired of being that guy, and it's time to start being the man I was before my life turned to shit. The one I know I still am deep down inside.

I offer him a sad smile, hating that there was ever a time I pretended he didn't exist. I might not be able to control what my father does about his past indiscretions, but I can control what I do about them. So, I promise only what I can.

"I'm not going anywhere, kid."

CHAPTER 23

SKYLAR

WINTER BREAK HAS STARTED, and though it's only been a few days since I've worked with Graham, I miss seeing him every day. Not that I would ever admit that to him. We might be getting along more than usual these days, but he'd probably laugh his butt off if he knew I was sitting at the bay window, watching the snow fall with a cup of coffee in my hands, while thinking about him and wondering what he's doing.

I know his relationship with his father is a tumultuous one, and I wonder if he'll find any joy in the holiday season, or if he's just waiting for it to be over.

I know he took the Christmas shift at work. Last I heard from him, his parents were livid he'd be working most of the day, and though he was glad for a reason to get out of the house, I feel sad at the thought of him manning the desk all alone. He's only eighteen. He should be opening presents and eating cookies for breakfast, not working as a way to avoid his family.

I sigh and lift my mug to my lips and take a sip, letting the warm brew take away the chill I always get when I sit by the bay windows during the winter.

JD is in the kitchen making dinner, and I'm supposed to be working on my entry, but my thoughts are too scattered to sketch. I only have a couple weeks to finish my entry for the Siddhartha Art Gallery's Amateur Art Competition, I've yet to settle on what to draw that falls under the subject of fate, and instead of working on it, I'm daydreaming about a boy.

What is wrong with me?

I growl and sit my mug down on the window ledge, then pick my charcoal and notepad up. My head tells me my parents are the perfect subjects. Their love was fated from the start. They'd been high school sweethearts, attached at the hip since the age of fourteen. They fell hard and were lucky enough to have the kind of love that lasts a lifetime. It's no wonder that after my mother's death, my father didn't last more than a year before he died from a broken heart.

Yet every sketch I have of them feels inadequate. It's like my heart knows something I don't. These sketches won't win me the contest. They're missing something—the little bit of magic that takes a piece from great to incredible—but I don't know what.

"Ready to eat?" JD calls from the kitchen.

I lift my head from the blank page and swing my legs down to stand where I mosey into the dining room. JD has already set the table, so I take my usual spot across from him, both of us on either side of the head of the table where we've sat for as long as I can remember. Neither of us want to claim our parent's place.

"Ready for this?" he asks. Grinning, he lifts the lid on the pot in front of us and begins to ladle its contents into the bowl on my plate. "Seafood stew."

I stare at the bowl, brimming with a red broth, giant shrimp, and black clams, and my stomach rumbles. "I haven't had this since that trip we took to South Carolina."

"I know. It was surprisingly easy to make, but don't get used to it. Do you know how hard it is to find good clams and fresh shrimp in Northeastern Ohio this time of year?"

"You know a guy, though, don't you?" I ask with a chuckle as I pick up my spoon. Any time something is hard to come by, JD somehow pulls a rabbit from a hat. It's become the running joke between us for years.

"Of course I know a guy." He winks, then nods to the bowl. "Tell me what you think."

I take a tentative bite, careful not to burn myself on the hot stew, then another, this time scooping up a massive piece of shrimp.

I close my eyes against the flavors bursting in my mouth and murmur my approval. Sometimes, I think being deaf, even with implants, heightens all my other senses. I swear I can taste every spice, all the nuances of flavor. It's probably one of the reasons I love food so much.

Mal and I once did a blindfold test where we tried different flavor combinations of foods. She got a third of them wrong while I got all of them right.

I also feel things more. The slightest breeze. A hint of rain in the air. Mounting tension. Thunder rumbling in the sky.

And because of it, I treat every opportunity to experience one of these senses as a blessing. "It's delicious, maybe better than when we had it the first time."

"Nailed it!" JD slaps a hand on the table, his grin a mile wide.

"You know, for someone who loves food so much, I should probably learn how to cook."

"Nah. Why cook when you have me?"

I shift in my seat as guilt tries to worm its way into this moment. "Well, you never know. If you get sick or want to go on a trip or . . ." I trail off while JD flashes me an amused look.

"If I ever go on a trip, you'd be with me."

"True." I drag my spoon through my stew and give a tiny little shrug. "But it would be nice to treat you to a home-cooked meal sometime. For your birthday or even on a holiday. Or when you get sick. I'm getting older, and I want to be an independent—"

"Woman," he finishes for me. "I know. But there are plenty of women who don't cook. In fact, it's more of a modern development than anything. There's Uber Eats and takeout."

A crusty loaf of Italian bread sits in between us on the center of the table. JD rips off a hunk, then pushes the loaf toward me, so I do the same, letting the subject drop as I pick up a knife and slather it with butter.

"I have a confession to make," he says, eyes bright. "I made this meal as a sort of celebration."

My eyes widen slightly. The first thing that comes to mind is that, after giving it some thought, he's come around to the idea of me going to college and he wants me to accept Chicago's offer. But I push the thought away, knowing it's impossible. It was only a short time ago he angrily shoved the acceptance letter in my face and demanded an explanation.

My ears perk, my gaze drawn to him.

"I know I should wait with Christmas so soon, but I thought it would be fun to give you an early present." He turns and picks something up off the chair beside him. It's an envelope that he slides toward me.

"You really can't wait two days?" I ask with a laugh.

He shakes his head. "Open it."

I arch a brow and my lips quirk. Every year he spoils me, all while making it more and more impossible to find him something for him in return.

Taking the envelope, I lift the flap and pull out a brochure along with a printed confirmation for Panama City in Florida, and I gasp. "The senior trip?" I glance up at JD, a question in my eyes as his smile spreads, splitting his face in two.

He nods, confirming the contents. "I booked you a suite—"

Without waiting for him to continue, I jump out of my seat and fling myself at him, nearly spilling my stew in the process as I wrap my arms around his neck. "Thank you!"

His laughter rumbles deep in my chest as he pats my back, and I drop a noisy kiss to his forehead, then plop back into my seat.

"What changed your mind?" I'd approached him about the senior trip to Panama City months ago, and he'd been less than thrilled. At first, I thought it was about the money. The trip wasn't cheap, and even though I promised to pay for it myself, he'd put me off. Eventually, I let it drop and told Mal I couldn't go.

If he was worried about my safety, the last thing I wanted to do was heighten his concern at a time when I'd soon be asking his blessing to go to a college four hundred miles away. As much as I wanted to go on the senior trip, I want SAIC more.

JD gives me a sheepish smile. "You're eighteen now. I said no out of a place of fear, which isn't fair to you. You've been nothing but responsible. You get good grades, always come home at curfew, and you don't drink or smoke or get into trouble like some teens do. Lord knows I gave Mom and Dad a run for their money when I was your age." He laughs. "You deserve this, bug." He reaches across the table and takes my hand, squeezing it in his. "You're responsible, and I trust you to be careful. Merry Christmas."

I swallow over the lump forming in the back of my throat. It's everything I've imagined him saying about college, and even though he's not talking about me going away to school, it gives me hope.

He'll come around. Rosa's right.

I just need to give him time, prove to him I'm more than capable of taking care of myself, so he won't worry when I'm gone. And this trip is another way to do it.

I clutch the brochure in my hands and give out a little squeal while I kick my legs. "Ah, thank you! I can't wait to tell Mal," I say, practically bouncing in my seat. In fact, the second I finish this delicious dinner, I'm running straight to my room to call her and share the news.

JD laughs. "Well, I would've waited until Christmas, but I figured the sooner I tell you the better, so you guys can book a flight together. The longer you wait, the more expensive they'll get."

"Yes! I'll call her right after dinner." I beam.

"You'll take your Aqua+ and wear it at all times, unless you're actually going for a swim," he adds, referring to the water-resistant accessory for my implants.

"Absolutely. Don't worry about that. The last time I went to a pool party was in seventh grade before I had the accessories, and I missed half of the inside jokes." For weeks, my classmates referred to Mikey Nelson as Squints from Sandlot because he kept trying to get the college-aged lifeguard to rescue him in the water, and I didn't catch onto the nickname until way after the fact.

JD rolls his eyes. "I was thinking more along the lines of you being able to hear if someone screams there's a shark in the water or some other emergency situation."

I laugh like this is the funniest thing I've ever heard because for such a strong man, JD has a ridiculous fear of three things: sharks, snakes, and spiders, while nothing scares me.

"Though I'm not afraid of aquatic animals, I can see the benefit in that," I joke. "Remember that time I was at the lake and those boys were playing volleyball?"

JD snorts. "You mean when they yelled for you to duck, but you couldn't hear them?"

I nod. "I had to walk around with a welt on my face the size of Texas for a week. Talk about mortifying."

JD nods his agreement. "We don't want welts the size of Texas."

"There's only one problem with this trip," I say, playing with the brochure.

"What?"

"I told you I would pay for it."

JD shrugs. "Well, now it's a gift."

"But—"

"Business is good. In fact, I'll be paying for you and Mal both to fly first class. No arguments. The last thing I want is for you to be wedged beside some creepy dude leering at you."

I stifle a laugh. JD always seems to think guys are looking at me when they're most definitely not. "First class is unnecessary."

"Didn't I just say no arguments?" He stabs the spoon in my direction. "Giving you things brings me joy. So let me *enjoy* it."

I exhale, staring into his eyes as I wonder what I did to deserve him. Everything he does, he does for me. Sometimes I imagine what my life would be like if he hadn't been so selfless and went off to build a life of his own without me in it, instead of staying and making it his life's mission to raise me right. What would I be like had I been raised by my uncle? Would I be living with him in Connecticut now?

I like Uncle Pete, but I'm not so sure he was cut out to raise a child. He's a little rough around the edges, due to being a bachelor his whole life. I don't remember much about the time we spent with him after my father died, but from what JD told me, he wasn't around much. He traveled a lot for work and often left without filling the fridge. He didn't cook and barely knew how to run a washing machine. We were crammed in his tiny two-bedroom apartment until JD found a way to provide for the both of us and took me in on his own.

"What if I want you to spend your money on yourself for a change," I say. "Maybe you could take a trip, too." I smile to myself, liking the idea. "Because that would be amazing. You could go anywhere you want. Reconnect with old friends, or take a special lady friend." I wink, and his cheeks flush.

"You know I can't leave work," he says, his tone an admonishment.

"You can. You just don't want to relinquish control," I point out.

He purses his lips. "I'll think about it," he says, even though I know he won't. He's just trying to get me to drop it, so I do. There's no use in arguing, and once I go away to school, he'll be forced to put himself out there and create a life for himself.

CHAPTER 24

GRAHAM

WINTER BREAK HAS ONLY just begun, and I'm already going stir crazy, which is precisely why I agreed to go shopping with the boys. It's the last thing I'm in the mood for, but tomorrow is Christmas Eve, and I hate the thought of being stuck in the house for one more second while my father plays the doting husband. This morning, he gave my mother a shoulder massage while she ate her eggs and I almost puked. Now, he's off in his office catching up on some endorsement stuff before the holiday while my mother wraps Christmas presents. Later, he promised her wine with dinner and a Christmas movie. It's like stepping inside a fucking Hallmark movie.

I change out of the athletic shorts and a T-shirt I wore to work out, and put on a hoodie and a pair of jeans, then swipe my keys off the dresser and start down the hallway. I pass one of the guest rooms on my way to the stairs—the one Atlas occupied only a few short months ago—thinking about how it felt just like yesterday he was here and my biggest problems were perfecting my game on the field and keeping my hold on Mackenzie.

Now, I have a whole new host of problems eating away at me that I'd trade in a heartbeat. It's been several days since I heard from Crenshaw after the poker game with Miller, and I can't help but wonder when I'll hear from him again.

Nervous energy shoots into my limbs at the thought. It's part of the reason I need to get out of the house. Sitting around feels like waiting for the other shoe to drop, and I'm not sure how much more anxiety I can take. Sitting on pins and needles doesn't suit me.

I race down the stairs and grab my sneakers from the laundry room at the back of the house when my mother calls out from the den. "Graham, is that you?"

I pause, my fingers gripping my shoes as I contemplate ignoring her and slipping out the door. I've done a lot of that lately. Mostly because I don't want to face her. I hate looking her in the eyes and knowing I hold a secret that would rip her life off the hinges.

Unable to escape my guilt, I finish slipping my shoes on, then straighten and make my way through the laundry room out into the hallway to find the door to the den ajar. I lightly knock, then peek my head inside. "Did you need something?" I ask.

"Graham, come inside." My mother waves me in, her expression bright as the sun. "Close the door." She motions to it just as excitedly, so I turn, shutting the door behind me as I wonder what this is all about.

"Are you going somewhere?" she asks, noting the keys in my hands.

"Uh, yeah. The boys are going Christmas shopping, so I figured I'd join them."

"Speaking of Christmas"—she comes closer, her face split into a wide smile—"I know it's only a couple days away, but I just got the best news. Can you keep a secret?"

I have a feeling I don't want know whatever it is, but Mom's so excited, I can't burst her bubble. So instead of saying this or making an excuse to leave, I force a smile and shove my hands in my pocket. "Sure." I say. "What is it?"

"I just finalized the last details for your father's Christmas gift. I wasn't sure if I'd be able to get the venue I wanted, so I had to wait and see, but I just found out a spot opened up, and if I don't tell someone, I might burst."

I run a hand over the back of my neck while my stomach churns, torn between telling her he's a selfish fuck who deserves nothing and acting like I care for her sake. Thankfully, I don't have to make a choice because she can barely contain her excitement. She's vibrating with it as she covers her mouth as if she can't hold back. "We're renewing our vows," she blurts. Squeezing my arm, her eyes glitter as she adds, "In Maui."

Ice fills my veins and my tongue swells, thick and rubbery. "What?" I mutter.

She laughs like I don't understand something as simple thing as the concept of renewing wedding vows. "I planned the whole thing," she says, heading toward the sofa where she picks up a couple of brochures and shows me. "The resort I wanted was booked, so I've been on a waiting list, but I found out this morning that they had a cancellation. We leave next month, just the two of us." Her sandy hair bounces as she does a little hop in place. "I know how much your father likes to get away in the off-season, and this resort is absolutely gorgeous. They take care of everything, from flowers to candles and music. We'll have a night ceremony and renew our vows under a blanket of stars, right on the beach, and then eat a candlelight dinner."

"Couldn't you get him just, like, a tie or something?" I ask, too stunned to come up with anything better.

Her smile fades, and I instantly feel like shit.

"I thought it was romantic? You don't think it's a good idea?"

For a happily married couple of twenty-five years, I think it's a great fucking idea. I want to tell her that, but little does my mother know their marriage has been anything but happy. Or monogamous.

I stare into the bluish-green of her eyes, and it boggles my mind how my father could have someone as thoughtful and beautiful and amazing as my mother, yet fuck it all up. It's like winning a lifetime supply of filet mignon, only to turn around and send it back to the kitchen.

How could he ever want someone else when he already has everything?

I shake my head, trying to clear the anger clouding my vision and choking me like a thick fog. "Of course I think it's a good idea." *Liar.* "It's very thoughtful. I just . . . He doesn't deserve it, Mom. He doesn't deserve you."

She rolls her eyes and shrugs off my statement as she heads to her desk, rifling through some brochures. "I know you and your father don't see eye to eye, but—"

"Mom." My chest tightens, and I'm not sure how much more I can take.

"I also realize he can be obstinate at times—"

"Mom . . ."

"And I get that you've had your differences this year—"

"Mom!"

My mother freezes while my heart pounds, rising to my throat as my voice reverberates through the room.

Her mouth parts in shock. Over the years, I've had plenty of arguments with my father, but have never raised my voice to my mother. Not once.

"Mom, there's something you should know." I swallow, uncertain whether I can do this. Lord knows I've thought about telling her the truth a thousand times.

"What is it?" She reaches out a tentative hand, a pinch in her brow as she places it on my arm. "What's going on?"

I exhale, the air leaving my lungs like a deflating balloon. Once I tell her, there's no going back. I can't shove the words back in or dull their impact. Secrets like this destroy lives. They change them forever, and I have no doubt this one will change hers in the same way it's already changed mine.

My mind races as I try and force the words past my lips. My mother's a strong woman, but she's been dependent on my father for as long as I can remember. It breaks my heart to think there's a possibility she might blame herself or think for one fucking second it's because she's not pretty enough, thin enough, or as interesting as she once was.

I don't want to break her, but I'm not sure I have much of a choice.

I picture the tears. The heartache. The betrayal.

My lips tremble and my throat closes up, the words on the tip of my tongue, turning to mud in my mouth–heavy and wet, too thick to swallow down or spit out.

A choking sound gurgles from the back of my throat, and I drop my gaze.

I can't do it. I can't tell her, and I hate myself for being such a coward.

"I just, uh . . ." I hedge.

"Is this about football?" she asks.

My head jerks up, my brow creased. "What?"

"If you think I haven't noticed you're not exactly enthusiastic about playing in college, you're wrong. I've noticed. Your father's noticed, too, and, Graham, I know I mentioned it when we went to Penn State, but whatever you do, we'll support you."

I shake my head because she's wrong. About everything—about what's ailing me, about my father.

"He'll come around." She gives my arm a little squeeze, and I want to laugh. I want to rip my hair out and scream.

She gives him far too much credit. She always has, and maybe she always will: a fact that terrifies me more than anything. Even after everything—all his infidelities and all his lies—she still might forgive him and sweep it under the rug. Wash away his sins as if they never happened.

But I do the only thing I can—I pretend. I've become really good at pretending these last few months.

Pretending that my life isn't falling apart.

Pretending that I'm not hurting. That I'm not in trouble.

Pretending that I know what the hell I'm doing with my life.

I bow my head and inhale a shaky breath, forcing an even shakier smile as I say, "Thanks, Mom."

CHAPTER 25

GRAHAM

"To what do we owe the pleasure of your company," Jace says the moment I slide into his truck.

The last time all five of us were together in the same vehicle was the night we won States and they kidnapped me and we crammed inside Teagan's Prius. I'd like to say the memory is a fond one, but it's also the night Atlas fell and wound up in the hospital—the same night I finally and truly realized Mackenzie might not ever care for me the way I cared for her, and I made the decision to let her go.

"I needed to get out of the house," I say, sounding every bit as exasperated as I feel.

"Trouble in paradise?" Jace grins.

"Something like that."

"These days, the rest of our lives are dull in comparison. You and Atlas are our only source of entertainment, so if you'd like to share . . ."

I chuckle, but it's devoid of humor. "My mother's Christmas gift to my dad is a surprise trip to Maui where she's planned a romantic renewal of their wedding vows," I spit out.

"Oh, shit." Jace's smile deflates like a flat tire, and I can all but feel Atlas's dark gaze boring into me from behind, but I ignore it. I already know how he feels about my father, and we're on the same page. "I was not expecting *that*," Jace says.

"That's fucked up," Teagan supplies.

"Yup."

Jace glances over at me before he jerks the wheel of his truck. The tires shudder over the rumble strips, and then he brings us to a stop on the side of the road. "Punch me."

"What?" I ask, glancing at him like he's crazy.

"Punch me. Come on." He curls his fingers, beckoning me. "We both know it'll make you feel better. Physical aggression is your MO these days."

I pierce him with a look, not in the mood for his theatrics. "I'm not fucking punching you."

"Just one to the jaw. I can take it." He taps his chin. "Come on, Scott, don't be a pussy."

"Shit. If you don't, I will," Atlas mumbles from behind him.

"Hell no," Jace shoots back. "And no sloppy seconds either. This face is Graham's and Graham's only."

He's so serious, I would laugh if I weren't so annoyed.

"You really want me to punch you in the face?" I ask.

"If it makes you feel better, it'll be worth it. Just don't break my nose. The ladies love a symmetrical face, and mine is perfect."

"I snort. What if I aim for your jaw and miss?"

Jace sobers, staring me dead in the eyes. "Don't. Fucking. Miss. We're literally a foot apart."

"I'm still not punching you." I shake my head, turning away from him.

"Do it!" he shouts. "Let's go."

"For fuck's sake, get it over with so we can get our asses to the mall and help Atlas find the perfect gift for Mackenzie," Teagan shouts, and silence descends on us—a brief lull where I wonder if his mention of Atlas and Mackenzie is purposeful, because it's enough to make me snap.

"Punch me!" Jace shouts once more at the same time I whirl around and my fist connects with the side of his face.

His head jerks, nearly knocking into the window as his hand shoots up and clutches his cheek.

"Fuuuuck," he moans, as I shake my fist out.

"You asked for it," Teagan says.

Jace works his jaw and gives his head a shake, like a dog shaking water off his fur. "Damn. Why'd you do that?" He turns to me, shouting, "You're such a dick!"

"Are you serious?" I throw my hands up.

"Nah. I'm just fucking with you." He breaks out into a smile, the right side of his face red and inflamed from where my fist made contact.

I can't help it, I laugh and run a hand over my weary eyes.

"You feel better, don't you?" Jace asks, still grinning when I drop my hand.

"Kinda," I admit.

"See?" He punches the air in victory.

"Can we just drive, please?" Teagan asks. "My nuts are so smashed they're turning to peanut butter back here."

"Says the guy with the Prius." Knox huffs.

I sober, staring out the window as Jace pulls out into traffic once more, my thoughts drifting back to my mother. "She has no fucking clue." I swallow, calculating how much I want to say when I blurt, "I almost told her."

"Seriously?" Jace glances over at me. "What stopped you?"

I shake my head and stare out the window, at the blur of snow-dappled trees glittering in the sun. "I don't know. I guess I just... I don't want to be the one to break her heart, you know?"

"Marie and Storm aren't going anywhere," Atlas chimes in from the back seat, and I catch his meaning.

Eventually she'll find out one way or another.

"I know," I say, turning to him. "That's why I spoke with Storm."

Jace, Teagan, and Knox all turn to me at the same time.

"You did?" Atlas asks, his tone gruff. I know how protective he's become of his little brother, and I'm sure he's wondering what kind of interaction it was.

"I saw him tossing around a ball and gave him some pointers," I say, with a shrug, not wanting to make a big deal out of it, but also wanting to let Atlas know I heeded his advice. That I'm trying. Or maybe it was Skylar that ultimately convinced me to reach out to him. Either way, I finally did the right thing. "Storm said something about needing to make friends because they're here for the long haul, and it just kind of clicked. They're not going anywhere."

The truck falls silent.

The guys know how much I despise my father. They also know I've been struggling with the news that I share a half brother with Atlas, and so, admitting I willingly conversed with the kid is pretty monumental.

We stop at a red light and Jace turns to me with a dopey grin on his face. "Look at you," he says as he reaches out and ruffles my hair while I swat his hand away, "all growed up and shit."

"Get the hell off me, you jackass."

"I'm proud of you, man," he says, his voice velvety soft and warm like molten lava.

"Stop looking at me like that."

"Me, too, bro." Teagan places a hand on my shoulder.

"Group hug?" Knox suggests.

Before I know what's happening, all four of them unbuckle and come at me. Even Atlas, who piles on top, squeezing harder than the rest. Eight muscled limbs curve awkwardly around my slumped form while I try to breathe through the tiny gaps of their massive bodies pressed into my face.

The light turns green, and the car behind us lays on their horn.

"I can't fucking breathe," I say, gasping for air.

"We love you, too, man," Jace says, as he falls back into his seat.

One by one, they release me, and I take a deep breath, lungs burning. But when Jace puts the truck back in drive and peels off, I smile.

SKYLAR

"I'm so excited I could puke," Mal says as we browse a massive rack of sweaters. "Why can't they sell swimsuits this time of year?"

"Probably because it's thirty degrees outside and snowing," I say, to which Mal rolls her eyes.

"It seems unfair that we have to wait until right before our trip to go shopping. I hate Ohio weather."

My lips twitch. "Are you going to keep complaining or help me pick out something amazing for JD?" I ask. So far, I have an engraved money clip for him but nothing more. Not exactly earth shattering.

"Okay, you're right. What do you get the guy who has everything and wants nothing?"

"I don't know," I moan.

"There's nothing he needs or wants?"

"Well, he needs a girlfriend," I point out.

Even if he doesn't know it.

"Okay, so maybe one of those inflatable dolls."

I grimace. "I am *not* buying my brother a sex toy."

"It was just a thought," she mutters.

With a sigh, I gaze around the department store at all the glass cases filled with cosmetics and cologne and the racks of clothes, feeling more hopeless than ever.

"Why don't you book him a flight somewhere?" Mal suggests.

My head jerks toward Mallory. "What?" I blink as the idea settles.

"Send him somewhere. You suggested he take a trip while we're on spring break, right? So, force his hand. Book him a flight."

"To where?" I ask, intrigued by the idea.

"Anywhere. Who the hell cares as long as it gets him out of here."

I nod. "I could send him to a singles resort," I say, trying the idea on for size, finding it fits like a warm pair of fuzzy socks.

"Exactly. And if you send him while we're gone, it has the added bonus of distracting him so he's not sitting at home worrying about you the whole time."

"And I won't have to worry about him being lonely."

Mal smiles. "And if all goes well, he'll meet someone."

I sag a little. "But even if he does, they won't be from Ohio. It could only be a fling."

Mal rolls her eyes. "Stop being so practical. Not every relationship has to be serious."

My thoughts drift to Graham, and I flush. Lately, I've been thinking about him so much it hurts, and I wonder if maybe I'm developing feelings far beyond that of a coworker or even a friend.

"First of all, a good old-fashioned fling might do your brother good," Mal points out as she picks up a bottle of cologne and sniffs it. "Second, your brother might be modest, but we both know he makes enough money he could fly anywhere he wants as much as he wants, if it means making something long distance work."

"You're right." I smile. "I'm totally overthinking it."

"Now that we have that settled." Mal brushes her hands off in front of her. "My work is done. Shall we head to the food court and get one of those milkshakes they disguise as coffee?"

I laugh. "A frappe?"

"Whatever." She waves the correction away, and I follow. "We can discuss where to send your brother. I'm thinking somewhere slightly naughty like Vegas. You might get lucky.

He might drink far too much and wake up with a woman wrapped around him, only to discover he got married in a cheesy chapel with an Elvis impersonator like in one of those cutesy rom-coms."

"You're ridiculous."

"Hey, one can dream, right?" She whips around toward the exit of the department store. We head toward the food court when we approach a group of guys walking in our direction.

There are about five of them, all of them tall and muscled. From the looks of it, they're all ridiculously good-looking, too.

"Holy hotness," Mal mutters under her breath.

I'm about to agree, when I notice something familiar about one of the boys in the back. His head is turned away as he talks to someone, but I recognize the confident way he carries himself.

My gaze flickers to the messy, sandy hair, the square jaw, and . . .

When he lifts his head, I freeze. Butterflies flutter in my stomach while my pulse pounds in my ears, and I curse myself for not shopping in the city like I wanted to.

Goose bumps crawl over my skin as I try to regulate my body's reaction to him, knowing I'm being ridiculous. But for some reason, seeing him outside of work with his friends, dressed casually in a hoodie and sweats, sends a punch of heat in my gut.

"Is that . . .?" Mal glances over at me, and the question dies on her lips when she takes in my expression.

Trying my best to recover, I glance the other way, but it's too late.

"Oh, this should be fun," she says with a clap of her hands.

GRAHAM

An hour into shopping, I'm already over it. Though hanging with the boys has provided me with a much-needed distraction, the effects of their company and the empty banter is a temporary salve to my situation at home. Or maybe it's watching Atlas's bright-eyed expression as he picks up Mackenzie's Christmas gift that puts me back in a funk.

My thoughts keep drifting to the gold necklace he got her, the one with the dandelion charm. I know it holds some special meaning between them, and I'm ashamed to say I give the symbolism far too much thought. Not because I'm jealous he's with Mackenzie. That ship has sailed. It's more because I want the same thing. Some people become jaded after they get their heart broken, and I often wonder if that would be easier for me, to completely give up on love. But instead, it made me want someone special in my life even more.

Ripping my gaze away from the jewelry bag in Atlas's hand, I glance ahead at Jace, who's currently roasting Teagan for the gift he bought his sister, Brynn.

"Dude, she's gonna be so pissed when you give her that. Can I be there to watch?" Jace asks, not even bothering to hide his smile.

"Hell no. I happen to think it's the best gift I've ever given."

"You're so lame. If I gave my sister a T-shirt that said 'my brother is my bodyguard,' I'd get punched in the nuts."

"You don't even have a sister, dipshit."

I roll my eyes at them. "You guys fight like an old married couple," I say, at the same time I spot a familiar face up ahead.

My steps falter as I do a double take, shocked to find Skylar standing only a few yards away. She looks like a fucking dream in a loose-knit sweater, tight jeans, and knee-high boots that show off her amazing legs.

"Fuck, check these two out. Dibs on the brunette," Jace mutters under his breath.

My head jerks in his direction, my gaze murderous.

"Or not?" he says, arching a brow.

"Damn. Look at that. One of them is waving us over," Teagan says, and my gaze whips toward them to find her best friend, Mallory, waving while a pink-cheeked Skylar grapples with her, half-turned away from us in an effort to stop Mallory from drawing attention.

I grin, and though I've appreciated Skylar before, I've never felt territorial over her—until now.

I slap my hand on both Teagan and Jace's chest to stop them from getting any ideas. "She's waving to *me*, you jackasses."

"You? What makes you think that?" Jace asks, and I can practically hear the pout in his voice.

"Because I work with her."

"Wait. This is the chick you work with?" Jace points as we slowly make our way over. "Now I totally get it."

"Hey, Graham." Mallory flutters her fingers, her smile wide.

I lift my chin in greeting. "Guys, this is Mallory and Skylar," I say, not wanting to delve further into introductions. Mostly because I'm afraid Jace will say something stupid.

"Actually, this is great timing because I need to shop for Skylar's Christmas gift. Would you mind taking her off my hands for a few?" Mallory asks while Skylar narrows her eyes at her.

"Funny, you said nothing about needing to split up *before* we ran into Graham."

"Because I didn't want you to know, silly." Mallory playfully swats at her, then pats me on the arm as she passes. "Thanks a bunch. Keep her as long as you want," she says, then quickly saunters away, leaving me and Skylar to stare at each other in her absence.

I shove my hands in my pockets and chuckle as Skylar says, "I'm gonna kill her."

"Just punch her in the face," Jace says from behind me. "It solves everything."

Beside him, Teagan jabs him in the gut. "Seriously, dude?"

"Ow," Jace whines. "What did I say?"

"Um, wanna get a coffee?" I ask, jerking my head toward the food court.

"Definitely." Skylar smiles and it lights up my insides.

"What, you don't wanna hang with us?" Jace says as I brush past him.

"Nope," I say as I reach behind me and grab Skylar's hand, dragging her away from them. "I'll catch up with you guys later."

"So, those are your friends?" Skylar asks once we're out of earshot as she glances over her shoulder.

"Don't look," I hiss. "They're like stray dogs. They might follow."

When Skylar laughs, I puff my chest with pride.

"Do they play football, too?" she asks.

"What gave them away?"

She shrugs. "They're all . . . big. And muscley."

I snort before I frown at the prospect of her checking out my friends.

The further we walk, the more I become aware of her hand in mine. The warmth of her palm sinks into my skin, and holding hands feels more intimate now that we're alone.

I check out of the corner of my eye to see if she looks uncomfortable, only to find her pink-cheeked with a soft smile touching the corner of her mouth.

Clearing my throat, I give her hand a playful squeeze. "What brought you out here, anyway? Isn't this kind of far for you?" I ask.

"It's really only about twenty minutes from my place, and Mal hates shopping in the city, despite being closer to Oak Ridge, so this is the next best thing."

I nod. "You're Christmas shopping, too?"

"Yeah. For my brother."

"JD, right?"

She grins shyly up at me as if my remembering something as simple as a name means more than it should, and my heart pinches. "Yeah. He gave me one of my presents early and it's amazing, so the pressure is on to find him something just as awesome."

"Any luck yet?"

"I think I'm on to something, yeah."

We step into the food court, and make our way toward the coffee shop, then get in line to wait our turn. "What flavor of coffee candy are you getting this time?" I ask, unable to hide the humor in my voice.

Her lips purse, but she can't hold back a smile as she says, "Gingerbread. So, sue me. I like my coffee sweet."

"If it's that sweet, it's no longer coffee, but I digress."

After we order, the barista gives us our total and I whip out some cash when Skylar shoves my arm away. "I'm paying," she says.

"No way." I push the cash over the counter and add, "Coffee was my idea."

"Maybe, but Mal pawned me off on you."

I snort. "Hardly. She did me a favor and saved me from Jace and Teagan's bickering."

We stare at each other, facing off, waiting for the other one to crack when Skylar manages to hip check me out of the way. "Hey," I protest with a laugh.

Skylar shoves a ten-dollar bill toward the barista who's looking between us, confusion lacing her brow like she has no idea what to do. When the girl tentatively takes Skylar's money, she spins around and points in my face. "Ha!" Skylar shouts in triumph.

"I've never met a girl so happy to cover the bill before."

"Well, you haven't met anyone like me, then."

No, I haven't.

"Besides, it was seven bucks, not seven hundred," she says with a roll of the eyes.

When the barista returns with our drinks, we take them to a little bistro table outside the shop and sit across from each other.

Skylar wraps her hands around her paper cup and takes a sip of her drink, moaning with pleasure. "So good."

I smile and realize how much my mood has lifted since running into her. "Will you be real with me for a minute?"

She glances up at me, her expression open and honest as she waits for my question, and I realize that's one of the things I like about her. There are no pretenses where Skylar is concerned. What you see is what you get. She's nothing but genuine, no matter the circumstances. It wouldn't be hard to know your place with her or where you fit into her life. Something tells me she wouldn't make you guess. She'd lay it all out on the line.

I hesitate, distracted by the pink lipstick ring on the rim of her paper cup, before I lift my gaze again and ask, "Your parents died when you were young, right?"

She nods. "I was only two with my mom and three when my father died."

"And you were born deaf." It's not a question but a confirmation, so she only nods waiting for me to get to my point. "What was that like?"

She exhales a distant look in her eyes as she stares off behind me. "Hard. It was surgery and years of speech therapy. I went to a school for the deaf my first few years, but it was a far commute and expensive and JD's career was just taking off, so I switched to Oak Ridge in fourth grade. Then it was a few years of kids making fun of me while I struggled." She glances down at her coffee a small smile touching her lips. "But it worked itself out. I learned to stand up for myself. I met Mallory, and speech therapy paid off. By the time I was in junior high, I no longer needed it, and kids no longer saw me as all that different, so they left me alone."

I tilt my head, eyeing her with admiration. "You had a lot stacked against you, and yet, you're so . . . I don't know . . . unflappable, strong despite your circumstances," I say, coming up short of the perfect word to describe her. "You're so sure of yourself and completely unapologetic for who you are in spite of the obstacles in your life. And I just wanna know how."

I think of Mackenzie and how she needed me for so long after the accident. I'm not sure Skylar would ever need anyone. She's too independent. Too resilient. And I can't help but wonder what the difference is. What gives one person the ability to bounce back while another flounders?

She blows out a shallow breath, her eyes lost in thought as she gives my question her full attention. "I don't know. Maybe it was my brother or maybe it's just how I'm made, but the way I see it, everyone has something bad in their lives. At some point or another, each of us has our own cross to bear. You can take the bad and let it destroy you, or you can give it purpose. Happiness is a choice. And I choose happiness. Every time."

Happiness is a choice. It's that simple.

I think about my own life and the problems eating away at me. Could I really just choose to be happy instead of letting them destroy me? Could everything that's gone on in the last couple months serve a greater purpose in my life? Can something good come out of my debt with Crenshaw? Is it really all that simple?

I honestly don't know.

But I'd like to think she's right.

"What if sometimes it's too hard to find the good in something?"

Her eyes soften as she tilts her head. "It's all about perspective, no? I could sit here and think of all the things in my life that are harder because of my deafness, or I can think about all the things that are better because of it. How I rely more on my other senses. I taste more, feel more, and see more. I'm more patient because of it. I can read body language and my gut is more in tune with my surroundings. I understand that perfection is overrated. Look"—she reaches out and grabs my hand—"you can let your father's affair destroy your outlook on love, or you can vow to never be that kind of man. You can promise to do better. You can have a relationship with Storm. You don't need to be a reflection of him."

"Am I that obvious?" My chest tightens. "Or are you just that good at reading people?"

"Maybe it's neither," she says, her gaze steady on mine. "Maybe I'm just good at reading *you*."

Heat spreads through me, unfurling like bird's wings. My gaze flickers to her mouth, and I want to kiss her. It's not the first time I've had this thought. It's less impulsive than the first time—the other day at the office—but the desire is there all the same.

Over the last few months, I've watched two marriages crumble on their foundations. First, through Mackenzie when she found out her mother cheated and had filed for divorce prior to her death, and then, my own parent's relationship. I had my heart shattered by my best friend. I have every reason not to believe in love. To want nothing to do with it. Yet, here I am, finding myself drawn to someone when it's the last thing I should want.

"What's your biggest fear?" she asks.

"Discovering I'm just like my father. Being so selfish that I don't care who I hurt in the process."

"You're not like him." Skylar squeezes my hand. "If you were, you wouldn't care this much."

"Why do you draw?" I ask, watching the way her eyes light up at the question.

"I don't know. I guess I've always been artistic, but I started when I was young. It just . . . sort of makes me feel alive inside."

I exhale. "I remember a time when football made me feel that way."

"But it doesn't anymore?" she asks, her gaze intent on mine.

I shake my head. "No, but then I think about quitting, just giving it all up, and it scares me because it's all I've focused on for so long. Sometimes, I wonder if I even know who the hell I am without it."

"Maybe all you need is to let go of who you think you need to be because it's taking away the focus on the person you already are."

I swallow, feeling the weight of her words in my heart.

She grips her paper cup, staring down at it as if it holds the wisdom spilling from her lips. "Sometimes I think people search so hard to find themselves when the answer is already there in all the little things, the tiny details of everyday life. We're not just *one* thing, Graham. We're a million tiny things put together."

A lock of hair falls in her eyes, and I reach out, brushing it aside. My thumb grazes her cheek, bringing a flush of color to her fair skin.

If that's the case, then I want to know all of the things that make Skylar who she is. Every single thing about her. Her favorite food. What kind of music she listens to. The books she reads. The face she makes when she's tired. I want to know if she's a morning person or a night owl. I want to know her favorite season. How she looks when she wakes up. Her worst fears. Her greatest dreams.

I want to know every thought inside her head and everything in between, and this scares me more than anything because I have no idea if it's reciprocated or not. The last time I felt this way, I thought I knew, only to discover I was wrong.

I have no idea how much time passes as I sit there across from her, talking about everything from movies, books, her favorite season, and her plans for the holidays to what it was like growing up deaf.

"Do you believe that things happen for a reason?" I ask.

"Like fate?"

I shrug. "Yeah, maybe."

"I don't think so. To believe in fate seems, I don't know, sort of cruel. Like we have no say in our lives. No control over what happens to us. Why?"

I never believed in fate. Before now, I thought shit just sort of happened, the bad and the good. But now I'm not so sure. Now I'm wondering if maybe everything that happened with my father and Crenshaw brought me right here, to this moment and to Skylar. Maybe I was meant to meet her.

But I don't say that, because it makes me sound crazy. So instead, I say, "I don't know if I was meant to meet you. If it was fate or just a coincidence, but I'm glad I did."

Skylar's mouth curves.

"You give me a new perspective. You make me feel like I can turn the bad in my life around. You're like this big ball of sunshine, spreading your light on everything in its path."

She dips her head, her voice turning shy as she says, "I don't know about that. I just see things differently, that's all."

"Skylar?" I place a finger under her chin, tipping her head so I can meet her eyes.

"Yeah?"

"You need to learn how to take a compliment."

She grins. "Noted."

CHAPTER 26

SKYLAR

I SHOVE ASIDE MY second cup of coffee, which has long since grown cold.

"You want another?" he asks.

"No. I definitely think I've hit my caffeine intake for the day." Something sad drifts through his expression, and I allow my mind to race. To imagine it's because he doesn't want to leave just yet.

"I have an idea," I say, reaching my hand out, my eyes twinkling with mischief. "Come with me?"

He narrows his eyes, but his lips twitch revealing his amusement. "What are you up to?"

"I would never lead you astray," I say, making a slashing motion over my heart.

"Well, in that case . . ." Graham pushes back from his seat. "Is crossing your heart as binding as a pinky promise?" he asks, his tone teasing.

"Duh," I say, grabbing his arm as he laughs.

I pull him out of the food court back into the main part of the mall, passing a steady stream of shoppers buying last-minute presents for their loved ones.

Excitement bubbles in my chest. I hurry down the corridor toward the giant Christmas display with the twenty-foot tree towering in the distance. Christmas music drifts toward us the closer we get, until we're standing directly in front of it. Giant bulbs shine from pine limbs, and bright, twinkling lights glow from the tree's massive branches. At the foot of it sits a large velvet armchair where a pudgy real-life Santa, complete with red suit, wire-rimmed spectacles, white beard, and red hat talks to a little girl. His elves hover nearby, helping to move the line along while they pass out candy canes.

"I'm afraid to ask what we're doing here," Graham says, his tone wary.

"Isn't it beautiful?" I practically vibrate with joy.

Graham glances down at me while I cling to his arm with excitement. "Definitely the most beautiful thing in the room," he says, and the way he says it makes me think he's not talking about the tree.

I swallow, my gaze drifting to his perfect mouth, the masculine angle of his jaw, and I clear my throat, feeling silly. *Of course, he's not talking about me.*

"Are we here to look at the decor?" he asks, bringing me back to the moment.

"Of course not." I shake off my thoughts, and return my gaze to Santa. "You're going to sit on his lap, silly." I slap him playfully in the chest as his eyes widen in horror.

"Uh, no. No way."

I roll my eyes. "Come on. How are you supposed to get what you want for Christmas if you don't ask for it?"

"Um, not by sitting on some pervy old guy's lap, that's for damn sure."

My lips twitch, but I fight my smile, instead piercing him with a sharp look. "That's not fair. You have zero reason to think this guy is a perv. Maybe he just loves kids?"

"*Exactly* what I'm saying."

I scoff. "You know what I mean. Men exist who love children in a very non-pervy, cherish-their-innocence, fatherly or brotherly kind of way."

"If you say so . . ." he trails off, eyeing Santa like he doesn't believe it.

"Come on." I yank on his arm, trying to move him toward the line, but he's as solid as rock. I grunt once more, but he won't budge from where he's rooted to the floor. "Graham," I whine.

"Skylar," he mocks, while his eyes glitter with amusement.

"*Please,* just trust me."

He arches a brow and jerks a thumb toward Santa who lets out a raucous laugh, stomach shaking like a bowl full of jelly.

"Give me one good reason why I should sit on that guy's lap like I'm an overgrown three-year-old."

"Because telling him what you want for Christmas will mean speaking your desires out loud, and speaking your desires out loud will manifest what you want. Positive attraction, self-fulfilling prophecy and all that."

"Even if I bought that, what if I don't even know what I want?"

I grunt with frustration. "Weren't you the one telling me I gave you a new perspective just moments ago. That I was like a ball of sunshine? Just . . . trust me." I step forward and take his hand in mine, ignoring the way it fits perfectly, sinking tiny hooks in my flesh. "Look, I'll go if you go."

"You'll go up there and sit on Santa's lap and tell him what you want for Christmas?"

I nod. "Absolutely."

"And I can take a picture to keep as evidence?"

"Not only can you take a picture"—I lean toward him and bop him on the nose—"but the elf will take one for you."

He purses his lips as if he's mulling it over, but I can see in his eyes that I already have him.

"Fine," he mutters. "But I have another condition."

"Okay?"

"If you utter a word about this to my friends, I let the kissing virgin out of the bag."

I gasp in mock horror. "You wouldn't."

Graham's green eyes gleam as he leans forward. The heat of his breath tickles the side of my face; his lips graze my ear. "I would."

A shiver races down my spine, and as he leans away, my thoughts drift back to the when he stole my sketchbook and asked me to kiss him to get it back.

I should've taken him up on his offer.

Hell, who am I kidding?

I wanted to, even when I was pissed at him. I just had too much pride to admit it.

The line lurches forward, and Graham steps away from me, jolting me from my thoughts.

"So, how do I do this exactly?" he asks.

I blink, taking in the crease between his brow. "*Wait.* You've sat on Santa's lap before, right? Like, as a kid?"

He shakes his head. "No."

My eyes widen and I stare at the side of his face in shock. "Not ever? Not even when you were, I don't know, three or four? Or a baby just for the photo-op."

"Nope. Never. My father thought stuff like this was tacky."

I massage my forehead, releasing the tension forming in the crease of my brow. "Oh, wow. That's just . . ."

"I mean, my dad's an ass, but I don't think it's that big of a deal. Right?"

"I didn't even have parents, and I've gone to see Santa plenty of times," I point out.

"Maybe you're the abnormal one?"

I bark out a laugh. "That's highly likely. However, you're definitely not getting out of this now. Sitting on Santa's lap is a childhood tradition."

Graham fidgets with his hands, and I get the impression that he's nervous, which is so freaking adorable I can hardly stand it, so I decide to put him out of his misery. "Okay, so all you do is go up there, and he'll ask you if you've been a good boy this year—"

"Ah, *yeah*," he drawls. "I think I've seen this film. Only Santa's elves looked"—he tilts his head—"a little different."

"I'm sure they did, you creep, but this isn't an adult film. So, when he asks you—if he asks you—whether you've been a good boy, *lie*."

Graham laughs.

"And then he'll ask you what you want this year, and you tell him. This is your green light to ask for whatever you want."

"Seriously?" He grimaces.

"Seriously. When I was five, I asked for new ears."

Graham's gaze shoots to mine, and I shrug. "My implants were fairly new and I was struggling with my speech and hearing and kids making fun of me at school. It was . . . a lot."

Something I can't read passes through his expression before he turns his attention back to Santa. "Do I really have to sit on his knee?"

I press my mouth together, stifling a laugh. "Yes."

Of course, he doesn't *have* to. But seeing his muscled, six-foot-three frame on Santa's lap is going to be the highlight of my year.

I watch as the little girl in front of him finishes her turn, and then the female elf calls for the next in line to take their place, eyeing Graham skeptically.

Huffing out a breath, Graham shoots me a murderous look before he hurries down the candy cane lined pathway right up to Santa's lap where he plops down on one leg like a sack of rocks.

Santa winces, readjusting himself while his cheeks turn red, and I pinch my lips closed in the monumental effort to stop myself laughing.

I quickly snap a picture with my phone as Santa goes through his normal routine. I can vaguely hear their voices from my place in the front of the line, but I can't make out their words due to the familiar notes of "We Wish You a Merry Christmas" playing in the background. It's hard to say whether I'd be able to hear them with normal hearing or not, but the only sign I have of what they're saying, is by watching their lips move.

I lower my phone and slide it back in my pocket. I'm pretty sure Santa just asked the million-dollar question: *"What do you want for Christmas"*?

Graham sobers, his eyes staring at something in the distance. He looks so serious, I wonder if he's thinking about what I told him. That in order to manifest what he wants, he needs to ask for it, voice it out loud.

I have no idea what Graham's going to say, but I figure it can go one of two ways. Either he'll answer with something ridiculous and make a joke of it, or he'll say something profound. One of the perks of being deaf is the ability to read lips, and as his mouth moves, I read his words as he speaks them, even though I know I shouldn't.

And they're not at all what I was expecting.

He's dead serious, and his throat bobs with emotion as he answers.

"To have direction again. To find my way."

His words split my heart in two like a fault line in the earth.

The ground feels unsteady beneath my feet as he jumps down from a stunned Santa, completely oblivious to the fact he just punched a hole in my heart. I watch as his sober expression transforms as he turns to me, forcing a smile I'm not sure he really feels beneath the weight of his words.

"All done," he says, his tone light.

My lips part, but I'm at a loss of what to say. I'm not supposed to even know what he asked for.

It's my turn.

The elf is calling for me to take my spot, but I can't seem to put one foot in front of the other with the heaviness in my heart.

Graham's forehead pinches and he nudges me in the side. "Flaking out on me, Sky?"

Warmth courses through me at the sound of my name on his lips. It's the first time he's used a shortened version of it, and I can't help but feel like maybe it means something, but there's no time for contemplation.

With a rueful smile, I hurry toward Santa where I gently sit on his lap as he peers down at me, his wire-rimmed spectacles at the end of his nose. I could be wrong, but I swear he ogles the swell of my cleavage visible through the V-neck of my blouse. And is it my imagination, or is his hand a little too low on my back?

"Have you been a good girl this year?" he asks, eyes south of mine.

His hand shifts, brushing the top of my ass, and my face burns with righteous anger. Suddenly, I'm furious that this lecherous impostor heard Graham's most private wish, the desires of his heart, and before I can think of what I'm doing, I reach up and flick Santa's spectacles right off his fugly face. Then I flick him again, this time in the eye.

"Aargh!" Santa flinches, rearing back as he clutches his eye and shoots out a string of curse words, nearly knocking me off his lap.

I scramble to my feet at the same time I see a pissed little elf barreling toward me, and run for the velvet ropes where Graham stands, wide-eyed, mouth gaping like he doesn't believe his eyes.

"Go, go, go!" I yell as I jump the rope bordering Santa's village and take Graham's hand in mine.

Behind me, Santa yells something about security while I run as fast as my feet can carry me, pulling Graham around the corner at the end of the corridor.

Laughter bursts from his chest as I push him against the wall and press a hand against his mouth. "Shhh. You're going to get us caught," I admonish.

Peering around the corner, I expect to see them coming for us any minute, but the coast is clear, and when I turn back to Graham, he's no longer laughing. I become aware of every pinpoint of touch between us as his green eyes latch on mine.

My hand over his lips.

His breath, warm on my skin.

My chest pressed against his.

Our thighs touching.

I'm breathless and my lungs burn—from the run over here or Graham's proximity, I'm unsure. My face is only inches from his, and as I slowly remove my hand and drop it to my side, his gaze shifts to my mouth.

Time stands still, and then his mouth is on mine.

My eyelids flicker closed as his lips explore mine, tentative, uncertain like the brush of a butterfly's wings. Shivers race down my spine as a soft sigh bursts from my chest, and I pull him closer.

He angles his head, his fingers threading through my hair as he takes control. His tongue brushes the seam of my mouth and I allow him access, opening up to him like the petals of a flower, unfurling in the moonlight while the woodsy scent of his cologne surrounds me.

My head spins at the same time my knees buckle, but his arms catch me, pressing me tighter against his chest.

If this is a first kiss with Graham, I don't want to know what a second kiss would be like. One is enough to make me lose my mind. Two might kill me.

My senses erupt as he expertly moves his mouth over mine. One hand presses against the small of my back while the other moves up my side, leaving goose bumps in its wake, until it's cupping my jaw.

Graham's kiss is everything I thought it would be—confident, soft, yet unyielding—and it doesn't take long for it to consume me. Until his every breath is my own, and I can't tell which heartbeat is his and which is mine.

A few minutes later, his lips slow, and he pulls away, leaving me to stare up at him, dazed and wondering if it affected him as much as it affected me.

He leans down and presses his forehead to mine. "*Damn*," he whispers, unknowingly giving me all the answers I need. Then he pulls back, a laugh rumbling from the back of his throat as he cups my neck. "Did you really just flick Santa in the eye?"

CHAPTER 27

GRAHAM

*T*HIS GIRL . . .

Finally back in my bedroom, I scrub a hand over my face as I brace my weight against my dresser, thinking about Skylar. Her sweet face. Her lips. The feel of her body pressed against mine.

Fuck. I knew I was in trouble the moment I kissed her.

Hell, maybe I knew I was in trouble the moment I laid eyes on her at O'Malley's.

The whole ride home from the mall, I had to listen to the guys give me shit about her, too. And though I'm not sure if I'm ready for something more, I'm also not sure I have a choice in the matter, because when it comes to her, I can't seem to stop myself.

I groan as I walk backward to my bed and flop down on it, replaying every nuance of our kiss in my head. It was Skylar's first kiss, but it didn't feel like a first kiss to me. It felt like the last one you have before you find someone you want to kiss for the rest of your life.

Did I really just fucking think that?

I chew on the inside of my cheek, flipping through my memories of the afternoon for some sign that Skylar and I are bad for each other. Some sort of red flag to indicate she and I should never cross the line and try and be anything more than friends, but I find none. She's not perfect. No one is. She's obstinate and independent to a fault. From the little I've seen, she's quick to anger. She certainly had me pegged wrong from the start. But none of those imperfections come even close to outshining all the perfect parts of her.

Every time I'm around her, all I want is more. Simply put, Skylar makes everything better.

So, I push aside the niggling doubt in the back of my head, the one that's terrified of getting hurt again. I ignore that tiny voice telling me I might not be ready, that it's too soon, and I doze off, dreaming of amber eyes and lips every bit as sweet as the coffee she drinks.

Christmas Eve is uneventful. I go to church with my parents, and we smile and pretend that we're the perfect family. Once we get home, everyone goes their separate ways, and I spend the rest of the evening dreaming of Skylar.

I want to text her, but something inside of me hesitates. I have no idea how she felt about our kiss, or if she's thinking of me like I'm thinking of her, and the part of me afraid to get hurt again holds back.

I grab the remote off my nightstand and turn on a movie, flicking the channel until I find *National Lampoon's Christmas Vacation*. I laugh at the funniest parts, but I find myself wishing for company, someone to share all the tiny moments of life with. I'm so tired of being alone, and I can't help but wonder what kind of movies Skylar prefers. Does she like those cheesy Hallmark movies, chick flicks, comedies, or action? Would she laugh hardest at the part in *National Lampoon's Christmas Vacation* where the uncle's wig catches on fire, or where Eddy dumps the shitter in the sewer?

Fuck it.

I snatch my phone up beside me and shoot off a text.

Graham: *What are you up to?*
Skylar: *Hey, just watching a movie with JD. Why? What's up?*

I wondered if she might think it's weird that I'm texting her, but the fact that she's acting like it's totally normal, brings a smile to my lips.

Graham: *I was just sitting here wondering what your favorite Christmas movie is.*

Skylar: *Oof. That's a tough one. But I'm a traditional girl, so I'm gonna have to go with* A Christmas Story, *followed by* The Grinch.

Nice. So, maybe she does like comedies.

Graham: *You'll shoot your eye out.*
Skylar: *Aaah, fra-gee-lay. It must be Italian.*

I tip my head back and laugh at her quote, but I have to one-up her.

Graham: *Only one thing in the world could've dragged me away from the soft glow of electric sex gleaming in the window.*
Skylar: *Crap! That's a good one. Did you look it up?*
Graham: *Pinky swear, I didn't.*
Skylar: *Well, I must believe you now. We know how I feel about the pinky swear . . .*

I prop a pillow behind me head, getting comfortable.

Graham: *So,* The Grinch, *huh? The animated original or the one with Jim Carrey.*
Skylar: *The original, of course.*
For some reason, this makes me smile, and I find myself wishing I were there with her and we were watching it together.

I type several responses to this effect but delete them all, afraid to sound pathetic or like I'm moving too quickly when a text from her comes through.

Skylar: *Can you be real with me?*
Graham: *Sure.*

My heart leaps as I wait for her question.

Skylar: *Was it okay? The kiss?*

I swallow, thinking about the kiss we shared, unsure of how to put it into words. I may have pined for Mackenzie for years, but I'm no saint. I've kissed plenty of girls, and done other stuff, too. But the kiss with Skylar was different. Memorable in a way I can't explain. Meaningful. Quite frankly, I can't wrap my head around it. I've known her for three weeks, yet she's managed to somehow burrow under my skin.

If she only knew . . .

Graham: *You tasted like gingerbread, and it's all I can think about.*
Skylar: *The gingerbread or me?*
Graham: *You.*
Graham: *Most definitely, you.*
Skylar: *Okay, good, because I was worried. You know, since I've never . . .*

Damn, this girl gets to me.

Most girls I know wouldn't come right out and ask. It takes balls. Instead, they'd stew over it, maybe dig for compliments or some other way to find out if the guy was into it, but not Skylar. She just comes right out and asks. And again, I find myself enamored with the fact that I always know what she's thinking, how she's feeling. With Skylar, I'll never have to guess, and it's refreshing as fuck.

Something she says flashes in my mind. About wanting her first kiss to be done right. *Whoever he is, I want him to be worth it.*

Graham: *Was I worth the wait?*

Although we were equal parties in the kiss we shared, I'd be lying if I said a small part of me wasn't a little concerned she might be upset I took her first.

I wait with bated breath, but she doesn't make me wait long.

Skylar: *100%*

I wake up on Christmas morning, feeling slightly lighter than I had the day before. Last night, Skylar and I texted for an hour before her movie ended and she finally called me. We talked for so long, I fell asleep on the phone.

Even my mother's gift to my father can't get me down. Instead, I think about Skylar as I roll out of bed, take a quick shower, and pull on sweats and a T-shirt. I have more than an hour before I have to leave for work, since I have the Christmas shift, and I don't even mind because it gets me out of the house. Plus, I have my thoughts to keep my company, because I plan on daydreaming about a particularly sexy brunette all afternoon.

I pad down the hallway in bare feet and find Mom and Dad already on the couch, his arm wrapped around her shoulder as they sip their mugs of coffee. A tray of Christmas cookies which Mom ordered from the bakery sits in front of them on the coffee table.

"Hi, sweetie," Mom calls out.

"Morning," I mumble as I take a detour into the kitchen. I pour my own cup of coffee, not just because I need the jolt of caffeine, but to mentally prepare myself before I go into the living room and face them. It's only a matter of time before my mother finds out the truth and her world is shattered. The least I can do is be present for the moment and give her an hour of my time in which I pretend we're not falling apart, and I'm not itching to get the hell out of here.

I take a sip of my black coffee, letting the bitter brew warm my gut before I head into the living room and take a seat in a chair opposite them.

Around the base of the tree presents are scattered about, smaller in size now that I'm older.

After a few minutes, Mom starts the festivities and motions for me to start opening some of my gifts. With as much enthusiasm as I can muster, I unwrap several sweaters, a hoodie, and some new sneakers. I open several small boxes with gift cards for my favorite stores, and unload a stocking filled with snacks. I give Mom the necklace I bought her and a framed photograph of us at the lake over the summer, which makes her cry.

We're almost finished when Dad hands me a package, and I blink over at him in surprise. "Open it." He motions to the box. "It's just a little something I got you when your mother wasn't looking."

Mom smiles at him, the same surprise in her gaze I'm certain is mirrored in my own. I try not to expect too much as I slip off the shiny wrapping. In my eighteen years, I'm not sure my father has ever picked out a gift for me himself, so this is a first.

The last of the wrapping falls away, and I lift the lid on the box, pushing aside the tissue paper to reveal a white-and-blue Penn State jersey.

I stare down at it as a prickling sensation claws up my spine.

"It's the first of many, I'm sure, but I thought I'd get a head start," Dad says, pride in his voice.

My insides twist as I lower the box and glance up at him. "But I haven't even signed with them yet."

"Sure, but it's a given, right?" He pats my leg, like my signing with them is a foregone conclusion.

And I guess it should be.

But I've made no decisions where my future with football is concerned, and I wonder what he'll do if I decide I'm done. If I walk away, what will he say?

Part of me wonders if it's even crossed his mind as a remote possibility.

Probably not.

And for the first time ever, I feel the slight stab of fear that he might completely disown me, which in turn, pisses a part of me off that doesn't give a shit what he thinks.

"Right. Thanks," I mutter, but inside I'm numb.

"Well, as long as we're giving out surprises . . ." Mom smiles and stands, walking over to the tree where she retrieves an envelope from the branches. She's practically giddy with excitement and my stomach turns over.

I swallow, knowing what's inside the envelope she hands to my father, and I can't watch. Getting to my feet, I clear my throat and announce, "Well, I hate to do this, but I'd better get ready for my shift at the hotel."

"What?" Mom's head jerks in my direction. "I thought you'd try to change your shift?" she asks, incredulous.

"Yeah, sorry. They needed someone to cover the holiday shift, and everyone else who works the front desk has kids," I lie. "It seemed like the right thing to do."

Mom's shoulders droop, but her expression softens. "I guess that makes sense, but I hate the thought of you leaving and being gone all day on Christmas."

I set my coffee cup down and lean across the sofa, pulling her into one of my giant bear hugs. "You won't even know I'm gone. You and Dad can plan your trip," I whisper in her ear. "Besides, I'll be back tonight, and we can watch a movie and eat cookies, okay?"

"Promise?" she mumbles into my shoulder. "I only get the rest of the school year with you before you leave."

"Promise," I say, leaving out the fact that I haven't decided where the hell I'll be going. "Thanks for the gifts, Mom," I say as I pull away, then give her a quick kiss on the cheek.

"Are you sure you don't want to stay for the surprise?" she asks, waving the envelope out in front of me.

I swallow. All I want to do is to get the hell out of here. Away from my father and his expectations. Away from the reminder that he's a liar and a fraud. Most of all, I need to be anywhere but here when she gives him that present.

So, I shake my head and say, "Nah, I'm good." My eyes harden on my father, then return to her. "Merry Christmas, Mom."

I knock on the door to room 208. The familiar sounds of "I'll Be Home for Christmas" trickles through the closed door, along with a burst of laughter. Leaning against the doorframe, I close my eyes, remembering a time when my home carried the same sounds; a time when it wasn't all bad.

The door swings open, and I straighten.

Marie stares at me warily, her brow creased. I'm sure she's wondering what the hell I'm doing here, maybe even wondering if I'm here to stir things up and cause trouble. I've never given her any reason to think I want her here in town. And even now, as I stare at her, I have to fight back my repulsion. An image of my mother gifting my father the trip to renew their vows swiftly flickers in my head, and I have to remind myself my father was a married man; *he* broke his vows, not her.

I clear my throat. "Is Storm around?" I ask, my voice gruff.

Marie crosses her arms over her chest and takes a tentative step out into the hallway, her posture defensive. "Graham . . ."

"Look, I know I'm interrupting, and it's Christmas. But regardless of how I feel about you or my father, Storm's my brother. I'm here for him. I'm not gonna hurt him, and I won't stay long. My shift starts soon, anyway."

Marie nods and opens the door wider, waving me inside, and I think I see a flicker of something in her eyes not present a moment ago—something that looks a lot like respect.

"Graham!" Storm perks up at his spot by a little Christmas tree. It's probably three feet high and filled with ornaments and colored lights with a dozen presents spread out beneath its small branches. An empty plate, save for a single carrot stick and some cookie crumbs, sits on the table beside him, evidence that Santa came. Whether Storm still believes in him or not, or it's just tradition, I don't know. We've spent some time chatting during my shifts over the past week, but the subject never came up. Regardless, the sight of it makes my heart pinch painfully in my chest. Even more so, when Storm stands and comes toward me wearing his football PJs.

Sometimes it's easy to forget how young he is; right on that cusp before he starts turning from a boy into a man.

I swallow over the lump in my throat, hating that he had to spend Christmas at a hotel instead of in a place he can call home. I think of our massive house with our three intricately decorated Christmas trees and the spread of holiday food my parents will have later, and hate my father more in this moment than I ever have.

Emotion swells inside me as I reach out and ruffle Storm's dark hair. "Hey, buddy!" I say, trying to sound happier than I feel. "Merry Christmas."

"I didn't know you were coming today," he says, trying to fight a grin.

"Well, I only stopped by for a minute." Storm's smile falters. "I'm working today, though, so you'll come visit me on my shift, right?"

His eyes brighten and he nods.

"Maybe we could even sneak in a movie on my phone. I'm sure it'll be dead down there today."

"I can bring some of Mom's Christmas cookies," he says, his voice rising with excitement. "She makes the best snickerdoodle and sugar cookies."

I reach my fist out, and Storm bumps it with his. "Deal."

"I just wanted to give you this." I slide my hand inside my pants pocket and pull out the little box with the green bow.

"Sorry it's not wrapped," I say, holding it out. "The bow was all I had."

Storm blinks up at me, eyes popping. "A present for me?"

I nod, the corners of my mouth curling as I motion for him to take it.

Behind us, Marie watches. I can feel her gaze boring into me, but I ignore it. I don't blame her for being protective of him. I'd be the same in her shoes.

Storm lifts the lid on the little white box and takes the black wristband out, glancing up at me with a question in his eyes. "Cool," he says unenthusiastically, and I laugh.

Stepping forward, I slide it on his wrist. "This is my lucky wristband."

His eyes flicker to mine, clinging to my every word.

"I don't even remember where I got it, or when, but I was probably about your age. I've worn it at every game since I was twelve, and it's never let me down."

Storm cocks his head, his gaze intent on the band around his wrist as he homes in on the letters of my last name embroidered into the black cloth. "Like a good luck charm?"

"Exactly like a good luck charm. I haven't played a day without it."

"Did you wear it at States?" he asks in awe.

"Sure did."

"Wow, that's so cool." He grins for a moment before his smile slides, his eyes turning serious. "But I'm not a Scott."

My heart pinches, so I bend forward, forcing him to meet my eyes. "You're a Scott in all the ways that matter."

He spares a quick glance at his mother, his throat working before he offers me a dubious expression. "But—"

"Hey, am I a Scott?" I interrupt.

He nods.

"Is Atlas a Scott?"

He nods again.

"Well, we're your brothers, which makes you a mother-freaking-Scott. You hear me? That also means you were born to play football, and you're bound to be good."

His frown melts. "Yeah, okay. Thanks." He nods, almost to himself as his eyes brighten. "This is pretty dang cool." He spins around to his mother, who quickly swipes at her eyes. "Mom, are you crying?" His tone conveys he thinks it's the most ridiculous thing in the world.

"No, of course not," she says, her voice thick. "Why would I cry?" She rolls her eyes at me and I stifle a laugh.

"Did you see what he gave me?" Storm holds his wrist out like Marie didn't just witness the whole exchange firsthand. "I have Graham Scott's good luck charm on my freaking wrist!"

He pauses in his dancing, a furrow in his brow as if something just occurred to him. "Wait. But won't you need it in college?"

I swallow, my chest tight. "Nah. It's time for someone else to carry the torch for a while."

Any good luck it gave me wore out a long time ago.

CHAPTER 28

SKYLAR

CHRISTMAS MORNING PASSES QUICKLY. JD and I wake before the sun rises and open presents. As predicted, his plane ticket to Mexico for a "singles trip" doesn't go over well, but he slides it in his wallet for safekeeping, so I take that as a win. We eat a giant brunch at midmorning and proceed to decorate gingerbread houses, both of us trying to one-up the other. Like every other year, JD eventually gives in and eats part of his, and then we watch Christmas movies while we drink hot chocolate with extra whipped cream, all while never changing out of our pajamas.

And despite having a wonderful holiday like we always do, my mind is elsewhere. All I can think about is Graham. No matter what I do, I can't seem to get him off my mind. The taste of his lips. His moss-green eyes and the way his calloused hands cupped my face, gripped my waist. How we talked for hours on the phone last night.

I wonder how his morning went before taking the day shift at the hotel. I hate the idea of him working today. Even more, I hate the idea of him being lonely or bored. On Christmas of all days, he should have a little joy.

"Something on your mind?" JD asks, eyeing me from his spot on the couch.

"What makes you say that?" I pick a piece of lint off the throw blanket on my lap, avoiding his knowing gaze.

I risk a glance up at him and catch his answering smirk.

"Okay," I drawl, feeling the telltale heat of a blush rising to my cheeks. "It's nothing bad. I was just thinking about . . ." I clear my throat, wondering why it's so hard for me to tell JD I have a crush, though the term crush feels like downplaying it, which might be the reason for my hesitation. I'm not really sure what Graham is to me, but he feels like a whole lot more than a friend or even a crush. "There's a boy," I blurt before I can overthink it."

JD raises a brow, angling his body toward me. "A boy? Where'd you meet this *boy*?" he asks, and I don't miss the emphasis on the word.

"Um, a few weeks ago when I was out with Mal." I bite my lower lip, purposely leaving out the part where he also works at the Bardot. "We've hung out a few times."

"And you like him?" he asks as if it's so hard for him to believe.

A smile slowly spreads across my face, and it's all the answer JD needs. He glances away from me, his throat bobbing. "Do you want to date him?"

"I don't know," I say. "Maybe?"

"Is this you asking for permission?"

I scoff, feeling a stab of irritation. "Do I need your permission?"

His expression smooths, the irritation making way for concern. It's hard to be annoyed with him when he's looking at me like that. "I'm sorry. Of course you don't need my permission. You're eighteen, and I trust your judgment. I just . . . I don't ever want to see you get hurt."

"I won't," I say, though I have no idea if that's true or not. "It's not serious."

Yet, I think. Though if I'm being honest with myself, I want it to be.

He nods, his relief palpable.

"But even if I were, I can't live my life never putting myself out there because I'm afraid of getting my heart broken," I say, and for the first time I wonder if maybe I've been wrong all along about the reasons behind JD's lack of social life. Maybe it's not because he's too focused on me or work. Maybe it's because watching our mother die first, and our father follow on the heels of heartbreak was enough for him to put a guard up. I wonder if he's afraid.

JD exhales. "How'd you get so wise?"

The corners of my mouth lift. "I have a pretty smart brother who taught me everything I know."

My answer seems to appease him and he grins, returning his attention back to the television screen. A while later, when I notice his eyes start to flutter during the tenth replay of *A Christmas Story*, I slink off to my bedroom and change. I pull on a warm sweater, a pair of jeans, and boots, only taking the time to tie my hair up and quickly swipe on a little mascara and cherry ChapStick. As an afterthought, I grab my canvas tote, the one that holds my sketchbook and the piece I've been working on.

By the time I return to the living room, JD's eyes are closed, his chest rising and falling with his breath. I tiptoe toward him and give him a soft peck on the check and murmur, "I'm heading to Mal's for a bit."

"Be back for dinner," he mumbles, then sprawls out on the couch, snuggling into the cushions.

I lift the throw blanket off the back of it and tuck it around him before heading for the door and snatching my car keys off the console table.

I enter the Bardot and the warmth of the lobby thaws the cold from my bones. As crazy as it sounds, I've been working here for so long, it's almost like a second home to me. I nod and greet the bellhop as I pass, basking in the warm glow from the tree lights by the fireplace.

"Couldn't stay away, huh?" The sound of his voice heats my insides like a shot of whiskey, and my gaze finds him instantly.

"I heard they have a catered lunch for employees today." I step up to the desk and fidget with my hands on the strap of my tote, realizing how much I want to pull him in for a kiss. But even if this were the place for it, and we talked about the kiss briefly, I don't know if it's the kind of thing he plans on repeating, and I don't want to make any assumptions.

"Is that the only reason you came?" he asks, arching a brow.

"Not the *only* reason," I say. "There's this boy . . ."

"A boy, huh?" His lips quirk.

I nod. "Yeah. You see, the other day when we were together, he kissed me." Nerves twist in my stomach. "And now it's all I can think about."

"Is that so?" He leans over the counter, eyes sparkling. "So, you're no longer a kissing virgin?"

I shake my head, desire fisting in my chest.

"Nope. But the memory is kind of hazy, so I can't be sure."

He exhales a breathy laugh. "I guess he'll just have to refresh your memory."

I flush and my smile spreads with the promise.

"Go out with me," he says, like it's a demand rather than a question.

"When?"

"As soon as my shift ends in an hour."

Unable to hide my smile, I nod. "I have a few hours to spare."

"Good. Will you be bored in the interim?"

I roll my eyes as if it's even a question. "Of course not. But even if I do get bored, I have this." I lift the sketch pad out of my bag and wave it in front of him. "Speaking of, I want to show you something."

I flip through the pad, turning to the correct page and hand it to him.

The sketch is of my parents. It's all clean lines and crisp edges. The man in the picture is crying as he cradles his wife's face. Though I sketched it initially in charcoal, I painted it with watercolors so their facial features pop from the page where they embrace, their bodies intertwined.

"What do you think?" I ask, wincing, afraid he'll hate it.

"It's . . ." He falls silent for a moment as if searching for the words. "Skylar, this isn't just a drawing. It's . . . a connection. An emotion. A *feeling*."

I feel the compliment hit its mark and my stomach turns inside out.

"What does it make you feel?" I ask, hopeful this time.

"When I look at this"—he shakes his head, and I see the muscle in his jaw work—"I get that gut-deep feeling, the one that tells you that you can't live without someone. The kind of wanting that feels like holding your breath whenever you're apart. A love that twists inside you like a knife, because even the mere thought of losing them or living without them tears you up inside. The realization that life will never be the same again now that they're gone, and the fear that for the rest of your life, you'll never want another person as much as you want them."

I swallow while my heart hammers in my chest.

I want to laugh his answer off, to take it for the compliment it is and move on, but I know he's thinking about Mackenzie—his best friend, the girl he was in love with not all that long ago—so I can't.

My eyes gloss over, and an emotion I can't label helicopters around my heart. "What was she like?" I ask, my voice soft.

When he frowns, indicating he has no idea who I'm talking about, I add, "The girl who broke your heart?"

He says nothing and for a moment, I think he might not answer. When he eventually begins to speak, I'm not sure I want to hear it.

"Mackenzie was—*is*," he corrects, "pretty amazing. She's been through a lot, yet she's one of the kindest, most forgiving people I know. She doesn't quit on people. Instead, she fights fiercely for them, and she's not afraid to take what she wants out of life."

"And she's beautiful." I know she is without confirmation, and yet I want the answer all the same, even if I hate myself for it. I've never been self-conscious, even with my disability. Yet with Graham, I feel a vulnerability I'm not accustomed to, along with the unfamiliar fear I might not be enough.

His eyes flicker. "She's attractive," he says, and he sounds like he hates admitting it.

"Well, she's not perfect, at least." I reach out to take the sketchbook from him, and a jolt of electricity snaps at the skin where we touch. "Because I already know at least one of her flaws."

He frowns. "What's that?"

"She missed out on you."

I keep Graham company for the next hour while he finishes his shift. The lobby is empty, and work is slow considering there aren't a lot of people coming and going from the hotel on Christmas Day. We pass the time by playing cards and talking until his shift is over, and we can finally get out of here.

He takes my hand, dragging me from the lobby into the cold outside.

I have no idea where he's taking me, but I follow him to his car. He opens the passenger door for me and ushers me inside. "I know you're Miss Independent," he says in response to my arched brow, "but I have manners."

I inhale, sinking into my seat and breathing in the scent of leather and Graham's cologne when he takes the driver's seat and starts the car. In one fluid motion, he checks his mirror and pulls out into traffic. He drives with one hand on the wheel, the other resting near the gear shift in the center between us, and I can't help but wonder how he'd react if I laced his fingers in mine.

"What?" He smiles over at me.

I shake my head and bite my lip as I glance away. "Nothing."

As if reading my thoughts, I feel his hand curl over mine, intertwining our fingers, and I smile at the window.

"Did you have a good Christmas?" he asks in his smooth baritone.

"I did, but it's not over yet." He gives my hand a small squeeze. "How's your mom?" I ask.

"If you're asking if she knows yet, she doesn't." He sighs. "Unless something has changed in the short time I've been gone. I know I need to tell her. It's becoming increasingly clear my father won't, but I haven't found the courage yet."

I wonder what it would be like to shoulder a secret like that, knowing it would crush someone you love.

"You'll instinctively know when the time is right."

"Do you think I'm wrong or selfish for not telling her?" he asks.

I jerk my head toward him. "No, of course not." That's the last thing I want him to think. "I think your father is the selfish one for expecting you to hang onto this. He should be the better person and tell her himself so you're not burdened with the choice in the first place."

He exhales, relief flickering over his face as if my opinion matters to him, and for some reason, the knowledge it might does funny things to my heart.

"Thanks," he says, his tone soft.

"No need to thank me for the truth," I say, wishing I could help him in some other way.

When he pulls over to the side of the road and parks, I'm surprised. We've only gone a short distance, and when I stare out the windshield, I note we're in the heart of the city. The sidewalks are mostly devoid of people, with a few stragglers milling about. If it weren't Christmas, I'd assume we're going to dinner or shopping. But most places are closed, and I can't imagine what we're doing here otherwise.

"You don't mind a short walk?" he asks.

I shake my head. "Where are we going?"

"You'll see." He slides out of his seat and rounds the car. When I join him on the sidewalk, he takes my hand and we're off. A little over five minutes and a few blocks later, the town square comes into view with its towering pine Christmas tree, strung with thousands of twinkling lights, bright in the waning daylight.

My eyes flicker to the massive outdoor skating rink at the base of the tree. Skaters zip over the smooth surface of the ice, couples hold hands, and kids scream. I imagine it's the only thing open on Christmas day, so I assume it's what we came for.

I point to the ice and laugh. "Are we . . .?"

"We are."

Oh boy. "Is this a bad time to admit I've never been ice skating before?"

"Seriously?" His brows reach his hairline. "Not even as a kid?"

I shake my head, my stomach jumping with nerves. "Never."

"Damn, Davenport. I'm even more excited now than I was a few minutes ago."

I scoff. "Why? Because you know I'm going to fall on my ass a dozen times?"

He purses his lips like he's mulling it over. "I mean, I won't mind picking you up, that's for damn sure. This is bound to be entertaining."

I punch him in the arm and laugh. "Not funny."

"I think I could get used to this, though."

"What?"

He leans into me, his hands on my waist as he lowers his mouth to my ear and says, "Being all your firsts."

He pulls away and heads to the desk, totally nonchalant. And I stand there, staring after him and trying to deal with the millions of fireworks currently launching through my chest.

I may only be eighteen and completely inexperienced, but that was the hottest freaking thing anyone has ever said to me.

He glances over at me to find me rooted to my spot and winks, then lifts his chin, a subtle nod to join him.

Once I'm finally able to make my feet work, I head to his side and give him my shoe size, then take the skates the attendant hands me.

"Ready?" He tugs on my hand and guides us to a bench, kneeling down in front of me and gently gripping my right foot.

"What are you doing?" I ask.

Grinning up at me, he says, "Putting on your skates."

I arch a brow. "You know I can do that, right?"

"I know, but I wanna do it for you. Is that okay with you, Skylar Davenport?"

I purse my lips as he slides one of my boots off and gently cups my foot, tugging the skate on in its place and flooding my body with heat in the process. I watch as his fingers make quick work of the laces, deftly tightening and tying them. If Graham telling me he wants all my firsts is the sexiest thing to ever happen to me, then this is the second.

Once he finishes, he begins working on his own.

"So, on a scale of one to ten, how bad does it hurt when you fall?" I ask, warily eyeing the ice. I tried skiing once and wound up with a bruised tailbone after only about ten minutes.

"It's not bad unless you fall really hard, but I'll be there to help you."

"Be prepared to help *a lot.* I don't exactly have the best balance," I say, tapping my ear.

"Oh, shit." Graham's eyes widen. "Skylar, I didn't even think about that. If you don't want to—"

"No." I rush to say, placing a reassuring hand on his. "I want to." A rueful smile curls my lips. "But just know, that if I go down, you're going down with me."

More than an hour later, despite Graham's expert skill and his ability to catch me when I slip, my ass hurts from the number of times I've fallen. True to my word, I've also taken down Graham more than a time or two.

"I'll have you know that when Mallory gets annoyed with me because I'm limping around tomorrow, I'm telling her to call you and complain."

"Damn, you're hanging with Mallory tomorrow?" he asks, glancing down at me.

"Yeah, why?"

He shoots me an impish grin. "I was kinda hoping we could hang out again after your shift."

Something warm unfurls in my stomach. "I might be able to squeeze you in."

"Oh, you can, huh?" He nudges me playfully in the side, but when I almost fall, he catches me and we laugh.

Later, when we finally make our way off the ice, I walk like a penguin stiffly over the platform where we stowed our shoes on the rack. I notice Graham pause, moving around in front of the shoe rack, his gaze searching wildly.

"Is something wrong?" I ask, sensing his distress.

He exhales, then turns to face me with a grimace. "So, you want the bad news?"

"Is there good news to choose from?"

"Afraid not." He bites his lip, and I try not to stare at how soft it looks beneath his teeth. "Someone stole your shoes."

"What?" I shriek and shuffle-step my way to see for myself, sure he missed them, but lo and behold, my black Steve Madden's are missing from the slot right beside his.

"What kind of asshole steals someone's shoes?" I ask, waving my arms.

Graham bends down and starts unlacing his skates. One by one he pops them off while I mourn my life choices. "Clearly, I owe you a pair of boots," he says.

"No. It's not *your* fault, but I'll admit, I'm not looking forward to walking the three blocks back to the car in my socks."

"Come on, let's get your skates off," he says, motioning for me to sit on the bench behind me.

After he slips the skates off my feet and straightens, he heads to the clerk at the rink and turns them in, then jogs back to my side. "Ready?" He claps his hands and wiggles his fingers.

"Sure." Resigning myself to frostbitten toes, I take a step forward at the same time Graham dips down and sweeps me off my feet.

I yelp in surprise and give my feet a little kick. "What are you doing?"

He stares at me like I'm stupid. "Did you really think I'd let you walk back to the car with no shoes?"

"Well . . . *yeah*. It's kinda far."

"So little faith in me," he says with a shake of his head.

"Graham, you can't possibly carry me the entire way," I protest as his arms tighten around me and he walks toward the sidewalk.

"Why not?"

"Because I'm a whole human being."

He snorts. "A whole human being? As opposed to a half human?"

I poke him hard on the chest. "I'm serious."

"First, jabbing me in the chest while I'm very gallantly trying to carry you several blocks through the city is probably not the best idea if you don't want me to drop you. Second, I bench over two-twenty-five. You're a shrimp in comparison," he says, lifting me up and down like a human barbell to prove his point.

"Okay, okay, I get it," I say with a squeal as I tighten my hold around his neck.

He chuckles, gripping me to him until I start to relax, melting against him as he walks. My head rests on his upper chest, just below the crook of his neck, while his strong arms bear my weight. I'm all too aware of every square inch of my body touching his, and when I inhale, I'm rewarded with the clean scent of his skin—a combination of soap and cedarwood that makes my head spin.

A few minutes pass, with me enjoying this far too much, before he asks if I had a good time despite my stolen shoes, and I answer with the truth: a resounding yes. Then we proceed to joke the rest of the way about how awful a skater I was.

"Did you see that little girl that kept skating circles around you?" Graham asks, a smile in his voice. "I swear every time you fell, she rolled her eyes."

"Punk," I say, so serious we both burst out laughing.

Once we reach the car, he opens the passenger door and slowly lowers me into the seat, his body grazing mine as he sits me down. Heat spikes in my veins while my pulse pounds in my ears as he pulls away from me ever so slightly.

The darks of his eyes dilate, until I can barely see the green encircling them as his gaze dips to my mouth, and he says something I don't catch, but I read it on his lips. "*You have the sexiest mouth.*"

The breath stalls in my lungs, and I want him to kiss me again so badly, everything inside me aches with desire. My hands still grip his neck, willing him to close the gap between us as I toy with the hair at the nape of his neck, tugging the silky locks through my fingers.

His nostrils flare before he leans forward, his breath hot on my skin—so close I can practically feel the press of his mouth already and we're not even touching.

Every nerve in my body tenses in anticipation.

My back straightens, urging him even closer. And, finally, like an answered prayer, he closes the infinitesimal gap between us and lowers his mouth to mine.

I hum in approval as our lips lock, and I'm not disappointed. Our first kiss wasn't a fluke or beginner's luck, because this one is every bit as amazing.

Our breath mingles as my skin heats, and the world falls away.

His hands cup my face, pressing me further back into my seat as a guttural moan bursts from the depths of his chest that makes every nerve in my body come alive.

When he releases me a few minutes later, my heart stutters while I struggle to slow my breathing.

The world slowly comes back into focus as I blink my eyes open, and I know with complete certainty I'm in trouble because it's only been a few weeks and two kisses, and I can already feel myself falling.

"You're so much different than I thought you'd be," I murmur against his mouth.

He brushes a lock of hair from my face, staring at me with so much intensity, it makes my heart rate spike again. "How did you think I'd be?"

"Just . . ." I shake my head as I bite my lower lip. He's far from the cocky, sarcastic boy I thought he was. I almost can't put it into words. "I don't know. You surprise me, that's all."

He leans back, and I mourn the loss of him, but he interlocks my hand with his, glancing down at how well we fit together, like we're two pieces of a puzzle and says, "You surprise me too."

CHAPTER 29

GRAHAM

"Where did you say your parents were again?" Jace asks, rounding the island in our kitchen.

"The ballet." I grimace.

"Oh shit. You dodged a bullet there."

"Yeah, I'm not crying over it." I turn and grab a glass from the cupboard, then fill it with water from the fridge.

"Have you made any decision yet on who you'll sign with?" Teagan asks.

I shift on my feet uncomfortable with the question because I'm no closer to knowing what I want than I was months ago. "Nah."

"Word is you're going with Penn State."

My gaze snaps to Teagan. "Who said that?"

Beside him Jace leans forward, bracing his weight on his elbows. "Your dad's been going around town talking to everyone who will listen about how both his son and nephew are headed for the Big Ten."

The Big Ten is the oldest division one collegiate athletic conference and generally consists of the same top ten schools. Penn State and Ohio State being two of them. I know Atlas is planning to sign with OSU, but I've made zero verbal commitments.

"He needs to shut up and let me figure it out," I mumble, not wanting to get into it with them, mostly because I have no idea what the fuck I want to do.

Crossing the kitchen, I open the pantry, grab a pack of Chips Ahoy! and toss it on the counter in the hopes of deflecting the conversation.

"Score!" Jace practically leaps over the island, grabs the pack of cookies, and rips it open before cramming one in his mouth. "Don't you have any Christmas cookies?"

"Nope."

Jace frowns. "Why do I feel like you're holding out?"

"My mom gets that shit catered," I say.

Jace grimaces. "Right. So does mine. Lifestyle of the rich and famous," he says in a mock tone before he glances over at Teagan, his gaze expectant. "I bet your sister made cookies, didn't she? See if I can stop by on my way home and grab some."

Teagan snorts. "Even if she *did* give you cookies, they'd probably be laced with cyanide."

Jace grins. "True. That's why I'd make you eat one first, just to be sure."

I chuckle. As long as I've known him, Jace has had a hate-hate relationship with Teagan's twin sister, Brynn.

"So, what's up with you and this Skylar chick? You serious?" Teagan asks.

"What?" My head jerks at the sudden change in subject. "Um, no. Not really. What made you think that?"

Jace and Teagan exchange a look.

"What?" I ask, crossing my arms over my chest.

"You're just not really the casual type," Jace says.

Teagan snorts. "Yeah, take that from the player who's an expert on casual."

Jace simply shrugs. "I accept my title proudly."

I blow out a long breath and scrub a hand over my face before I brace my hands on the counter. In truth, these last few days have been amazing, but they've also scared the shit out of me. The way I feel when we kiss almost reminds me of the way I felt about Mackenzie. And I'm scared to go back to that place, one where I'm vulnerable to getting crushed again.

"I can do casual?" I say, although it comes out like more of a question than a statement.

"*Right*," Jace drawls, eyes wide as he grabs another cookie.

"I can," I insist. I have to. I don't want to lose whatever this is with Skylar.

"Then what's the problem? You like her, right?"

"I do." I shift on my feet, unsure I want to have this conversation with them. "I mean, I think I do. She's fucking amazing. Fun to be around. Honest. Sweet. And talented as fuck."

"Not to mention smoking hot," Jace points out. "Hey, do you have any milk?" he asks, waving a hand toward the refrigerator.

I cover my face with my hands for a moment—he's like a kid, sometimes—then turn and grab him a glass and the jug of milk from the fridge, knowing he won't be able to focus until I do.

"Wait. You do find her attractive, don't you?" Teagan asks when I don't say anything.

"Of course I do. Hell, when I work with her, I find myself torn between staring at her cleavage and her ass all fucking day. It's almost to the point of exhaustion."

Jace nods, serious as he says, "She has a nice rack."

I shoot him a murderous glare, and he holds his hands up. "Got it. Don't go there. So, you *do* like her?"

I place my elbows on the island, leaning toward them as I say, "Yeah. We've hung out and kissed a few times."

"Yes, dude!" Jace slaps a hand on the island making me jump. "For a moment, I thought you were totally letting her friend zone you again."

I shoot him a dry look, then shrug. "Maybe we're better off friends."

"What? No!" He shakes his head. "No, no, no, no! You're *never* better off as friends." Jace glances at Teagan for backup. "T, do you hear this shit?"

When he turns back to me, he jabs a finger at the island. "Look at what happened last time you were 'just friends,'" he says, making air quotes with his fingers. "You wound up being in love with her for six freaking years and getting your heart and your ego railroaded."

"That's different."

Jace arches a brow. "How? Face it, bro, you're a sentimental schmuck who wears his heart on his sleeve. You don't know how to just be friends as much as you want to pretend you do."

"So, what? Are you suggesting I just dive into a relationship again? I'm not sure I'm fucking ready for that after everything that happened. Hell, I don't think I'm even capable of truly falling for anyone again after . . ." I trail off, letting them fill in the blanks. "And even if I were, I'm not sure I fucking want to."

"So, then it stays casual." Teagan shrugs like it's simple, and Jace points a finger at him as if to say he's right.

The front door slams, followed by footsteps and a familiar voice. "What's up, assholes?" Atlas saunters toward us, and I shoot Jace a meaningful look to drop the subject.

Knox follows behind him, glancing between us while Jace presses his lips closed for half a second before he blurts, "Not much. Graham here is just telling us about his fucked-up love life."

"What the hell, man?" I ask, throwing up my arms.

"What?" Jace shrugs. "It's not like they don't know."

Teagan crosses his arms over his chest and fills them in. "It's the chick he ran into at the mall the other day. He's smitten but scared because he's not over Kenzie yet and doesn't know if he can ever let anyone in again."

I drill him with a glare. "Remind me not to talk to either of you ever again."

Atlas shrugs. "You just need to get back on the saddle."

"Yes, thank you!" Jace snaps his fingers.

"Why don't you ask her to the banquet? Do you have a date yet?"

"I don't know . . ." I hedge.

"Dude, listen to the man. He knows what he's talking about. He landed Mackenzie, didn't he?" Jace asks, his eyes glittering with humor.

I flip him the bird, but I laugh in spite of myself. "You're such a dick."

"Again, I wear the title proudly."

"I'll think about it," I say.

"When's the next time you're seeing her?" he asks.

"Tonight."

"Damn, bro." Jace laughs. "You really can't do casual."

When I head to pick Skylar up later that night, my conversation with the guys is all I can think about. I know I shouldn't be ready to start something with anyone. It's far too soon. Hell, just a few weeks ago, I thought I might never be ready. Yet I can't help but want to spend my time with her. Skylar makes everything better. She views the world with rose-colored glasses and is the exact brand of positivity I need in my life.

And, yeah, if I'm being honest with myself, I can't get enough of her mouth—the taste of her lips and the sound of her soft sighs. Her smooth skin beneath my fingertips. At night, I lie awake, breathing in the scent of her floral perfume still lingering on my skin, petrified of what this means and where it will lead. Sky Davenport is my newest addiction.

I think of my conversation with the boys.

I can't afford to get hurt again, yet I struggle to hold the people in my life at arm's length. *Can I do casual?*

I want to. I really do. Because the alternative is staying away from Skylar altogether, and I'm not sure I can do that. I know I don't want to.

I follow the GPS directions to Skylar's place and pull up to her house, prepared to meet her at the door when she appears in the entryway, a white paper box in her hands as she hurries toward the car. "Hurry," she says, swinging her door open, "before my brother sees us."

"Is there a reason we don't want your brother to see us?" I ask, even as I follow orders and pull away from the curb.

"It's just easier this way. No questions. No explanations. I don't think he'd be too thrilled with the fact I'm dating a guy from work." She rolls her eyes. "Besides, do you want to face my very overprotective brother and explain what your intentions are?"

My stomach clenches at the thought. I'm not even sure what my intentions are, so explaining myself is low on my list of priorities.

"That's a definite no."

"Exactly." She snaps her seatbelt on as I turn off her road. "Anyway, the last thing I want is to play twenty questions with him over our relationship, especially since we're just . . . friends?"

My body goes numb.

Friends. We're just friends. She said it herself, and here I am overthinking everything like I always do.

Fuck.

"Yep," I say, quickly, trying my best to ignore the sting of rejection.

This is what I wanted, wasn't it? Casual.

"Oh, I almost forgot." When we stop at a red light, she pushes the white paper box toward me. "These are for you."

I flip the lid open and I'm hit with the heady scent of sugar and butter. My mouth waters as I stare down at the assortment of Christmas cookies, then glance at her in question.

"I always freeze extra cookies, and I saved you some." She shrugs.

My chest squeezes as I reach down, pick up a peanut butter blossom, pop it in my mouth, and chew. A moan of approval rumbles in the back of my throat as I try a small iced Santa next. "Shit, these are good," I say between bites.

"Slow down there, champ. I don't want to be responsible when you choke." Skylar laughs.

The light turns green, and I reluctantly close the lid and press on the gas. "Those are probably the best cookies I've ever had."

"Well, it's probably the only thing I can successfully make without burning, so you're in luck."

"Do you know how long it's been since I've had homemade cookies? Thank you," I say, reaching out and squeezing her hand.

Her cheeks turn pink, and I can't help but notice how damn cute she is when she's flushed.

Ten minutes later, we're sitting in a quiet movie theater, a bag of popcorn between us, while I regret our choice of activity. All I can think about is turning to her and pressing her back into the seat, crushing her mouth to mine. It takes everything in me to try and focus on the movie instead of the way her leg brushes my knee or the soft sound of her laughter, and how all I want to do is nip at her lower lip with my teeth.

Afterward, as we're walking out, Skylar grabs my hand. "Hey, you okay?"

Clearly, she notices my mood is off.

"Yeah." I sigh, frustrated with the push and pull of my emotions. "I'm just . . . in my head, I guess?"

"You need comfort food," she says, so matter-of-fact, she even has me convinced. "There's a little diner two minutes down the road. Come on, it's my treat."

Once we're sitting in the diner across from each other and we've placed our orders, she takes a sip of her Coke, eyeing me over the rim of her glass. "Tell me what's eating at you?" she says.

"What makes you think something's bothering me?" I ask.

"You're too quiet, and that's never been a problem with us. So, spill." She wiggles her fingers.

"I don't know how to do this," I say, waving between us.

She stiffens as she asks, "Do what?"

"I don't know—whatever *this* is. Friends, but not friends. More, but not more." I growl, tugging at my hair, frustrated with her evasiveness. I sound like a fucking girl.

"Just say it, Graham. Whatever's on your mind and on your heart, say it out loud. Life is too short to hold back."

"The last thing I need is to fall for anyone again. The last time . . ." I trail off, my jaw tensing as I think of how badly I spiraled.

"Graham, we don't have to—"

"But I fucking *want* to," I growl. "That's the problem." I shoot a hand through my hair. "Hell, I used to believe in forever, in fucking fairytales, soulmates, rainbows, and everything in between. But now, I'm not sure what I believe anymore. I've lost my faith in a lot . . . including myself."

My throat bobs, and the urge to bottle everything up and keep my mouth shut rises to the surface, but I shove it back down. "All I know is that I'm scared as shit to ever feel as hopeless as I felt when I lost Mackenzie, and maybe I'm afraid for nothing because maybe love just isn't in the cards for me. But what I do know is that I like you. A lot." My face contorts. "And that scares me, especially when you get in the car and call me your friend."

Despite what I said to the guys yesterday, it's my worst fucking nightmare to get stuck in the friend zone again.

Skylar's throat bobs. "Graham, I like you, too," she says, her voice soft. "More than like you. The only reason I called you my friend was because I didn't know how to put a label on us or to even broach this conversation with you, and I was afraid of scaring you off." She huffs and glances down at the table, shaking her head as she places a hand to her forehead. "I'm new at all of this. It's a first for me."

Relief swells inside my chest. I reach out, placing my fingers under her chin so her eyes meet mine. "Another one of your firsts?"

She bites her lip, and my stomach flutters.

"We don't have to have all the answers," I say. "In a lot of ways, this is a first for me, too."

Mackenzie was a given. My feelings for her had always been there in the background. Meeting someone new and falling for them is an entirely different experience.

"That's good, because I don't have any." She licks her lips. "What if we just enjoy each other's company and don't worry about labels or the future? Can we just be in the moment?"

I close my eyes, thinking about my heart, battered and bruised inside my chest, and I wonder if something so broken can be mended. I think about Crenshaw and the mess I've made for myself.

I'm damaged goods. In need of repair, only I don't know how to fix myself.

If only she knew how badly I want to shove aside the fear and jump.

"I don't want to hurt you," I whisper.

"You won't," she says so fiercely I blink my eyes open.

I want to ask her how she knows—how she has so much faith in me when I have none in myself. Hell, I don't even know who I am anymore. My life is so fucked up right now, I don't know which way is up.

But all I know is that when Skylar and I are together, I can think clearly. Life makes sense, and it feels a little like I'm getting a piece of myself back again. Like maybe I've finally found direction again.

And maybe it's selfish, but I want more of that.

"There's a football banquet this weekend," I hear myself saying. "Will you go with me?"

Her smile spreads, and she offers me a nod. "I'd love to."

CHAPTER 30

GRAHAM

I TAKE ONE LAST look at myself in the foyer mirror before I shrug on my coat. Though my father will be in attendance tonight, the parents usually do their own thing while the team hangs together. Regardless, I'm determined to have a good time with Skylar there.

A hand clamps over my shoulder, and I immediately tense.

My father's reflection comes up behind me. He's already dressed even though he and my mother have nearly two hours before they need to be at the banquet hall. For some reason, this irritates me more than it should. "Your mother and I just wanted to see you before you left for the night. I know once you get there, you'll be too busy with your friends to pay us any mind."

My mother's robed form flits behind us, and my father turns to her. "Ah, there's my beautiful wife," he says, as she goes to him.

My stomach clenches as he folds her in his arms. Leaning down, he gives her a quick kiss while she stares up at him in adoration. "I just got out of the shower, so I'll start getting ready now," she says, and when her eyes turn to me, they grow wet with tears. "It's hard to believe it's our baby's last year."

My father nods, and I fight the urge to call him out in front of her because I know better. There's not a damn sentimental bone in the guy's body.

Instead, I return my mother's affectionate gaze. "Love you, too, Mom."

"This time next year, he'll be a Nittany Lion," he says.

My brow creases and I open my mouth to protest as my mother reaches out, taking my hand. "Your father told me you made a decision."

My head jerks, cheeks burning with indignation. "He did?"

Mom's smile falters. "Well, yes . . ." She glances up at him, a question in her eyes as if she's second-guessing herself.

Did my father really make the fucking decision for me?
Who am I kidding? Of course he did.

The muscles in my jaw lock, making it impossible to speak. All I can manage through the haze of my anger is a slight nod.

"Anyway, I better go get ready," Mom says, "but you have fun tonight, dear. You deserve it." With one final squeeze of my arm, she hurries from the room, leaving me alone with my father.

Silence stretches between us while I struggle to get a rein on my anger. "You told Mom I'm taking the offer from Penn State?"

His gaze focuses on mine. "They needed an answer, Graham."

I bark out a laugh. "So, you just took it upon yourself to give them one? You didn't think to, I don't know," I say, waving a hand in the air, "consult me first before deciding my future?"

"It was the obvious answer. Between them and Texas A&M, they're the better school."

That's part of the problem. Dad thinks I'm trying to decide between schools—between teams—when really, I'm trying to decide on football at all.

I scrape a hand across my jaw, my thoughts burning a hole through my head, my stomach sick.

Dad slaps a hand on my arm. "None of that matters tonight, anyway. Tonight is your night. You played a great season. You have a lot to be proud of, son. It's only up from here."

His words echo inside me. I've longed to hear him say something similar for as long as I can remember, but for some reason, they don't pack the punch I thought they would.

I snort. "*Now* I can be proud?"

He drops his hands, stuffing them into his pockets. "Of course," he says, sounding affronted.

I spin to face him, my jaw a hard line. "All year, all you did was tell me how I wasn't good enough. Every time I fucked up or fell short, you were there to rub it in my face."

He opens his mouth to speak, but I barrel forward. "I don't think you said one positive thing to me all year, despite our win at State. And now you have the audacity to stand there and tell me I should be *proud*?" I shake my head, a sardonic laugh bursting from my lips. "You've got to be kidding me."

When I turn to leave, he stops me with a hand on my chest. "Don't think for one second that everything I did wasn't for you. I saw your potential. You have the chance to be something great, even bigger than I ever was, and so I pushed you."

"Is that what you call it?" I smirk.

"Graham . . ."

I hate the way his voice sounds coming from his mouth, like he's pleading with me to be reasonable when he hasn't been reasonable with me a day in his life.

"Did you ever stop and think that maybe I didn't need a coach? Maybe all I needed was a father." I brush his hand off me and reach for the front door, leaving with his gaze burning on my back.

Because Skylar worked the morning shift, we agreed I'd pick her up from the hotel, where she'd change, and we'd head straight to the banquet. While I wait, I call up to Storm's room to see if he wants to hang out. When he answers the phone, he's more than thrilled to meet in the lobby and we play War with a deck of cards he brought from his room.

"So, you're taking Skylar to the banquet?" he asks, eyeing me as he flips his card over.

"Yeah. Why?" I take both of the face-up cards and add them to mine.

"I thought you were just friends."

My brows rise to my hairline. "Friends can't hang out?" I ask, because it's easier than explaining I'm not really sure what we are.

He shrugs. "I guess. It's just . . . you're all dressed up," he says, motioning toward my dress shirt and tie, "and Atlas is taking Mackenzie as his date."

I swallow, silent for a moment. It's the first time I've thought about Skylar and Mackenzie meeting, and I'm not sure how I feel about it.

"Teagan's taking his sister," I say, as if that's proof my relationship with Skylar is nothing more than platonic.

"Really?" Storm scrunches his nose as we both turn over another card. "Why wouldn't he want to go with someone he likes?"

I shrug. "Teagan's pretty low-key. I'm not sure he's interested in anyone, and taking his sister means he can go without worrying about entertaining a date."

I grin to myself as I think about the real reason Teagan's taking her. Apparently, he foiled her plans of driving to Ohio State to visit some freshman guy she'd been talking to for a while, with the promise of spending the night. He'd all but threatened to show his parents the text thread if she didn't go with him tonight so he could keep an eye on her.

"I don't think I want a girlfriend," Storm says as he grabs the high cards and places them under his pile.

"Why not?" I ask with a frown.

"It's too much trouble."

I bark out a laugh. "Isn't that the truth."

"I mean, look at my mom and Cal and your mom," he says, licking his lips. He glances up at me warily, like maybe he shouldn't have said anything, though I have no doubt it's weighing on his mind. "The last thing I wanna do is wind up miserable and messed up like them."

I flop back in my chair, my stomach sinking to my feet.

I open my mouth but can't seem to find my voice. I'm at a loss for words. I want to tell him not to be jaded. That not all relationships end like theirs. That just because our parents fucked up doesn't mean it has to be like that for everyone else.

And then I wonder what it says about myself that I want him to believe in something I'm scared to believe in myself.

"Ready?" Skylar's voice breaks through my thoughts.

"Whoa." Storm's voice is a distant sound behind me as I turn my head and lay eyes on the girl in front of me.

The words catch in my throat as I soak her in. The loose, dark waves piled at the top of her head, showcasing the slender line of her neck and miles of smooth skin. A little black dress clings to her every curve as silver heels showcase her long legs.

I swallow, then remember my manners and stand. "Uh, hey," I choke out.

"Is it . . ." She touches her hair. "I don't usually wear my hair up, but Mal insisted," she says, and I realize her meaning. She's nervous about her implant being visible, but her hair covers most of it, save for the small flesh-toned pieces that curl into her ears.

"No. Mal's right, it's perfect. You look . . . God, you look beautiful."

Her cheeks flush, and I fight the urge to reach up and touch the blush with my fingertips, aware that Storm is watching us and I just told him Skylar and I are nothing more than friends.

I clear my throat and offer her my elbow. "You ready?"

"Ready," she says, biting her lip as she adjusts the black shawl around her shoulders and hooks her arm through mine.

When I glance back at Storm to say goodbye, he rolls his eyes and mutters under his breath, "Just friends. *Right.*"

By the time we arrive at the banquet hall, it's already abuzz with conversation and laughter. I take Skylar's hand in mine, pulling her past the front of the room where the coaches, staff, and parents mingle, and toward the back where my teammates already form a huddle.

I pause a few feet from them, turning toward Skylar before they spot us. "You know, it's not too late to bail. We could go somewhere, just the two of us . . ."

"And have you miss your senior football banquet?" She arches a brow, leaning her cheek next to mine. "I know you're not sure about a future in football, but that doesn't mean you shouldn't celebrate all your hard work. Or have fun with your teammates."

She pulls back and our eyes lock. "While that may be true, my parents will be here. Are you really prepared to meet the asshole who raised me?" I ask her.

She tilts her head. "I'm here for you, Graham, and that means doing whatever you need me to."

Shit, she's perfect.

I exhale, trying to relax and wondering why the hell I'm so nervous. "Ready to meet this crazy group?" I nod toward my friends at the same time they spot me.

"Scott!" Jace cups his hands around his mouth, yelling like a banshee. "Graham Cracker, come here." He waves us over and I shoot Skylar a look that says this is her last chance to bail before it's too late.

When she chuckles, I cross the remaining space between us and pull her close to my side as we greet each other, shaking hands, giving fist bumps, and slapping each other on the back.

"Mall girl," Jace points once we're finished.

"I guess that's me?" Skylar says with a chuckle.

I roll my eyes. "Everyone, this is Skylar. Skylar, this is Jace, the clown of the group and one of our receivers. Teagan, the sensible, chill one, also a kick-ass tight end." I point to Knox, who towers over the tallest of us which is saying something.

"Knox, the friendly giant who's a beast as our running back, and Atlas, resident bad boy, and one of the best damn receivers in the state." Then I gesture to the girls of the group. "The blonde, here, is Teagan's twin sister, Brynn. The redhead is Knox's girlfriend Carrie, and this is Mackenzie." I motion to her before I quickly tear my eyes away.

"Um, excuse me," Jace says, stepping forward. "I take offense to those introductions. Mine was especially lackluster. Why'd you introduce everybody as being the best in their positions except me, huh? All I got was, Jace the receiver, while Atlas got *best in the damn state*."

"I mean, Riverside didn't win States until I came along." Atlas smirks.

I point at my cousin. "That. That, right there."

Jace flips both of us off.

Everyone laughs, but it immediately dies down as a shadow falls over us, and I turn to see my father. I tense when he stops beside me, his cool gaze landing on Skylar, then immediately flitting back to me. "I see you arrived safely, son." He glances around him, taking in my teammates. His gaze quickly darts away from Atlas when his jaw tightens. "Congratulations, boys. It's been an amazing run, and an even better season." He lifts his drink to his lips and takes a sip.

"What do you want, Dad?" I ask, frustrated with interruption so soon after getting here.

"You must've missed the memo where you're supposed to get your picture taken with your family upon arrival?" He motions toward the front of the room to the photo booth left of the door.

"Who said I missed it?" I spit back, my gaze hard on his face.

I should've known he'd do this here: put on a friendly face and play the supportive, doting father. Normally, I'd go along with it because that's what I do, but I'm not in the mood tonight. "It's my night. You said as much at the house, remember?"

He chuckles under his breath and raises his hands out in front of himself. "Fair enough."

My eyes round in surprise that he'd relent so easily when he glances over his shoulder. I follow his gaze to where my mother stands, alone, a drink in her hand. "I just figured you'd want to for your mother. We both know how proud she is . . ."

My jaw locks. Of course he'd use her, knowing how completely guilt ridden I am at having to keep his secret from her so he gets what he wants.

"You're right. I would like a picture with Mom. Speaking of mothers," I turn to Atlas whose eyes are drilling a hole through my father. "Atlas, will Marie be coming tonight? I know you guys have gotten closer this last month."

Out of the corner of my eye, my father's face puckers, his cheeks redden while Atlas continues staring at him, daring him to meet his eyes. "Unfortunately, she had to work. You know, so she can support her other son. Did you know she has another son?" he asks, turning to me, feigning innocence.

"*Right.*" I snap my fingers. "I think I did hear that some-where. In fact, I think I heard he's also my—"

My father jerks my arm, cutting me off as he spins me around to face him, his fingers digging into my flesh. "Enough," he hisses. Then, even more sternly, "Don't forget, it's not just *my* reputation you'll ruin." His gaze shifts to my mother once again, and I wrench my arm from the hold he has on me.

Stepping away from him, I turn to a wide-eyed Skylar and hate myself for making her uncomfortable when she's been here all of five minutes. "Will you be okay for a minute?"

"Of course." She smiles, but her eyes dart to my father un-kindly, then back to me.

"Be right back." I squeeze her hand and brush past my father without saying anything as I make a beeline toward my mother. I take her hands in mine when I reach her and give her a kiss on her cheek, before I tug her toward the background they have set up for the photographer and wait as my father joins us so we can pretend we're one happy fucking family. The photographer leans into his camera, holding up a finger for us to pose, and a second later, the flash goes off.

When we're finished and I return to our group, I take Skylar's hand and brush my lips over the soft skin of her knuckles. When I glance back to my friends, they're watching with interest. Jace's mouth curls as he assesses us with a knowing gaze, and I mouth *fuck you* to which he tips his head back in laughter.

An hour later, I can't remember why I was so nervous about bringing Skylar here. We sit in a large group around a table.

Half-empty soft drinks which Jace spiked with rum when no one was looking litter the table. Atlas and Mackenzie sit to our right while Teagan and his brooding sister sit directly across from us. Jace, who came solo, sits on Brynn's other side, offering snide remarks and commentary that make her roll her eyes, while Knox and his girlfriend sit to my left. I know Skylar can sometimes have trouble hearing in crowded places with large groups, so I be sure to repeat anything she misses and talk clearly, turning to her so she can read my lips if she needs to.

I've spent the better part of the last hour catching her up on each of us; from Jace's player status to Teagan's tree-hugging ways, and now they've seemed to move on, regaling her with questions and making it their life's mission to fill her in on the gritty details about me that she may have missed.

Jace leans across the table, nodding in her direction and I brace myself for whatever dumbass thing he's about to say.

"So, Skylar, we've been talking to you for a while now, and I can't help but notice the tone of your voice. You've got this kind of gritty Miley Cyrus vibe going, but if I don't know better, you have a hint of an accent. Where are you from?"

I tense, fighting the urge to cover my eyes with my hand, instead shooting him a look that could kill.

"I'm from here. I'm just deaf," Skylar says, deadpan.

"Come again?" Jace blinks like an idiot, and now I really do think I might murder him.

"I'm the deaf one and he needs me to repeat myself," Skylar says, and everyone laughs.

"Oh, shit. I'm sorry. I didn't know," Jace says, shooting me a pointed look. "I'LL BE SURE TO SPEAK LOUDER SO YOU CAN HEAR."

I close my eyes and shake my head. "You jackass, she's deaf. Speaking louder won't help her hear you any better."

"What the fuck do I know?" Jace flops back in his seat, glancing between us before his eyes settle on her. "So, if you can't hear, how are you getting all of this?" He waves around the table.

Skylar's lips quirk. "I have cochlear implants. Without getting technical, it's a medical device that allows me to process sound."

"That's cool," Teagan says, looking genuinely interested.

I watch on with pride as Skylar briefly explains her situation.

"And I read lips a lot, too. Especially if I'm in an environment where it's noisy, or maybe someone is really softly spoken. In fact, I'll probably be doing it a lot tonight, since there's so much background noise, but it's become almost habit, something I automatically do, so I don't even have to think about it."

"So, you just go around staring at everybody's mouth while they talk?" Jace asks as his brows rise.

Skylar lifts a shoulder. "More or less."

"*Damn.* That's fucking hot."

"Watch it," I warn, feeling territorial.

"What?" Jace shrugs while Knox and Teagan snicker, knowing he's going to dig himself into a hole. "I can't help it. Bro"—he leans toward me, eyes bright—"if I had a hot-ass chick like this staring at my mouth every damn time I talk, I'd have blue balls twenty-four seven."

"You're *such* a pig," Brynn growls.

Jace winks at her before he focuses back on me with a shrug. "Just speaking the truth."

"Well, maybe you should stop, because if you keep talking about how hot she is and mention her and your balls in the same sentence again, I'm going to cut your dick off."

Jace laughs and throws his hands in the air. "Noted."

"So, Skylar, give it to us straight," Teagan says, completely unfazed by the conversation that just ensued. "Do you even like football?"

"I guess I never really thought about it," she answers honestly.

Jace gapes, then glances around him. "She never really thought about it," he mutters.

"I like the uniforms," she says, grinning.

"I'll second that." Mackenzie's lips quirk.

"Third." Brynn raises her hand.

"Just so you know, my ass looks better than Graham's in my pants," Jace says motioning between us.

I snort. "Is that why you're always slapping mine on the field?"

"What can I say, when I play, I get a little handsy." Jace winks at me. Everyone laughs, except for Brynn, who just looks disgusted.

"This guy is a beast on the field," Atlas chimes in, surprising me. "It's too bad the season is over and you can't watch him play."

"Well, there's always next year," Teagan says.

I feel Skylar's gaze heavy on the side of my face as she asks, "Are you all going to different schools?"

"That's yet to be seen," Teagan fills her in. "Signing day is in February. It's kind of a big deal. Local media covers it and everything. That's when players who got recruited for college, officially sign and commit to their school. Some of us are being more tight-lipped than others about where we're headed, though," he says with meaning as he stares pointedly in my direction.

"I'm taking the offer from Penn State."

"Yeah?" Jace straightens, eyes bright as he offers me his fist. "Congrats, man."

I bump it, and try for a smile, but it feels forced as I sense Skylar's questioning gaze beside me. Turning to her, I shoot her a look that says I'll fill her in later. She nods and reaches out to squeeze my knee underneath the table. "I'm hitting the bathroom," I say, standing. "You good?"

"Yeah, I'm perfect."

Jace stands, too. "I could take a piss."

"I'm not holding it for you," I say as he rounds the table.

"What if I ask nicely?"

"Fuck no."

Skylar laughs while Atlas shakes his head, then turns to Mackenzie. "Wanna dance?"

"Teagan, watch my girl, here, will you?" I ask.

"You know it."

I lean down toward Skylar, looking her in the eye as I say, "I owe you a dance when I get back."

"Promise?" she asks me, eyes glittering as her gaze drifts to my mouth.

"Absolutely," I say, then lean even closer, my voice dropping an octave. "Jace is right. It *is* fucking hot."

I pull away, satisfied when I see her cheeks flush, then nudge Jace in the back before he can make any more dumbass remarks.

CHAPTER 31

SKYLAR

I STARE OUT AT the dance floor, watching Mackenzie and Atlas sway to the music. They make for a handsome couple, I'll give them that. Joy stretches across Mackenzie's face as Atlas spins her, then pulls her into his arms. I'd be lying if I said she didn't intimidate me just a little. This is the girl who held Graham's heart, then crushed it beneath her palm. The one he probably compares every other girl to, including me.

She's beautiful and vibrant with eyes the color of polar ice caps that penetrate right through you with a single glance. I don't have all the details of what happened between them, but I can only imagine the kind of pain and heartache that comes with falling in love with your best friend, only for her to choose your cousin in return.

Not that I begrudge them their happiness. Maybe she wasn't Graham's person, but someone else is, and the more time I spend with him, the more I can't help but hope and pray it's me.

"Losing Kenz really did a number on him," Teagan says from behind me.

I glance over my shoulder, and he rises, rounding the table and taking the seat beside me where we both gaze out at the dance floor. "He told me about it; I mean, a little." I admit.

"Probably one of the hardest things is seeing one of your closest friends lose themselves and having no clue how the hell to bring them back. It's nice seeing him happy again."

I assess the boy beside me. Blond curls frame a cherubic face with bright blue eyes and a gentle smile. Based on the little Graham has told me about his friends and what I've seen today, he's the most reserved of the group.

"Graham's a great guy. I'm just lucky to have met him."

"He's been through a lot in the last year, and not just with Mackenzie. The guys and I are pretty sure some stuff is going on that he hasn't told us about, but in the last month he seems happier—better."

I'd like to think the change is due to me, but it feels self-absorbed and maybe even a little wishful to assume.

"When I first met him, I thought he was a total horse's ass." I give a little laugh, tucking a loose curl behind my ear. "Totally pegged him for a narcissistic misogynist."

"Graham?" Teagan eyes me with surprise.

I nod. "I was wrong. I know that now."

"Other than myself, Graham is one of the least self-absorbed people I know. He's a protector, and he'd do anything for his friends and the people he cares about. Hell, if anything, he's too much of a people pleaser."

"I can imagine that it was hard being needed so much by Mackenzie, then being left hung to dry when she found someone else."

He turns toward me, his gaze sharp. "Observant, aren't you?"

I shrug. "He didn't tell me everything, but I've been able to put some of the pieces together."

"Mackenzie got in a car accident with her mother. She was driving. When she woke up, she discovered her mother had died. Only she survived. It tore her up inside. She couldn't remember the circumstances of that day for a long time, but she blamed herself. To make a long story short, she leaned heavily on Graham during that time. He was her pillar, and being the protector he is, Graham fell even harder for her than before. Don't get me wrong, he had serious feelings for her even before the accident, but when he almost lost her, I think panic set in and his feelings deepened. The more she leaned on him and he lifted her up, the more he fell."

I swallow, hating the thought of Graham loving someone else so wholly, but knowing it's necessary to understand him better. "Do you think he'll ever fully get over her?" My heart rises to my throat, almost afraid to hear his answer.

"I think he's more over her than he realizes."

I release the breath in my lungs, relaxing as he continues.

"Mackenzie was never what Graham needed. In a way, they enabled each other. As long as she was a victim and hurting, she needed him. And every time he put her back together again, he fell apart."

"A vicious cycle," I say, getting it.

Teagan nods. "She was his vice, and so when he started losing her, he went a little sideways." He meets my gaze, his expression sober. "He needs someone strong and independent. A girl who knows exactly what she wants. And maybe I'm wrong, but you seem to be exactly that."

I swallow, surprised at how good it feels to hear him say it. "I'd like to think so."

"Just be patient with him. Graham wears his heart on his sleeve. When he falls again, he'll fall hard. But he might resurrect a wall first before he allows it to crumble."

"He's scared," I say, gleaning that much from the candid conversation he and I had the other day.

Teagan places a hand on my shoulder and leans into me. "So, carry a sledgehammer, Skylar." He reaches up and taps his head. "Just know the right time to use it."

"What the hell? I'm gone for five minutes, and you're moving in on my girl, T?" Graham towers over us, a grin stretching across his face despite his words.

Teagan raises his hands out in front of him and his dimples pop. "She's all yours. Just keeping your seat warm, bro."

Graham snorts. "Dance with me?" He reaches out and takes my hand, placing his other one on my lower back as he guides me forward, but he pauses halfway there, his attention on something in the distance. When I follow his gaze, he's staring at the gorgeous woman I recognize from earlier as his mother.

He sighs and turns to me. "I've been avoiding my father, but it's no reason not to make my mother's night. Do you mind?"

I shake my head, a smile lighting up my face because I love that he cares.

"Are you sure meeting my parents doesn't freak you out?"

"Of course not. I want to meet all the people in your life," I say, realizing how true it is and wondering what that means.

"Mom?" he asks as we approach.

She turns her gaze to him and her expression comes alive. A warm smile spreads over her face. From her elegant black dress to her long, light brown hair, his mother is divine. "Darling." She pulls him toward her, clasping his free hand in hers. "Your father just went for my coat. I was hoping you might stop by for a quick chat before the night winds down."

"I just wanted to introduce you to the girl I've been seeing," he says, glancing down at me, his gaze warm. "Mom, this is Skylar. Sky, this is my mother, Sheila Scott."

I smile and accept her outstretched hand. "It's a pleasure to meet you, Mrs. Scott."

"Oh, please, call me Sheila." She gives my hand a little squeeze. "My goodness, you're beautiful."

When my cheeks heat, she chuckles. "Sorry to embarrass you, dear, but I call a spade a spade. I assume you're the reason my son had a huge smile on his face every time I glanced his way this evening?"

My blush spreads from my cheeks and straight to my neck as I eye Graham, wondering what he'll think of her comment.

He grins then winks at me, and my stomach swoops.

"Here you go, dear," a masculine voice breaks through my thoughts. I jerk my head forward to see Graham's father handing his mother her coat, his eyes hard as they flicker between me and his son. "Great. Is this your latest distraction?"

Graham's jaw ticks while his hands fist at his side. I catch the muscle bunching in his arms, and for a moment, I'm so afraid he might strike his father, I rise on my toes, leaning into him as I slide a hand across the hard plains of his chest.

"I find the *best* relationships actually heighten a person's drive, rather than detract from it. Wouldn't you say?" I ask him.

His father rocks back on his heels, clearing his throat. "Well, yes, I suppose that's—"

"I also find that when I focus solely on *my* relationships instead of the ones around me, I'm much better off."

Graham chokes on a laugh.

His father opens his mouth, but he closes it again like a guppy while Sheila beams at me. "Well, I say we let these two enjoy the rest of their evening," she says, patting her husband on the shoulder and offering me a wink.

We say our goodbyes and watch them leave. Once they're out of earshot, Graham leans down, his mouth against my ear as the deep bass of his voice rumbles through my chest, "I think I just developed a fetish for you putting my father in his place."

"I told you I can take care of myself."

He bites his lip and smooths a hand down my hair, staring at me in awe while goose bumps spread over my skin. "You're the sexiest fucking thing I've ever seen."

He leans even closer, and I part my lips, sucking in a breath while I anticipate his next move, but just when I think he might close the gap between us and claim my mouth, he tugs me toward the dance floor. "Come on."

I laugh at myself as I follow and a new song comes on; something slow and moody. He splays one hand over the bare skin of my back while he intertwines my fingers with his other, holding our clasped hands against his chest.

Every nerve ending in my body comes alive as he begins to move, his thighs brushing mine as he follows the slow cadence of the music. "So, how much do I need to apologize on behalf of my friends and father tonight?"

Though I find it difficult to focus through the butterflies in my stomach, I grin. "They're great. Jace is hilarious, Atlas seems quiet but introspective, and Teagan is a sweetheart. And Knox is a little of them all."

"That assessment's fair."

"You didn't tell them I was deaf?" I ask, curious about his answer.

Graham shrugs. "I guess I didn't see the need to. Does that bother you?"

I bite my lip and give a subtle shake of the head, loving that he doesn't see an issue with my lack of hearing. So many times, I enter a new environment with a friend or someone at school and I'm already pegged as "the deaf girl." It's nice to just be treated like I'm normal.

With a sigh, I lower my head, pressing it against his chest and listening to the steady rhythm of his heart while my head spins. I like Graham so much more than I ever dreamed I would. Maybe that should scare me, but somehow, it doesn't because every time I'm around him, I can't help but want more.

We stay like that, moving to the music for the next couple of songs. His hand leaves mine, gliding down the bare skin of my back, leaving a trail of fire in its wake while my own wander over the back of his shoulders. The muscles tense and move at my touch. His dress shirt is crisp against my fingers as I shift directions and bury them in the hair at his nape, wanting nothing more than to tip my head up to his, stand on my toes, and find his mouth with my own.

He dips down, pressing his forehead against the top of my head, a move I've almost come to expect from him. A gesture I love.

"Wanna get some air?" he asks in the silence between songs.

It's not even a question what my answer will be.

"Yeah," I say with my heart beating in my throat.

"Come on." He tugs me off the dance floor, and into the hallway. We walk in silence, my pulse the only sound in my ears.

Every nerve ending beneath my skin buzzes as I wonder where he's taking me, until he pauses by a door at the end of the building and pulls me inside.

"The boy's locker room?" I say, with a laugh. "This is a first for me."

He grins and stops beside a bench in front of a row of lockers, tugging me toward him. Reaching down, he brushes his thumb against my cheek, and my breath catches in my throat. "Well, I did say I wanted *all* your firsts."

Nerves twist in my belly. I'm both petrified and exhilarated at the thought of finally being alone with him. "Is your locker in here?" I blurt, suddenly nervous.

He grins and slides his hands down my arms. "It is." He jerks his head to the left and reaches out with one hand, lifting the handle of one of the bright red lockers so that it pops open. Inside, a football uniform hangs in place as if waiting for him to put it on.

"I wish I could've seen you in it," I say, grinning as I stare over at the Lycra, imagining how hot he'd look in it.

He arches a brow. "You wish, huh?" he asks, stepping away from me toward the open locker. "Lucky for you, I'm in the habit of granting wishes." He winks, then slowly loosens the tie from his neck before he flicks it open and unbuttons the top of his shirt.

I clasp my hands over my mouth, a nervous chuckle erupting from my chest. "You're putting it on? *Now*?"

He nods, biting his lip as his hands work his buttons, sliding down the rest of his shirt until he shoulders it off, followed by the white T-shirt he wears beneath it.

My laughter dies in my throat as I take him in. I knew Graham was built. I could tell by the feel of his firm chest and the way the fabric of his dress shirts strain against his arms, but the reality of Graham is so much more than the fantasy.

My mouth turns to dust as I take in the defined pecs, arms cut with muscle, and rippling abs. I try to speak but find I can't when his laughter interrupts whatever nonsense was about to spew from my mouth.

"Eyes up here, Skylar." A rueful smile crosses his lips while my cheeks heat, but I'm too stunned for words. "Is this the first time Skylar Davenport is speechless?" He chuckles and the muscles ripple in his stomach, drawing my gaze to a flash of something dark on his side, just below his arm.

I reach out, tentatively touching his torso, experiencing a zap of something electric as I urge him to turn angle toward me, so I can have a look.

When he does, the dark spot over his skin comes into focus, and I realize it's not a bruise or a play of shadows, or even a birthmark. It's a tattoo about the size of my palm. A compass.

My eyes flicker to his. He's watching me intently, waiting for me to ask him about it, but I don't have to. Because my thoughts drift to the day at the mall, when he sat on Santa's lap and asked for direction and to find his way, and my stomach clenches.

"It's beautiful," I say, as I trail my fingers over the ink. "When did you get this?"

He shivers at my touch, goose bumps pebbling the surface of his skin. "Almost two months ago now." His throat bobs. "You're the first person to see it."

"I've never been a fan of tattoos," I admit, and he frowns. "Until now."

"And now?"

I arch a brow, biting my lower lip as I tear my gaze from the ink to meet his eyes. "So fucking hot."

His lips split into a wide grin, and before I can register what he's doing, he starts to unbuckle his belt.

My eyes widen, homing in on the movement. "What are you doing?" I stutter out.

"I can hardly put my uniform on in suit pants." A wicked gleam enters his eyes, and he drops his slacks without a second thought, while I try as hard as I can to control my breathing.

Don't look down. Don't look down.

I focus so hard on his eyes, my vision doubles while his dance with amusement, daring me to hold his gaze instead of peeking at what he's packing.

I bite my lip so hard I nearly draw blood.

My nostrils flare as I breathe deeply.

I concentrate on keeping my eyes north of his waistline. And then in an act of betrayal, my gaze darts south.

I catch a glimpse of tight black boxer briefs, which he fills out so well my entire body flushes. I bite my lip so hard it could split and spin around, giving him my back.

Holy shit!

A low chuckle rumbles from his chest, shooting straight up my spine, igniting a ball of fire low in my gut. Swallowing I manage a weak, "I'll give you some privacy while you change," which only makes him laugh harder.

A few minutes later, my cheeks are still burning as his hands fall on my shoulders, and he turns me to face him.

My heart kicks at the sight of him in his uniform. He's so hot I can barely stand it.

"Well . . .?" He spreads his arms out and a sandy lock of hair falls over his forehead and into his eye.

I want to push it out of the way so badly my fingers burn to touch him.

I want to trail kisses down all that smooth, tan skin.

I want to embed myself in his heart like he's etching himself into mine.

I want to do a lot of things I probably shouldn't.

Instead, I shake my head, giving him my best poker face. The one that says I'm not nearly as affected as I am. "You are ridiculous, Graham Scott. All these poor girls at Riverside had to watch you from the sidelines every Friday?" I inhale as I step closer. "You're a closet heartbreaker," I say, poking him in the chest.

His lips quirk. "A closet heartbreaker?"

I nod. "There's no way there aren't a million girls pining after you just hoping for a chance."

"I love that you think that," he murmurs, reaching for me, and his touch shoots hooks into my flesh.

"I love that you don't."

A devilish grin spreads over his lips as his gaze trails down my body. "Now it's your turn to try it on."

I slap a hand over his chest. "Nice try, but I'm not stripping in front of you."

"Damn." He grips my arms in his hands while my heart riots. "Not even part of the uniform?"

I tilt my head, giving it a moment's thought. "Okay. *Part* of it," I say, my voice heavy.

His eyes glitter and he reaches for the hem of his jersey at the same time I turn for the helmet in his locker and slide it over my head. "You asked for it," I say.

Graham laughs so hard, it rattles my bones. "So unfair."

"You should've stipulated." I wag a finger at him, then place my hands on my hips and give him my best pose. "How do I look?"

"You look . . ." He draws closer, his voice husky. "So fucking hot," he says, repeating my words from moments ago.

He reaches out, curling a finger around the face mask of the helmet. With a tug, I stumble closer. His scent surrounds me as his eyes darken, his intentions clear as his gaze dips to my mouth.

My lungs seize the moment he grips the sides of the helmet and slowly slides it off. With deft movements, he places it on the bench beside us, his gaze never leaving mine as he does.

His finger tips my chin at the same time he lowers his mouth to mine, stopping within an inch of my lips. The sweet warmth of his breath ripples over my skin, forcing me to pull in a ragged breath as my heart beats like a bass drum.

Anticipation slides through me. The frantic fluttering of butterfly wings floats inside my belly. If I didn't so desperately want his mouth on mine, I might be embarrassed at how much I want this—want *him.*

I close my eyes, parting my mouth, the word, *please,* on the tip of my tongue. I'm ready to beg, to plead with him to put me out of my misery, afraid that if I don't taste him soon, I might combust.

And then his lips crash against mine.

They're soft, yet confident as they move, yielding to my own. He kisses me like he might die if he doesn't. Like I'm a work of art he's determined to study. He kisses me like I draw my sketches, taking his time, focusing on all the tiny details.

He slides his hands into my hair, angling my head as he pulls me against him where my chest molds to his. His thumb strokes my cheek, and his mouth moves to my throat, to my ear.

I almost pull away, self-conscious of my implant, but if it bothers him, he doesn't show it. He nips my earlobe with groan before I have the chance to push him back, then returns to my mouth.

The image of his perfect body flashes through my head, sending a wave of heat roiling through my gut as his tongue brushes mine. I moan as my hair forms a curtain around us, and I realize I don't want this to end. Not just right now, this kiss, this moment. But us. I don't want *us* to end.

CHAPTER 32

GRAHAM

A WEEK HAS PASSED since the banquet. I spent New Year's with the boys, wishing Skylar were with me. She had plans with her brother, and though I felt our relationship changing and shifting into something deeper, I know how much he means to her, so I didn't want to interfere. Besides, meeting him would take us to another level. One I'm not sure I'm ready for. I keep telling myself to slow down, to take the scenic route. But no matter how much I try to lay off the gas, each time we're together, we're throttled forward and I push the pedal a little more.

School starts back, and between work and classes, Sky and I manage to see each other nearly every day, no matter how brief. On the days we miss each other, we call or text. Jace and Teagan are right. I can't do casual. I'm just not built that way, because I believe when you find something worth keeping, you fight like hell to hang onto it.

I drive thirty minutes to Oak Ridge. Tonight, I'm picking Sky up and showing her around our little town of Riverside since we didn't have the time for it the night of the banquet—not that there's much to see. We'll grab a coffee at Roasted, dessert at Sugar Shack, and catch a movie at the cineplex. I'll drive her through the town square, and we'll peruse the boutiques before we head over to Crow's Creek. I plan on taking her back there once the weather thaws and we can put on one of our Rebels' bonfires, but for tonight, it's simply a place we can go to have some privacy, because if there's one thing I can't get enough of, it's her mouth.

My GPS tells me to take a right, and I'm almost at her house. One more turn, and I'll hit her street. Even though I've picked her up from her house before, I'm still not all too familiar with the route to know it off by heart. I'm hoping that will soon change.

My phone rings beside me on the center console, and when I glance to my right, my stomach sinks at the name illuminated on the screen.

Crenshaw.

I debate ignoring it. Whatever he wants can't be good. It's also likely to ruin my night.

I tighten my grip on the steering wheel, my jaw clenched. Though the ringing stops, the lull is short-lived, and when it starts ringing again a moment later, I curse and answer it.

Crenshaw's voice blasts through the car's speakers, his tone clipped. "I have an assignment," he barks.

I grind my teeth together at the same time my GPS alerts me that I missed my turn. "When?" I ask. *Please, say tomorrow.*

"Now."

Shit. Not only does the idea of canceling on Sky last minute completely suck, but disappointment instantly sweeps through me at the prospect of not getting to see her. "And if I can't?" I ask.

His dark laughter rumbles through the phone. "How much do you value your kneecaps? What about that pretty little brunette of yours?"

Ice fills my veins.

"I don't know who you're talking about," I lie.

"Oh, no? You think I don't do my research, Scott? You think when you started coming to me and gambling, I didn't know what had you so torn up? It's my job to watch my back, so when the new guy has an interest in the police chief's daughter, I take notice."

I close my eyes as relief surges through me, replacing the fear in my bones. For a second, I thought he was talking about Skylar. I wonder if she's in danger, if my mistakes will come back to haunt more than just myself.

Just the thought makes me sick.

I want to tell Crenshaw to fuck off. I want to tell him to pound salt, consequences be damned. But now that he's threatening the people I care about, it's not an option. I might be willing to risk myself, but I'm not willing to risk Mackenzie or Skylar.

"Fine." Every muscle in my body tenses in protest. "What do you need?"

"Meet Frankie outside the hotel. He'll be waiting. When you pull up, he'll climb into your car and you'll pay one of our clients a little visit. They owe me money—a lot of money. It's your job to get it back, by any means necessary. Don't return empty-handed."

I swallow. This was the moment I've been waiting for, the one I feared might come. For weeks, I worked at the front desk at the Bardot, thinking I got off easy. But really, Crenshaw was just waiting for the right moment, the right assignment, to make me pay.

"Don't you have thugs other than Frankie to handle this sort of thing?" Surely, he wants someone less morally inclined for the job. Someone whose heart is as black as his.

The memory of Frankie towering over me, a crowbar gripped in his meaty paws flickers to life, and I shudder.

"You're one of my thugs now, Scott. Consider it your newest title."

Bile rises to the back of my throat. "Why? I blurt out. "Why are you doing this to me? You know I'm not cut out for this shit."

Is he punishing me because I owe him. Because I'm young and stupid and fucked up? For the life of me, I can't figure it out.

"Graham," he chides. "You don't give yourself enough cred-it."

"Why can't Frankie go alone?"

"Because shit goes wrong. Sometimes there are surprises, and if there's two of you, it's less likely. He also doesn't owe me ten fucking grand. Any more questions?"

I clench the steering wheel tighter, my knuckles whitening over the wheel. "Nope," I grind out.

"Good." The amusement in his voice deepens my ire. "Next time, don't question me."

I bang the steering wheel with my hand when the line goes dead, then make a U-turn at the next intersection. As much as I don't want to, I dial Skylar, and she answers on the second ring. "I just finished getting ready. Are you almost here?"

My chest tightens at the sweet sound of her voice. "Skylar, listen, I uh . . ." I swallow, plunging a shaking hand into my hair. "I hate to do this, but something's come up and I have to cancel."

"Oh." I can hear the disappointment in her voice, but she does a good job of smothering it. "Is everything okay?"

"Yeah, it will be, anyway. Just some family stuff. Can I get a rain check?" I ask, hating myself for lying to her, but seeing no other way around it.

"Yeah, of course."

I tell her I'll call her later and hang up, taking the turn at the next light, gunning it as I head toward the city, knowing it's only a short drive from here. The closer I get, the more my chest tightens and the faster the miles pass. I try not to think about the job before me as I pull up outside the hotel and park, but my mind goes there regardless.

Crenshaw expects me to use force to get his money, but there are certain lines I won't cross. Even out of self-preservation, I don't have what it takes to be one of his thugs. I can't break another man's back in order to save my own.

Over the last couple of months, I've done so many things I regret. Made too many mistakes to count. But I'm done sacrificing my integrity. I'm done failing. Which leaves me with the only recourse I've got, paying Crenshaw's client a visit and praying like hell I can convince him to give me the money.

My passenger door swings open, breaking through my thoughts as a blast of cold air sweeps inside. Frankie fills the car, his imposing presence taking up even more space than his hulking form, and before I can say a single word, he's rattling off directions.

Ten minutes later, I pull up to a large brick house. A pink sled is propped up against the garage door, a rogue pair of child-size rainbow boots on the porch.

A knot tightens my stomach at the same time Frankie turns to me, his beady eyes hard on my face. "We're here to see Daniel Miller. As you know, from the poker game you helped us rig, he owes us thirty grand. Crenshaw's given him several extensions, and he keeps jerking his chain. Today, we collect." His jaw hardens to stone. "By any means necessary."

"And if he just doesn't have it?"

Frankie's lips thin. "We make him pay, regardless," he says, his meaning clear.

My gaze shifts back to the front porch. Dread swirls in my stomach. "But how does that help anyone?"

I'm stalling for time, afraid of the man I might become once I walk through that door.

"You don't get it, do you?" Frankie leans toward me, his tone flat. "It's not just about him. We make him pay as a warning to others. It sends a message. Dick us around, and we break your legs. We key your car. Burn the fucking skin from your face. Carve an ear off your head."

I swallow, my breathing shallow as he reaches out and grabs my hand. Turning it over, he places something heavy and cold in my palm. I pull it toward me, staring down at the switchblade gleaming under the streetlight. "Whatever it takes," he says.

I can't breathe as I stare at him in the darkness, wondering what he'll do if I refuse. Will he use the switchblade on me?

Daniel Miller isn't the only one who owes Crenshaw a debt, but I have a feeling going against direct orders and breaking our arrangement will lead to far worse repercussions than money ever could.

"Once you're in, I'll check the perimeter, then watch the door to ensure no one joins us," Frankie says, plowing forward, regardless of whether I'm ready. "If I say we need to roll, you need to get your ass back outside. Otherwise, finish the job. You're either coming out with the money in full or blood on your hands. We don't leave empty-handed," he says, echoing Crenshaw's sentiments.

I stare at him for a moment longer as my blood turns cold.

I need to bail, I know this. I can't bring myself to do what he's asking, but I also can't turn back when I know what the consequences will be.

I'm not sure which makes me the bigger coward.

I swing open my car door and hurry over the concrete sidewalk where I plant my feet and ring the doorbell. A moment later, Miller opens the door. His gaze immediately darts from me to Frankie—who's turned toward the street, surveying our surroundings—and his eyes widen.

"Um, w-wh-what are you doing here?" he stammers out.

"Daniel," I say, forcing a bravado I don't feel. "It's good to see you again. Now, let's get straight to the point, shall we? Crenshaw wants his money. And he wants it now."

Fear dilates his pupils, and I can read his next move before he even makes it.

He steps back and slams the door, but not before I stop it with my side. The wood reverberates backward, and I push my way inside. "Where's the money?"

"I–I–I don't have it. I'm sorry," he says, his voice thick. "I can get it in a few weeks, but I need more time."

"Seriously?" I scrub a hand over my face, contemplating my next move.

The floor creaks behind me. I don't need to look to know it's Frankie, and suddenly, I'm pissed Daniel is making this hard on me. Why can't he just have the fucking money?

Why couldn't I?

I lunge forward and grab a handful of Daniel's shirt. A yelp escapes his throat as I shove him back, his feet stumbling over the carpet.

In the background, the sound of a game show on the television fills the room. Light from the screen flickers over the walls, and the scent of whatever he had for dinner still permeates the air.

I wrench him closer to me, teeth clenched as I grind out, "Where's. Our. Money?"

"I told you." His voice shakes. "I promise I can get it in a few weeks, but I need more time. Please. I'll do anything," he pleads.

"Now. Crenshaw wants it tonight."

"I can't—"

My fist plants into his face, swallowing his words as his head snaps back. His legs crumple, and he falls into a heap on the carpet. I hover over him, my breath coming in short, shallow gasps.

"I don't think you understand," I say, my voice a frantic rasp in my throat. "Do whatever you need to. Borrow it. Fucking sell your car. I don't give a damn how you do it, but get me the money tonight."

Daniel raises his trembling hands in front of his face. "If there was a way I could, I would . . ." The flesh around his eye is red from my fist and already swelling. It's a far cry from what Crenshaw and Frankie expect of me if he doesn't produce, but it makes my stomach churn all the same.

Crouching down, my teeth clench as I fist his shirt in my hand. Frustration bubbles inside of me, hot and thick like lava. I want to scream at him. I want to tear his house down and shake him, rattling his bones until he understands.

I feel Frankie behind me, his gaze boring into my back. "You don't fucking get it, do you?" I hiss, careful not to let Frankie hear what I'm saying. "If you don't give me the money you owe, they won't let me allow you to walk away from this."

A sob rips through Daniel's throat as he shakes his head, and all I see is black.

My insides quake as I contemplate my options, knowing I have little choice.

I wonder what they'll do with my body when they're through with me, because I won't hurt this man. I can't. I may have made mistakes in the past, but I refuse to sacrifice the rest of my character.

On a wing and a prayer, I reach inside my pocket and pull out the knife Frankie gave me, flicking it open in one clean, swift movement. On the off chance he's bluffing, I'm hoping the threat of it will turn the tide and change his mind.

Daniel's eyes flicker to the weapon and a whimper escapes his throat. "Please. I have a little girl upstairs," he says, his voice thick. "She's four."

I swallow and my heart squeezes inside my chest. I suspected as much when we pulled up to his house, but his confirmation only makes the dread swirling in the pit of my stomach worse because he doesn't agree to give me the money. He doesn't acquiesce, or change his mind. He doesn't have it, and if I'm reading him right, he never plans on getting it either.

My hand, the one holding the switchblade, begins to shake as I lean into him. "Do you see the man by the doorway?" I whisper.

His gaze flickers, and he nods. "He won't let me leave here with nothing. Either it's your blood in my hands, or your money. And if I don't finish the job, he will. So, please, if there's any way . . ."

Daniel closes his eyes, pulling a ragged breath into his lungs. "I have seven grand. It's—it's all I could get. I can give you that now and the rest later."

The muscle in my jaw flickers. "That's not even half," I grind out.

A creaking sound to my left draws my attention, and when I glance toward it, the breath catches in my throat. A little girl with braids stares down at me, her eyes round and wide, and her lip quivering beneath them. "Daddy?"

"Shit," I hiss and yank away the knife, pressing it to my side.

"It's okay sweetheart. Daddy's fine. I'm just talking to my friend here, and then I'll come tuck you in. Go back to bed, sweetie."

Her gaze darts to Frankie in the doorway. Tears glisten in her eyes.

"Listen to your father," I say, my voice calm and soothing. "It's okay. We're just having a chat."

When she finally turns away and scurries back up the stairs, I exhale and wipe the sweat beading my brow on my arm, knowing what I have to do.

"Is there a problem, Scott?" Frankie asks, as if he already knows the answer.

I straighten, motioning toward the stairs. "He's got a kid here," I say, hoping this might sway him.

"And . . .?"

"And I'm not a fucking monster," I snap. "Maybe that's your MO, but it's not mine. He's got seven grand. Let's take it and go. Crenshaw can collect the rest in a few weeks."

Frankie's dark eyes flare to life. "No."

I growl as I run a hand through my hair and turn my body toward the living room where the guy slumps, his gaze dull and lifeless as they meet mine as if he already knows his fate.

"This is fucking stupid," I say as I whirl on him.

"Good thing you don't call the shots." He steps forward, his hands bunching into fists, and I do what I should've done weeks ago when Crenshaw dragged me into his car and that secluded stretch of woods.

I push my shoulders back, my muscles coiling, preparing for a fight. I have no idea if he's armed or not, but I'm willing to take my chances. I'll fight to my last fucking breath if it means protecting the people in this house. "We're leaving. Now."

Frankie barks out a laugh. "Is that so?"

"Daniel will never show his face again around the Bardot or the Gentleman's Club." Beside me, Daniel frantically nods his head in agreement. "Then we're going to get in the car and leave, and tell Crenshaw he didn't have the money, but we took care of it. As long as Daniel never steps foot near him again, he'll never know the difference."

Frankie scoffs. "You've got some balls on you, I'll give you that."

He runs a hand over the back of his neck before he takes a few steps toward Daniel, but I place a palm on his chest to stop him, my intentions clear. "I won't let you do that."

Something flickers in his eyes. "You got a death wish, kid?"

"If I die on this hill, so be it. I won't be Crenshaw's puppet again."

Frankie stares at me, his jaw ticking. To my utter shock, he nods, then glances at Daniel. "You have the seven grand?"

Daniel scrambles to his feet. "It's in the safe."

"Get it," Frankie snaps.

Daniel hurries from the room, returning a few minutes later with a bag of cash he hands over to Frankie. "If Crenshaw ever sees you anywhere near his establishment again, he'll kill you, and your little girl, too. Do you understand me?"

"Yes." Daniel's throat bobs, his eyes bright with relief as Frankie turns away from him and for the door, motioning for me to follow.

Once we're outside, I inhale, nearly giddy with relief. "What will we tell Crenshaw?"

The muscle in Frankie's jaw ticks for a minute before he says, "Let me handle Crenshaw."

After I drop Frankie off at the hotel, I'm jumpy. Antsy with the need to see Skylar and take my mind off everything that just happened.

My mind races as I replay the evening. I still have no idea what made Frankie change his mind, but I can't help the sinking in the pit of my stomach, telling me it's not over yet. If Crenshaw catches wind that I went soft on the guy and let him go, I'm a dead man. No amount of pleading my case will persuade him to go easy on me.

I shudder as I stop at a red light, realizing I need Skylar because she's the only thing capable of drowning out the images dancing in my head. Those amber eyes, her gravelly voice, that gorgeous smile . . . I press my lids closed and try to push away the picture of the little girl with the braids, but it's seared in my head along with the look of fear in her small, round eyes.

My hand shakes as I pull out my phone and shoot off a text to Skylar.

Graham: *You still home? I finished up early, and I really need to see you.*

Skylar: *When you canceled, JD took me to dinner, but we just got here. You should join us.*

I exhale and run a hand over the back of my neck, unsure of whether I'm up for meeting her brother under the circumstances. JD means so much to her and it's imperative he like me, but my head's a fucking mess. I can't stop thinking about everything that just transpired and what the aftermath might be.

Skylar knows nothing about Crenshaw, nor my past mistakes with gambling. What would she think of me if she did?

I hate the thought that her feelings might change.

I chew on the inside of my cheek as all my insecurities rise to the surface, making my need to see her even stronger.

Graham: *You're sure he doesn't mind?*

Skylar: *Not at all. It was his idea.*

Skylar: *Pleeeaase come.*

A grin spreads my lips as another text pings with a pin to her location.

I click on it, opening my GPS. The restaurant is only ten minutes away, so I get there quickly and find a parking space in the back.

I get out and make my way inside, giving myself a little pep talk as I enter. The restaurant is small but crowded. Waiters brush past me, heading toward the kitchen. My gaze flickers over the crowded bar and desire slides through me. It would be all too easy to numb the details of my evening with something stronger than water. But because I'd rather have Skylar, I keep walking.

I weave past the first couple of tables when I spot her seated in the back of the small dining space at the same time she lifts her head and catches my eye. Her smile is instantaneous, and it's exactly what I need to loosen the vice on my chest.

Dark hair spills over her shoulders and her eyes brighten under the pendant lights above. "Hey!" She stands to greet me, and I pull her into my arms, breathing her in.

My face presses into her neck. She's like a salve to my wounds. Now that I'm with her everything is better, and when I quickly pull away, I remember myself again and glance to the chairs around her to find them vacant.

"Your brother . . . ?" My eyebrows pull together.

"In the restroom."

I nod, grateful for the moment to collect myself as I take a seat beside her. The warmth of her palm seers into my skin as I reach out and take her hand in mine, pretending like the last hour never happened. Pretending for a moment that meeting her here with her brother was always the plan.

"Everything okay?" she asks with a little laugh.

My fingers lace through hers, and I close the distance, brushing a soft kiss over her mouth. "It is now," I murmur. "I just needed to see you."

"Glad I could help." Her grin says it all as she leans into me once more and steals another kiss.

Someone clears their throat beside us, and we jerk apart. Skylar chuckles at the same time I glance up to find the source of our interruption, and all the blood drains from my face.

Crenshaw.

My lungs seize as I try and draw a breath.

I think of all the reasons he might be here at the restaurant standing before me, the most plausible being that Frankie told him I flaked. Not only did I fail to get him his money, but I disregarded his orders.

I straighten in my seat, slightly angling my body in front of Skylar in a protective stance when I register both surprise and anger flaring in his eyes, and I frown.

Something tells me he's every bit as shocked by my presence as I am his.

My mind races as Skylar pushes her chair out and stands, then places an arm around him.

My eyes zero in on the place where they touch, her bright smile, the pride shining in her amber gaze, and my stomach takes a nosedive.

No . . .

A chill creeps up my spine, and even as the words leave her mouth, I don't want to believe them. My mind won't compute.

"Graham, I'd like you to meet JD."

CHAPTER 33

GRAHAM

I CAN'T WRAP MY head around what my eyes and ears are telling me, that JD Davenport and Darrell Crenshaw are one and the same.

What. The. Actual. Fuck?

If I weren't staring up at him with my own two eyes, I wouldn't believe it.

Skylar's smile slowly fades the longer I stare without saying anything.

I haven't budged an inch, and though I know I need to do something or say something, I can't seem to make my body cooperate.

Miraculously, it's Crenshaw that makes the first move. He extends his hand to mine as I manage to push back my chair and stand on rubbery legs. "Nice to meet you," he says, taking the lead.

His gaze is full of meaning.

It tells me not to say anything, to keep my mouth shut.

I clear my throat. "Um, yeah, you, too," I force out, hoping it doesn't sound as strained as it feels.

I don't need to ask to know he's none too pleased that I'm the boy Skylar's been spending time with. I can feel it in the way he squeezes my hand a little too tightly, and I can see it in the tight set of his mouth.

Not that I give a fuck what he thinks.

When he releases me, he and Skylar take their seats while I hover on my feet, unsure of whether to stay or flee.

"You didn't tell me the boy you were seeing worked at the hotel," JD says, his voice tight with accusation.

Skylar's eyes flicker to me, and the concern creasing her brow forces me back in my chair. "Um, I didn't?" she asks, tucking a lock of hair behind her ear.

"No."

My gaze narrows on Crenshaw, unhappy with the dickish tone he's taking with her.

"Well, I'm sorry. I thought I had," Skylar says, her tone flippant, and this time, it's my turn to be pissed. How could she not tell me JD owned the fucking hotel? How could she keep this from both of us, like it's an insignificant detail?

Even if I didn't know JD elsewhere, it's the kind of information a guy would want to know before jumping into a relationship with the boss's little sister.

A vein in JD's forehead pulses. "No. You told me you met when you were hanging out with Mal."

"Well, we did, actually," she says, smiling as she likely remembers that day at the bar. "I was shocked when he showed up at work a couple days later."

JD nods along with her story before he turns his icy gaze to mine. "Interesting."

My mind races as I recall everything I know about Skylar and her brother, looking for clues I missed that might have led to the truth.

A memory flickers to life as I remember the charcoal sketch in the office of the Gentleman's Club. It was hers, I'm almost certain of it now.

Then there's the way she rushed out of the house when I picked her up so he wouldn't know she was seeing someone at work, and how readily she agreed to keeping us quiet with our coworkers.

JD's desire for her to stay on at the hotel, even after graduation, suddenly makes a lot more sense. It's the family business—her legacy.

I can't help but feel duped. Bamboozled.

"Why didn't you tell me your brother owned the hotel?" I ask.

Her throat bobs. "I just assumed you knew. It's not like it's a secret." She gives a sheepish shrug. "And okay, maybe I didn't specifically mention it because I didn't want to remind you.

I hate people thinking I get special treatment. It's one of the reasons I work so hard. Is it really that important?"

"You should've told me," I say, ignoring her question.

Because it's not just important. In this case, it's fucking paramount, and I have no idea what this means. All I know is a giant flashing caution sign is going off in my head, and I don't know what to do about it.

When Skylar deflates, I take a calming breath, trying to ease the anxiety ratcheting up my spine. She can't help who her brother is any more than I can, and though she should've told me, it's not like she had reason to believe JD and I already knew each other in a whole other, less pleasant, capacity.

I reach underneath the table and give her knee a little squeeze. The last thing I want is to make her feel bad about it, especially when my gut tells me she has no idea who her brother *really* is. Hell, I don't even want to entertain the idea that she might, because as it is, our situation is already fucked.

I can feel Crenshaw's eyes peering over at me in the tense silence, but I refuse to meet them. Instead, I keep my gaze focused on Skylar when a waitress pauses in front of us. "Is everybody ready to order?"

"Can we have a few minutes?" Skylar asks.

The waitress tells us to take our time, and once she's gone, Skylar turns to her brother. "Are we good?" she asks, and if I didn't already know how much his opinion matters to her, I can see it in her eyes.

"Of course," he says, forcing a smile. "If you're happy, I'm happy. That's all that matters to me."

I call bullshit, but her relief is palpable as she turns to me and squeezes my hand. "See? It's all good. I'm just going to use the restroom while you're looking at the menu." She pats my shoulder and stands. "Why don't you two talk, get to know each other." Then, before I can stop her, she walks across the dining room, leaving us alone.

My gaze is still on her back when Crenshaw's voice slithers through me like a snake. "I thought you were busy tonight? Don't you have a job to do?"

So, he doesn't know we've finished, which means he hasn't spoken with Frankie.

I'm not sure whether to be relieved or worried.

"Frankie hasn't updated you yet?" I *tsk* and shake my head. "Sounds like a communication problem with your right-hand man."

"Did you finish the job or not?" he snaps.

"I'm here, aren't I?" My back prickles with sweat. "Did you know Daniel's daughter would be at home when we paid him a visit?"

Crenshaw's eyes narrow, but he says nothing. It dawns on me in that moment that he has just as much to lose as I do, if not more, when Skylar finds out who he really is.

"Tell me, does your sister know about your other line of business? What do you think she'd say if she did?"

The vein in his forehead pulses despite his poker face, and I have my answer. "You're done seeing my sister," he says, so matter-of-fact, it makes me laugh.

"Sorry, but you might be able to tell me what to do in my professional life, but not my personal one."

"That's where you're wrong, you naive little fuck," he hisses. His face twists with rage as he leans closer. "I own you, Scott, and don't you forget it."

"What about your sister? Do you own her, too? Because it seems to me she's perfectly capable of deciding who she wants to date."

I'm a fool for not keeping my mouth shut, but I can't seem to help myself. Crenshaw might be pissed I'm the one Skylar's seeing, but I'm fucking enraged that the one girl to break through my walls and make me feel something other than Mackenzie is my debtor's sister.

Crenshaw leans back in his chair, eyeing me for a moment as his lips curl in a cruel smile that's somehow more frightening than his ire.

"I'll give you tonight," he says, toying with the rim of his water glass. "You can have your little dinner with her and drive her home, then you'll break it off. And if you don't," his eyes glitter, "I'll have Frankie take care of you like you took care of Daniel tonight."

A light bulb goes off. *If he hasn't spoken to Frankie yet, why does he assume Daniel didn't pay?*

"You knew Daniel wouldn't have the money," I say.

His grin turns serpentine and he chuckles. "Of course I did. Guys like him never have the money." His expression grows serious. "Desperation has a scent."

My hands fist on top of the table, drawing Crenshaw's eye. "So, you don't want Skylar dating someone like yourself, is that it?" I ask, allowing him to think I actually did my job tonight—that I took Daniel out.

"Of course I fucking don't!" he shouts, causing several people to glance our way. "She is everything we're not. She's innocent and sweet and everything good in this fucked-up world, and you'll keep your dirty paws off her, you hear me?"

My resolve hardens. "If you force my hand, I'll tell her about you."

A beat of silence stretches between us, the air around us sharp with tension, like the crack of a bullwhip.

A smile touches his lips, but it doesn't reach his eyes. "If you did that, it would implicate you as well, and you don't want Skylar knowing about your extracurricular activities any more than I do. Tell me . . ." he says, tilting his head, eyes narrowed on my face. "Do you really think Skylar would be interested in a loser like you, if she knew who you really were?"

I flinch at the force of his words. Because they're true, and they play on every single vulnerability I've ever had where Skylar is concerned. That I'm not good enough for her. That I'm broken and flawed. Lost and wandering.

That if I fall for someone, I'll only wind up getting hurt again.

I say nothing as I turn my head, hating how much his words hit the mark.

"That's what I thought." He scoffs at my reaction. "You're nothing more than a spoiled brat with a gambling habit who can't hold his liquor."

My nostrils flare, and I want to tell him he's wrong, that I care about her more than I ever thought possible, especially after getting my heart broken, but I can't seem to make my mouth work.

"Skylar is going places," he continues, pushing back his chair, "and you're not going with her."

He pulls a wad of cash from his wallet and throws it on the table with a flourish as he looks me in the eye one last time. "You have until midnight. After tonight, I won't be so forgiving." He winks as he skirts the table. "Dinner's on me."

He turns and finds Skylar on her way back from the restroom, and like a car crash, I can't help but watch the man I hate say something to her I can't hear, pulling a smile from her lips before heading out the door.

CHAPTER 34

SKYLAR

WHEN GRAHAM PULLS UP to my house a few hours later, my insides twist with worry.

He turns the car off, hesitating a moment before he glances over at me in the moonlight, his eyes soft. After JD begged off, claiming an emergency at the hotel, we stayed and had dinner together, and though we ate and talked, something felt off. And if the way he's looking at me—like it's for the last time—is any indication of what he's thinking, I'm not going to like what he's about to say.

Reaching out, he tucks a lock of hair behind my ear, and I have half a mind to ask him to come inside before I think better of it. I have no idea when JD will be home, and he seemed none too pleased about my dating Graham as it is. Somehow, I doubt he'd appreciate my being alone with a boy in the house without his knowledge.

"See you tomorrow?" I ask, hopeful I'm just imagining the tension between us.

"Uh, actually, I can't make it tomorrow." He ruffles a hand through his hair as an emotion I can't decipher flits through his eyes.

"*Okay*. How about Sunday? We could have lunch together?"

"I'm actually going to be pretty busy."

My stomach clenches. I know I'm getting the brush off, but I don't want to believe it. "That never seemed to stop us from seeing each other before."

He nods. "I know. It's just with signing day right around the corner and the pressure from my father, I need to figure out what I'm going to do, you know?"

I do know. Everything he's saying makes perfect sense. Though he told his friends he was signing with Penn State, he confided in me it was his father's decision, not his. Yet I can't shake the hollow feeling in my chest that says there's more to why he can't see me.

"Okaaaay," I drawl, trying not to take it personal.

"Thanks for understanding." He reaches out and squeezes my hand.

"Is something else going on?" I ask. Not one to sit with my emotions, I meet his eyes and straighten, preparing myself for whatever comes of the conversation we're about to have. No matter what, I can handle it. I'm strong. Resilient. Independent. I can handle anything that comes my way. "Because I'm sensing a shift between us, like something's happened that I'm not aware of."

"No," he answers immediately. But then his brow creases and his green eyes cloud over. "It's just . . . I don't know. So much is in the air for both of us. Soon, we'll be going to different colleges. I don't know how long I'll work at the hotel, so it'll be hard to even see each other. Maybe we'd be better off, I don't know, cooling it for a bit? Before we get even more invested."

His words hit me like a lightning bolt. They were the last thing I expected.

I can't breathe. Can't even think. I knew something felt off, but I thought he was merely upset with me for not telling him JD owned the hotel.

I count to five in my head, trying to get a handle on my thoughts. I have no right to feel the sharp stab of devastation. It's not like we're serious. We've only been seeing each other a couple of weeks—known each other only one short month—but I don't want us to end. I don't want to put the brakes on no matter how complicated things might be.

I open my mouth to speak, surprised when my voice works. "Us going to college never seemed to bother you before."

"Things just feel more complicated now. I mean, your brother's my boss, Skylar."

"Is that what this is about?" I ask, feeling like we're only halfway to the truth. "You just said so yourself, you're not sure how long you'll even be working at the hotel, so who cares if JD owns the Bardot?"

"It's not all about that, but I feel like it matters."

"Then I'll quit." It's rash, but I mean it. I'd leave in a heartbeat if it meant keeping Graham. I don't plan to be here this time next year anyway.

"You can't do that." He shakes his head. "Your brother needs you."

"No. JD *wants* me to work there. He wants to control me so I can never leave him, and he feels secure in believing nothing can ever happen to me if I'm nearby," I say, realizing how true my words are. "But I've told him I don't want that for my future. And maybe he doesn't want to listen to me, but it doesn't make it any less true. If I leave my job now, before I even graduate, maybe he'll finally accept that I'm not going to stay forever like he wants."

"Listen . . ." Graham soothes my ragged nerves as he reaches out and takes me in his arms. It feels like home, even though home is outside this car door. "Don't quit, okay? Whatever this is," he says, looking in my eyes, "we'll figure it out."

I fall silent, willing him to say something else because his words are telling me we still have a chance, but the resignation in his eyes is telling me we don't. "So, we're still going to see each other?"

"At work, yeah." He nods, his throat bobbing. "We'll figure the rest out later."

"Right." I drop my gaze, recognizing the rejection for what it is. He's clearly through with me; he just doesn't want to hurt my feelings. "Is this the part where you say you want to just be friends? It's not you, it's me?"

"Skylar . . ."

I hate the pleading in his tone. Loathe it, in fact. Because that's all it is—a plea for me to somehow numb my feelings, to magically feel good about the end of us when he's all I want.

I bite the inside of my cheek, finding the courage to speak through the tightness in my throat. "I get it, honestly," I say, my voice even. "Like you said, we're both busy. It's probably best I focus completely on my project for the competition, anyway. Now isn't the time for distractions."

I want him to call me out on labeling him a distraction, but he doesn't. Instead, he simply nods, his mouth parting as if he wants to say something else but doesn't know if he should.

He sighs and presses his lips together as if strengthening his resolve before he stares out into the dark street.

I wonder why he's so determined to bury us.

With every ounce of dignity I have left, I push my shoulders back and place my hand on the door handle, hating that we're ending our night like this—with him pushing me away instead of pulling me in for a kiss like I want him to.

"It was fun while it lasted," I manage, and then I brace myself for the wave of sadness that hits as I step out into the cold.

CHAPTER 35

SKYLAR

A FTER SCHOOL, I SIT with Mal at Dixie's, one of the local hangouts in Oak Ridge. It's my day off, but Graham's working, and after spending the entirety of my shift on Saturday wishing and hoping for him to drop by and see me, I decided I needed to get out and clear my head. If I don't, I might pop by the hotel, and the last thing I need to do is show my face there like I'm a stray dog that can't find its way home, especially when Graham made it clear he wants distance.

I slurp the dregs of my milkshake through the straw, desperate to consume every last drop like it holds the key to all my problems.

"So let me get this straight." Mal wrinkles her nose. "He cancels your plans, shows up a little over an hour later, thrilled to see you, and then, after an awkward dinner where he met JD, he basically breaks things off on the ride home?"

I grimace. "Basically."

"It makes no sense."

"It doesn't," I agree, shoving my empty cup aside.

"Something had to happen between the time he arrived at the restaurant and you left. Did you check out another guy? Say something to piss him off?"

"No. What makes you so sure this is my fault?" I ask defensively. "I mean, I admit he seemed a little bothered by the fact that I hadn't told him JD owned the hotel, and JD was surprised the guy I've been hanging out with works there, but—"

"Do you think that's it?" Mal asks, her eyes bright.

I bite my lip, thinking it through just as I have done for the past couple of days, and I still don't have an answer. "I don't know. We've been quiet about the fact that we were seeing each other, but I'm the owner's sister, it's not like we're gonna get fired over it. Besides, I don't even think JD has anything to do with who gets hired and fired; that's Frankie's job since he manages the place."

"Are you sure he sees it that way? Maybe Graham's worried about keeping his job?"

"I doubt it. He even said something about not working at the hotel for long." I screw up my face. "Something about this whole thing seems off."

"So, what else, then? JD left dinner early. Do you really think he had a work emergency, or could it be he was pissed about Graham? He's so overprotective, I just can't imagine him not seizing the opportunity to stay and grill the boy you're seeing."

My mouth parts as I consider it. "You're right. I suppose JD might have said something to him in my absence. But do you really think he'd do that?"

Mal arches a brow. "I'd bet my life on it."

My chest tightens. "But I told JD we weren't serious, that we'd just been hanging out. Like, I really downplayed us to him. He had no reason to get so protective, and after his initial shock, he seemed cool about it."

"I'm sure JD can read between the lines." She reaches a hand out to me, placing it over mine. "Hell, I've only seen you two interact a few times, and I can tell you firsthand, you'd have to be blind not to see sparks fly. I mean, do you really think JD expects you to tell him that you felt him up the other night in the boy's locker room while he pressed you against his locker with his tongue down your throat and a hand up your shirt?"

"Mal!"

"What?" She laughs and spreads her arms out. "Are you telling me you lied and that's not what happened when you recounted every minute detail to me in perfect, steamy precision?"

My cheeks flush as I smash my lips into a thin line.

She's right. I know JD too well. This is new territory for him. Sure, I've had crushes on boys in the past, but never anything like this. And I've never had anything close to resembling a boyfriend. I have no idea how JD would act in such a situation, but if past behavior is any indication, he wouldn't handle it well.

My teeth clench as I think of the possibility. The more I mull it over, the more it makes sense.

I fist my hand, pounding it on the table in front of me. "I swear, if JD had something to do with this, I'm going to strangle him."

"Down girl." Mal grins. "I don't disagree with throttling JD. In fact, I'll even do it for you, but first, you need to do some damage control."

I sigh, at a loss of how to make things better. "I'm not sure there's any changing Graham's mind. Besides, he's my first kiss, Mal. No one ends up with their first kiss," I say, hating that it's true.

I recall the look on his face and how resolute he sounded. Cooling things off is most definitely what he wanted. And after what happened with Mackenzie, his best friend, he's already guarded. He won't want to risk getting his heart broken again. He probably thinks he's protecting himself.

But then, I remember what Teagan said about how when Graham gets scared, he resurrects walls around himself. I just need to carry the sledgehammer. The only problem is I can't be certain that's what's happening here.

I like Graham—more than like him. In fact, I'm hesitant to put a label on this uncontrollable feeling inside me because it's unlike anything I've ever felt before.

And because it's too early.

We've only been hanging out for a month. It can't be anything more than like or lust. All I know is that every moment I'm not with him, I want to be, and until the other night, I thought he felt the same way.

"Your parents were high school sweethearts," Mal points out.

"And their love never died," she says.

I huff out a breath, thinking about it.

From everything I've been told, Graham fought for Mackenzie and lost. But who's fighting for Graham?

Maybe it's about time someone does.

Maybe Teagan's right. Maybe I've been carrying around this sledgehammer, and now is the right time to use it.

CHAPTER 36

GRAHAM

A WEEK HAS PASSED since the night I broke things off with Skylar, and Crenshaw has yet to confront me about my inability to follow through with Daniel, or check in with me about whether I broke things off with Skylar. I can only assume he confirmed the latter, but I have no idea why he has yet to approach me about Daniel. I can only imagine he has several reasons for why he hasn't beaten my ass for going against direct orders. Either Frankie hasn't told him, or he's choosing to let it slide. The latter seems unlikely, considering he's already pissed about me and Skylar. Or maybe he's picking his battles. Who knows?

I'm still reeling from ending things so suddenly with Skylar. Even if Crenshaw hadn't made demands, I can't imagine how she and I could ever work under the circumstances. Being with her would mean either telling her the truth about her brother and crushing her, or maintaining Crenshaw's secrets.

It's like the situation with my father and mother all over again. And I fucking hate it.

If I hadn't broken up with her, every day forward would be a lie. I know what kind of monster he is, and he's seen the worst parts of me. He knows my sins probably better than anyone else. Even if he allowed me to date Skylar, his presence would be a constant reminder of everything I hate about myself.

Every day since that night, I've been trying to convince myself that breaking things off with her was for the best, the right thing to do. I told myself I wasn't ready for a relationship, not after Mackenzie. I remind myself we'll both be moving away at the end of the summer and relationships are hard enough without putting the added strain of long distance between us. I tell myself a lot of things that all sound like bullshit because none of them trump the simple fact that she makes me happy, and ever since she came into my life, she's made it better. So much better.

Seeing her in passing all week has been excruciating. I don't know if she's doing it on purpose, but I swear every outfit she's worn has been carefully curated, all of them to perfectly show-case her curves. On the days she's not working, she still comes into the office, each day with an excuse. One was to reclaim the sweater she left. Another to have lunch with Rosa. Yesterday, she worked with fucking Brad on some damn wedding that's coming up. The days she's not here, I can smell her perfume lingering at the desk like she pumped it through the vents. It's driving me fucking crazy.

Even now, as I sit at one of the tables in the lobby across from Storm, I can't help but watch her out of the corner of my eye. After all this time, I'm struck by the sight of her. My heart beats faster in her presence like I'm fucking twelve again with my first crush.

The palms of my hands grow damp with sweat, and something inside my chest pinches as she tosses her dark hair over her shoulder and smiles at a male patron.

"*Hello*, earth to Graham." Storm snaps his fingers in my face, and I jerk my head, turning my attention back to him.

"Sorry. I zoned out for a minute."

Storm snorts. "Ya think? You and Skylar still not talking?"

"We're talking," I grumble. Sort of. In truth, I'm not sure I've mumbled so much as a hello to her since our ill-fated dinner.

"Right. She told me you broke things off."

My eyes narrow at him. "She did?"

He shrugs. "Pretty much."

"Well, what did she say about it?"

Storm glances up at me from his hand of cards and scoffs. "Wouldn't you like to know."

"Hey, am I your brother, or is she?"

"Since you decided to dump one of the hottest girls I've ever seen, maybe I've decided to disown you."

My jaw drops. "You little shit," I hiss once I recover. Storm laughs as I mumble, "And I didn't dump her."

He arches a brow, calling me on my shit, and I bow my head.

In the past few weeks, he and I have been spending a lot more time together, but since cooling it with Skylar, I see him nearly every day. He keeps me company while I work, and I've taken to helping him with his homework after school. Several nights, I've even watched him while Marie works late.

"Chill, bro," Storm says, sounding like one of the guys. "All she said about it was that you're right, and it's probably for the best."

I frown, straightening in my chair as I risk another glance at her. I should be happy she isn't heartbroken, comforted that she sees the sense in the bullshit excuses I gave her.

But I'm not, because my reasons for breaking it off were just that: bullshit.

I turn back to our game of cards with a heavy heart.

"If you like her so much, why'd you end it?" Storm asks, seeing straight through me.

"Who said I liked her that much?"

"Dude, I might be ten, but do I look blind to you?"

I sigh, barely restraining myself from lowering my head to the table in front of us and banging it against the hard surface. "It's complicated."

He lifts a shoulder, playing his hand. "You like her and she likes you. Doesn't seem all that complicated to me."

I'm about to give him some generic explanation when Marie bustles through the front door of the hotel and heads toward us. "Sorry I'm late," she says, dropping a kiss on Storm's head.

"They had me doing some last-minute paperwork so that I can start collecting benefits."

I stand, shoving my hands in my pockets, not yet totally comfortable in Marie's presence. She and I don't have the best relationship for obvious reasons, but I know I need to make it work for Storm's sake. I like to think she and I have come to a kind of impasse—one where we don't speak about my father or the fact that her entire presence in town will likely flip my family on its side. Instead, we focus solely on Storm, and so far, it's worked for us.

"It's no problem." I glance at my watch. "I don't start for another five minutes, anyway."

She nods, giving me a small smile. "Thanks for keeping an eye on him."

"Sure thing." I reach out, slapping Storm's hand. "Later, man."

When I turn around, I catch Skylar's eye, only for her to quickly drop her gaze and busy herself with something on the computer.

I take a deep breath and make my way to the front desk, hating the pit in the bottom of my stomach. It's the first day we've been scheduled to work together since I cooled things with her, and I expect it to be brutal. In truth, I'm shocked Crenshaw didn't fire me on the spot. But then, he takes the debts owed to him seriously, and I also can't help but feel like this might be some kind of test to see where my loyalty lies. If I've learned anything about the man over the course of the past couple of months, it's that Crenshaw might not stalk his prey, but he likes to play with his food.

I round the desk as Skylar bends over her sketchbook. Her dark hair falls to the side of her face, obscuring her sketch from view, which only makes me want to reach out and look at it even more.

"Hey," I say, scuffing the floor with the toe of my shoe.

"Hey," she snaps the sketchbook shut, glancing at me in surprise like she hadn't seen me. "Glad you're here. Brad needs some help with seating arrangements for that big wedding next month and asked if I could help. If you don't mind manning the desk, we'll probably just work back here." She motions toward the little nook behind us, decked out with an end table and a couple of chairs.

"Sure, no problem." My brow furrows as she snatches up her phone and taps out a text message without even looking at me.

"Great. If you need anything, just give a holler." She stands so fast my head spins, brushing past me as if she can't get away fast enough.

My arm darts out, and I grip her wrist in my hand. "Hey, are we good?" I ask, waiting for her answer, even though it's a stupid question. Of course we're not fucking good.

She frowns like she has no idea what I'm talking about, and I have the urge to shake the unflappable expression from her face to get down to the real emotion beneath. "Yeah, why wouldn't we be?" She flashes me a small smile, like I'm the weird one for thinking we might not be okay.

I drop her arm, unsure of what I expected as I ignore the wrenching inside my chest and clear my throat. "I was just checking."

She nods and no sooner than she steps away from me to one of the chairs in the corner does Brad appear. In his arms, he carries a laptop and some paperwork. He sits them down on the table between them before he catches me staring. A smug smile spreads across his cocky face, and he winks as he pulls Skylar's chair out for her.

Fucking asshole.

I turn away from them and log into the reservation portal with my employee ID, trying to busy myself. The last thing I want to do is give Brad the impression that him spending time with her bothers me.

Despite my best intentions, thirty minutes later, I'm in agony. The soft murmurs of their voices drift toward me. And no matter how much I try to drown them out, I can't. Their laughter claws at my back, and I have to fight the urge to spin around and ask what's so fucking funny. Instead, I turn and leer at them like a creep.

Skylar wears a broad smile on her face as Brad hovers over her to mark something on the papers spread out in front of them. Another laugh rumbles from the back of her throat, but this time, Brad presses a finger to her lips to silence her, and I see red.

The muscle in my jaw twitches as I stare at the finger over her perfect lips.

I hate that she's even talking to him, let alone laughing and flirting with him. I hate that he's touching her. I hate that this is all my fault.

But what gets me the most is how she's doing it right in front of me.

A throat clears at my back and I begrudgingly spin around to wait on a guest. I check the woman into her hotel room, run her credit card, and activate the keycards, which I grumpily push over the counter to her. It wasn't all that long ago, I was flirting with the female guests to get under Skylar's skin, and it pisses me off that the tables have turned.

A few minutes later, I note the time and glance over my shoulder, annoyed they're still huddled together. What the hell could possibly take so long to figure out a freaking seating chart? Just put some names at some tables and be done with it.

"Isn't it time for your dinner break?" I ask. Her shift started well before mine, and I know for a fact she's been here nearly five hours.

"You hungry?" Brad asks, and I want to punch him in his stupid mouth.

"I could eat." She smiles, and before I know it, they rise from their seats *together* with me staring after them. "We'll be back in thirty minutes," she calls behind her.

My nostrils flare as I watch them leave together, a heavy feeling inside my chest sinking into my gut and burning up my insides like acid.

I try to busy myself while she's gone. I refill the water pitcher in the lobby and make fresh coffee. I organize the desk and clean the computer screen. I even rearrange the fucking brochures and takeout menus. But nothing helps to take my mind off what they're doing at dinner and what they could possibly be talking about. I thought she despised Brad.

Later, once they return, Skylar takes a seat on the couch in front of the lobby fireplace while Brad heads down the hallway, and I seize the opportunity to confront her.

Crossing the room, I stop at the foot of the couch, towering over her. "Are you flirting with him in front of me on purpose?"

Her eyes widen, shock brightening the amber to gold. "What?"

I cross my arms over my chest, eyes narrowed on her as if I'll be able to interrogate the truth out of her. "You've been flirting with him ever since I got here," I say, waving a hand toward the hallway where he disappeared.

"We're working on that huge wedding next month. It's a massive account, and he needs help planning some of the details. I'm helping him."

"Right." I roll my eyes, hating how bitter I sound. "It takes two fucking hours to put some faceless names at a table."

She stands and throws her hands up. "What do you want from me, Graham? First, you break things off, and then you're pissed I'm talking to another guy, even if it's just a work thing? What the hell do you expect me to do? Wallow in the corner?

Beg you to change your mind? I tried to make you see sense that night in your car and it didn't work."

I take a step closer, breathing her in. Every muscle in my arms aches for me to reach out and draw her into my chest. If she only knew how much I wanted her, she wouldn't think twice about talking to Brad, or anyone else for that matter.

But she's right. I'm being an asshole. I can't expect her to be miserable just because I am.

I glance away from her, staring out the window as I debate on what to say to her. I hate the thought of her thinking I don't want her when it couldn't be furthest from the truth. There are a lot of things I haven't told her—things about my past, the gambling—things I'm not proud of. But for some reason, this is one omission I can't bear the most.

I open my mouth, ready to tell her I still want her just as much as I always did when I catch fucking Brad out of the corner of my eye, making his way toward us.

Apparently, they're not done.

His gaze dances between us, a glimmer of a threat in his voice as he asks, "Everything okay over here?"

When Skylar doesn't answer right away, he leans into her like I can't hear him, asking, "Is he bothering you?"

"I'm right fucking here," I growl.

Skylar shakes her head, turning her back on me as she tells him no, and I feel her dismissal in every bone of my body.

I want to yank her to me and wrap her arms around me. I want to press my lips against hers, feel her throaty moans against my tongue.

I want a million things I can't fucking have, and it makes me furious.

I turn away from them, watching as they take a seat beside each other on the couch and resume working like I was never there.

Hovering beside the coffee station behind them, I fix myself a cup, even though caffeine is the last thing I need. I don't even try to pretend I'm not eavesdropping. They're too lost in conversation to notice anyway.

"You know, Skylar, I owe you an apology," Brad says.

I nearly spill coffee down my shirt. Tensing, I wait for whatever BS he's about to spew as I add a gallon of creamer to my coffee cup.

"It was wrong of me to sway my mother with the scholarship," he says. "You should've won. You by far have the most talent out of anyone at Oak Ridge."

You think, asshole?

"So, why do it?" she asks. "I had nothing to do with Graham throwing those punches," she says.

I grimace.

"You really don't know?" Brad barks out a laugh as I stack several sugar packets together and tear the top off, pretending it's his head. "Skylar, I've been in love with you for years. I thought I was obvious, but apparently not. It doesn't make what I did any less shitty, but I was having a rough week, and I just thought . . . I hoped when I saw you at O'Malley's that night you'd finally give me a chance. But, not only did you turn me down once again, some stranger's coming to your rescue, and I thought . . . hell, I didn't know if you were with him or what, but my pride was crushed, and I made a mistake."

Silence follows, and I want so badly to turn around and see the look on Skylar's face, to read her expressive eyes to tell what she's thinking. It's then, I glance down at the empty pile of creamers and sugar packets, and I realize I've been fixing Skylar's coffee.

Behind me she sighs, and I'm sure she's about to put him in his place when she says, "It's fine, Brad. I mean, it sucked, but it's over now, and I'm not one to hold a grudge."

What. The. Fuck?

She's just gonna let him off the hook like that?

He clears his throat, sounding nervous as he asks, "Well, if you'll let me, I'd like to take you out sometime and make it up to you."

I stiffen.

Say no.

A pause follows, and I squeeze my eyes closed, bracing my hands on the counter of the coffee bar knowing her answer might kill me.

I have zero claim to her. I know it, and yet I still can't help but turn green at the thought of her going out on a date with another guy so soon after we decided to cool it. Especially with fucking Brad.

As if sensing her coming rejection, Brad says, "Just think about it."

"Um, yeah, okay. Sure."

Sure, she'll go out with him, or sure, she'll think about it?

Shit, I feel like I'm losing my damned mind.

My heart pounds in my chest as I remind myself she's free to date whomever she wants. She and I were never official, and whatever we had I broke off last week.

I scrub a hand over my face and push away from the counter, turning to find her eyes on mine. Brad is no longer sitting beside her, and I wonder how long I stood there, brooding and too jealous to notice anything else.

She breaks eye contact first, then gets up and heads toward the hallway where she disappears, only to return a few minutes later with her winter coat.

Her shift is over. Brad monopolized what little time I had with her, and it pisses me off even if it shouldn't.

I stare as the doorman opens the door for her, allowing her to exit, and she fades from view.

My legs twitch to follow, and before I can stop myself, I'm running after her. I burst outside. The cold bites at my cheeks as I glance around for her. Snow falls in huge white tufts, blanketing the sidewalk in a frothy layer of white as I search for Skylar and come up empty.

Frowning, I skirt the building, checking the parking in the alleyway, and sure enough, I spot a glimpse of her red coat. "Skylar?" I call out, but either she doesn't hear me or she's ignoring me, so I try again. "Skylar, please wait."

This time, she pauses, turning at once as I shorten the distance between us.

Snowflakes fall against her dark hair and cling to her lashes. She's so beautiful, it takes my breath away.

Her pert nose scrunches in confusion. "Graham, what are you—"

I crush my mouth to hers and swallow her words as she stiffens in my arms, and I will her to kiss me back.

Her chest rises with her breath. Time slows as I grip her waist, pressing her back against the building when she suddenly comes to life beneath me. A soft moan rumbles from deep inside her throat as she angles her head, moving her mouth against my own.

I slide my hands inside her coat, feeling the warmth from her body as it molds to mine. My fingertips trace the curves under her soft sweater, groaning when they come to rest on the bare sliver of skin above the waistband of her pants.

I brush my tongue against hers before leaning back and pressing soft kisses to her jaw, her ear, and the pulse point at her neck. When I return my lips to her mouth, she shivers beneath me, so I press into her. Our bodies align perfectly, and I quickly become aware I'm practically dry humping Skylar fucking Davenport outside her brother's hotel.

She's so off-limits, she should come with a warning label, yet I can't seem to help myself. "You're not going out with Brad," I practically growl as I take her lower lip in my teeth.

"That's what this is about?" She pushes me back, her cheeks flushed and her breathing heavy as she blinks up at me. "You can't stand the thought of me going out with someone else, so you think you can come out here and kiss me like this, and . . . and, what? What's exactly your goal, Graham?"

I take a step back and the warmth of her body fades. "Fuck, I don't know." I run my hands over my face, watching how Skylar's expression crumbles.

She slides away from the wall, shaking her head as she points a finger at me. "You don't own me, Graham. I'm not yours to play with when you want and dispose of when you don't."

Shit, she's right. I know she is. Just like I know I should let her walk away. She's so much better off thinking I'm an asshole, because Skylar and I together will only end in disaster.

But I can't. Because I'm a selfish prick. A fool. I'm a million different things. None of them good.

She shoots me one last sorrowful look, and it's all the confirmation I need to tell me she's been as miserable as I have this past week without her. I reach out and gently take her in my arms, her back pressed to my chest. I'm relieved when she doesn't pull away.

"I was wrong," I say against her hair. "I was wrong, okay? I don't want to take a break from you. I need you, Skylar. I want you in my life."

A breath shudders through her chest as she let's go and leans in. Twisting, she cranes her neck, her whiskey gaze meeting mine, and I drink her in like an endless bottle I can't get enough of. "But what about everything you said?" she asks. "About needing to focus on deciding what comes next, and college, and football, and us working together?"

"All of that is true." I reach down and cup her face in my hands. "Maybe we *would* be better off curbing this, but I don't want to. I can't. It's torture without you." I have no idea what I'm doing—what I'm saying. Inside, my head is screaming no, that I have a death wish and will most certainly get myself killed, while my heart is screaming yes.

"But JD . . ." She trails off when I stiffen at the mention of his name. "He said something to you, didn't he? Mal and I talked about it, and we decided that could be the only explanation." When I don't immediately answer, she searches my gaze, and anger blooms in her cheeks. "I knew it!"

Her tiny hands fist at her side, but I cup them in my hands, unfurling her fingers. "It's fine," I rush to say, because the last thing I want her to do is confront JD about us.

"It's not fine. Not at all."

"What if for now, we keep things quiet. We can be low-key at work and see each other after hours. There's no need to advertise our relationship."

Skylar nods her head in agreement. "Yeah, okay. It's going to be enough of a shock when I tell him my plans for college, and I know he'll have to adjust, but for now, one thing at a time might be easier. Besides, once I'm away at school, he'll have zero say on who I date."

I sigh and press my forehead to hers as relief swirls inside me like a typhoon, even while I hate myself for caving so quickly and not holding my ground.

But when she stretches up on her toes and softly brushes her lips against mine, I can almost convince myself this will work. I can keep us a secret from Crenshaw.

CHAPTER 37

GRAHAM

I'M IN THE MIDDLE of texting Skylar when something hits the side of my head.

I frown and lower my phone to see a sugar packet lying on the table and roll my eyes. "Real mature," I say to Jace who's currently glowering at me from his spot on the couch across from me.

"Come on, man. This is supposed to be our time, you fuck-er."

I laugh at him. He's such a girl sometimes.

"I've spent the past hour sipping my coffee while you two quote poetry about how nice of an ass Josie Lynch has."

"Damn, it's so fine." Jace bites his knuckles, and I shake my head.

"And now it's time for me to go." I stand, earning a round of groans from the guys.

"Keeping it casual, I see?" Jace grins, and I flip him the bird. "Shit, you're worse than Atlas now. That lasted, what"—he turns to Knox and Teagan—"all of five minutes?"

"What can I say?" I shrug. "I know a good thing when I see it."

"Mmhmm," Jace murmurs as I shove my phone in my pocket and turn for the door. "Tell the wife I said hi!"

I flip him the middle finger for the second time which earns more laughter, then find my car on the street outside Roasted and make my way to Crow's Creek. For the sake of being extra cautious, Skylar and I have decided we shouldn't be seen in public together, so we've resorted to parking at Crow's Creek and hanging out inside my car. It's not exactly the most romantic, considering it's too cold to enjoy the property around the cabin, but it allows us to share a meal or play cards, and talk without worrying about any outside pressure.

I pull into the gravel drive, parking right in front of the cabin. Jace's parents haven't used it in forever, so I don't need to worry about any of them showing up. Hell, he probably would've given me the keys if I asked, but I don't want to impose, and I also don't want Skylar to think I expect anything from her more than the little we've messed around. I know she's less experience than me, and I'm not in any rush to push the envelope. What we have right now is enough.

A rush of anticipation shimmies through me as I see her car crest the hill behind me, coming up the drive.

I catch a glimpse of her dark hair, and my heart beats a little faster. Every time we're apart, I have a way of questioning whether I'm an absolute fool for pursuing her when I know it can only end poorly. But when I'm with her, the moment I see her again, my heart has a habit of remembering why I can't stay away.

SKYLAR

It's been nearly three weeks since Graham and I got back together again, and so far, we've been able to see each other without arousing suspicion with anyone at work or my brother.

JD eyes me over the takeout containers on the island. I sit, perched on a barstool, shoving sesame chicken in my face, in an effort to hurry out of here and meet Graham to go over the sequence of events for tomorrow.

"What?" I ask, wiping at my mouth. "Do I have food on my face or something?"

JD shakes his head, unusually quiet. "Just . . . you seem different."

I swallow. "Different how?" I ask, taking another bite of chicken, though I know what the difference is—it's the boy I'm about to meet. Following the dinner when I introduced JD to Graham, he could tell I wasn't myself, so I confessed that Graham and I split up. He hasn't said anything about it since, and I know he assumes we're still broken up, which is just as well. I don't need his influence or disapproval coloring my relationships. Despite our sneaking around, in the last few weeks, Graham has quickly become my world.

"I don't know," he answers, toying with the food in front of him.

I drop my gaze, feeling heat flood my cheeks as I lift a shoulder. When it comes to JD, I'm a terrible liar. "My senior year is almost over, and I'm getting older," I hedge, hating that I'm hiding something from him. It doesn't matter how many times I remind myself things are easier for me and Graham if JD doesn't know about us, omitting something so important to me still fills me with guilt.

Once I win the scholarship and tell him about school, then I'll quit at the hotel, and it won't matter if Graham still works there or not. I'll tell JD how serious I am about him, that my feelings for him have evolved into something I've never felt before. Something I don't recognize. Something I'm afraid to put a label on for fear of what it might mean.

"You remember I'm sleeping over Mal's tomorrow, right?" I ask.

"Yeah, sure," he tells me, seemingly distracted. "Where did you say you're going again?"

My stomach sinks with his question, afraid he's growing suspicious of the story I fed him last week about visiting her grandparents in DC.

I wipe my clammy palms on the front of my jeans. "To visit her grandparents, remember? It's their fiftieth wedding anniversary, and they're throwing a party?"

While it's true Mallory will be traveling to visit them for the impending celebration, I will not. Instead, I'll be touring SAIC with Graham. It's a five-hour drive from here, so the plan is to leave early and drive straight back. We'll then crash at his place since his parents are in Hawaii renewing their vows.

"And her parents will be with you guys?" he asks, his eyes on mine.

"Of course." The lie falls from my mouth like lead, sinking into my stomach like a brick.

He nods and goes back to eating his dinner, seemingly accepting my answer.

Five minutes later, I'm in my car on the way to meet Graham in our usual spot at his friend Jace's property at Crow's Creek. I try and tamp down the worry that JD senses something's off. When I pull into the gravel drive, Graham is already waiting for me, so I quickly park and round his car, where I open the door, shielding out the cold and sink into the soft leather. "Hey," I say, breathless at the sight of him.

His sandy hair is rumpled and sexy like he's been running his hands through it, which makes me instantly want to do the same.

"Hey, back," he says, pulling me in for a kiss.

His lips are warm and soft, and his mouth tastes like cinnamon.

"Everything okay?" he asks when we break apart, placing his fingers under my chin so my eyes meet his.

I nod. "Just excited and maybe a little anxious for tomorrow."

"Me, too." He grins. "And you're sure this is a good idea?" His brow creases with worry as he waits for my answer.

"Yes." I reach up and smooth out the wrinkle in his skin with my fingers. "I told JD I'm traveling with Mal for the anniversary party this weekend, and Mal knows. If he calls her, she'll cover for us."

"Okay." His throat bobs, and I can tell he's still worried, so I change the subject. "I submitted my entry this morning." I bite my lip, thinking of how nervous I was to hand over my sketch.

"For the competition?" His eyes brighten.

"Yep."

"So, what now?"

I take his hand in mine, glancing down at how well we fit together. "Now, we wait."

"I'm sure it's perfect." He lifts our intertwined hands to his mouth and brushes a soft kiss across my knuckles.

One of the things I love most about Graham is how affectionate he is. He's always holding my hand, wrapping his arms around me, touching my hair, or pulling me in, like we're both magnets and he can't stay away for too long.

"Did you wind up entering the sketch of your parents?"

I shake my head. He doesn't know it, but I submitted a sketch of him. Lately, I've given a lot of thought to the theme of fate—an invisible force that somehow predetermines events in our lives—and I can't help but wonder if maybe there isn't something to the concept, after all. Maybe we were meant to be together all along.

I have no idea what led him to O'Malley's that night, but it's hard to believe our meeting at the bar, and then a couple days later at work, wasn't kismet. It's like we defied the universe the first time, parting ways as enemies, so it threw us back together again. Mother fate refused to allow us to deny each other.

"No. I took a risk," I say, staring into his eyes, lost in the mossy green. "I went with something different."

"Whatever it is"—he gives my hand a little squeeze—"you're a shoe-in."

I laugh and roll my eyes. "You don't even know what the other submissions are like."

He laces our fingers together, staring into my eyes. "I don't need to see them to know you're the most talented person I've ever met."

"Speaking of talent and the future, have you given any more thought to school and what you're going to do on signing day?"

He sighs, and when his eyes darken, I instantly regret asking. I know how torn up he is about what he wants to do with his life beyond high school. I hate that I can't help make the decision for him, but no matter what he chooses, I'll be here.

"I don't know. Some days I think I'm a fool to pass up an offer from one of the Big Ten, but then other times . . ." He worries his lower lip with his teeth.

"Others times?" I gently prod.

"I feel sick at the thought of another four years of the pressure. Of my father coaching me and critiquing me; of battling on the field when it no longer brings me the joy it used to. I can just imagine him calling me to check up on me, going to my games and giving me a rap sheet of everything I did wrong. I've thought a lot about it, and part of me loves football. It's in my blood. But there's no denying the part of me that sometimes resents it."

He sighs and runs a hand over his face. "I don't know. Maybe I'm overthinking it. Maybe it would be different away from home, where I can put distance between me and my father, but if I'm being honest, football never really felt like mine. It always felt like his, and this whole time I've just been borrowing it from him like a worn-out shoe that won't ever fit no matter how many times I try it on."

Tears fill my eyes as I think of the compass etched in his skin. Graham's been trying to find his way for so long, it's no wonder he's lost.

Seeing the emotion in my eyes, Graham reaches out, cupping my face and brushing my cheek with his thumb. "*Hey,*" he says, his voice so soft I'm forced to read the words on his lips, "*I didn't mean to make you sad.*"

"I just want you to be happy," I say through the lump in my throat.

I want him to find something that brings him as much joy as art does for me. Something that's truly his.

"You make me happy," he murmurs, and then his gaze drops to my mouth before he stretches across the seat and kisses me.

I sigh as I angle my head, deepening the kiss at the same time Graham lifts me up, sliding me across the center console on top of his lap. My hands rake in his hair, breathing in the scent of his skin. It's like standing in the middle of the woods surrounded by cedar and pine, a scent so distinctively Graham.

Our kisses become more frantic; the breath heavy in our lungs. I bite his lower lip, gently pulling it into my mouth and his answering groan spikes low in my gut.

I can feel how much he wants me when his mouth drops to my neck, and I'm so close to saying the words. That I want him, too. I want this, but I hesitate, too nervous to utter them out loud.

Aside from some heavy make-out sessions and some groping, we haven't gone much further. I have no idea how much experience Graham has; I only know he has some. He wasn't a saint while he was waiting for Mackenzie, at least not before her accident. But if I know Graham at all, I'm sure he would never take me in the front seat of a car—especially knowing it's my first time.

Still, it doesn't stop me from testing the waters. I taste his neck, sliding my hands up the front of his shirt and feeling the hard ridges of muscle while his hands do the same. They toy with my bra, graze the tops of my panties, and slide over my backside. We kiss and nip and taste until our breathing grows ragged.

When he reluctantly pulls away sometime later, he stares straight into my soul with his jade eyes.

My heart thumps, and a flood of emotions rush me at once, sinking into my bones, and though it's foreign to me, there's no mistaking what it is.

But I don't say it out loud. Those four letters hold too much weight.

Because what's even scarier than the notion that I'm falling hopelessly in love with Graham Scott, is that he might not feel it, too.

CHAPTER 38

GRAHAM

THE DRIVE TO CHICAGO goes as well as expected. True to form, Skylar exerts her independence and insists on taking her car, so I tease her the entire way about her driving skills while we laugh and chat about everything from school to work, and what we'd like to do over the summer. We only stop once for coffee and snacks, and we make great time, arriving before noon, so we grab a quick bite to eat before heading toward campus.

For reasons I can't explain, I'm more nervous for this trip than I was when my father made me tour Penn State. My stomach twists as we find parking on a side street, then make the walk toward downtown Chicago.

The university is interspersed right inside the city, and because this isn't an official tour, we don't have a tour guide. We're left to our own devices as Skylar opens a map up on her phone and steps aside so she can figure out where we need to go. I'm well aware we look like total tourists, lost in a foreign city, but I'm finding it hard to care. Everyone is on the go, everything is busy. Life unfurls around us, and it's so different to Riverside with its quiet streets and slow pace. Though I see the advantages of both, I can't help but be drawn to the activity of city life.

"This way." Skylar points, glancing up from the screen.

She begins to move, and as we walk downtown, exploring the area and several of the campus buildings, it becomes clear that SAIC is focused on city-centric life.

I see the excited gleam in Skylar's eyes and can easily imagine her here, thriving in such a culturally rich environment. It's the perfect place to find inspiration for her art, and the more we see, the more animated she becomes. She talks about the fine arts program and the faculty. We spend more than an hour in their museum, the Art Institute of Chicago, taking in the exhibits, and her eyes are wide with awe. Afterward, we explore The Hyde Park Art Center, Homan Square, and take a look at some student housing.

The more we see and the more she talks, I find my chest growing heavy with envy. I think about how little reaction I had to stepping foot on the hallowed ground of Beaver Stadium and find myself asking if I've ever been as excited about football as she is about pursuing a career in art.

At one time, football was everything to me, but as the day passes, I realize just how much my desire to play was tied up in my desire to earn my father's approval. I walked in his shadow for so long because I hoped to make him proud. But I've changed. I'm not the same little boy anymore. I want something that makes me burst with hope for the future, a path that's my own—one I can grasp with two hands and hold onto.

Most of all, I want the freedom and space to decide what that is.

We quietly stroll through Millennium Park near campus. The giant metal archways of the Jay Pritzker Pavilion loom in the distance, and when we pause in front of a massive shiny metal object, Skylar stares up at it. "This is the Cloud Gate or 'the Bean.' Want to take a picture?"

I nod, wanting to commemorate this day with her. I take her phone and extend my arm until we're both on the screen with the Bean in the background. Once I take a few photos, we find a seat on one of the nearby benches, and Skylar turns to me, a grin curving the corners of her mouth. "So, what do you think?"

"I think it's amazing, and you're going to love it," I say, idly playing with the back of her hair.

She bites her lip and nods as she glances around her, a look of contentment smoothing out her features even as she says, "Tuition is crazy expensive. I really need to win that scholarship."

I instantly conjure an image of the Gentleman's Club, and my brow pinches. I know for a fact he can more than afford to send Skylar anywhere in the world for school, much less Chicago. "Your brother's been pretty successful. I'm sure he could help you out. All you need to do is ask," I suggest, unsure of whether I should say anything at all. I already know how

Skylar feels about asking her brother for help, and if she knew the money used was made through illegal means, I can't imagine she'd want it.

"Maybe," she says, sounding like she's not all that sure. "But even if he was willing to pay for me to go away to school, how fair is that? He busted his butt for me when I was young. He gave up his youth, sacrificed his time, and endless hours building his business. He's done so much for me already; it feels unbelievably greedy asking for more."

I clench my jaw and grind my teeth, hating that she has no idea what a monster he is when he's been nothing but a godsend to her.

"I can see something going on in that head of yours. What is it?"

I shake my head. I don't even know how to vocalize the sheer number of things that have been running through my mind since we got here. "I guess I'm feeling . . ." I trail off, trying to feather out a single emotion. ". . . a little jealous, I guess."

"Jealous?" She frowns, turning so her amber eyes are all I can focus on. "Of what?"

"You know what you want, and you're not afraid to go after it. I want that."

"Most people don't know what they want to do with their lives at our age. Some are still figuring it out in their thirties and forties. It's okay to not have it all mapped out."

I stare at Skylar and realize with complete certainty she's the one thing in my life right now I *am* sure of. She's the one thing that fits, that feels right. "I think I'm going to turn down Penn State," I blurt, surprised at how good it feels to finally make a decision.

"Okay," Skylar says, waiting as if she knows there's more.

"I have no idea what the hell I want, but I'm confident it's not football anymore." I glance around while Skylar squeezes my hands in silent support. "I think I'd like to go to school somewhere different, somewhere busy and chaotic and teeming with life. Somewhere like here."

Skylar grins. "Thinking of suddenly taking up art?"

I laugh. "Not a chance. I have the artistic ability of an ant, but that's okay," I say, tucking a lock of hair behind her ear, "because my girlfriend is the one with all the talent in our relationship."

Skylar's breath stutters, catching in the back of her throat at the label, every bit as affected by hearing me call her mine as I was by saying those words.

It's the first time I've called her my girlfriend out loud, and damn, it feels good.

"And I know we could do the long-distance thing," I say, "but I don't want to. If you're going to be here, in Chicago, then that's where I want to be, too."

I spent years pining after a girl who was never going to love me in return, thinking it was the real thing only to discover it wasn't.

But Skylar makes me feel things I didn't think possible. She came barreling into my life at a point when I was at my lowest and somehow brought me back to life again. She gave me direction when I had none. And I may have done some foolish things in the last year, but I'm not a fool enough to risk losing that for even a second.

"You'd really leave everything behind and move here, for me?" she asks, wide-eyed.

"Skylar," I shake my head, wondering how she doesn't get it, "I have nothing waiting for me in Riverside. Everything good I have is right here, with you. And if there's ever been a person who will help me figure out my path, it's you. When I'm with you, it's like the clouds part, and everything becomes clearer."

The moment the words leave my mouth, snow starts to fall. I blink up at the sky as Skylar holds her hands out, catching the white ice crystals in her palms. "It's snowing," she says as she jumps to her feet and spins around.

Tipping her head back, she catches the flakes with her tongue and laughs while a hand fists in my chest, pounding against my heart.

Sometimes I think life is nothing more than a composite of singular moments. Time passes, and with it, our memory fades. But there are certain little glimpses in time we remember, like the snapshot of a camera. And it's at those times that life really happens. A single instant, a significant event, a critical choice, a crucial consequence, or a defining moment. Some action or feeling that changes your course.

This is one of those moments.

I watch Skylar, her face raised to a gray sky as snowflakes dust her freckled cheeks. There's not a single ray of sunlight to be found among the clouds, but it doesn't matter because she is the sun, touching everything and everyone in her light. Including me.

Especially me.

A smile graces her perfect lips as she laughs, and the sound sinks into my skin, warming me from the inside out like a shot of whiskey.

And it hits me all at once.

I'm in love with her.

My feelings for Skylar aren't born out of desperation or deepened by tragedy.

She and I were two sparks colliding from the very start. Starting slowly from an ember before we burned. At a time when I was at my lowest, she lifted me up, numbing all the broken parts of me and healing me from within. My life without Skylar was dark and lonely. And I was lost, traveling a path with no end in sight, no vision of where I was going, only that I was tired of spinning my wheels.

But with her . . . I no longer have to be everything to everybody. Being so wholly and unapologetically herself allows me to do the same.

She takes me as I am and loves me for it. I don't need to hear her say it in order to see it in her eyes, to hear it in her words, and read it in her actions.

Skylar loves me.

Me.

And for the first time in years, I'm excited about my future. Because it has her in it. Because Skylar is my compass, and as long as I have her, I'll never be lost.

CHAPTER 39

SKYLAR

A FIRM HAND SHAKES my shoulder, and I groan. When I blink my eyes open, it's completely dark. I rub the bleariness from my eyes, taking in my surroundings and realize we're in a garage.

I straighten in my seat. We must be back in Riverside already.

"I fell asleep. Why didn't you wake me?" I ask in an accusatory tone as I frown over at Graham.

He chuckles and brushes the hair off my forehead. "Because you were clearly tired and you looked so peaceful."

"I know, but I wanted to spend time with you, keep you company while you drove. After all, this was my car and my trip." I yawn. "What time is it?"

"Just after midnight, and no worries, because you were talking in your sleep, which was entertaining enough to keep me awake."

My eyes widen, and my whole face flushes. "Oh no. What did I say?"

He presses his lips together, holding back his smile. "It's my secret, but let's just say my name was called a time or two, and I'll be storing it in the ol' memory bank to pull out from time to time."

I groan and cover my face with my hands. "How mortifying."

Graham laughs, and the sound rumbles through my chest as I peek at him through the gaps in my fingers, unable to help the grin splitting my lips.

Something clicked in him since we left Chicago. He's lighter somehow. Brighter.

And maybe it's the weight of indecision where his future is concerned that's gone, but I can't help but feel like it's more than that.

"Ready to go inside?" he asks, and I nod.

Reaching into the back seat, he grabs my duffle bag and slings it over his shoulder as he steps out of the car. I join him in his garage and I follow him to the main door.

He takes my hand and leads me inside, flicking the lights on in the kitchen as I remember that day a few weeks ago, when I followed him here and he told me about his father. As if reading my thoughts, his eyes darken as he glances around the empty kitchen, his gaze falling to the island and a handwritten note. He steps closer and picks it up. Based on the feminine handwriting, I assume it's from his mother. It has the name and phone number for the resort they're staying at in case he needs to get a hold of them.

"Are you okay?" I ask, placing a hand on his arm.

"Yeah." He sits the note back down and turns to me. "I mean, I hate the thought of my father renewing his vows to my mother when they clearly mean so little to him, but . . ." He shrugs. "I think I'm starting to accept that I didn't do this to them. The burden of responsibility isn't mine."

He runs his hands up the sides of my arms. "You hungry?" he asks.

I shake my head as goose bumps cover my skin and a prickling awareness settles at the base of my spine. We're alone. Completely and utterly alone.

My heart pounds a staccato rhythm as I gaze at his mouth. "You must be tired."

His Adam's apple bobs. "Strangely, I'm wide awake."

"Me, too," I breathe. "Why don't we get ready for bed?"

He nods as he turns and tugs my hand, pulling me out of the kitchen and guiding me down the hall toward his bedroom. I've never been as nervous as I am as I step inside and close the door behind me.

Graham stands in front of his dresser, filling the room with his presence. He kicks off his shoes and pulls the sweater he's wearing up over his head while the breath catches in my throat.

The white T-shirt beneath fits snugly over his muscles, and I can't help but stare as I close the gap between us, remembering how smooth and tan his skin was that day in the locker room when he tried on his football uniform.

I reach out to him, sliding my hands over his chest and to his back when my gaze snags on a photograph taped to his mirror, and I freeze.

Frowning, Graham glances behind him, his gaze following mine to land on a picture of him and Mackenzie. They're in a photo booth, and while she stares straight ahead at the camera, he has nothing but eyes for her.

I already knew about her, of course. He told me himself how she broke his heart, but to see in his eyes, plain as day, how much he adored her, and to know he still has a picture of her tacked to his mirror . . .

I take a tentative step back, feeling the damper close on my mood.

Graham reaches out and takes the photo, then moves away from me toward his closet where he pulls out an old yearbook and slips the photo inside before he snaps it closed. "Mackenzie is my past, Skylar. I left that one up there a while ago, and quite frankly, forgot it was even there. If you haven't noticed, I don't spend a lot of time within these four walls anymore."

His mouth tips up in a smirk as he draws closer, catching my face in his hands as he meets my eyes. "I've been spending all of my time in between school and work with another girl. She's pretty fucking special. So special, I forget anyone else even exists because she means damn near everything to me."

I place my hands over his, wanting to believe him. "She does?"

He nods, a furrow in his brow, like it pains him that I even have to ask. "Do you really *not* know how much you mean to me?"

I close my eyes shake my head. Because I do know. Of course I do.

I can feel it in his touch. Read it in his smile.

I don't need to ask to know.

"I'm sorry. When I saw it, I just . . ." My heart pounds as I think of how much I care about him, that elusive word dancing on the tip of my tongue. "Sometimes my feelings for you scare me. I forget what I ever did to pass the time before you, and the thought of losing you—"

He places a finger over my lips. "You're not going to lose me. I'm right here," he says lowering his mouth until his lips are all but brushing mine. "And there's no place in this world I'd rather be than with you, in this moment."

In the dim light of his room, his eyes glitter. His mouth parts, his breathing deepening, and when he leans toward me, pressing his forehead against my own in a move that's become as familiar as breathing, desire unfurls in my stomach. It stretches inside of me like a vine, curling around every part of me as his hands move into my hair.

His nose slides down mine, every inch of skin tingling with his touch as his breath washes over me. Anticipation tugs on my chest as his lips barely graze mine in a kiss so soft, I'm not sure it's happened yet.

And then he presses his mouth more firmly to mine, parting his lips ever so slightly to mold with my own, while I match his every move. Hands tug through my hair as his body pushes me backward, until we tumble onto the bed where we become all tangled limbs, parting lips, and exhalations.

I shiver as his hands move to the skin at my waist, burning me up with his touch while my own push beneath his T-shirt until I yank it up over his head. My shirt follows, then my jeans. For a moment, I forget what garments I'm wearing beneath them, until I glance down and am relieved to see I'm wearing a pair of black lacy underwear and a matching bra.

Graham pushes back from me, and I try not to shy away from him as he rakes his eyes over me, drinking me in. Instead, I let him look. Because I trust him. More than I realized until this moment, because it's enough to give him all of me. Body. Mind. Heart.

I'm a gift I desperately want him to accept.

"Fuck, you're beautiful," he says, his voice a quiet rasp, and then he dips his mouth back to mine. A small brush of lips. Then fuller, deeper. Nerves wrench at my gut, but I push them away, instead focusing on the delicious trail of Graham's mouth over my neck, down to the swell of my breasts, as the heat between my thighs threatens to ignite if I don't extinguish the flames. "I think about this, about you constantly," he hisses as his mouth slides to my neck.

I want to say something back, because the reverse is true, but I'm too caught up in *feeling*, too in the moment to form any sort of coherent thought into words. So, I show him with my hands as they skim down his abdomen and inside the top of his boxer briefs before I push them off. I feel all of him, taking my time, and he explores me in return.

Graham shifts on the bed, rummaging in his nightstand, and when he returns, he's ready for me. My desire reaches a fever pitch as I bite my lip and we come together, skin to skin. Our hearts one singular beat. Our breathing syncs. Our souls intertwine.

My mind goes blank, save for the boy pressed against me—the boy loving me—as the world stops. Everything in it falls away but him and me and this moment I try to memorize with every exhalation, sweet kiss, and brush of the hand. Each murmured whisper gets locked away, placed in the memory bank. Every touch and adoration seers into my mind and my heart as we each let go.

Afterward, I lie encapsulated in Graham's arms, my back to his chest. I can feel the rise and fall of his breath against me, along with the beat of his heart. A few minutes pass, and when he leans over and kisses me again, it's gentle and sweet, not the feverish, passionate kisses from moments before.

Rolling over, I press up on one arm, needing to see him.

I slide my hand over his torso, and his abs clench, the muscles rippling with my touch until I smooth my fingers over the ink on his skin.

"I love you," he whispers, and I freeze.

I glance up at him with wide eyes, unsure of whether I heard him right, until he leans forward and brushes a soft kiss on my shoulder and whispers again, "I love you, Skylar Davenport."

I bite my lower lip as tears blur my vision, because I feel it, too, and his saying it gives me the courage to say the same, to speak my heart.

"I love you, too."

CHAPTER 40

GRAHAM

"S TAY." I PRESS MY hand over her chest, feeling the beat of her heart, soft as butterfly wings.

She laughs and the vibration from it travels through my arm. "You know I can't. I have to get back or JD will get suspicious, especially as I'm working tonight." She yanks my Riverside Rebels sweatshirt over her head and sits up straight, inadvertently pushing her chest out as she does. "How does it look?"

My gaze travels down the length of her. In nothing but her lacy panties and my Rebels hoodie, she looks like a fucking dream. "That gives us hours yet," I say, then reach up and yank her to me.

A yelp escapes her lips as I roll her over, pressing her onto her back. I brush my lips against hers and groan. She tastes like mint toothpaste and strawberry ChapStick: a lethal combination that turns me on far more than it should. I'm so fucking addicted to it, I might suffer withdrawals when she leaves.

"Stay," I murmur again, this time with a soft press of my lips to her throat.

Skylar sighs, a contented sound. "You, Graham Scott, are trouble."

She has no idea.

Gripping my hair in her hands, she crushes her mouth to mine, and for a moment, I think she might reconsider and stay. We kiss until we're breathless and gasping for air. Until she presses her palms gently against my chest, and says, "I really do need to go."

With a groan, I roll off her, lying flat on my back while I watch her finish getting ready—leering at her like a voyeur is more like it.

Once she's dressed, I walk her downstairs and she declines my offer of coffee, correctly guessing it's a stalling technique. I lean against the wall opposite the door in nothing but athletic shorts as her gaze tracks my body, and she grins.

Even after last night, she still turns pink-cheeked at the sight of my bare chest, and I'm almost certain Skylar blushing is something that will never fucking get old.

She finishes putting her shoes on and reaches out, interlacing my fingers with hers. As ridiculous as it is, I can't help the sinking in my gut—the feeling in the pit of my stomach that's telling me this is the last time we'll be together. I'm probably being paranoid. After everything that happened yesterday—the intimacy we shared and telling each other "I love you"—my emotions are high.

It's perfectly normal for me to be scared under the circumstances, I tell myself. Getting my heart broken again would crush me. Losing Skylar would be insurmountable. What she and I share is different. Falling for Skylar, however quick, has been an awakening. Like the birth of the most beautiful sunrise, my feelings for her emerged slowly off the horizon, blinding in its beauty, until it quickly became the center of my universe.

I swallow hard as she falls into my arms for a hug and tells me she'll see me tomorrow, promising to visit while I'm at work. I nod and give her a kiss goodbye, then watch as she takes a step backward and heads out the door. A small wave, and then she's sinking into her car like the sinking in my gut. The car engine rumbles to life, reverberating in my chest, and then she backs down the driveway until she's out on the road and driving out of sight.

I stand there a moment longer, arms braced over my bare chest against the cold as my heart pounds like a jackhammer. I try to ignore this feeling inside of me. I try to smother it down and tell myself it'll be okay.

My relationship with Skylar will remain a secret until we graduate and we're both away at college. Then we can be together openly. It won't matter who knows we're a couple once we're in a new city.

But we can't remain a secret from Crenshaw forever, and I've already ruled out telling Skylar the truth about who he really is.

I just pray it won't cost me, and if she ever finds out, she can forgive me for keeping it from her. Not because I don't want her to know about the mistakes I've made—I don't give a damn about myself—but because JD is one of the most important people in her life, and in the same way I don't have the heart to tell my mother about my father, I can't crush Skylar like that, either.

I huff out a breath before I close the door and head for my room to get dressed. I know exactly what I need to do.

No matter how much it kills me, even if it hurts my pride, I'm going to pay Crenshaw a visit.

And beg for his blessing.

I enter the Bardot at half past noon. Skylar isn't due into work for another couple of hours, which gives me plenty of time to find Crenshaw in the Gentleman's Club, talk to him, and get out before she's none the wiser. With any luck, I'll be paying her a visit at the front desk where I'll be able to pull her into my arms and kiss her without the fear of who might be watching and will report back to the boss.

I enter the elevator and swipe my badge through the card reader, waiting as I make my descent. The doors ding open and I pause outside the entrance to the club so I can catch my breath.

The entire ride here, I thought about what I might say to him. How I can somehow convince a shark that I'm worthy of his little sister, who is like a daughter to him, when he's had a front-row seat to how much I've fucked up. I'll explain how the gambling was a foolish mistake, born out of desperation. I'll swear on everything that is holy I haven't had a drink since that night at O'Malley's and have zero intention of touching another drop. I'll tell him I plan on going to college. How I'm going to make a good life for myself. I get good grades. I'm respectful. Responsible. A good guy that simply made a couple bad choices and paid for them.

Above all, I'll tell him how much I love his sister. How I've completely fallen head over heels for her in the short amount of time I've known her. I'll explain that she feels the same way I do, and if he gives me his blessing to be with her, I'll never speak a word to her about the Gentleman's Club or who he really is when he's not with her.

Keeping his secrets will be my penance. My sacrifice. The price to pay for being with Skylar. Because she's worth it, and as long as I can have her, I can do anything.

I exhale and start for the entrance when my phone rings, and I glance at the screen, hoping for Skylar and the extra boost of courage it will give me. Instead, it's Atlas.

I ignore it and make my way inside the empty club when it rings for a second time, and I frown. Atlas rarely calls me just to talk, so whatever he needs must be important for him to call twice.

I press the phone to my ear and answer, hovering just inside the club as I say hello.

"Where are you?" Atlas asks, a tremor in his voice.

Fear needles my spine. "The hotel. Why?"

"It's Storm," he says, his voice thick. "He's been hurt."

"What do you mean he's been hurt?" My heart jumps in my throat. "Is he in his room? Was it an accident?"

I turn, making a beeline for the elevator again when Atlas's voice stops me. "No. He's at my place. Someone jumped him."

I pause, squeezing my eyes closed, trying to think over the thunderous beating of my heart. "Is he okay?" I ask, sick to the stomach at the thought it might be worse than I imagine.

"I think so. Listen, just get here, okay?"

I nod, shooting one last lingering look behind me at the club before I get back in the elevator. As much as I want to clear the air with Crenshaw, it'll have to wait if Storm needs me.

I fly down the highway and over the familiar roads to Atlas's place. Soon, I'm back in Riverside and pulling into the driveway of the trailer he shared with his father before he died. I hurry up the walkway and enter without knocking, freezing just inside the doorway when I catch sight of Storm sitting on the couch.

I suck in a sharp breath as my gaze flickers over him.

He's far worse than I imagined.

After Atlas called, I thought I'd arrive to find him with a couple bruises, maybe even a puffy lip. But Storm's face is swollen twice its size. His right eye is completely swollen shut, while the left is inflamed and black. Bruises cover the pale skin of his jaw, below a split lip and a bloody nose which Atlas is currently inspecting, a bag of frozen peas on his lap.

"What the hell happened?" I hiss, somehow moving my feet as I cross the room and kneel in front of him.

"Miraculously, I don't think it's broken," Atlas says to me, his forehead creased with worry as he places the bag of peas back over the bridge of Storm's nose. He sighs, then turns to me. "He got together with a bunch of kids from school. They went sledding at Boyd Park. When he left the hills to make his way to the parking lot where I was waiting to pick him up, a guy jumped him."

"Should we take him to the hospital?" I ask, my stomach roiling with concern.

"I tried, and he got pissed. Marie's insurance sucks. I offered to pay, but he insists he's fine and is being a stubborn little dick," he says, enunciating the words for Storm's sake. "I promised to at least wait until you got here and see what you think."

"Money isn't an issue," I say, meeting Storm's eyes.

I'll make sure Cal fucking pays.

"Are the injuries just to your face?" I ask, inspecting him.

"Yeah. It hurts, but other than that, it's fine, I swear. Mom will just worry. I asked Atlas if I could spend a couple days here, so she doesn't have to know."

I frown, a crease in my brow. "Is not wanting to worry her the only reason you wanna crash here? You didn't get in a fight with one of your classmates, did you? You worried about getting into trouble?"

He shakes his head.

"Is someone bullying you?"

"No, I swear. I'm just afraid if she gets freaked out, she'll wanna leave or something. And I really want to stay in Riverside. I've just started making friends and"—his throat bobs—"I have you guys now . . . both of you . . ." He trails off, his chin quivering with emotion, so I place a hand on his knee, letting him know it's okay.

"All right." I glance at Atlas. "We'll just keep an eye on him for now. You don't think he has a concussion or anything?"

"I checked him out, did some dilation tests. I think he's good."

I nod, unsure of how I feel about this, as my mind works. "Did you get a look at who did this?"

Atlas growls. "No. Lucky for them, because I swear if I found whoever did this, I'd tear him limb from limb. Storm said it happened too quickly. All he can say for sure is that the guy wore a ski mask. Said he was huge. So, it must've been a fully-grown man and not a kid. What kind of sick fuck jumps a kid just for the hell of it?"

A creeping sensation rolls up my spine, and I straighten.

The guy wore a ski mask. Said he was huge.

My eyes widen as this piece of information clicks, along with another thought. Whoever did this only touched his face, the most visible part of him. Which means they were sending a message, rather than just trying to hurt him.

My heart pounds so hard against my ribs, I think they might crack.

Bile rises to the back of my throat as my thoughts race faster than my mind can process.

Because I know what kind of sick fuck would harm a kid.

My phone pings in my pocket, and I flinch. With shaking hands, I reach inside and slide it out to find a text from Crenshaw.

His timing is impeccable, and I know without a doubt what I'll find when I open it up.

My stomach rolls as I read, and all of the blood drains from my face.

Crenshaw: *I warned you. Next time will be worse. Don't test me.*

My knees buckle as I brace a hand against the couch to stop my fall.

Somewhere in the back of my head, I hear Atlas's voice. He asks if I'm all right, but it's foggy and distant, like a thick wall is separating us rather than a few feet of empty space.

Crenshaw's threatened to go after Storm if I don't stay away from Skylar.

I should've suspected the moment Atlas told me something happened to him. But maybe I was in denial. Maybe I never really thought Crenshaw would stoop this low despite his threats. Or maybe I simply allowed love to cloud my better judgment so much I couldn't think clearly.

Because now he's made good on his promise.

CHAPTER 41

GRAHAM

I STUMBLE OUT OF Atlas's house on wooden legs. I'm sure he's wondering what the fuck is happening. What had the blood draining from my face and me running from his place like my feet are on fire, mumbling some excuse about running to the drugstore to grab stuff for Storm. I'm sure I'll have some explaining to do later, but there are more important matters at hand and before I know it, I find myself back where I started an hour ago, in the basement of the Bardot.

I barrel toward to Crenshaw's office in the back, but I don't even have to get that far before he emerges from his lair with Frankie by his side, still wearing the black clothing he jumped my brother in, minus the ski mask.

I don't even think. Don't even pause to assess the situation. Instead, I jump.

My hands wrap around Crenshaw's throat, fingers pressing over his trachea for one glorious moment before I'm thrown off him, into the side of the bar. The wind knocks out of me, and I struggle to get to my feet as Frankie comes at me.

"It's okay, Frank," Crenshaw calls out, and Frankie immediately stops, nostrils flared, eyes wide with bloodlust as he stares down at me.

I straighten and get to my feet, intent on telling him I'll fucking kill him if he touches my brother again, when Crenshaw blocks my path. "That was your one shot, kid. You don't get another."

I turn my eyes on him, and every ounce of hatred I feel for him burns in my veins. "If you want to teach me a lesson, teach it to me. Go ahead," I say, spreading my arms. "Take your shot. But don't hurt a kid. He's fucking innocent."

Crenshaw shrugs, his lips curling. "It's much more effective going after . . . Thunder? Lightning?" He frowns. "What was his name again?"

My jaw hardens. "You're an even bigger asshole than I ever imagined. Tell me, does Skylar's happiness mean *anything* to you?"

"Oh, it means everything." His gaze hardens to stone as he takes a step closer. "Which is precisely why I'll do everything in my power to keep you from her."

I bark out a laugh. "Why? Because I made a dumbass mistake, drank too much, and gambled more than I had? Is that so fucking bad that you'd stoop to this level to keep her from me? That was one stupid moment in time. One mistake. *One.* It doesn't define me, and it's sure as hell not who I am."

"Oh, I know exactly who you are, Graham." He points. "And I don't want Skylar with someone like me. I want her with someone better. Someone worthy, because she's everything fucking good in this world. I've sacrificed everything for her, done things I never thought I would just to ensure she has a legacy, to make sure she's taken care of and never has to worry about a damn thing. If you think, even for one second, that I'm going to let her waste her life on a guy that would rather stoop so low as to do my dirty deeds just so he doesn't have to beg his daddy for money, then you're wrong. Because that kind of man will choose himself and his pride. Every. Fucking. Time."

My mouth gapes, and I try to respond but my mind draws a blank.

Because in a roundabout way he's right.

I did choose to work for him, knowing the kind of shit he might have me do.

My mind conjures an image of Daniel and his daughter. I may not have followed through with him, but for some reason, Frankie hasn't told him. As far as Crenshaw's concerned, I made him pay—I did as he asked.

I wonder what I would've done had Crenshaw's request been something less violent, maybe slash someone's tires or bash their windshield in. What if he asked me to pass along a package that contained threats, drugs, or blackmail material. For all I know, the envelope I delivered that night could've been any number of those things. I know the answer, and it makes me sick, because I would've continued doing as he asked, anything as long as it meant fixing the mess I made on my own.

"That's not who I am."

I wonder who I'm trying to convince, him or me.

Crenshaw scoffs and turns to leave, but I'm not done with him yet. I follow after him, nipping at his heels.

"I'll tell her everything," I bark out.

Crenshaw pauses, slowly turning around, head cocked.

"If you come near Storm again, or you get in the way of us," I continue, "I'll tell Skylar all about who you really are."

"And you think she'll believe you? Over me?"

"I know she will," I say, although a part of me worries she won't, and even if she does, will she still want to be with me after everything?

A smile spreads over Crenshaw's face, but it doesn't reach his eyes. "If you tell Skylar, you won't have a brother to worry about, I can promise you that."

I swallow. Something tells me Crenshaw will make good on that promise because it's not just Skylar at stake. He has a hell of a lot more to lose if anyone finds out about what he's really doing here.

"Do you even know her like I do?" The muscles in my arms bunch and my throat bobs as I try and restrain my rising panic. "You say you love her and everything you've done is for her, but if that were true, then you'd know how incredibly talented she is. And you'd know that to waste that talent would be a crime. You'd know SAIC is the best art school in the country, and getting early acceptance is next to impossible. You'd know how badly she wants to go there. So badly, she's applying to every damn scholarship she can get her hands on in the hopes of paying her own tuition just so she can."

I take another step closer, and Crenshaw's eyes glitter darkly. Clearly, he doesn't like my questioning his love for his sister.

"You'd also know how guilty she feels at the thought of leaving you. How she worries about you being lonely when she's gone. How she frets over the fact that you've given your life up for her. She's torn up inside at the prospect of throwing the things you've done for her in your face by heading to Chicago in the fall. And if you truly loved her like you say you do?" I shake my head. "You'd let her go. Without hesitation, you'd give her what she wants. I would."

A muscle in his jaw ticks while his hands bunch into fists. I watch as something flickers through his eyes and then flares to life, like a lightbulb turning on. "You're right," he says, his voice deathly quiet.

My body tenses. They're not the words I was expecting, and somehow, they're worse than a threat.

"I'll make you a deal." He slides a hand inside his suit jacket and pulls a cigar from his pocket. Looking at it, he holds it out and Frankie steps forward, clipping the end of it while I stand there, losing my patience. "Walk away from Skylar, and not only will your brother and all your loved ones remain unharmed, but

I'll give Skylar my blessing to go to SAIC. I'll even pay for it. Every last dime."

My heart skips inside my chest. It's not the bargain I'd been hoping for when I sought him out earlier, but it surprises me all the same.

My thoughts splinter, scattering in a million different directions. I can't lose Skylar. Just the thought of it sends a lance to my heart. But something tells me Crenshaw will make good on his promise if I tell her the truth. If he's willing to hurt a child just for ignoring his wishes once, what would he do if I ignore him again? If I take it one step further and tell her everything I know?

I don't really have a choice but to accept his offer. I can no longer sacrifice the people I love by ignoring his threats. Where would he stop? And how would I find a way forward with Skylar after this, even if he let it go? If I tell her who JD really is, will she resent me someday? Will she blame me for the loss of the most important person in her life?

I wish I could go back in time and never step foot in the Play House. I wish I could go back and stop gambling the first few times I lost. I wish I could rewind to the day he and Frankie showed up at my door and just asked my father for the money. Because as much as I didn't want to lose my pride and admit I needed his help, anything would be better than this.

I inhale, my chest aching from the effort, like someone's put my lungs in a vice grip.

If I walk away now, Skylar will only suffer one heartbreak, not two. At least this way, she can go to SAIC and work on her art without the burden of guilt.

I imagine her in the city, walking the crowded streets with her friends and classmates, and I know she'll find happiness there. She's the kind of person that radiates light wherever she goes, that makes the most of what she's given. Which is how I know she'll move on. She'll find a way to mend her broken heart, and when someone special comes into her life—and I know they will because she's too damned special—she'll love again.

And so, I look Crenshaw in the eyes, and for the second time, I accept his deal.

CHAPTER 42

SKYLAR

I'VE BEEN CALLING GRAHAM nonstop for a week straight. I haven't spoken to him since the morning I left his house following our Chicago trip when I walked away on cloud nine, promising to see him the following day. Since then, I've replayed that magical day and night over and over in my head, looking for some subtle sign it wasn't as perfect as I thought it was, some sense of impending doom, but I find none.

No matter how many times I call or text, I get no answer. Even when I showed up at his house, either no one was home, or he ignored me.

Graham doesn't have much in the way of a social media presence, just a couple of old accounts that haven't been touched at all in over a year, so I get no clues from stalking him online.

I've never been connected to someone the way I am with Graham, which is why his sudden disappearance feels a little bit like walking around with a hole in my hand.

I have no idea why he's ghosting me or why Frankie told me, just this afternoon, that Graham won't be returning to work at all. There must be some sort of explanation, some reason to account for why, only a week ago, I fell asleep in his arms, and now he's virtually gone missing.

My mind conjures a thousand different scenarios, none of them to do with me and everything to do with something out of his control that's gone awry. Maybe his parents came back from their trip and told him they're getting a divorce. Or he finally decided to tell his mother about his father's affair and he's dealing with the aftermath. Maybe he's injured or sick. Maybe he had a family emergency.

I have no idea the reason for his sudden absence. All I know is I'm worried about him, because whatever reason he has to go radio silent on me can't be good, and when I tried to find Storm to ask about it, I was told by his mother he was staying with Atlas for a few days.

I finish checking in a guest and hand them their keycards. I don't even have it in me to so much as smile when I wish them a good night. My nerves are ragged with worry, tinged just the slightest with another emotion I'm afraid to name—fear.

What if he regrets what we did?

What if he regrets me?

"Still haven't heard from Graham?" Rosa asks, her accent thick with her worry. I told her everything yesterday after going to his house and finding it empty.

I shake my head. "Nope. And Storm isn't here, so I can't ask him. I could track down Atlas or one of his friends, but . . ."

How much should I really chase after him if he doesn't want to be caught? He'll find me when he's ready.

I push the thought aside, certain I'm being paranoid and his vanishing act has nothing to do with me, and everything to do with one of the other dozens of scenarios I conjured.

I'll hear from him soon. I have to believe that.

Rosa frowns and pats my hand just as the doors to the hotel swing open, and a breath of fresh air—in the name of Graham—bursts inside. My eyes lock on his, noting the turbulent shade of green, and I don't know whether to be relieved or further worried.

He comes to a stop in front of the reception desk, head bowed, as he says, "Hey."

It's not the greeting I wanted, considering the passion in our last exchange followed by a week of silence, and as I stare up at him, I search his expression for some sign I'm overreacting, that things are fine and I'm being paranoid, but I find none.

"Um, can we have a minute to talk?" he asks, lifting his gaze again. I focus on him, taking in his bloodshot eyes and the crease in his brow, and my stomach drops.

I nod, unable to say anything through the lump in my throat as I turn to Rosa. "Can you watch the desk for a minute?"

"Sure. Go ahead," she says, and when I round the desk and join Graham, I don't know what I expected, but it's not for him to pull me further into the lobby by the fireplace.

I reach out and grip his arm, begging him to look at me, to take me in his arms and tell me the last week has been as excruciating for him as it has for me. But instead, he shoves his hands in his pockets, sending a spike of disappointment under my skin so deep it scars.

"Graham, where have you been all week? You haven't been returning my calls, and you haven't shown up to work. Then, just this afternoon, they tell me you quit. I've been so worried, not to mention—"

"You were right," he says, cutting me off.

For a moment, I'm not sure I heard him right.

I shake my head. "Graham, what are you talking about. Right about what?"

His Adam's apple bobs. "That night, when we went to my place, and you saw the picture of Mackenzie still on my dresser, you thought I wasn't over her." He shoves a hand through his hair, and though a part of me knows where this is headed, I won't let my mind go there. I won't let myself even begin to think I might be right. "And I thought I was, I really did, but then . . ." His voice breaks, his sandy hair disheveled as he drops his hands. "After you left the next day, I ran into Mackenzie and everything became clear. All my feelings, everything I'd been holding back for so long, hit me like a tidal wave. I'm not over her. I think maybe it took being with you—being with someone else—to realize I still have feelings for her. So, I told her, and as it turns out, she feels the same way. I think we're finally going to give us a shot."

My jaw unhinges as I blink up at him. Of all the things I expected him to say, this was the last thing I ever imagined.

I press my fingers to my forehead, trying to ease the pounding ache blooming at the front of my skull. I can't wrap my head around what he's telling me. Like a tongue twister I can't decipher, I repeat his words in my head, as if they might suddenly make sense.

"So, what are you . . ." I clear my throat, trying to clear my thoughts. "Are you saying that sleeping with me made you realize you're still in love with another girl?"

"That's exactly what I'm saying."

"No . . ." My ribs crack, and my heart cleaves in two, accepting what my brain won't.

"Skylar, I'm sorry. I never meant to hurt you." His green eyes glisten with unshed tears, adding to my confusion.

I take a small step back, knocking into a chair behind me. "You can't be serious? But I . . . But we . . ." I swallow, thinking about everything I gave to him, and everything he took from me. My first kiss, my first time, my whole heart. "You said you loved me," I say, clinging to the desire to believe this is some kind of mistake. Some misguided fear. Some misunderstanding.

"I know," he says, his voice a thick rasp, barely recognizable over the beating of my heart. "In the moment, I meant it."

His words stab me.

I take another step back, and this time I let myself fall into the chair behind me. The cushion meets my back and supports my rubbery limbs as they go numb because I can hear what he's not saying.

In the moment, I meant it. But now, I don't.

I might be able to get past him loving both of us at once. I might be able to get past accepting he has residual feelings for her. After all, they have history, years of friendship.

But I can't get past him not loving me.

It's as insurmountable as crossing the ocean with nothing but your own two feet; no scuba gear, buoy, life raft, or paddle to help.

The first sob rips through my throat like a shot—fast and painful with the force to blow me over. But the second one comes softly, and as I collapse into a heap of tears, I realize I don't even have a life vest to keep me afloat.

GRAHAM

I push outside the hotel. My feet can't move fast enough to carry me away from here. The cold air bites at my cheeks as I step foot onto the city sidewalk, and it's like releasing the lever on a well pump.

Tears spill from my eyes onto my cheeks as I pause a few feet outside the Bardot's doors and I swipe angrily at them.

I bend in half, placing my hands on my knees in an effort to pull air into my lungs. I'm fully aware at the people gawking as they pass, wondering what this grown-ass man is doing standing in the middle of the sidewalk, crying like a fucking child. But I can't help myself as I replay the stunned expression on Skylar's face over and over again in my head like the replay of a football reel.

I straighten, gasping for breath before I turn back around, heading for the doors once more because I can't do this. I can't leave her like this, can't let her think for one second that she's second best to anyone. That she doesn't hold my entire fucking heart in the palm of her hand.

My hand grips the cold metal of the door handle and I can see inside to the front desk where Rosa cradles Skylar in her arms as she cries. Skylar has someone to console her, to wipe her tears and help her mend her broken heart, and it's not lost on me I don't. There's no one in the world capable of healing the holes in my heart Skylar's absence will cause.

I start to open the door, but my arm is as weak as my resolve and I let it fall shut again. I take a step back. Turning, I pace in front of the building, asking myself what the hell I'm doing. I can't change the game just because I don't like the way it's being played.

I pass by the doors and my face crumples at the sight of her wiping her eyes with a tissue.

I pass by again.

Rosa hands her a bottle of water.

Again.

Skylar starts gathering her things.

Again.

She presses her phone to her ear, saying something I can't hear to someone I can't see, and I wonder if she's leaving, going home early.

I wonder if weeks from now, Brad will dry her tears and she'll finally give him his chance. The thought chokes me. I can barely swallow through the thickness in my throat.

Because the fact of the matter is, whether it's Brad two weeks from now or two years, eventually someone else will be there. Someone else will be hers, and there's not a damn thing I can do about it.

I watch a while longer, taking stock of what I've done, how much I hurt her. I let the excruciating pain of witnessing her come unglued engulf me, knowing I'm responsible for it and that might somehow absolve me of my sins.

I remind myself of why I did this. Breaking up with Skylar and allowing her to hate me is the best way to push her to move on with her life; it's the best thing for everyone. Storm will stay safe. Skylar will never know what a monster her brother is, and she can go to school in Chicago, free of worry and guilt. She can build a life for herself, one full of love and laughter.

And I . . . I'll get to live with the peace of knowing I did the only thing I could in this situation to make this easier on her. I made myself the bad guy.

I used to scoff at the proverb, *If you love something, set it free.*

I always thought it was such bullshit. If you love something you fight like hell for it. You do everything in your power to hang onto it because life isn't exactly in the business of handing out happy fucking endings. Quite the opposite. So, when yours rolls around, you grasp it with both hands and hold on tight.

But I guess that's not the case here.

I have to let go.

I have to.

I was wrong about Skylar weeks ago, when I said she was like a ray of sunshine. She's not. She's a fucking star, hot and bright, burning up the universe with her light. Whereas I'm the night. Dark and lonely and vast as the sea. Only she lights me up. She fills the void inside me until I'm no longer empty

My chest constricts, and I bring a hand to the burning under my solar plexus, as if rubbing out the pain of a broken heart is as simple as massaging a sore muscle. But when the pain only intensifies, I drop it.

Then I do the only thing I can. I turn around and leave.

CHAPTER 43

SKYLAR

ONE WEEK. SEVEN DAYS. One hundred and sixty-eight hours. Ten thousand and eighty minutes. That's the amount of time it's been, give or take a few seconds, since Graham broke up with me at the Bardot, yet it feels like forever. Only the bullet hole he put in my heart is every bit as raw and painful as the day he put it there.

I swirl my spoon in the melting pint of ice cream Mallory dropped off earlier when she tried to convince me to go out with a couple people from school. They were hitting a roller rink, which I'd enjoy almost any other time. But a roller rink means loud music, laughing, yelling, and tons of chatter, which makes it next to impossible to hear, and I'm not in the mood to work so hard at hearing tonight. I'm not in the mood to read lips or smile or laugh or do any number of things. Fun is low on my list of priorities, when I suppose it should be on my highest.

I sigh and take another small bite of ice cream and grimace. It's mint chocolate chip, my favorite, but it tastes off.

Or maybe it's just me.

Maybe I'm the problem.

I groan and scrub my hands over my face, wishing I could pull myself out of my funk. I should've gone out with Mal, I know this, but it's like I want to stew in my misery for a while longer.

I hear the front door open with a creak, then close shut, and I straighten. JD bustles into the kitchen a minute later with a large pizza box in his arms, a bright pink gift bag balanced on top.

I force a smile, although if it looks anything like it feels, it's not very convincing, though he doesn't seem to notice.

"Hey, bug. How about pizza and a movie?" he asks before his eyes shift to the melting treat in front of me. "Dessert first, huh?"

I nod, rolling my lips inward before I say, "I guess it's been that kind of day."

He sets everything on the counter, and braces his hands on the island in front of me. "Seems like it's been that kind of week." He takes the spoon from me and scoops a bite of the icy treat into his mouth.

I sigh and shove the carton of ice cream away from me and fold my arms over my chest. "I miss him," I say, my voice thick.

JD's eyes soften. "You deserve so much better, bug. And one day you're going to get it, too." He shrugs. "Besides, you knew him, what? Six weeks? Two months? Give it time." he reaches out and places a hand on my shoulder. "It'll get easier."

"What if it doesn't?"

"It will."

I want to ask him what makes him so sure. What if I have to walk around for the rest of my life with this giant scar where my heart used to be?

Instead, I say nothing. Something tells me he won't understand, and honestly, the last thing I want to hear is how I'll forget about Graham one day. Because I don't want to forget about Graham. Ever.

"I just might have something that will help cheer you up," he says, his eyes bright.

I perk up just a little as he grabs the pink gift bag and slides it toward me, rubbing his hands together like a kid on Christmas. "Open it."

I lower the gift bag onto my lap, pushing aside the tufts of white tissue paper to reveal a sweatshirt. With as much enthusiasm as I can muster, I pluck it out, thinking it's just a regular gift until I notice the giant SAIC embroidered in big bold letters across the front, and I gasp.

My mouth parts as I stare at the sweatshirt, surprise and confusion twining around my thoughts. "Why did you get me an SAIC sweatshirt?" I ask, not wanting to read too much into the gesture until I know.

"Because you're going there in the fall, and if you're going to attend the *best* art school in the country, you need a sweatshirt to prove it."

My eyes widen, and I try to think of something to say, but I'm so shocked by what he just said, I'm speechless. "But . . .?"

"I'm sorry, Skylar. When I first saw the brochure, I freaked out instead of being happy for you, but I'm so proud of you. You're the most talented person I know, and that talent would be wasted if you stayed here. Though I'd love nothing more than for you to help me run the Bardot after high school, I also understand that's my dream, not yours."

"Really?" I ask, my throat tight with emotion, afraid to believe my ears.

He nods, his eyes glossy with tears. "I've been selfish in pressuring you to stay. I want you to go, and I'm going to pay for it, too.'"

"JD, no." I shake my head, pushing the sweatshirt back toward him. As much as I want to go there, I don't want it to be on his dime. I don't want it to be another sacrifice in a string of so many I can't count them all. "It's too much."

"When it comes to you, Skylar, nothing's too much. There's no price I wouldn't pay to ensure your happiness."

I frown for a minute. Something about the way he says it is off, but I can't put a finger on what it is or why it unnerves me.

Shaking off the thought, I hold the sweatshirt to my chest and bite my lip. For so long, I've waited for this moment, dreamed of JD giving me his blessing to leave for Chicago in the fall. Only in all the scenarios I conjured, none of them involved him coming to me. All of them involved me breaking the news to him and begging for acceptance.

It almost seems too good to be true.

"Thank you, but I am gonna pay for it. There's this scholarship—"

"Why don't we worry about the logistics later, huh? Right now, we have a very large pizza to consume," he says, opening the box, "because celebrations are in order."

A smile splits my face in two as giddiness bubbles inside my stomach, popping like champagne.

I can't wait to tell Graham.

The thought hits a wall, and my smile free falls.

I've received some of the best news of my life, yet it feels meaningless without him.

Mallory and I exit Bed and Bath World, back into the main corridor of the mall. Though I didn't purchase anything, I was able to push aside my thoughts of Graham to enjoy the moment and make a huge list of things I want to buy to take with me to Chicago in the fall.

But now that we're leaving the store, thoughts of him return like they always do, hovering over me like a thick fog I can't shake.

"It's equally amazing and perplexing how JD all of a sudden had a change of heart, isn't it?" Mal asks as she pauses to stare at a dress in a shop window.

I shrug. "I'm pretty sure it was on account of all the moping I'm doing."

Mal turns to me. "True. When I came to pick you up today, he seemed pretty worried. For a minute there, he looked so thrilled at the prospect of me taking you out to cheer you up and look at stuff for your dorm, I thought he was gonna lay one on me."

I let out a half-laugh. "That'd be the day."

When Mal starts walking again, I match her pace. "What will you do if you don't win the scholarship money? Will you really refuse JD's money?"

"I don't know," I say my voice flat. "I guess we'll see."

Mal turns to me, a knot in her forehead, the frustration in her eyes evident. "Come on, Skylar. Even I'm starting to worry about you. I know you're hurting, and you have every reason to be pissed. In fact, you should be mad at him," she says, and I know she's purposely avoiding saying his name. "You should be furious that he freaking took your first kiss and your virginity, and then told you he loved you only to break up with you a week later. Anger would actually be a huge relief if you'd just allow yourself to feel it rather than this . . . this . . . walking around like a zombie, like you're numb, or . . . I don't know . . . dead inside."

She reaches out and takes my arms in her hands while my eyes fall to her face. I want to give her some kind of reassurance, some kind of sign I'm okay. And I'm trying, I really am, but I'm just not there yet. "That's because I *am* dead inside. That's exactly how I feel."

"But aren't you mad? I mean, you pegged Graham for a narcissistic asshole from the start. Maybe it's time to admit that you might've been right. Maybe this other version of him you thought you saw was just him faking it. Maybe he really is just an asshole, and he used you, Skylar."

"See, that's the thing," I say, my voice thick, "he's not. And he really is a good guy, Mal."

She sighs, clearly frustrated with me for reasons I understand. I'd be frustrated with myself, too.

"I'll be okay, Mal, I promise," I say, even though I'm not sure I believe it. "Just, don't give up on me, okay?"

Mal scoffs. "Like I could ever give up on you." She bumps me with her hip. "I'm just so used to you being the strong one. You're so unflappable. Nothing ever breaks you, so this is new for the people who care about you, and it scares us. But I get not being able to be strong all the time, and I don't want you to feel like you have to pretend, okay?"

Mal's words hit their mark, because she's right. I don't do defeated. I never have. Maybe that's why my heartbreak feels so different than any other disappointment I've ever had in my life; it's like I'm wading through molasses instead of water, like it's too thick to swim and I'll never pull myself out.

But she's right. It's okay to not be okay for now—not that I have much of a choice, but for some reason, her giving me permission makes it easier.

My lips curve a little into something resembling a smile. It takes a lot of effort, but it's progress. "I appreciate that."

Lifting my head, I'm hit with a wave of memories as I'm faced with the empty spot where the massive Christmas tree stood only weeks ago. The same place Graham and I waited to see Santa. It's where we shared our first kiss. *My* first kiss.

I feel a pang of sadness so sharp and sudden, I gasp.

My hands fly to the pain in my stomach as tears sting the back of my eyes, and I remember Graham's Christmas wish—to find direction, where he belongs.

I wonder if he's any closer to finding his way. And I wonder if his time spent with me brought him closer to his path or further away from it.

I swallow over the thickness in my throat as my eyes catch on two familiar figures up ahead. They're headed toward us, but my brain can't process what my heart already has as they draw closer and she spots me, her expression brightening. A smile of recognition lights up her face.

"Skylar?" Mal tugs on my arm, clearly confused as to what's holding my attention here.

As Mackenzie and Atlas approach me, the pain and grief wash away, leaving in their place a slow, rolling anger, like the first clap of a thunderstorm. My gaze drops to their hands, which are intertwined between them, and my stomach roils.

Closing the distance between us, I storm up to them, anger stabbing my insides like a dagger.

"Skylar, right?" Mackenzie says as I come to a stop in front of them.

I narrow my eyes, and her smile wavers before I turn my gaze to Atlas, my face contorting with my rage. "You're still with her after everything? After what she told Graham?"

Atlas blinks, shock marring his masculine features as he glances over at Mackenzie in question. His mouth parts, and he returns my gaze with a small shake of the head. "Uh, I don't know what you're talking about."

"What I said to Graham?" Mackenzie frowns. "I think you might be confused."

"So, are you saying when he told you he still has feelings for you, you didn't return the sentiment? You didn't lead him to believe he still has a chance with you?"

Her brow creases as she flinches. "What?"

"Um, Skylar." Mal tugs on my arm. Her voice is soft as she tries to diffuse the flame of anger burning through me. "Maybe we should—"

"Graham," I say, rolling my eyes, not in the mood for her to play stupid. "He told me everything."

Her face remains blank, so I sigh and turn to Atlas once more. Maybe I can get through to him since she seems so hell-bent on playing dumb.

"A week ago, Graham came into work and broke up with me. He told me he realized he still has feelings for Mackenzie, and that when he confronted her about them, she confided she felt the same way. He broke up with me, saying he owed it to himself to explore whatever might remain between them."

"This is news to me," Atlas says, his dark gaze turning to Mackenzie, but something tells me he's not buying what I'm selling. Instead of looking pissed, he only looks confused, maybe even concerned.

"Graham never spoke with me a week ago. I mean, we see each other occasionally, but it's always when I'm with Atlas or we're hanging with the guys." She frowns, her brows drawing together as I try to process what she's saying. "Skylar, I'm sorry to tell you this, but we never had that conversation. As far as I know, Graham has moved on." She waves a hand toward me. "I thought he'd moved on to you. Ever since I saw him with you at the banquet, he's seemed so happy. Different. Lighter. I thought it was because you two are together."

She turns to Atlas, but he's no longer looking at her. Instead, he's staring at me with eyes dark as night, some emotion swirling in them I can't decipher. "You said it was a week ago? When, specifically?"

I tell him the date, going on to further explain how he came to see me at work and broke the news.

Atlas's gaze shifts to the floor where he stares, mumbling something about Storm and how it must've been just after he got hurt. I'm not entirely sure because he's not speaking clearly enough for me to hear, and I can't get a good read on his lips.

Mackenzie touches his arm. "You think his breaking up with Skylar has something to do with Storm getting hurt?"

I shift on my feet, not following. "Storm got hurt?"

What the hell is going on?

Atlas nods, his jaw tight. "If Graham broke up with you when you say, then it was after Storm got hurt. Someone jumped him, beat him pretty good. Maybe it freaked Graham out. Maybe…" Atlas exhales and shoves a hand through his hair. "Hell, I don't know, but it seems like a pretty big coincidence."

That it does.

Because Graham and I were just together that morning. He must've found out about Storm later that day, after I left. Then, the following week, he broke up with me. But that doesn't make sense. Why would Storm getting hurt have anything to do with me?

I shake off the thoughts because they only confuse me more. I close my eyes and take a step back before I refocus on them. "So, you're saying the conversation between you two never happened?"

"No. It never happened. I've hardly even seen Graham these past two weeks. He's been particularly elusive."

"Same," Atlas chimes in. "Other than the time or two he's quickly stopped by to see Storm, but I've always been on my way out."

So, he didn't break up with me for another girl? And he doesn't still have lingering feels for Mackenzie? The night at his house, he was telling the truth when he said he was over her.

Which begs the question, *Why the hell did he lie?*

GRAHAM

I hiss as I let the weight bar come down, then push it up again, my arms trembling with the effort. The radio blares in the background, loud enough to drown out my thoughts.

Most of them, anyway.

My parents, football, school, Storm, all of them are distant thoughts. The only thing I can't seem to get my mind off no matter what I do—the one thing I need to forget the most—is Skylar.

But I don't mind so much. Thinking about her is a special kind of torture, one I'm not hell-bent on quitting any time soon because the moment my thoughts of Skylar and how much I miss her cease to exist—if they ever do—it will make our breakup feel a whole lot more official.

And acceptance feels a lot like giving up.

I know we have no chance of reconciliation as long as Crenshaw is in the picture. Any shot I had at fighting for her and winning has long since passed. But it doesn't mean I can't allow myself the pleasure of dreaming some cosmic event might somehow bring us back together again. Like maybe that stupid fucking proverb I hate *is* true: *If you love something, set it free. If it comes back, it's yours.*

I inhale through my nose as I bring the weight bar into my chest once more and conjure an image of Skylar's face. I picture her smile, the sprinkle of freckles across the bridge of her nose, and groan as I push the weights back up and rest them on the bar.

I wipe the sweat from my forehead with a towel, my breathing heavy as I sit up. I take a pull from the water bottle beside me, glancing to the entrance of our home gym when the door bursts open and my father walks in.

My muscles instantly tense.

"Getting some training in?" Dad asks, leaning against the doorframe.

I grind my teeth and inhale a calming breath through my nose. Everything's about fucking football. "Something like that."

I stand and head to the free weights where I pick two out and start some bicep curls.

"Our trip to Hawaii was really something else," he says, a smile in his voice. "The place was beautiful, and the weather was perfect. She really outdid herself. We—"

"I don't give a fuck," I snap.

Dad freezes, his eyes wide, mouth rounding with the words I cut off. For a moment, I think he might finally understand how angry I am, how much I despise him and what he's done to us. But then, he blinks and says, "Excuse me?"

I grunt and curl a few more while he watches before I sit them down and cross the room, staring him dead in the eyes. "Do you really think I want to hear about your trip with Mom after everything I know?"

His face hardens, a hint of anger behind his words as he says, "That was in the past."

"Yeah, it feels real past, Dad." I lower the weights and place my hands on my hips, my gaze narrowed to pinpoints. "With Storm, it's never going to be 'in the past.'" I make air quotes with my fingers. "Just when, exactly, are you going to wake up and see that? You have a child, Dad. A child," I say when he drops his gaze from mine. "You can't just ignore him; pretend he doesn't exist. They're not going away and they shouldn't need to."

I spin around, taking all the anger and frustration of the last few months out on the wall as I pull my fist back and let it fly. My knuckles punch straight through the Sheetrock, and the spike of pain instantly assuages the one in my heart.

I pull my fist out of the wall, my knuckles raw and split as my breath snags in my lungs. "Do you even know what this has done to me? How stressed I've been?" I ask, my voice thick with unshed tears.

I brace my arms against the drywall around the hole, letting it hold me up while I lean into it. "You've put so much pressure on me with football, to be the best, to push myself, and now this . . . I've had to keep your secrets, knowing that they hurt someone I love." I turn around, staring at him through my watery gaze.

"Graham . . ." He steps forward, hand out.

"No." I point a finger. "No. I'm done with whatever sorry ass excuses you have." I step toward him once more, wishing the wall I just tore up was his face. "Losing Mackenzie was hard enough, but I might've coped without all the other shit weighing me down. Did you know, after I discovered everything you did, that in an effort to cope I started gambling?" A bitter laugh escapes the back of my throat. "Drinking, too. There was plenty of that. How about the fact that I ended up owing ten grand to some goon?

"Remember when I disappeared during your precious make-up holiday dinner for the son you wish you had?" I say, referring to Atlas. "Yeah, it wasn't because I'm just an asshole or an insensitive prick. It was because they came to the house and jumped me. Shoved me in their car and drove me to an empty field where they would've broken my hands and legs had I not paid."

"That's not possible. No." My father shakes his head. "Why the hell didn't you come to me? Why didn't you—"

"You don't get it, do you?" I huff out a breath, surprised at how cathartic spilling the truth is. "The job I got? It was the only way I could repay the guy I owed. I've been working off my debt, because I'd rather owe a thug than turn to you for help. That's how little I can rely on you."

"I would've helped you," he says, his tone firm. "I still will. Just name the price, and tell me how I can fix this, and I'll find a way."

I think about Skylar, and for the first time since I fell in love with her, I realize I never would've met her if not for my debt to

Crenshaw. She was my light in the dark, the one good thing to come out of my mistakes. My greatest accomplishment.

And I can't have her. It's too late.

"It's over," I say, sagging with the words. "Taken care of."

All the anger and hate drain out of me as I turn and grab the towel off the weight bench, slinging it around my neck. "And just for the record, I've made a decision about next fall. I'm not playing football. I want nothing to do with you or your fucking legacy. I'm done. And the second I graduate, I'm out of here.

CHAPTER 44

SKYLAR

T HE SECOND MAL PULLS into my driveway, I fling open my car door. As soon as I confronted Mackenzie in the mall and realized Graham lied, I insisted she take me directly home so I could grab my car and confront him.

"Are you sure about this?" she asks, leaning her head toward me to catch my gaze before I take off.

"Positive. I need to talk to him."

"And you're sure you don't just want me to take you?" She gazes up at me, concern creasing her brow. "Maybe it's better you have someone with you, in case you need it for moral support or whatever."

"It's better I go alone, trust me. I might be there a while."

Because I'm not leaving until he gives me an explanation for why he lied and tells me what the hell is going on.

"I love you." I blow her a kiss. "Call you later, okay?"

She nods and leans back, so I can shut the door. Then I take a deep breath before hurrying inside to snatch my keys off the console table by the door before JD has a chance to realize I'm home. The last thing I want to do is answer questions as to why I'm home early and where I'm going, considering he seems to always know when I'm lying.

Heading to my car parked in the driveway, I hop inside, turn the ignition, and glance in my rearview mirror before I begin to back out. The car pulls to my right, making a weird thumping noise.

Something doesn't feel right, so I put the car in park and get out. Rounding the vehicle, I glance at the tires to see I have a flat and curse.

Lucky for me, I can change a tire. JD made sure of it before I started driving, but I still resent the time it will take because all I want to do is get to Graham.

I hurry to my trunk where I keep the spare, jack, and tools.

With a grunt, I lift the tire out and set it on the ground at my feet, then take the jack, along with the wrench I'll need to the front of the car. I place them behind the wheel well and start to work the car up by pumping the lever. With any luck, I'll have the tire changed and be out before JD realizes I'm home.

Once I get the car up, I begin to loosen the lug nuts, noting the nail in my tire—the source of the flat. Using my weight to help me, I shimmy the flat tire off and roll it to the side when something on the car catches my eye and I double back.

A little black box, about four inches in length, sits just beyond the tire well. I've never noticed it before, and for a moment, I wonder if it's simply because the tire hides whatever it is from view, but on closer inspection, it doesn't look like it's part of the car. It looks foreign, like someone put it there.

With a frown, I reach for it, removing it with ease to see the letters GPS emblazoned on the back of it, along with the word "Trax," which I assume is the brand name.

I drop down in front of the tire to the cold concrete beneath me. With shaking hands, I slide my phone from my pocket as my breathing quickens. a Google search confirms my suspicions.

This device is a GPS tracker.

Someone's been watching me.

I swallow and my chest tightens so much I feel like I might choke. I lift my head and stare at my house—the one I've shared with my brother since I was kid. The one he bought for us after he opened the hotel and it was an instant success.

There's only one person I could even fathom wanting to know my whereabouts so badly they'd have me followed or track my whereabouts, and he's inside that house.

Without thinking, I slide the device inside my pocket, then manage to finish changing the tire with shaking hands and my churning thoughts.

Once I'm finished, I return the flat, along with the tools to my trunk, then snap it closed and head for the house. When I enter, it's quiet. I hear nothing as I tiptoe down the hallway to the kitchen, only to find it empty. Upstairs, I hear the sound of water running. JD's door is cracked open, so I peek my head inside and confirm it's coming from his shower.

I quietly slip inside, being careful not to make a sound as my eyes make quick work of his room, looking for his phone.

I find it on his nightstand and make a beeline for it. Trackers like these are controlled by an app, so if it's his, I'll know.

I take a deep breath and close my eyes as I clutch it in my hands. I don't know what I'll do if I see the app on his phone. Such an invasion of privacy is not okay. Not to mention all the other things it might imply.

I blink my eyes open, cognizant that I might only have precious seconds before he gets out of the shower, and scroll through his apps. I even do a search for "Trax" but find nothing.

With a sigh, I put it back on the nightstand, torn between feeling relief and fear at who the hell is tracking my whereabouts if it's not him, when a buzzing sound draws my attention.

My brow furrows as my ears perk, and I try to trace the source.

It's coming from my right, so I open the drawer of his nightstand and shuffle through ChapStick and some old magazines, when I gasp. A small red iPhone I've never seen before is buried among his things. But that's not what has me drawing in a breath.

A notification flashes across the screen.

It's from the Trax app, and it says, "Target moving."

The water in the bathroom abruptly shuts off, and my heart leaps in my throat. I scramble to put the phone back exactly as

I found it. I hear the clang of the glass shower door as I cover it with the magazines, then quietly close the nightstand.

Standing, I scurry for the door as the garbled drone of my brother's singing reaches my ears, and I let myself out into the hall.

I close the door the way I found it with a racing heart before I hurry back downstairs and outside. Taking a minute to catch my breath, I try to wrap my head around the fact that my brother has a hidden GPS tracking device on my car.

I have no idea what to do with this knowledge, let alone what the hell it means.

My mind races as I shove a hand through my long hair, but I can't discern one thought from the other. All I know is the minute JD checks that phone and sees the car is in the driveway, yet the tracker is telling him it's not, he'll know I moved it.

Without a second thought, I hurry toward my car and stick the device back on the car behind the tire. It's magnetic, so it clings easily to the undercarriage.

When I head back to the house and swing open the front door open again, I find JD standing in the hallway. My heart leaps into my throat, pounding in my trachea. "You scared me," I say, my voice an octave too high. I press a hand to my chest, shrinking under his scrutiny, worried he might've seen me.

He frowns, his eyes taking me in, and for a moment, I think he's gonna call me on moving the GPS. But instead, he says, "You look pale, and you're breathing heavy. Are you sure you're all right?" He cranes his neck to peer out the door window.

I shift in front of it, like he might somehow know what I discovered just by looking. "Uh, yeah. Like I said, you just scared me. I don't feel well, actually." I press a hand to my throat and scrunch my face as his eyes dart back to me.

"What's wrong? Are you getting sick?" He frowns, placing the back of his hand over my forehead to check for a fever. "The flu's going around."

"I'm sure it's just a cold," I say. "But my throat's sore and I'm kinda tired. If it's all right with you, I might just head up to bed and rest."

"Okay. I'll make you some soup."

"No." I shake my head, rushing to add, "It's okay, really. I'm probably just gonna sleep, anyway."

He offers me a soft smile. "Okay, if you're sure. Let me know if you change your mind."

"Sure thing," I say as I brush past him.

For the second time in the last five minutes, I make my way upstairs, only this time, I head to my room. Closing the door behind me, I turn and press my back against it.

JD has a tracker on my car.

JD has a tracker on my car.

I repeat this over and over until it and all its implications sink in. Because if JD's been tracking me, then he knows I didn't go with Mal to DC for her grandparent's party. It means he knows I went to Chicago.

My face blanches as another revelation sinks in.

It also means he knows I spent the night with Graham.

My thoughts surge forward at full speed, but the road I'm headed on is foggy and feels like taking a dark and windy turn. Everything that happened these last two weeks starts adding up, and I don't like the math.

The awkward dinner with JD, when he bailed on us for no good reason.

Graham putting the brakes on us and using work as an excuse, when he never really seemed all that concerned about it in the first place.

Storm getting his butt kicked by some random dude in the park.

Graham dumping me. *Again.*

Him not showing up for work, then quitting his job.

My brother's completely unprovoked change of heart and sudden acceptance of me going to SAIC.

Discovering my brother has been tracking my car using a mystery device I didn't even know he had.

He knows I lied about where I was the weekend I went to Chicago, yet he pretended he didn't.

Why?

None of it makes sense. But something tells me it does. Something tells me they're all connected, only I'm scared to look too closely to find the reason why because if I'm being honest with myself, my intuition tells me all fingers point back to JD.

And my intuition is rarely wrong.

CHAPTER 45

SKYLAR

I STARE UP AT my bedroom ceiling, watching the light from a passing car slide across it. I can't sleep. I've been awake since I crawled in bed hours earlier. It's now four a.m., and my legs are restless along with my thoughts.

I keep thinking about the tracker on my car and how intrusive it is. I should be pissed, and maybe I am, but I'm too afraid to notice because my gut tells me there's a much bigger picture here that I'm missing. It's like I'm staring down at a puzzle with enough missing pieces I can't make out what it is, but from the little I can glimpse, I know I'm not going to like it once I'm done.

I swing my legs off the side of the bed and stare out the window at the darkened street below. I'm certain JD holds the answers, just like I'm certain he won't willingly give them. I can't exactly sneak into his room and take the iPhone I found in my quest to find out the truth. It's too risky considering he's lying right next to it. That leaves my hunt for information elsewhere.

Typically, we're both open books with each other. Or, at least, I thought we were.

My thoughts drift to the Bardot. He spends more time there than anywhere else.

Graham worked there.

Maybe that's where the connection lies.

JD doesn't have an office at home where he might keep private documents, but he does have one at the hotel.

I straighten as I mull it over. His office is in the basement at the Bardot. I never really thought much of it before. There wasn't space for one on the main floor because of the employee break room, the lobby, and banquet room. It made sense he might want one and putting it on the floor below made more sense than taking up a hotel space on the floor above it.

But now . . .

No one goes to JD's office. And I mean, *no one*.

The only time I've ever even been inside was once or twice just after the hotel was built. That was nearly eleven years ago. It's a known fact that it's forbidden. No one even has access to it except for him and maybe Franklin because he manages the hotel.

Suddenly, I'm certain if there's anything to find, I'll find it there.

I jump up from the bed and hurry to my dresser where I replace my PJs with a pair of sweats and a long sleeve T-shirt, not bothering to grab my cochlear implant off the charger.

I don't plan to be gone long, just like I don't plan on talking with anyone. This time of night, the hotel is blessedly quiet. The only person around will be Jack who'll be working the front desk, and most nights he falls asleep in his chair. Sneaking past him without explanation won't be difficult.

I head down the stairs, taking pains to be quiet on the way down, and once my feet hit the landing, I turn for the foyer. My heart pounds in my chest as I slip my coat off the hook by the door and stare down at both of our lanyards with our work IDs.

Guilt swims in my gut as I swipe his badge off the console table instead of mine, aware of the fact I've never once defied my brother. Then again, he's never given me a reason to, and I'd say the tracker I found on my car is a pretty damn good reason.

Shoving the guilt aside, I slip the badge in my coat pocket and snatch my keys off the table. The air is crisp and the night sky is clear as my breath fogs out in front of me while I hurry to my car.

I hurriedly remove the tracker, dropping it in the driveway, unwilling to take any chances he might wake and see where I'm headed.

I drive the familiar streets into the city, and when I arrive at the Bardot, I park in the alleyway between buildings where I sit for a moment, staring at the side of the building with a sinking in my gut. Once I go inside and start snooping, whatever I unearth can't be covered back up.

I close my eyes, reminding myself of the GPS device he installed on my car and allow myself to feel the sting of betrayal, the invasion of privacy. Searching JD's office is no different. I have no reason to feel bad when he clearly has no problem doing the same to me.

I swallow, pushing my reservations aside and step out of the car, deciding to make my way to the back entrance of the hotel instead of bypassing Jack on the off chance he's not asleep at the desk. The last thing I want is to explain why I'm here on my day off just after four in the morning.

I remove JD's badge from my pocket and swipe it in the card reader on the door, letting myself inside. The door closes softly behind me as I hurry toward the elevators at the end of the corridor. Once the doors slide open, I step inside and swipe the badge, then hit the button for the basement. I wait as the car lurches and I descend. The doors ding and I step out into a small opening. My feet carry me forward slowly, as if I'm waiting for something to jump out at me as my gaze skims my surroundings. It looks different from what I remember. Lush, somehow. I don't remember the expensive lighting or the sconces on the walls.

When I spy the set of double doors in front of me, I frown. Part of me wonders if JD is slowly renovating the basement to make it another usable space for the hotel: conference rooms, another ballroom, or a massive gym. It wouldn't be a bad idea, all things considered.

I scan his badge in the reader once more, yank the doors open, and my heart plummets.

I blink while the breath stalls in my lungs.

This is a dream.

It has to be.

There's no other explanation for what I'm staring at other than the fact that it can't possibly be real.

Somehow, I manage to draw a breath and move my feet as I take in what appears to be a casino.

A fucking casino.

In the basement of the Bardot.

There's not a soul in sight as I launch myself forward, past the poker tables, through a room filled with so many slot machines I can't easily count them all. I touch one of them, feeling the smooth surface beneath my fingertips. A yank of the lever would produce flashing lights. I wonder if it makes a sound, if there's sound all around me; I wouldn't know since I left my implant charging at home.

I swallow and my mind races, but I don't allow myself to contemplate what I'm seeing. Not yet. I'm not done here, and if I pause too long for reflection, I might lose the nerve to finish what I started.

I don't know much about gambling or casinos. Even though I'm eighteen, I've never stepped foot in one. Never gambled a day in my life, and the only times I've ever played poker was when I was a kid. JD taught me a couple times. Cards have always been something we've done together, along with board games like Scrabble and Clue.

I spot a small alcove just past a massive bar with an impressive display of liquor, and make a beeline for it. Bathrooms flank the hallway before I see the door in the back which I know is JD's office, only the last time I was down here, the floor was concrete rather than polished tile, and the walls were unfinished plasterboard.

I inhale through my nose, my nostrils flaring as I approach the door and see the card reader. With shaking hands, I swipe JD's badge and wait for the little green light to flash, then push it open.

The inside is rather modest compared to the rooms I just walked through. It's furnished like a regular office with a large black desk, leather chairs, and bookshelves lining the far wall.

I hurry behind the desk and take a seat in the chair. A laptop sits on the gleaming surface of it, and when I open it and power it up, I say a prayer that it doesn't ask for a password. My prayers fall on deaf ears when the prompt pops up, and I curse. Quickly, I try every password I've known JD to use and I hit on the last one: the street name of our first home paired with my birth date.

The home screen appears and illuminates the darkness in the room.

I have no idea what I'm looking for, so I go to the hard drive and start scrolling through folders. I find one marked "Total

Revenue" and balk at the numbers on the screen. Another is marked "Debts", and when I open it, my stomach sinks.

A list of names, some familiar, stare back at me from the spreadsheet with another column listing a dollar amount, some of them so large, I can hardly believe my eyes. And then my gaze hits on the name I've been searching for, and I freeze.

The bold letters jump out of the screen, mocking me as ice chinks through my veins, a painful slog to my heart.

Graham Scott.

Debt owed: $10,000

My hands begin to tremble as I try to move the mouse and take a peek at the other columns, but I'm shaking too much.

I bring my hands in front of me, wringing them out as the heavy thump of my pulse reverberates in my chest, and I flop back in my chair.

I don't want to believe what I'm seeing.

I can't.

I shift in my seat uncomfortably as I try to breathe though what feels like a million tiny spiders crawling under my skin.

Pulling out my phone, I take several photos of the files, then slam the computer shut. I stare at the closed door of the office and think about the casino beyond, praying for another explanation other than the one my brain is hammering into my skull.

JD is running an illegal casino and gambling ring. And from the looks of it, he's been doing it for years. It's how he's made his money, and he must be . . . laundering it through the hotel?

Worse yet. The worst truth of all . . . Graham owes him money.

I have no idea how he lost so much cash to JD, only that it couldn't have possibly been through the casino at the Bardot because until that night at O'Malley's, I had never seen him before. I would remember him. Those eyes and that face aren't easy to forget, and though not all of the names on the list of clientele are recognizable, a lot of them are. Most of them are regulars at the hotel that stay monthly.

My thoughts pinwheel. I think back to the dinner where Graham met JD for the first time and how he seemed surprised. How he seemed upset to discover JD, my brother, owned the Bardot. It stands to reason our affiliation would be a problem for JD. The straight and narrow is the only path I've ever taken, and integrity is something I value. All Graham would have to do is let everything he knows about JD slip. If he told me even a morsel of truth about my brother's secret business—his secret second life? I don't even know what to call it—he'd know I'd be broken, devastated. I would never approve of what JD's done.

And losing me is JD's worst nightmare.

It suddenly makes sense. Giving me his blessing to attend school in Chicago is a cakewalk compared to the consequences of me discovering the truth.

The only part I can't understand is how Graham came to work at the Bardot in the first place. It had to do with JD, that much is obvious, but then, how did Graham not realize JD owned the hotel? Did he keep it a secret? Does he have someone else working for him? Does he go by an alias?

My mind shifts to Franklin, one of JD's only friends from high school to stick by his side after all these years, and suddenly, I'm certain he knows. He's working with him.

I draw in a shaky breath. I have a thousand unanswered questions to replace the ones I came here with. But I'm certain JD is the reason Graham broke up with me. There's no other explanation, and though the tracking device, concealed double life, casino, and the gambling ring slay me, this revelation guts me the most. Because for the past week, JD has watched me cry and walk around the house like a zombie. He witnessed me become a shell of myself over a boy I loved, when all this time, *he* was responsible for Graham breaking my heart. He had the power all along to make it right. He held all the cards, and he played them seamlessly when he needed to. He made sure he won and Graham lost. The only problem is I was the unsuspecting bystander that got gunned down in the process.

I stare down at my phone. It trembles in my hands as I open my contacts and pull up Graham's number. I'm not thinking clearly, but then again, why the hell would I be after everything I just uncovered?

I start a new text, wishing I could call him instead, but it's not an option since I don't have my implant in. Besides, I'm not sure I'd manage to actually speak over the pounding of my heart in my throat and the thoughts rattling around in my brain like an old bag of bones.

Even through text, I'm too stunned to form a coherent thought long enough to string words together to form a cohesive sentence. I'm too flabbergasted to think of what I actually want to say. So, I keep it short.

Skylar: *WTF?*

After I hit send, I attach some of the photos I took of his name in the documents on JD's computer because they're explanation enough as to what I'm referring to. I fully expect not to hear from him for at least a couple hours, since it's not yet daylight, but he surprises me when my phone rings almost immediately.

I decline the call since I can't hear him anyway, and instead, shoot off a text.

Skylar: *Can't talk. I don't have my implant in.*
Graham: *Where are you? And how did you get those documents?*
Skylar: *I'm in JD's office in the basement of the Bardot.*

I hold my breath and wait to see his reaction; if he knows what's down here.

Tiny bubbles dance on the screen, indicating he's writing, but as quickly as they started, they disappear. I wait several more minutes, wondering what he's doing, if he's even going to answer at all, when finally, another text pops up.

Graham: *Why are you down there?*

Evasive. But I'm not opposed to pushing.

Skylar: *Did you know JD had a GPS tracker on my car? He knew I wasn't with Mal the day we went to Chicago. He knew I spent the weekend with you instead.*

When he doesn't respond, I growl, frustrated with his continued silence. Clearly, he's still afraid to say anything about whatever the hell is really going on, and this conversation would be a whole lot easier if I had just grabbed my damn implant before I left the house.

Skylar: *I ran into Mackenzie, Graham. I know you never spoke with her.*

I wait but a moment to let that sink in before I send another.

Skylar: *Just like I know JD is the reason you dumped me. Clearly, he runs an illegal casino, and based on these documents, you owe him money. But he had too much to lose because of our relationship, so he forced your hand in breaking up with me. How close am I?*

I expect him to dodge the question or try and skirt around the truth, so when I get his incoming text, I suck in a breath.

Graham: *Pretty damn close.*

Skylar: *Did you already owe him money when you started working here? Did you know about the casino?*

Graham: *Yes and yes.*

Skylar: *I have a million more questions, too many to type over text.*

Graham: *I know, and I'll answer them. Don't move, okay? I'm on my way, and I'll meet you down there.*

I huff out a breath and lean back in my seat, then click open my photos. I scroll past some of Graham to the ones of me and JD from Christmas. A selfie of us on the couch sipping virgin mimosas. Our gingerbread houses. A picture of us icing cookies. JD opening the fuzzy socks I bought him. Cooking Christmas dinner.

My throat aches with the urge to cry as I continue, taking in each and every detail. The five o'clock shadow covering his jaw. His crooked smile and kind eyes. The way he looks at the camera—at me—with the love and devotion of the brother I've known and loved my entire life.

I try to reconcile myself with the two versions of him I now know exist. The one I know nothing about and my brother—my friend, my parent.

He's the same person who rocked me to sleep after I had a nightmare. Who brushed my teeth, bathed me, combed my hair, and put me to bed. The boy who dropped out of college so he could raise me, and busted his ass to earn enough to get me my first cochlear implants.

But with what money?

The question taunts me now. Does it matter if he paid for my implants with money from the hotel versus money some nameless, faceless guy who lost at the poker table? Has anything he ever given me come from legal means?

I don't have the answer to any of these questions, which bothers me maybe more than all the other ones I have about the casino and his seemingly double life.

The only thing that gives me solace is the fact that Graham will be here soon, and once he is, we'll figure this out together. I'll get all the answers I need, and though I have no idea what to do with this information, he'll help me process it. Now that I know the truth, there's no reason we can't be together.

As for my relationship with JD, I have no idea what to do. Part of me is disappointed he kept this from me, furious he'd do something so reckless, so illegal. I hate that he's not the man I thought he was. I'm pissed he forced Graham to break up with me. Upset he went as far as to track my whereabouts.

He has this whole life—this whole other side of him—I knew nothing about.

I'm at war with myself. Part of me wants to write him off all together. I want nothing to do with whatever legacy he's built here. But he's my brother. My *brother.* The only real family I have.

I click my phone shut and close my eyes, unable to look at him anymore. My brain hurts as bad as my heart. And if it weren't for Graham, I'd wish to go back in time to when I knew none of this because it was so much simpler living in the dark.

Sometimes, ignorance really is bliss.

CHAPTER 46

GRAHAM

I GLANCE AT THE speedometer. I'm pushing ninety, but it's still not fast enough.

My thoughts drift to Skylar, alone in the basement of the Bardot. I have no idea how she got access to it, nor how she found out I lied about talking to Mackenzie, but I imagine her surprise when she stepped off the elevator and stepped foot inside the Gentleman's Club.

I'd be lying if I said a part of me wasn't relieved she knew the truth and still chose to text me. She doesn't think I'm despicable for gambling. She doesn't hate me for lying to her about Mackenzie and breaking her heart. Most of all, she doesn't hate me for keeping the truth about JD from her.

At least I don't think she does.

Maybe once I get there, I'll discover I'm wrong and she wants nothing to do with me, I don't know. I wouldn't blame her if she didn't, but I sure as hell hope that's not the case.

My phone rings with an incoming call, and I go to answer it. For a moment, I assume it must be Skylar before I remember she doesn't have her implant in, so she won't be able to hear.

When I see Crenshaw's name flash across the screen, the bottom drops out from under me. My back breaks out in an instant sweat, and all I can think is, *he knows*. He knows where Skylar is, and he knows she's discovered the truth about everything.

I ignore the call, my mind racing.

What if he went into work early? What if he has some kind of alert system set up to indicate when someone's in his office, and Skylar tripped it. What if he thinks I told her everything instead of her discovering it on her own?

I swallow over the bile rising to the back of my throat when my phone starts to ring again. Instead of ignoring it, this time I hit answer and put him on speaker phone as I say, "What do you want?."

"Is Skylar with you?" he asks, his tone frantic.

"No." *But I know where she is.*

"Fuck," he hisses on the other line. "I woke up and saw she wasn't in her bed. I can't find her anywhere and her car is gone, so I thought maybe—"

"She's not with me," I snap, "so are we finished here?"

"Do you know where she is?"

I scoff. He's got some fucking nerve asking me that. "Like I'd tell you."

"Graham, I need to know. Stop messing with me. I already called Mallory, so if she's not with either of you, the only other place I can imagine she'd go is the Bardot."

I say nothing for a moment, but my silence speaks more than my words.

"She's there, isn't she?" he asks, his voice dropping to an ominous baritone. Then without waiting for a response, he mumbles, "She'll hear the alarms and get out. Someone will help her. It's fine. She's going to be fine."

A needling sensation pricks my spine. "What are you talking about? Hear what?"

"The alarms. There's been a fire at the hotel."

I shake my head, my posture rigid. "What are you talking about? I just texted her. She was fine. The Bardot is fine," I say, hearing the tremor in my voice.

"It's not. I just got the call maybe five minutes ago, I don't know. I went to wake her, to tell her I was headed there when I found her missing . . ."

The sound of my heartbeat thrashing in my ears drowns out the sound of Crenshaw's cursing. My vision blurs as I picture Skylar alone in the basement, with zero clue as to what's going on the floor above her.

I can't breathe.

Can't think.

"Why isn't she answering her damn phone?" Crenshaw shouts into my ear, breaking me from my stupor.

He doesn't know.

The knowledge Skylar can't hear the alarms sinks straight into my gut like a bag of rocks. I think I might be sick as I answer. "Because she doesn't have her implants in."

"What?" The word snaps over the line like a live wire.

"I tried calling her earlier, too, but she didn't answer," I say, numb. "Then she texted me back, saying she didn't have her implants in."

Crenshaw barks out a laugh, and I wonder if he's losing his mind? "If she doesn't have the implants in, she won't hear the alarms. But someone will usher her out. She'll see there's an evacuation," he rambles to himself. "Surely, the sprinklers will go off and she'll feel the water, see them going off with her eyes. She'll know."

Skylar is in the basement of the Bardot without her implants.

And there's a fire.

A fucking fire.

My car shoots over the rumble strips, and I jerk the wheel back to the road.

"JD," I say, the fear in my mouth cloying. "Please tell me there's a sprinkler system in the basement."

"That's what you're fucking worried about?" he asks, then, as if catching my meaning, his voice collapses in on itself as he says, "*No.* No, that's not possible. She can't even get down there."

"She's there." I swallow. "I have no idea how she got down there, but that's why she called me. That's how I know where she is. She knows *everything*."

He's silent for a moment, and I think it's because he's processing everything I just said—that Skylar knows who he really is. That she's discovered the Gentleman's Club and is aware of the debt he was holding over my head. But when he finally answers, his voice is thick with fear. "She won't hear the alarms," he mumbles. "She won't see or feel the sprinklers. She'll have no fucking clue."

My throat burns like acid. She can't hear a damn thing, much less the sound of the fire alarms. Even if she weren't in the basement, she could be standing right beneath them upstairs and not hear them.

She's completely screwed.

And all I can think of is how I told her to stay put.

CHAPTER 47

GRAHAM

P OLICE HAVE THE MAIN street cordoned off, so I park as close as I can get to the hotel and sprint. The wail of sirens whines in the distance. Only a small smattering of people gather to watch, considering it's still early, but the ones that do stare and point. A single fire truck blocks the road. It's a small crew and they appear to be doing very little, which pisses me the hell off as I break through the barricades.

My gaze scans the hotel to find the windows eerily dark upstairs. The lobby is bright, but not from the warmth of the chandelier or pendant lights. Instead, a flickering and sputtering glow which I assume is the fire illuminating the floor from within.

My heart drops to my feet, but as I take a step closer, one of the firefighters shouts, "Hey, what the hell are you doing, kid? You can't come through there!"

"I have to get through," I say, surging forward. "My girl-friend—"

The firefighter plants his hands on my chest and pushes me back while I fight his grip on me. I grapple with him, trying to break free. "I have to go after her!" I scream. "She doesn't even know about the fire."

"Almost everybody has evacuated. We're cross-checking the evacuees with the hotel's system and making sure everyone is accounted for. A small crew has been sent up to check the floors. If you wanna find your girlfriend on the list, check over there," he says with a flick of the head to a small crew behind me.

A line fifteen people deep snakes over the sidewalk.

I try Skylar's phone again with another text.

Graham: *Skylar where are you? Please answer.*

When I receive no response I try calling, but it goes straight to voicemail.

Despair inflates my chest like a balloon.

"She's not on the list." JD appears beside me, eyes wide as he takes in the sight before him. It's probably the only time I've ever been glad to see him.

Maybe with his help, we can save her.

Maybe he can get us into the hotel.

I stop fighting and stare the firefighter in the eyes. "She's in the basement, and she's deaf." The hopelessness of my words sinks into my bones.

His eyes widen, confirmation her situation is as bad as I think it is.

"If you don't let me go after her—"

"You can't go down there, son. As far as we can tell, it's an electrical fire that started in the ceiling. It's now spreading to the first floor. There's no telling how much structural damage has already been done. If and when the building collapses . . ."

I stop listening, and my eyes glaze over.

This can't fucking be it.

I can't lose her like this.

". . .we'll try and send someone down," he finishes, turning as a group of firefighters opposite us move one of the barricades to make way for a larger fire truck.

I glance up at JD, pissed he's not helping, when his eyes meet mine and he nods toward the alley beside the hotel.

We wait a moment until the fire officer directs the truck where to park, and then we make a sprint for it.

I round the building beside JD who calls to me. "With the fire spreading on the first floor, we won't even get to the elevators in the lobby. We'll take the back-door entrance, the one delivery trucks use for supplies."

We pause by the door when I remember I don't have my badge, and from the looks of it, neither does JD. "The alarms and security should be deactivated without power," he says, noting my momentary panic.

I wrench at the handle of the steel door, but it doesn't budge. "Shit!" I slam my hand against it.

I don't allow my thoughts to drift, to wander about what might have happened. She's probably finding her way out as we speak. It's why she hasn't responded to any of her texts. Skylar's smart. Resilient. A fighter.

"They must have only deactivated from the inside." He scrubs a hand over his face while my thoughts darken. This is all his fault. The fire. The club. The lies that led her here and in this moment, I hate him so much, I want to choke him. Wrap my hands around his neck and watch the life go out of his eyes.

But that won't help our situation.

As satisfying as it might be, attacking JD will just waste time when we have none to spare.

As if reading my thoughts, JD nods, his throat bobbing. "I know," he says, and with the look of pure unadulterated fear swimming in his eyes, he's far from the man I know as Crenshaw.

"Well, you can stay here if you want, but I'm gonna find my way inside."

"I'm coming with you."

I want to say no, to tell him to go to hell, but the fact of the matter is no one knows this hotel like he does. I need him.

"Come on. We'll see if there's a window somewhere on the first floor and pray like hell we can make it down the stairs. Outside the restaurant might be our best bet." He waves for me to follow and hurries around the side of the building, skirting the back of it so as to avoid the firefighters working out front.

Smoke is starting to billow out of some of the windows where the glass has shattered. We keep moving down the building until we find a spot in the corridor outside of the restaurant that appears calm.

"If there are any flames nearby, breaking the window will only make it worse, so get back." He waves me off as he grabs a mini potted pine, grunting as he struggles to lift it above his waist.

I hurry to his side and help. Together, we hoist it up chest high and count down before we chuck it at the window. The glass shatters and we duck to avoid the flying shards.

JD removes his jacket and drapes it over the window frame to protect us from any sharp edges—like I give a fuck about getting cut. Shoving him aside, I hoist myself up and through the window, hopping down onto the restaurant floor.

Everything is dark inside, pitch-black.

The air is filled with the acrid scent of smoke I can only imagine will get stronger the closer we get to the active fire.

Behind me, I hear JD's feet land.

"Which way?" I ask, and he motions to the hallway.

"We have to take the emergency stairs. Come on."

He pulls out his phone and turns the flashlight on as I do the same, fumbling in the darkness until I hit the right keys, but the beams don't carry far in the smog, and it only gets worse the second we leave the dining room and enter the hallway where the smoke thickens. It burns my eyes and kills the tiny beam of light. In the distance, the sound of crackling and the roar of flames plays softly like a distant melody I try to ignore.

We move quickly to the opposite end of the hallway, and I begin to cough as JD yanks open the stairwell door and we descend.

We reach the basement and he opens the door easily. There are no locks to disengage, no security system to bypass. Everything in the hotel is dead, save for the sound of the fire roaring above us.

Sweat trickles down my face the moment we enter the hallway outside the Gentleman's Club. It's got to be a million degrees down here, and my coughing worsens in the thick smoke. Lifting my shirt over my face, I use it as a partial shield as I try to breathe through the burning in my lungs, afraid of what we might find on the other side of these doors.

"Ready?" JD asks, through a fit of coughs. I can barely see him, hovering in front of the door, but it's obvious he's thinking the same thing as me. When he pushes through the door and we step inside the casino, our worst fears are realized.

We freeze. My body goes numb as I spot firelight through the smog, crawling at what I imagine to be the far end of the room.

It won't be long before it spreads to where we're standing.

Snapping into action, I move my feet as JD calls out, "Where is she?"

"In the office," I shout over the roaring flames.

Or at least she was.

"Hurry!" JD yells, and we wordlessly surge forward, bent over as we run.

"Shit!" I duck as a beam ten feet away collapses from the ceiling, sending a shower of sparks into the air.

I hack some more while my heart hammers in my chest. We skirt past the bar as sweat pours down my chest and back. The bottles of booze pop and explode like mini atomic bombs as we quickly move past it and head toward the alcove with the bathrooms that leads to JD's office.

We easily push open the door, and though no fire has reached the alcove yet, the smoke is somehow stronger here—so strong I can taste it.

I shove at the door and meet resistance. I realize it's a body the moment I step inside. "Skylar!" I yell, then immediately descend into a fit of coughs.

I reach for her and my arms knock into JD's. "She's unconscious," he says, the fear seeping through his voice.

My fingers move across her back to her neck, where I feel for a pulse, relieved when I feel the soft flutter under her jawline. Then, I note the soft rise and fall of her chest. "She's breathing."

"Let's get her the fuck out of here," he says with a cough, and I scoop her up in my arms myself before he even has the chance.

I cradle her against my sweat-soaked T-shirt, balancing her weight against my chest and focusing on putting one foot in front of the other.

My lungs burn like they're on fire, while I stumble through the dark with her in my arms, struggling to breathe. I can't stop coughing, and my chest heaves as I hack and gasp for air.

The exertion of carrying her makes it harder to breathe when she stirs in my arms. "Graham?" Her voice is weak from the smoke and husky without her implant, but I've never heard a more miraculous sound.

I give her a little squeeze, so she knows it's me. There's no way to communicate that JD is here with me, so I don't even try.

"The smoke . . ." she trails off.

"It's all right, baby," I manage between coughing fits, even though I know she can't hear me or see my face well enough to read my lips. "We're getting you out of here."

We push our way back into the Gentleman's Club and pass the bar, now backlit by the glow of flames. I walk aimlessly for a moment, until I'm far enough away from the bar and my hand meets what I believe is a wall.

Ahead, the orange glow of fire is larger. It flickers on the ceiling toward the front of the room, and several other spots as well. But it's too disorienting and I can't see a hand in front of my face, so I can't discern where the fire starts and where it ends.

I glance down at the girl in my arms. I can barely make out her face even though it's right in front of me. All I see are the whites of her eyes glimmering in the darkness, wide with horror.

"I tried to get—" she starts, then breaks off into a cough, and I squeeze her tighter, wondering how in the hell we're going to leave the way we came if the fire is worsening.

"We can't go up," JD says behind me, as if reading my thoughts. "Take the back door we tried earlier. Come on," he says, between gasps for air. "Follow my voice."

I don't bother asking Skylar if she can walk. She won't hear me, and I'm taking no chances of losing her in the darkness.

Instead, I adjust her in my arms and I surge forward until the heat above me grows. My scalp burns and boils, forcing me down to a crouch. It takes all my strength to carry her in this position, but my adrenaline is pumping and my resolve is solid.

I can't see anything. I have no idea where JD is until he calls again. "Over here!" he shouts, and I adjust my trajectory.

Across the room, the sound of snapping and crackling ricochets off the walls. Heat radiates from the floor. It's so hot, I can feel it in the soles of my shoes burning, like I'm walking on a bed of hot coals, and I wonder if the rubber is melting.

"We're close now," JD says, and I wonder how he knows.

Then again, he's more familiar with the place. He has the best chance of any of us to feel his way out.

I close my eyes against the stinging smoke, blindly following the sound of his voice as he hollers again.

"Right here. Right here," he says, hacking on the smoke. "It's the supply room door. Come on."

I feel my body weakening, but knowing we're so close, I surge forward. My pulse pounds a dull thud in my chest, and my lungs scream from the pain of breathing as Skylar grows heavier in my arms.

Each step is like walking through cement when the ground beneath me shudders, or maybe it's the ground above, I can't tell. I'm too disoriented; my senses are on overload.

A loud wrenching, screeching sound pierces my ears, loud enough to rise above the crackling inferno around us. It's a warning shot, a chance to duck and cover, but I'm too sluggish, too slow, and I have no idea where it's coming from until out of nowhere, pain engulfs my spine on impact.

The breath rushes from my lungs, and I drop to my knees, the sound of Skylar screaming the last thing I hear before the world goes black.

CHAPTER 48

SKYLAR

I HAVE NO IDEA what's happening. I can't see. Can't hear.

My world is as dark as my hearing is blank.

All I know is one second, I was in Graham's arms and the next I was falling. Heat engulfs my flesh as I hit what I assume is the floor, and it's several minutes until his arms scoop me back up again.

A minute later, we finally burst outside into the fresh air. I vaguely register the rising dawn lighting up the sky or the crowds of people. I'm too busy gasping, greedily sucking in air like a starving man inhaling his food.

My lungs heave, burning with the effort before I finally glance up at the face of the man holding me. The face I expect to be Graham's.

But it's not his.

It's JD.

My stomach plummets as panic sinks into my bones and my stomach roils.

What is he doing here?

I glance behind me at the building, hoping and praying he's behind us, but he's not. And when I don't see him, I turn back to JD who falls to his knees, gently placing me on the ground.

Nearby, firefighters rush to our aid and immediately try to attend to me. JD says something to them I can't hear, and I imagine he's telling them I'm deaf, though I don't know for certain because I can't focus through the buzzing in my head to read his lips.

I wait until he meets my eyes, his chest heaving with his own heavy breathing, and I ask, "Where's Graham? Is he in there?"

I wait for him to say no, but when his eyes darken and his gaze drops to the ground, I have my answer.

I scream and lurch forward as an EMT helps me to my feet, but two arms come around me from behind, restraining me.

I fight their hold on me, coughing like a madwoman as I try and break free.

I want to go after him just like he went after me.

I want to save him, like he tried to save me. Or at least, I want to die trying.

I jerk my body, pounding at the arms gripping my waist until my body gives out. I fall to the ground in a heap, giant sobs ripping through my chest like gunfire as tears clog my raw throat.

My heart swells. I can't breathe.

JD meets my gaze, his eyes glistening with unshed tears as he crawls his way to me. Reaching out, he cups my face in his hands and looks me in the eyes before he motions to his mouth, for me to read his lips.

"I'm so sorry." His face begins to crumple, but he blinks and his features smooth. Resolve flickers in his eyes, and his throat bobs as he mouths, "I love you."

Then he drops his hands, turns, and heads back inside the building.

CHAPTER 49

SKYLAR

WAITING IS TORTURE.

It feels like it's all I've done since JD saved me from the fire.

I waited after he went back inside the building. Part of me thought he'd never return. That I lost Graham, and now I'd lose him, too.

When he emerged from the door ten minutes later with Graham in his arms, it was a miracle.

But seconds after he dropped an unconscious Graham to the ground, he collapsed, and I knew the miracle was short-lived. Our luck was running out.

JD's heart had stopped, and it wasn't until they had him in an ambulance that they managed to revive him.

Once I got to the hospital, they checked me out and ran some blood work. A lump on my head revealed I'd passed out from a fall in my haste to escape when the smoke started, rather than smoke inhalation. Doctors credited being unconscious on the ground where the smoke was thinner, along with my slow, steady breathing, for limiting the damage due to smoke inhalation. Ultimately, they cleared me to go home with the condition I return if I experience any problems.

Now I'm waiting again.

Waiting to see a now conscious Graham.

Waiting for word on JD.

Waiting.

Waiting.

Waiting.

I sit in the hospital waiting room, arms wrapped around my knees and holding them to my chest while Mal sips a coffee beside me. I called her in a fit of tears just after I was released, and filled her in on everything that happened. Like the best friend that she is, she stopped at my house to grab my implants and rushed straight over.

The sound of footsteps draws my attention and I glance up to see a nurse approaching, her kind eyes on mine, and I've never been more grateful to hear again than at this moment.

"Miss Davenport?"

I drop my legs and straighten. "Yeah, that's me."

"You came here with Graham Scott, but are here for Josh Darrell Davenport as well, correct?"

"Yes, I'm his sister," I say, steeling myself for news, good or bad.

"I'm afraid your brother is fighting pretty hard right now. There's edema in his lungs and one of them has collapsed."

I suck in a breath, afraid to hear the rest of it.

"He's still unconscious and we had to intubate him. We're hoping to see some improvement with lung function, but if we see any more signs of failure, we'll do a bronchoscopy, which is a procedure where we look at the degree of damage to the airways. It also allows suctioning of secretions and debris, if necessary. Overall, it's touch and go, but we're still optimistic. We have the best team working on him, I can assure you of that."

I nod, closing my eyes for a moment to collect myself. "And Graham?" I ask, focusing on the nurse again.

She shifts on her feet, hesitating, "We can't give out information unless you're a relative or—?"

"I'm his sister," I lie.

She frowns. "You're his sister, too?"

Oops.

I clear my throat, ready to admit the truth when beside me, Mallory squeezes my hand, and chimes in, "Graham is her stepbrother."

The nurse glances between us, one brow raised. "Right," she says, and I know she doesn't believe us, but she must take sympathy on me because she drops her clipboard and says, "I have good news. Graham is awake and doing well. He did get a concussion and has some rather large contusions where a beam fell on his back, but other than that, he seems to be doing well. We ran some tests and though we're still waiting on some blood work, the preliminaries look good considering how much smoke he inhaled. Is your brother an athlete or . . .?"

"He plays football," I answer.

"Ah. Well, being an athlete just might have saved his life. If not for his age and being in prime condition, I don't know that he would have fared so well."

I bite my lip as my thoughts flicker to JD, who is older and undoubtedly not as in shape as a high school athlete.

"Can I see him?" I ask, pushing the thought aside.

"It's not quite visiting hours yet, but we're going to make an exception." She winks, and motions for me to follow.

My stomach flips as I pad my way down the hallway. The vinyl floors squeak under my sneakers and I catch the scent of Clorox and coffee in the air.

She pauses by room 308 and gives a slight knock before she pushes it ajar. "I'll be at the nurses' station. Just give me a buzz if you need anything."

"Okay, thanks." I take a deep breath before I step inside the room.

Butterflies rise from my stomach, fluttering into my throat as I take him in. Graham's inert form lies in a hospital bed, covered by a white blanket. An oxygen tube runs from a machine through his nose, and his arm is hooked up to an IV. The juxtaposition of his surroundings and the cotton hospital gown compared to his muscular biceps and hard chest isn't lost on me. The pale color of the soft material washes him out, or maybe it's the smoke he inhaled, giving his skin a grayish pallor. Either way, even ill from smoke inhalation, he's by far the most handsome man I've ever seen.

I draw closer, seeing what I couldn't through the smoke of the fire—things I know aren't from the short time he was inside the hotel. Like the thick stubble covering his jaw that tells me he hasn't shaved in days. His messy, slightly too long, crop of sandy hair. The dark crescent moons shadowing his eyes from lack of sleep.

I sink into the chair beside his bed and reach out, taking his hand in mine. He responds by opening his eyes.

His head lulls to the side and a soft smile touches his lips. "Skylar," he says, his voice deeper and slightly raspy from the smoke.

I swallow hard, feeling the events of the day rise up inside of me like an oncoming storm. "You scared me," I say. "I thought I almost lost you."

"Then that makes us even because I thought I lost you first." He reaches out and brushes his knuckles over the side of my face as his expression turns serious, his voice firm as he says, "I love you." He draws in a shuddering breath. "I thought I might never get the chance to tell you again."

"Hush." I press a finger to his lips. "Of course you're getting to tell me."

A moment of silence descends between us, but there are so many things left unsaid, and it's not long before Graham starts.

"I couldn't tell you the truth. About JD. I know I should've, but—"

"I don't blame you, Graham. I don't know what went on, and I want you to tell me about all of it, I do. But let's just focus on one thing at a time, okay? Like getting out of here."

He sighs. "I thought you might hate me for lying."

I swallow and shake my head because hate is the furthest thing from how I feel. "I could never hate you, Graham."

"God, it feels good to hear you say that." He smiles, but it's quickly replaced by a frown as his brow furrows. "Are you okay?" His gaze flickers over me with concern as if assessing for damage, and it's not lost on me he's the one lying in a hospital bed with an oxygen tube, yet he's asking *me* if *I'm* okay.

"They checked me out, ran some blood work, and I'm solid."

"When we found you by that door, I was petrified. I thought maybe . . ."

I shake my head. "It's so stupid. I started to smell the smoke and ran for the door. I slipped and hit my head. I don't know how long I was out, but it couldn't have been long. The doctors said the fact I had been enclosed in that room lying on the floor is probably the reason I didn't breathe as much smoke in."

He blinks his eyes closed for a moment, then opens them again like he can't believe I'm here. "When the debris fell on me and knocked me out, all I could think before I hit the ground was how pissed I was at myself for not getting you out when we were so close."

"JD grabbed me," I say. "He must have doubled back at some point when he realized you fell or weren't answering. I don't know, since I couldn't hear anything, but first he saved me, and then he went back in for you."

He nods, his throat bobbing. "The doctors and nurses told me. How is he?"

My chest tightens and I press my lips together, shaking my head in an effort to hold back my tears. "I don't know yet. Not good," I manage. "I'm so pissed," I say, blinking through the moisture in my eyes. "So mad he could do this to me, that he could lie to me about so much and do so many things to hurt me." A tear slides down my cheek, rolling into my mouth. "But he saved you. And he's still my brother. I still love him, and I don't know if I can shut that off."

Graham strokes a thumb over the moisture on my cheek as he hushes me in a soothing voice. "No one is asking you too, okay? You can still love him, Sky. Come here." He tugs on my arm, motioning for me to join him on the hospital bed.

I lay my head on his chest, breathing in the masculine scent of him, even through the acrid smell of smoke.

My ear presses over his breastbone, above his heart where I can feel it pounding against my cheek, steady and strong. I close my eyes and think of everything I almost lost. "We have so much to talk about," I say.

I feel his hands in my hair. A press of his lips on the top of my head.

"I know, but we have plenty of time for that. For now, let's not think about any of it. Let's wait to hear about JD and be grateful we made it out."

"I don't know what's going to happen," I say, scared for the first time as I think about the hotel, JD, and everything I discovered. "I'm scared I've lost him either way."

"I know. But it's going to be okay. I promise. I'll be here with you every step of the way, and we'll figure this out together."

I sigh and sink into him, so grateful he's okay. "I missed you."

"I missed you, too. You have no idea how much." He tightens his hold on me and I feel his breathing even out. "I think I might close my eyes and rest a bit," he says, his words heavy with sleep. "The doctors said I'd be tired, but I don't want you to leave."

"I won't leave," I say, closing my own eyes.

"Then, can I hold you like this, just for a little while?"

A smile touches my lips as I murmur, "You can hold me like this forever."

CHAPTER 50

GRAHAM

"**I**'M SO FUCKING SICK of hospitals, you have no idea," Atlas says as he walks into my room, followed by the rest of our crew.

"You?" Mackenzie says, eyeing him. "Sometimes I feel like the last year has been nothing but one big hospital stay, even though I know that's not the case."

Atlas reaches out and takes her hand as I watch them draw closer, and I realize that even though I was falling for Skylar at the banquet, it's the first time I see them together and it doesn't stir any sort of negative emotions inside of me.

"Yeah, thanks for giving us a scare, bro." Jace rakes a hand through his hair. "Can we please go a little while now without anyone getting hurt or having a brush with death? Is that too much to ask?"

I snort. "I'd like that."

"Glad you're okay, man." Teagan steps forward and offers me his fist. I bump it just as Skylar scurries into the room.

"Well, since you're all here, one of you jackasses can give me a ride home, so Sky can stay here with her brother," I say.

"Are you sure?" Skylar rushes to my side. "I don't mind."

"Seeing as how they waited until I was getting discharged to visit, it's the least they can do. I mean, we basically sat vigil around Atlas when he was in the hospital." I shoot him a meaningful look.

"Fuck you." Atlas laughs. "No one called us, and once we found out, you know damn well I was busy helping Storm and Marie move their stuff into my place since they had nowhere to go."

A grin curves my lips. "They all good?"

"Yeah, they're good. We'll find them a better place eventually."

"Aren't your parents taking you home, Scott?" Jace asks with a frown. "I mean, I know your dad's a dick, but I would've thought they'd be here."

"They were. They came yesterday, but I told them to go home and get some rest. My mother looked exhausted, and I don't know . . . my dad was being weird, even for him. It was stressing me out."

"How's your brother, Skylar?" Mackenzie asks, and all eyes swing to her.

"Um, he's hanging in there?" she says, like she's not really sure how true it is. "His lung collapsed, so they had to place a little tube in his chest into the space around his lungs to drain the air and help it re-expand. They're also watching his heart, but he's stable and making a little progress, so I think that's a good sign. The doctors say he'll have at least another week in the hospital, though."

Mackenzie offers her a soft smile. "Let us know if there's anything we can do to help, yeah?"

Skylar nods, then clears her throat, her smile sheepish. "I will, and, uh, sorry about the other day at the mall." Her gaze flickers between her and Atlas. "Obviously, I was wrong, and I shouldn't have approached you the way I did."

"It wasn't your fault," I say, reaching out and squeezing her hand. Sky told me all about how she ran into Mackenzie and confronted her, which is how she knew I lied.

"I agree." Mackenzie's gaze softens, and I'm grateful she's being so gracious. Then again, Kenz is good like that. "You have zero to be sorry for. We're all good," she says, and I wonder if she and Skylar might ever be friends. The thought is a little weird, but oddly comforting.

"Okay, hold up," Jace says. "I don't like inside jokes or secrets I'm not a part of. Does someone want to explain to me what happened?" he asks, glancing around at everyone.

I roll my eyes. "You don't need to know everything, man." I swing my legs off the hospital bed, glad to get the hell out of here.

"You're seriously gonna do me dirty like that?" Jace asks, following me as I sign the discharge papers Skylar retrieved from the nurses' station.

"Yep."

"Atlas, bro . . ." Jace glares.

Atlas shrugs. "I'm not sure I know what you're talking about. Kenz, do you remember what happened?"

"No idea," Kenz says, playing along.

Jace frowns, pointing between the four of us. "You're dead to me. All of you." Then he turns to Skylar. "To think that you were different. You could've been my favorite."

Skylar laughs while I sling an arm around her shoulders. "You wanna walk me out?" I ask, pressing a kiss to the top of her head.

"Of course." She stands on her toes and brushes her lips over mine before we turn and head for the door with Jace at our heels.

"Damn, that's cold. To think you were our team captain, our leader on the field, and now you're shutting me out?"

I laugh, shaking my head. "He's never going to let this go."

Skyler glances up at me. "Are you ever going to fill him in?"

I lift a shoulder. "Eventually. But it's fun making him sweat first."

She laughs, and I think it's not a bad way to leave the hospital—holding my girl with my friends all around me.

When Mackenzie pulls into my driveway, I thank her and Atlas for the ride, ignoring a pouting Jace and a sober Teagan beside me as I step outside and make my way up the path. I push through the front door, calling out to my parents that I'm home since they're expecting me, but the house is eerily quiet. My footsteps echo over the hardwood and into the living room where I find my father sitting in his favorite chair, bent forward with his elbows on his knees, his face in his hands.

When he glances up at the sound of my entrance, it draws me up short. He blinks up at me through bloodshot eyes, ringed with dark circles. His hair is mussed, and it looks as though he's wearing the suit he had on yesterday when he came to visit me in the hospital. An unkempt appearance is so unlike him and I stand there, not knowing what to say.

"Dad?" I ask at the same time my mother walks into the room.

My gaze homes in on her and the luggage at her feet. Wide-eyed, I glance back at my father once more, realizing what this likely means. His eyes fill with tears as he quickly suppresses his emotion with the clearing of his throat. "Uh, son, your mother is going on a little trip. I'll give you two a moment."

He stands on shaky legs, and I've never before seen him look so weak, like he's every bit his fifty-five years. It makes me wonder if maybe he did really love her. Maybe he regrets his past more than I thought.

Once he disappears down the hall, I turn to her, my hands flexing at my sides. "Mom?" I step closer and dip my head. "Are you okay?"

She reaches a hand up to my face and cups my cheek. "You never should've had to shoulder this, Graham. I'm so sorry you did."

My chest constricts. "I wanted to tell you."

"You shouldn't have had to." She offers me a sad smile. "That's on your father."

My throat bobs. "Are you leaving him for good?"

She sighs and closes her eyes for the briefest of moments. "I don't know. Part of me wants to. To say I'm angry and hurt doesn't even begin to describe how I feel. The worst of it all is feeling like everything I thought was real, wasn't. Everything I thought to be true turns out to be a lie." She swallows and her gaze focuses over my shoulder. I follow it to our family photo above the fireplace. "But part of me loves him and always will. So, I just don't know."

I reach out and pull her into my arms, surprised at how strong she feels as I hold her. She's not going to collapse into a heap of tears. She won't crumble under the weight of his infidelity like I feared.

When she pulls away, she sniffs and gives a half-laugh. "I'm going to the cabin," she says, referring to the log cabin we own in Maryland. "I need some time and space to think, alone. Are you sure you're okay, though?" she asks, her gaze flitting over me, along with her hands. "You could come with me, get away a while?"

"I'm fine," I say, grabbing her hands and holding them in mine. "I promise. As much as I'd love to take you up on your offer, I should probably stay here. I have school, and Sky's brother's still in the hospital . . ."

Mom nods. "I'll let you know once I'm settled. Maybe you could come for a long weekend and bring that pretty girl of yours." She winks, and my insides warm at the thought of Skylar coming to Deep Creek with me.

"Sounds good. Take care of yourself, Mom," I say, pulling her in for one last hug. "Call me if you need anything, okay?"

Once Mom leaves, I find my father in the kitchen staring into a cup of coffee.

He seems to be completely unaware of my presence as I lean a hip against the kitchen counter and take him in. "So, did she accidentally find out, or did you tell her?"

My father startles, nearly sloshing the contents of his cup as he turns to me. He sets the mug down on the counter and braces his hands on the island.

"I told her," he says, his voice a quiet rasp. "Yesterday, before we even knew you were hurt." He scratches the stubble over his jaw. "Otherwise, I probably would've waited, but I guess it's good I didn't. It's better you weren't here." He lifts the mug to his lips and takes a tentative sip.

I can't imagine what it was like when she first found out, but I'm also glad I wasn't here to witness it.

"What made you do it? Tell her, I mean."

He glances over at me, blinking as if surprised by the question. "As stupid as it sounds, I didn't realize how much this affected you until the other day, when you told me you were done with football." He sighs and reaches a hand to the back of his neck. "When you said you were quitting, it just sort of .

. . struck me. The gambling debt and how stressed you've been . . . I never wanted that for you, and I guess by hiding this, I got good at lying to myself, too. I told myself you were upset on principal, that none of it directly affected you. I told myself it was a long time ago, in the past, and that's where it should stay, but you were right. It's not, and your mother deserves to know the truth."

His hand drops to his side and his throat bobs as he meets my eyes. "I'm sorry for making you feel as though you had to keep my secrets."

Shock rolls through me. Never in a million years did I imagine him apologizing.

I shift on my feet, unsure of what to say. "Okay. Well, I'm glad it's done."

He nods. "I'd like to try and make it up to you. Maybe we can start fresh. I'd like to do better, turn over a new leaf."

"What about Storm?" I ask, knowing his answer to this question will determine a lot. My ability to forgive him, for one.

"I plan on talking to Marie in the next couple of days. I don't know how to approach him, how to go about gapping that bridge, but I will. I've already started looking for a decent place for them to stay now that the hotel isn't an option and their old place needed work. No matter, I promise I'm going to do the right thing. Your mother insisted on it, in fact."

Ah, so maybe his change of heart has more to do with Mom's demand than his desire for change. Time will tell.

"As for your debt—" he starts.

"Don't worry about that," I interrupt him. "It's settled," I say, not wanting to get into it, and knowing JD won't be collecting any time soon. The future for Skylar's brother is as uncertain as my parent's marriage.

I have no doubt in my mind investigating the fire will reveal his underground gambling ring and casino. The only thing I'm unsure of is how much they'll discover and what kind of charges they'll prosecute him with.

I turn, intending to head to my room when Dad clears his throat. "One more thing."

I glance at him expectantly.

"I'm sorry for pushing you so hard with football. I never meant to make you feel like you weren't good enough. You were, and always will be, a damn good player. I just wanted to make you better because I saw how much raw talent you had. Believe it or not, I always wanted what was best for you, even if I went about it all wrong."

I nod, my throat thick. The hot press of tears stings the back of my eyes as I hold them in. "Thanks, Dad, but my decision is final," I say, in case this is some final attempt to sway me. "I'll always love the sport, but playing on the field no longer brings me joy. I'm tired of feeling like I'm chasing happiness."

Mostly because I've finally found it. In myself, and in Skylar and whatever our future might hold.

My father steps forward, resolve in his eyes as he places a hand on my shoulder and says, "I know I haven't always shown it, but

I've always been proud of you, Graham. And I'll be just as proud of you with or without football."

Cameras flash, their lights going off like the pop of fireworks, as Coach Clancy approaches the podium. A couple whistles come from the back as he addresses the crowd of friends and families of boys on stage. One by one, Coach goes down the line. Each of my teammates are dressed in apparel from their school of choice, and after they're announced, they sign their letters of intent to a round of applause.

I stand, flanked by Mackenzie and Skylar, clapping and yelling for each one of my friends. When it's Atlas's turn, Marie and Storm scream like banshees from their spot behind me.

In the days leading up to signing day, I wondered what it would be like for me. Would I regret not signing? Would I have a change of heart? Would it be too late if I did?

But as I watch Coach speak on behalf of my friends, I'm surprised to find not a single part of me wishes I were on that stage.

I reach down and interlace my fingers with Sky's.

I'm right where I want to be.

After the local media fires off some questions for the guys, they descend, making a beeline straight for us.

"You should've been up there with us, bro," Jace says, clapping me on the back, "but I respect your choices, man."

Out of all our friends, Jace was the one who had the hardest time accepting I didn't want to play college ball. Everyone else took the news in stride. In fact, I don't think they were too surprised.

"Congratulations, boys," I say, glancing around at each of them. "It was an honor being your quarterback and your captain. You all earned this."

"Aw, shit. Are you gonna get sappy on us, Scott?" Jace asks.

I clap Jace on the back. "I'm not going to get sappy. Just remember, when you're doing two-a-days and puking in the summer heat, I'll be drinking an ice-cold beer somewhere. And when you play, I'll be with you in spirit, from the comfort of my couch."

Jace snorts. "Better watch out, freshman fifteen is a thing and without football . . .?" he trails off letting his meaning hang in the air.

I roll my eyes just as Brynn storms over to where we're standing, her blue eyes throwing daggers on the side of Teagan's face. "You . . ." she all but growls.

"Uh oh, incoming," Jace mutters under his breath.

Brynn comes to stand in front of Teagan and pokes him hard in the chest. "Why didn't you tell me he was going to AU?"

"Ow." Teagan takes a small step back, rubbing the spot on his chest. "Who?"

Brynn rolls her eyes as she crosses her arms in front of her chest. "The only one of you who will be playing for the Griffins at Arenac, you numbskull."

Jace snickers, and Brynn pierces him with a look.

"I didn't think it was relevant." Teagan shrugs.

"Didn't think . . .?" Brynn splutters, then closes her eyes, taking in a deep breath. "You know I just signed an early acceptance with them. But I would've held off for Maryland had I known *he* was going to go there," she says, waving a hand toward Jace.

"Should I be insulted?" Jace asks, glancing around him. "I feel like I should be insulted."

Brynn huffs and spins around, storming off toward her parents.

Okay, then . . .

When Teagan turns back to us, his eyes are wide. "Dude, you're coming to Crow's Creek tonight, right?" he asks me as if his sister didn't just become unhinged.

"I'll be there."

"Sky?" Teagan asks, and it makes me feel damn good that my friends care enough to ask her.

"Maybe later. I'm picking JD up from the hospital today, so we'll see how things play out."

"That's great." Mackenzie reaches out and touches her arm. "I'm sure you'll be glad to have him home."

Sky presses her lips together, and I know it's because she's thinking of all the things that happened between her and JD; all the things she's yet to confront him about of which my friends know nothing.

I give her hand a little squeeze, and though she smiles up at me, I can see the nerves dancing in her eyes. "You got this."

SKYLAR

I sit behind the wheel of the car while JD slumps back in his seat beside me, an elephant in between us. We're both quiet on the drive from the hospital to our house. JD stares out his window with the passing miles, and I have no idea what he's thinking, but I can only imagine the trajectory of his thoughts.

When we get home, I park in the garage and we enter the house in silence. My stomach twists in knots as I place my keys in the dish on the console table. I know we need to talk about everything that's transpired since the day of the fire, but just the thought of broaching the mammoth subject makes me sick. Learning the truth has forever changed us, and I've been taking it one day at a time ever since. First, waiting on Graham to get released from the hospital, then passing the time to see if JD would pull through. Now that he has, and the moment of reckoning has come, I'm not ready. I'm not ready for him to become the stranger I discovered in the basement of the Bardot.

I thought I might've lost JD to the fire, but I didn't. I got lucky—*he* got lucky and survived. But the moment we talk about everything he did and all of his lies, I'll lose him in a whole different way because once he puts everything out there into the world, I can't go back and unhear whatever it is I learn.

I slip off my shoes and pad my way into the kitchen, while JD hovers behind me like he doesn't know what to do with himself. Wordlessly, I open the drawer by the fridge and take out a menu from the local pizza place and dial in an order. Once I finish, I put the menu back and tuck my hands in my pockets as I meet JD's sorrowful gaze and face the inevitable.

"You saved me," I say.

JD nods, his throat bobbing.

I inhale and my nostrils flare. "And then you saved Graham and almost died doing it. You did die, actually," I say, remembering how for one frightful moment his heart stopped.

"It was the right thing to do."

I bite my lip and turn my head. *The right thing to do.* I wonder how long it had been prior to saving Graham that he'd done the right thing. I'm guessing a while.

He must read this on my expression because he steps forward, his damp eyes pleading with mine. "Sky, I know you probably despise me, and I don't blame you, not one bit. But I need you to know—"

"Can we, just, not?" I ask, holding a hand up. I blink the moisture from my eyes and stare down at my feet so as not to lose my cool. "I know we have a lot to talk about, and you have a lot of explaining to do. And I don't know whether saving Graham's life is enough for me to absolve you of everything you've done and find a way to move forward, but can we just not tonight?"

I glance back up at him, steeling myself for the impact of his gaze. "I thought I lost you. And despite all the things you've done, I'm glad you're back home. I'm so glad you're alive, and I don't want to have to think about everything that happened. Just for one more night, I want my brother. The old JD." I glance toward the hallway. "So, I'm going to go upstairs, have a hot shower, and pull my hair up in a messy bun. Then, we're going to sit on the couch with a pizza between us, instead of the lies I know exist, and watch a movie like nothing happened. Just for one night. And then tomorrow, we can face the truth."

CHAPTER 51

GRAHAM

ONE MONTH LATER

I STAND IN THE cold, glancing out at the quiet street as I hear the footsteps from within. Shoving my hands in my pockets, I contemplate all the ways this confrontation can go wrong while my stomach twists in knots.

The moment the door swings open, I turn my head and meet JD's gaze. "Graham . . ." He blinks in surprise. "Um, Skylar isn't here right now. She's—"

"Picking up her dress from the tailor? I know." I nod. The ceremony for the Siddhartha award is tomorrow. It's a big day for Sky, and she's been a bundle of nerves all week. "I came to speak with you, actually."

JD swallows, and for a moment, I think he might turn away before he motions me inside. I follow him, aware this is the first time I've ever been inside Skylar's home. His footsteps echo down the short hallway as he guides me into the living room where I sit on the sofa. He takes a seat in the single leather chair opposite me. If it wasn't for the circumstances, the scene would be reminiscent of a strange meet-the-parents-slash-older-broth-er scenario. Silence descends between us like a wet blanket while I collect my thoughts, but JD is the first the break the ice. "If you're worried about your debt, you owe me nothing."

"No," I shake my head, "it's not that. I came here to thank you, actually." I inhale, swallowing my pride because I don't owe JD much of anything, but I owe him this. "For saving my life. You didn't have to go back in the Bardot, but you did, and you almost died as a result."

He lifts a shoulder like it was nothing, but I plow forward. "I don't want you to think I take that lightly, or I don't realize you saved Skylar when I couldn't. If it weren't for you . . ." I trail off, hating to think what might've happened.

"If it weren't for me, she wouldn't have been there in the first place."

I say nothing for a moment because we both know it's true, and there's no point in denying it.

"I love her," I finally blurt. "With everything that I am, with everything that I have. I want you to know that."

JD's throat bobs while his dark gaze clouds with emotion. "Will you take care of her for me? While I'm gone?"

I nod, my throat tight. Tomorrow, JD signs his plea agreement, and he'll start his four-year prison sentence. It shouldn't mean anything to me that he's asking me to care for Sky, but somehow it does. "You have my word," I manage.

I rise to my feet, offering him my outstretched hand. It's as much as a peace offering either of us can give, and he accepts it, giving my hand a small shake before he says, "You're a good guy, Graham Scott. I'm just sorry I didn't see it sooner."

SKYLAR

I wring my hands out in front of me as Graham and I stand outside the Siddhartha Art Gallery. The worst of the winter has thawed with the arrival of March, but the air is still chilly in the evenings. Though the cold air isn't the only reason for the goose bumps cascading over my arms. I have no idea what to expect out of tonight, but once I step foot in those doors, whatever news I receive could either be enough to make me or break me. And now, more than ever, I need to win this scholarship.

"How do I look?" I ask, holding my arms out at my sides.

Graham's gaze trails over me, moving down my body in slow perusal, igniting a ball of warmth inside my chest. He steps forward, pulling me toward him and dipping his mouth to my ear. "I'm going to lose my fucking mind watching you in that dress all night. If you weren't going to win this award, I'd be dragging you out of here so we could be alone."

I shiver, despite the heat of his breath on my neck. When I tried on the shimmery gold dress, I'd hoped to drive him crazy. Looks like I succeeded.

"It's cold as balls out here." Mallory's voice cuts through the air, amid the click of her heels on the pavement. "Why the heck are you guys still standing outside?"

I smile and pull away from Graham, craning my neck to catch a glimpse of Mallory making her way toward us, looking gorgeous as ever in a little black dress.

"Hey, Mal." Graham slings his arm around my shoulders, taking the chill from my bones.

"Um, hello, handsome," she says, taking him in, and I have to admit, Graham in a suit is a sight to behold. "And you . . ." Her gaze flickers to me. "If I weren't as straight as an arrow, you'd have me reconsidering."

I tip my head back and laugh. Leave it to Mal to chase away my nerves in a hot minute. "Thanks, I think?"

"It was definitely a compliment." She closes the gap between us and grips the sides of my arms, her smile fading as her expression turns serious. "You okay, babe?" she asks, and I know she's not just referring to my nerves at whatever lies inside those walls.

I nod, worrying my lower lip with my teeth. This afternoon, JD took a plea deal. All things considered, it's a good one, but that's not why he took it. He did it mostly to save me from having to sit through his trial and the extra media attention it would bring. As of this afternoon, he surrendered all of his assets, including our house which is now for sale, and reported for the first day of his four-year prison sentence with Frankie to follow on his heels for only half the time.

As far as he and I go, we have a lot to work on, but I love him. Even though he's lied and done things I never thought he'd be a capable of, he's still my brother—the boy who gave up everything to raise me, and I can't just write him off. Deep down, he's still the man I know and love, and I recognize him for what he is. A person who's good at heart but did some bad things out of desperation, then got carried away with it all. He and I will find our way through this, I know we will, even if it seems impossible.

"I'm okay," I say, offering her a smile of reassurance.

Mal takes one last lingering look as if to discern whether I'm telling the truth and then she smiles. "Good. Now, let's get the hell out of the cold, shall we? I'm freezing my ass off out here."

With a shake of my head, I turn toward Graham who hooks his arm in my left, while Mal takes my right, and we enter the art gallery with a united front.

The lobby walls are painted a stark white with bright lights glowing above us. Abstract paintings on the walls are the only pop of color. People buzz about, chatting and talking in small circles, some of them pointing to a makeshift stage featuring a single easel underneath a spotlight, a large white cloth draped over the artwork on its limbs.

My stomach does a slow roll as I guess what the canvas is beneath it, praying it's mine. No one has seen my exhibit—not JD, or Graham, or even Mal—and I wonder what they'll think of it.

"Damn, this place is impressive," a familiar baritone calls behind us, and I turn to see Jace, Atlas, Mackenzie, Teagan, and Knox all enter. Each of them as impeccably dressed as the next.

"I didn't know you guys were coming," I say wide-eyed as Mackenzie offers me a side hug before greeting Mal.

Jace runs his hands over the lapels of his suit jacket and gives a little shrug. "You should know by now that we come as a package deal. Even all the way in Chicago, if you or Graham need us, we'll be there. Might as well deal with it now, Sky," Jace says with a wink. "Also, when you and Scott, here, decide to tie the knot one day, and you will, remember that I'm the only choice for Best Man. *Obviously*."

"Obviously," I repeat as Graham rolls his eyes. Then I glance up to him with a warm smile and mouth *thank you* because I know this was partly his doing.

"So, which one of these beauts is yours?" Jace asks, glancing around him.

"None of these ones. The pieces on the wall are for sale by the gallery. The winner of the competition will be revealed first," I say, pointing to the easel, "and then after the winner is announced, the rest of the gallery will open up to a display with all the entries."

"Shit, that's intense. So, they just announce the winner out here in front of everybody?"

"Yep," I say, with a pop of my lips.

"Damn. I'm nervous now." Jace runs a hand through his thick, dark hair and I laugh. "Okay," he says, rubbing his hands together. "You got this." Then he steps forward and starts massaging my shoulders.

Graham's murderous gaze falls to his hands, and Jace slowly removes them, palms up. "Geeze, dude. Message received. I'm just trying to shake the nerves here."

I press my lips together, stifling a laugh as Graham curls his arm protectively around me. I know I probably shouldn't enjoy it, but I love it when he gets territorial.

"Can I hold your hand?" Jace asks Mal, practically twitching with nerves. "I need to do something with myself or I'm going to combust."

Mal turns to me wide-eyed, looking a little bewildered, and this time I do laugh.

"Attention!" a voice calls up ahead, and a hush falls over the crowd as all eyes turn to the attendant at the podium. A middle-aged woman smiles down at us, gripping a microphone. "I want to thank all of you for coming out tonight to support all the wonderful emerging artists that entered this year's Siddhartha Art Gallery's Amateur Art Competition. After we announce our winner, we will open up the gallery for you to enjoy all of the wonderfully talented entries. We invite you to stay, mingle with the artists, and enjoy some refreshments, as this year's submissions were truly incredible."

The crowd around us breaks into applause, and the attendant pauses, letting the sound die down as she nods, a smile curling her lips. "As you may know, we asked entrants to sketch the theme of fate. It was a pleasure to see everyone rise to the occasion, and it was truly a tough decision by our panel, but ultimately, one sketch stood out above all the rest. So, without making you wait any longer, I'd like to announce our winner."

She straightens, opening a small envelope. "The winner of this year's Siddhartha Art Gallery's Amateur Art Competition is . . ."

She slides out a card, while I stiffen and close my eyes. Graham's arm tightens around me while Mal squeezes my left hand.

The attendant clears her throat, then leans into the mic, and says, "Miss Skylar Davenport!"

The blood rushes through my ears as applause erupts. I vaguely hear Mal screaming something at me, along with the boys cheering behind me, but I can't make out their words over the humming in my ears and the commotion in the room.

I stand, frozen in shock until two warm hands grip my arms and a familiar moss-green gaze find mine. My eyes flicker to his mouth, which quirks at the corners as I read the words coming from his lips, "Sky, you won. You won, Sky."

All the oxygen rushes from my lungs as I turn my eyes to the stage and see the attendant waving me up to accept my award.

On shaking limbs, I make my way toward the stage and take the stairs slowly, accepting the plaque the attendant gives me with a smile, along with one of those large cardboard checks you see people receive when they win the lottery. The snap of a camera flashes as I accept it, staring down at the check in awe as my eyes grow damp.

"Congratulations," the attendant says. I watch her lips to read her words, still unable to hear her through the din. "You deserve it. Would you do us the honors?" she asks, waving toward my artwork, which is still covered by the cloth.

Swallowing over the lump in my throat, I grip the white sheet and yank if from the easel. While every gaze in the room shifts to my sketch, mine falls to Graham.

I watch him take it in, note the widening of his eyes and the parting of his lips. The portrait of Graham is so detailed it looks as though it could be a photograph. Every line of his face—the hard curve of his jaw, and the depths of his eyes—are detailed with the greatest precision. A lock of hair falls in his eyes as he stares out at a road ahead of him, looking for direction as a shadowed figure waits in the distance.

When his green eyes flicker to finally meet mine, I hold my breath, waiting to see his reaction. Does he love it? Hate it? I have no idea how he'll feel about the fact that he was—*is*—my muse. But if there's one thing I'm certain of, now more than ever, it's that he and I were meant to find each other. Maybe fate is real, and Graham was mine all along.

His feet start to move, his gaze still focused on mine as he crosses the lobby floor, quickly closing the distance between us until he's standing at the foot of the stage. As gracefully as I can, I lower myself to ground level. My feet touch the floor and I smooth my dress.

"You drew me?" he asks.

I nod, biting my lip, and before I can say anything else, he draws me in and crushes his mouth to mine, and when he pulls back, he mouths, "I love you, Skylar Davenport."

Epilogue

GRAHAM

THREE MONTHS LATER

The air is warm and damp from an afternoon thunderstorm, but it's the perfect night for a bonfire. The fire flickers, sending a spark of orange in the air as Teagan adds another log. I glance at the familiar faces around me and feel a wave of nostalgia. It's hard to believe our senior year is over. Even harder to believe we'll all be going our separate ways tomorrow.

I glance down to the girl wrapped in my arms and press a kiss to her head. She smiles, finishing her conversation with Mackenzie before she glances up at me with so much love in her eyes it's sometimes hard for me to believe it's all for me. "What's that for?" she asks.

"Nothing. Just missing you."

She chuckles and turns in my arms to face me. "I'm right here."

"You're still not close enough." I grin.

"How about now?" She shifts closer, until her nose brushes mine, and I can smell the sweet scent of her skin on the summer air.

"Still not close enough," I murmur.

She tilts her head ever so slightly, moving closer until I can practically taste her lips, feel them hovering above my own like we're already touching. "How about now?"

I lower my mouth to hers, one hand on the back of her head as I draw her in for a slow kiss. Her lips are smooth and soft as butterfly wings as they mold to mine. I take my time, nipping at her lower lip, and sinking into her when someone clears their throat and tosses an empty beer can at my head.

I flinch and pull back, frowning as my gaze connects with Jace. "You jackass."

"Dude! We have this one night together. *One.*" He holds a finger out. "Let's try to save the face sucking until the latter portion when I'm too drunk to care, huh?"

I arch a brow at him and flip him the bird.

"Ooh, moody," Teagan chimes in.

"That's because Sky leaves tomorrow," Jace half-whispers behind his hand like I can't hear him. "I'd like to say it's on account of *us* leaving, but I'm afraid it's not."

I snort. "Definitely not."

Sky wraps her arms around my shoulders and slides onto my lap from her spot on the ground where I cradle her in my arms, knowing how much I'm going to miss it once she's in Chicago and I'm still here.

"I might be leaving, but you're going to visit every weekend, right?" she asks.

"Of course," I answer.

"And you're moving there in August. It's two months, dude. Suck it up," Jace says with a roll of his eyes. "I love you Sky, you know that"—he waves the hand still clutching a beer can—"but if I *ever* get this whipped over a woman, someone please put me out of my misery."

"I call first dibs," I say. "Just because you've hit a drought and your sorry ass is without a woman, doesn't mean you have to get salty, Taggart."

"Me? Salty?" Jace scoffs. "And I'll have you know, this is a completely intentional drought."

"Sure it is," Teagan says, tipping his beer back.

"Are you sure you boys should be drinking so much right before conditioning?" I ask with a smirk, and all of them groan simultaneously. "I'll take that as a no." I laugh.

They each had a couple weeks off after graduation, and now all of them start training with their new teams. Several of them are taking summer classes, which is encouraged by the coaches to lighten their load during the football season.

"It won't be so bad," Atlas says, stretching his legs out in front of him.

"You're only saying that because Kenzie's joining you in Columbus," I point out.

Atlas smirks. "It does help ease the sting of two-a-days knowing she'll be there to rub my sore muscles."

Mackenzie laughs and jabs him in the ribs. "I'm not your personal masseuse," she says, but there's no malice in her words as she drops a kiss on his cheek.

"I'll be ready, assuming I even arrive in one piece," Jace mutters. "Brynn will probably shank me before we even cross the Ohio line."

"You're driving Brynn?" I ask, choking on sip of beer.

"I'm taking our car with me to Maryland," Teagan says, "so I asked Jace if he'd give her a ride."

"Oh, shit." I cover my mouth with my hand, hiding a smile. "How'd that go over?"

"About as well as you'd expect." Teagan shakes his head. "I still have a bruise on my ribs from where she punched me."

"It'll be a long-ass drive to Ann Harbor." Jace groans.

"But at least I'll have someone to watch over her for me." Teagan slaps a hand on Jace's shoulder, but Jace just grunts.

As I listen to them bicker back and forth, I think about Skylar and how much I'm going to miss her over the next two months. I know I'll be visiting every weekend, but it doesn't mean it won't suck being away from her. Still, I promised Storm I'd stick around for the summer before I join her in Chicago. He and Marie close on their new house tomorrow. With the help of my father, they were able to find a small place in town, only a few minutes from the school, and I want to help them settle in, make it a home. Even though Storm's relationship with my father is only just developing, he's putting in the effort, and I'd like to see where it goes before I up and leave. Besides, there's no rush considering classes at Loyola don't start until August.

As far as Sky is concerned, it'll be good for her to leave for Chicago early. It's been three months since JD started his prison sentence, and I know every day she spends here is another reminder of everything that happened. When I told her about paying him a visit before he went to prison, I could tell how much it meant to her that he asked me to look after her. It's all I need to know she still loves him and hopes to rebuild some semblance of what they lost in the future. In the meantime, she's focused on a rebuilding her life, and with the closing of their home in only a couple of weeks, she has no reason to stay in Oak Ridge, nowhere to even go in the interim. A fresh start in Chicago will be good for her in more ways than one.

I reach up, grasping her wrist and bringing her hand to my lips, where I place a soft kiss over her palm. "Do you have all your stuff packed up?" I ask.

"Yeah. It's weird seeing everything in boxes. The movers come in the morning before I leave to take everything to storage, and then Mal and I are off." She presses her forehead to mine. "I wish you were coming with us."

"I know, me, too. But I feel like I've monopolized enough of your time with Mallory, and I think she wants this time just the two of you." With Mallory headed to a college several hundred miles away, she and Skylar will be apart for the first time since they met, and the last few times we hung out with her, I could tell she already missed her best friend.

Skylar sighs. "You're right. She's pretty excited about the prospect of moving me into my apartment. Thank you for being so understanding."

I tuck a lock of dark hair behind her ear, brushing her implant as I do. "Of course. Besides, before you know it, August will be here, and I'll be in Chicago with you."

"Pinky swear?" she asks with a grin, and I laugh.

Sticking my little finger out, I hook it through hers. "Nothing could keep me from you, even if it tried."

"Not even a few hundred miles?"

"Not even."

"What about my brother?"

She quirks a brow, and I choke out a laugh. "Not your brother, either."

"Not even a fire?"

"Nope. Certainly not a fire." I grin.

Her lips hover above mine. "Then I guess I'm one lucky girl."

About Gracie

Gracie is a contemporary young adult author who loves romance and writing fictional characters. When she's not busy telling lies for a living, she's likely wrangling her three kids, cooking subpar meals, and procrastinating. Feel free to reach out to her on social media! She loves talking to readers and chatting books!

Gracie's Gang (FB Group)

Facebook Page

TikTok

Instagram

Pinterest

www.ingramcontent.com/pod-product-compliance
Lightning Source LLC
Chambersburg PA
CBHW021409010826
48972CB00014B/955